INTO THE LABYRINTH

A Novel About One Woman's Journey to Healing and Transformation

By
Tracy Carreon

ISBN: 978-0-6151-9133-1

For Caleb, the definition of Love.

PART ONE: THE CALL

CHAPTER ONE

The story begins where all stories do, at the beginning...a beginning, as all are, ushered in on the heels of an ending - for it is when night passes into day that the seeds of awakening are sown.

I remember, first, the coming of morning…

It crept in slowly as if hiding from the night. The waking world called but I didn't want to go, so I lay still and held my breath, hoping to stop the movement of time. When it refused to cooperate I exhaled, turned on my side and stared out the window. Beyond the pane of glass, rays of sunlight streamed through branches of an ancient oak.

For what seemed hours I watched the still and quiet light. Then finally, with a sigh of regret I stretched, swung my feet to the cold wood floor, stood and walked into the bathroom.

Most mornings I ignored the mirror hanging above the sink and the empty worn eyes staring back at me. This morning though, something, a hint of life maybe, caught my attention. I leaned closer, hoping to chase it down. But the small flicker simply flashed and disappeared. All that was left was dark hair falling across my face, hanging in tangles halfway down my back. Skin, fair and freckled, wind-burned from yesterday's walk along the beach. And an echo in the back halls of my mind…my mother's voice telling me I was too thin. I shook it off. She might be right, but I knew if I could keep people from looking in my eyes they might actually believe I was still alive.

Tears began to well.

"Damn. Come on. Come on," I pleaded. "Please. No." I stared at my reflection until it blurred, until I believed I could will myself out of existence. "Brian. Brian, please," I whispered. With jaws clenched, I waited for what I knew would come.

Stepping back from the counter I grabbed for the door behind me, feeling for the knob to steady myself. And then it happened. Shooting through my heart, jolting me backwards. Using trembling arms as a straight jacket, I tried to keep the pain from escaping and swallowing me whole. But when it leapt from my throat, it came as a creature caught in a trap, alone and helpless, resigned to the inevitable.

The image in the mirror watched as the creature howled and sobbed, hands balled into fists, rubbing the sides of its head as though to erase memories of living. The sound ripped through its body, shards of glass tearing it apart, leaving only empty wounded space, burning with every breath. Finally the creature slid down the door, onto the floor, and held its head in its hands until the sobs turned to a whimper.

And all the while, the image just watched.

These episodes began when I first came to this land where mountain and ocean meet. I came alone to live, three months after Brian was killed in a car accident, exactly six months ago to this day. He had been tying up loose ends at his office and was hurrying home so that we wouldn't miss our flight. The light, witnesses had said, was yellow when he flew through it, only to be stopped by another car hurling through a red light. The car had hit Brian's on the driver's side going 50 miles an hour, killing him instantly.

I was home taking care of last minute details before we left. I was annoyed when he was 30 minutes late, angry at 45 minutes, worried at an hour. When the phone rang several hours after he was supposed to be home I was sitting at the dining room table thinking about the trip we were going on, refusing to allow the incessant ringing into my consciousness. I sat while daylight faded to dusk and then to darkness.

I ignored the phone and refused to answer the knocking on the door that attempted to interrupt my vigil. I sat imagining every moment of our trip, the trip we had dreamt about, the one that was to mark the beginning of the rest of our lives. I sat, refusing to let anything in that might dare to rewrite my future.

CHAPTER TWO

That was the way I wandered through the first two months. Hollow. Numb. I helped make the proper "arrangements," sat through the funeral without a tear and even smiled and said thank you to those who, for some reason, found it necessary to apologize for Brian's death. People would remark to my family how strong I was and how well I seemed to be handling it. My parents would nod and look at me with a worried smile.

They knew. They knew that I spent each night sitting in front of the window of my old room, staring into the darkness. It scared them. They would ask if I wanted something to eat, if I wanted to go out for coffee with the friends who would stop by, if at least I would talk to my brother who called nightly to check on me.

But I just sat. Staring. I'm sure it looked as though I was losing touch with reality. And I guess in a way I was.

What I was doing in the deep of night was living out my life with Brian, the way it was supposed to be, in my mind. I could see and hear him clearly - his soft gentle features, so out of line with his deep, teasing voice. I could picture the house we had just rented and hoped one day to buy. The one we were on our way to when he was late getting home.

The time I spent in front of the window was more real to me than anything else. Blindly I moved through the day, doing what I could to avoid the act of living, just waiting for night to descend and carry me back to the sweet respite found only in darkness.

And then I made the decision to stop living out our life in my head and actually go and live it.

What that required was packing up and moving thousands of miles from my home and family in Florida, to live in a place where I knew virtually no one. A place with snow in the winter. If at the time I had thought of it like that, or thought of it at all, I would never have done it. But I didn't think. I simply followed orders.

"You must go, immediately." The command had drifted in softly and wrapped itself around me. I clung desperately to the belief that the voice belonged to Brian. Finally he had come to tell me what to do. I would follow without question, never doubting that he would be there waiting with cockeyed smile and tousled hair, wondering what had taken so long.

Hugging my pillow, I fought back voices of reason that clamored to be heard and did what I could to squeeze out the ache that swelled beneath the surface. I let my emerging plan creep into every corner of my awareness and take over with a force so strong that nothing short of destiny's hand could have altered it.

When I stepped into the kitchen of my parent's home relief swept over their faces. It had been a long time since they had seen me smile, and I'm sure it was with blind hope that they accepted it as a sign that I had awakened from my walking slumber.

As I stood watching them, sitting as always at the little round table in the corner, a hand reached through the fog and threw back a thick black curtain, exposing for a fleeting moment those truths so carefully concealed. The scene before me, once familiar and ordinary, became completely alien. My parents, the people who tied me to this earth and tethered me to shore could not pull me in. This kitchen, and all the comforts of childhood were beyond my reach. I was disappearing, leaving behind only a shadow sheathed in skin.

For an instant I knew these truths, and then the curtain dropped.

I said it as though it was the most natural thing in the world, as though I was telling them I was going to the corner store. "I'm moving to Maine. Immediately. Isn't that wonderful?"

From a distance I watched as their expressions changed from surprise to disbelief, to something bordering on despair, or pity. My mother tried setting her mug down carefully but it teetered and sloshed coffee onto the table and her robe. My father just stared. Finally my mother spoke, blindly wiping coffee from her lap.

"Y.y.you're what?"

"I'm moving to Maine. It makes sense really. I mean, financially it's possible. You know that. Brian…he…he provided well for me. And anyway, we were all set to go, the house was ready for us, at least through the summer and fall. I've only missed two months. The house may still be available and I could just rent it for awhile until I find something." I spoke while seating myself across from them, sounding completely assured of my decision and totally unaware of any difficulties it might involve.

Such confidence is a gift, if born of faith, but mine was pure illusion. It was completely out of my nature to do something so independent and impulsive.

I was a child of habit. I didn't like change. I liked security and safety. Before now the foundation upon which I had entrusted my world had remained firm and served me well. My parents had laid that foundation and then built the walls around it, taking their promise to protect me seriously. In return I had become a master at hiding, fiercely upholding the sanctity of the status quo and believing with all my might that if I didn't create chaos it couldn't find me.

But it had hunted me down, and my poor parents had no idea what to do. This, they had been unable to save me from.

Since the accident they had done their best to maintain what they could of their well-developed safeguards. Never speaking of the details of Brian's death, or the details of my grief, they simply hugged me and told me they loved me and that everything would be okay. They were strong and kind and did what they could to keep me from my pain. Without hesitation or invitation they moved me out of the house I had shared with Brian and back into my childhood home. They packed up all of his belongings and answered the endless phone calls and letters that came in. I had not put up a fight. It was easier to live with my illusions without the physical reminders of his absence.

And as almost a gift they allowed me my nightly sojourns into the dark. In truth I am sure they were afraid to tread into that darkness, afraid of what they may find in those places, or afraid they wouldn't know how to return from them. Whatever the reason I was simply glad they didn't intrude.

But on the morning of my announcement, without knowing it, as perhaps is often the case, I put the first crack in our unspoken agreement to do what we could to keep the darkness in silence.

I believe at that moment my parents could see the shape of things to come. But they saw it through the lens of their own fear, and so resisted the deeper voice that whispered of salvation.

CHAPTER THREE

I pulled myself up from the bathroom floor, rinsed my face with cold water, and stumbled through the bedroom, grabbing the blanket from the end of the bed on the way out. Wrapping it around myself, I walked into the kitchen and put the kettle on the stove. While waiting for the water to boil I stared blankly across the family room, watching showers of light spill in through the French doors that lined the back wall, becoming lost in the sensual dance of shadows playing upon the wood.

The kettle's whistle called me back. Mechanically, I took a tea bag from the box on the counter, put it in a mug and poured the boiling water over it.

Pulling the blanket tighter around my body, I took the tea, crossed the room and opened one of the doors. Crisp autumn air brushed against my face and feet and sneaked into the folds of the blanket, tickling my bare skin. I inhaled deeply, loving the smell of morning dew mixed with pine.

A stone pathway meandered gracefully away from the house. Following the steps with my eyes, I was carried closer and closer to the edge of the earth, or so it appeared. I knew the path well, every stone and tree and chipmunk that called it theirs. Walking slowly, I savored the feel of each step, the smooth curves of the stone, the rough spots in-between.

Brian had loved to run down the path, always in a hurry to reach his destination, but I had liked to take my time, lightly touching the bark of each tree along the way. Every morning I would bring birdseed and wait for the nuthatches to come, perfectly content to let the world go by without me. But after a while I would sense Brian impatiently watching from the end of the trail, waiting for me to scatter the seeds and follow him beyond the trees, where always, I would be stopped in my tracks.

Now, here without Brian, everything seemed a little less of itself. But as I followed phantom footsteps out of the garden, and passed through a screen of barren branches, I couldn't help but be taken aback by the sheet of blue that rolled bravely toward the horizon. How often I wondered where to find that point where water's strength and sky's wisdom melded.

The small hill I stood atop bowed to a wide stretch of beach below. To the east, mountains claimed the land, while islands guarded the sea that stood between them and me. Making my way down to the beach, I walked to where the water lapped against the shore and sat just beyond its reach. Drawing my knees close, I hugged the blanket around them and dug my toes between the layers of wet rocks, searching for the course earth beneath.

Luckily, the beach appeared deserted. I'm sure I would have looked rather foolish to anyone passing by - alone, barefoot, and naked beneath a blanket, sitting by the water on a 40-degree morning. I wondered what the neighbors thought of the strange young woman that lived in isolation amongst them.

I spent all of my time alone, walking the shore, hiking the trails, or in one of the kayaks Brian and I had bought to christen our new life. When I had first arrived I had expected to find him on every street corner, feel his presence as I strolled through town - but I hadn't, and so I rarely went to town anymore, only for food and supplies, and once to see a movie in the little theater. It hurt too much to walk the streets that we had roamed, ducking into shops and stopping for ice cream.

From our first visit it felt like we had come home. Maine, with its deliberate beauty, quiet dignity and unhurried temperament called to us, telling us it was where we belonged. The whole Downeast area had a magic about it, something special that felt strangely familiar - something that drew us back time and time again.

The summer before Brian's death we had rented the little house for a week, after discovering it the previous fall.

We were staying at the Bay Ledge Inn, our usual bed and breakfast just north of Bar Harbor. It sat perched on a cliff overlooking the water, with a steep stairwell that led to a private beach where we loved to walk and sit and explore for hours. But on this particular morning we rose early, graciously ate the breakfast provided by our hosts, and set out to devour what we could of Mt. Desert Island. It was a ritual we followed at least once during every trip.

This time we sought out the unknown, winding in and out of hidden streets, until happening upon a narrow drive laced by maple trees, their autumn smock forming a canopy above us. The road was filled with potholes and we bounced along until it turned to dirt, wound its way out of the maples, and dead-ended into a row of towering pines that stood like guards at the gates of Eden, denying us a view of what lay beyond.

Here the roadway turned to the left and then curved widely to the right, depositing us on the other side of the pines. At the road's end a gently sloping hill with a patch of wood loomed glorious above us. Stopping the car we got out, and for a while just stood, holding hands and breathing in the sounds of the sea.

Four houses, nestled deep into the land, dotted the roadside, each opening up to a sweeping view of the ocean. We chose to walk in the opposite direction, between the last house and the thick gathering of trees, along a narrow strip that eventually widened, creating a natural pathway for us to follow.

We walked until we reached the edge of the hill and then carefully descended toward the beach. Once there we climbed among the rocks, bending down to investigate starfish and collect the colorful bits of tumbled glass that had washed ashore.

I'm not sure how we had missed it, but as if on cue we turned to discover it at the same time. From where we stood all that could be seen was a roof and stone chimney peeking out between a red and orange flurry of leaves.

With only a look and not a word we moved up the hill. Upon reaching the entrance to the woods we found the first stone step and together followed the curving path. Every footfall carried us deeper into the cloister of trees, each providing entrance through another doorway, as though whatever hermetic seal had long been in place was now being broken.

And at the end of the path it sat, as if patiently awaiting the sisters of Fate - planted firmly in the pages of its own history, yet somehow held outside the margins of time.

CHAPTER FOUR

I have no idea how long I'd been sitting on the beach when I sensed movement. In the distance I could just barely make out the faint outline of a figure. There wasn't another house for miles in the direction from which it approached, and I'd seen no one pass that might be on a return journey.

As the figure moved closer the blurred edges of the outline began to focus, and I could see that it was a woman. She seemed to float above the rocks, having no trouble maneuvering around them. I hugged my knees to my chest, drew myself in, and prayed she wouldn't notice me. All I wanted was to be invisible.

My discomfort was not so unfamiliar. I'd always felt a little awkward in the world. Reality overwhelmed me and life had proven itself to be too much a paradox - so beautiful on one side, like Brian, and so frightening and unpredictable on the other, like his death.

Growing up I had lived in a virtual cocoon, fibered by the arms of those who loved me. In college I had read a story about the Buddha that said that as a young man he had been shielded from life's hardships by being kept within the safety of his city gates. I too had lived behind such walls. The difference was that he had wanted to explore beyond them, and I did not.

The story continued that when the young Siddhartha sneaked out of his home he encountered various forms of suffering. For me, the suffering I witnessed on television or vicariously lived through movies and books, the suffering I saw huddled on the streets of the city and heard in the stories of friends, even the small sufferings I had known in broken hearts, lost friendships and growing up, were more than enough to suffocate and overwhelm. Some part of me was able to not only envision, but also physically feel, the magnitude and collective accumulation of human anguish, and the rest of me ran from it. It was as if my spirit had never quite recovered from leaving the arms of Heaven.

Throughout childhood and adolescence I had masked the confusion whirling within and made the safest of choices. I went to college, became a teacher and never lived too far from home.

The riskiest area of my life had been my choice in men. I had been drawn to those who lived as I didn't dare - sought out the wild and attempted to tame it. But then I met Brian. He was kind, funny and smart, and knew how to take care of everything, including me. Instinctively I knew that I would be safe under his wing. Young and already successful, protective and ambitious, with feet planted firmly on the ground, Brian was all that a man was supposed to be. With him, I had found my harbor.

The woman was only a few yards from where I sat. I remained very still, only my eyes following her movement. She stopped just short of reaching me, turned to the sea and walked toward it, the water wrapping itself around her ankles. She was barefoot but apparently unbothered by the cold. She moved in a fine mist of violet, and as a soft breeze blew, it whirled in layers around her.

Thick black curly hair sprouted from her scalp and grew aimlessly in all directions. Something in its willfulness, something in her posture, mesmerized me. A power that moved in waves like ripples on the water.

She turned and looked directly at me - my heart raced and a shiver shot up my spine. Silently, I begged her not to speak, not to come any closer. She stood looking at me, reading my thoughts it seemed, until finally she just closed her eyes and bowed her head slightly. Then turning, she continued on her journey.

I watched until the woman disappeared into the fog that had settled over the beach, my heart still thumping and my breath coming in short, shallow gasps. How, I wondered, could a stranger have such an effect on me? And more importantly, why did I have this sudden, gnawing certainty that she was anything but a stranger?

I sat until my breathing calmed, then picked myself up from the rocks and started home. My tea, half full and forgotten, was cold. I was cold. My nose, toes and fingers numb.

The house was not much warmer. Upon closing the door, I scurried to the fireplace, put on a new log, along with some paper and bark, and lit it. Sitting cross-legged on the floor I stared into the fire, the flame transporting me back to that fall day two years ago when we had played on the beach, the day we had found this cottage.

We had been drawn up the stone steps by an irresistible force and had followed them slowly to the back of the property. There we had stood suspended in time, swaddled in the restful arms of the garden, and though we didn't speak of it, I knew we both felt the unusual energy residing there. In the silence I could almost hear its breath and feel the beat of its heart.

"Life is a promise," whispered from all four corners. I wasn't sure what the words meant, but they drifted in clearly on the breeze. I looked to Brian but could tell he had not heard them.

Pulling ourselves from the garden, we had wandered around to the front of the house. There had been no car or any sign of life. After convincing ourselves that no one was home, we peeked in the front windows. I could feel Brian smiling beside me, mirroring my own delight. Deep golden wood everywhere - walls and ceiling, and floors covered haphazardly with throw rugs. A large open space served as family room, dining area and kitchen, all lined with French doors that led to the rear garden. Streams of light rested on the wood. It was perfect, absolutely perfect.

It also looked as if no one lived there, occupied only by an overstuffed couch and a couple of deep armchairs in front of a stone fireplace, a wooden farm table with chairs, and a spattering of miscellaneous pieces. And though everything looked comfortable and used, there was something about it that begged for company, like a once favorite toy now abandoned. Loneliness tugged at me.

Or perhaps it was homesickness, for a home I had never known, but knew I had just found. The future stories of my life took shape and danced before me on the other side of the window.

Suddenly, I was turned around and whisked off my feet.

"Well babe, what do you think? Is this where all of those dreams of yours end up?" Brian was laughing, looking up as he held me above his head, his arms wrapped tightly around my hips. Light danced in his eyes, a child with a secret, or the intention to create one.

Slowly I slid down his body, until we stood so close I couldn't tell whose heart I felt beating in my chest. Brushing a strand of hair from my eyes he leaned over and gently kissed me. His mouth was warm and salty and tasted of every pleasure I had ever known.

When he pulled away there was clearly a plan being written in the air around him.

"Wait here, just one sec," he commanded, and then scuttled away.

"Brian?" I called after him, but he had disappeared from sight.

In what seemed only a moment he came running back, grabbed my hand and dragged me to the far side of the house. We stopped in front of an open window and Brian climbed inside.

"Just what, may I ask, do you think you're doing?" With hands on hips, I looked at him incredulously.

"Come on, there's nobody here. I don't think anybody even lives here." And to the worried expression on my face, "Come on, it'll be fun. I promise."

We were in the master bedroom. The window we had crawled through was one of many that looked out into the woods protecting the house. By the time I had crawled inside and gotten my bearings, Brian was gone, scurrying quickly to check out all the rooms. I lingered awhile, peeking into the little bathroom, and then the closet, relieved to find no clothes hanging or tucked neatly into drawers.

Still, I felt like a trespasser, not just onto someone else's property, but also into someone else's life. I had been carried away by the fantasies, the hopes and yearnings that had been conjured up when standing outside looking in, but being on the inside filled me with fear and the instinct to run.

And I was prepared to do just that when Brian snuck into the room. Turning from the open window, I found him standing in the doorway with his arms crossed over his chest, staring at me. When he spoke, his voice was soft.

"It's okay, really Sara. I've checked it out. There's no one living here. It's so perfectly you, it just calls for you to come and enjoy it. To fill it up. Come on, you know you want to. Anyway, we can't go now." His grin grew to the width of his face, lighting his eyes with mischief. He reached for my hand and led me into the great room.

A fire blazed and a blanket lay in front of it. Jazz drifted softly about.

"Your fire awaits Madam." With a sweeping bow he invited me to sit on the blanket.

Relaxing a bit, I obliged, and returned his invitation with my own.

Without another word, he jumped on top of me. We laughed until our laughter melted into silence. The music and the warmth of the fire tucked into the spaces between us, filling them in, until there were none.

We stayed in the little cottage far into the evening, talking, dreaming and making love. As we drifted to sleep in the amber glow of the dying flame, I knew without a doubt that this place was magic and it held within its walls the best of who we were.

I stared into the fire, wondering why it never seemed as warm as it had that night. Again the pain gurgled up from deep in my chest, but this time the tears were silent. I wrapped my arms around my legs, lay my head on my knees and simply let them fall.

CHAPTER FIVE

Hot water flowed the length of my body. Running my hands over my hair, eyes closed, I lifted my face into the wet spray, the salt of tears lingering on my lips. The smooth rush of warmth became Brian's caress. Tears mingled with water, whirlpooled around my feet and disappeared down the drain.

I stayed that way as long as I could, until my skin shriveled and turned red from the heat.

By the time I combed my hair and threw on a sweatshirt and worn soft jeans, the fire was blazing and the house warmer. After making a small salad, bowl of soup and hot tea I sat at the table near the window and watched the birds and squirrels fight over food as I ate.

Another day lay before me and I wasn't sure what to do with it. My mind drifted to the woman on the beach. Who was she and why had I never seen her before? And most importantly, why had my reaction to her been so strong? I couldn't put my finger on the feeling she evoked: Fear? Anticipation? Curiosity? I decided it was a little of each, but as for why, I doubted I would ever know.

The phone rang and I just watched it, letting the answering machine pick it up. It was my mother. My stomach twitched as I went over and picked up the receiver.

"Hi mom. I know... I'm sorry. I didn't mean to worry you. I was out at the beach...Yes it's cold, but I'm staying warm."

I could hear the real questions beneath the ones she voiced. She asked if I was eating, if I was warm enough, what I was doing with my time, when what she really wanted to know was why I was living alone in a house by the water, thousands of miles from my family. Was there something seriously wrong with me? What had she done wrong? And, did I have any idea how difficult I was to explain to everyone?

I felt sorry for both of us. She didn't know how to ask and I couldn't give her the answers she sought.

I realized I hadn't heard her last remark. "Sara, are you there?"

"Yes mom, I'm sorry, what did you say?"

"I asked if you would like me to come up there next weekend? I could get a ticket and be there by Friday."

We went through our regular routine, with me telling her not to worry and that she didn't need to come, and her wanting to help, but not knowing how. I consistently warded off these offers to visit. She and dad had come once, early on, but up here it was more difficult for all of us to pretend that everything was okay, and yet we were unable to do anything else.

In the end, as always, we both retreated. But this time I promised to come home for Thanksgiving.

"Oh that would be wonderful. Maybe by then you'll have decided to leave that place and come home for good. I'll tell your father, it'll make his day." Her voice began to waver, but as always, she recovered quickly. I could almost hear the reassembling of composure.

I spoke to my father only briefly. His voice was gentle, his concern genuine. The sadness I caused him broke my heart, but I had no idea how to change it for either of us.

Mom came back on the line to say goodbye. "Take care now Sara, make sure you eat. We'll call again in a couple days."

"Okay mom, thanks. I love you."

"I love you too. Bye honey."

"Bye." But she was gone before I got the word out. The dial tone thundered in my ear. I was always left with mixed feelings after talking to my parents, or anyone from home - a mixture of guilt, loneliness and relief. The dial tone was a reminder of how far away they were. And the symbol of how alone I was.

For several seconds I stared at the receiver and then gingerly placed it back in its cradle. Taking a deep breath, I picked up my dishes and headed for the kitchen. From there I heard the shuffle of mail being dropped into the box next to the front door. I waited a few moments then grabbed the small bundle that had been left.

Grateful for something to do, I sat on the floor in front of the fire, poked at it, and then turned my attention to the few envelopes and cards I'd received. There was one from my brother. That was it for the personal mail.

I opened the card and then absently flipped through advertisements marked "occupant," credit card offers and other beloved junk mail. Just as I went to throw it all away, my eye landed on a small tattered postcard with a faintly familiar logo on the front, addressed to M. Jensen. On the other side was a short typewritten note that read, *"Dear Friend, Please join us for an informal gathering of friends old and new. We will be celebrating the talent of local writers, each of whom will be available throughout the day for signings and questions."* The card was signed, "Your family at *The Next Chapter.*"

The Next Chapter. The bookstore. That's why the logo had looked familiar. Scanning the card I looked for the date of the event and discovered that it was today. The postmark showed that it had been sent two weeks before but had obviously been lost in the mail.

Gatherings were far from being my thing these days and I would have discarded the announcement without a second thought if it had not been for the small tingling in the pit of my stomach. Although my old friend Fear stirred at the thought of so many strangers, the idea of getting out for a little while seemed, if not exactly exciting, at least distracting.

Otherwise, I sensed it would become one of those days that would find me curled up on the couch until dark, when I would drag myself into bed, hoping in the deep of the night, in the darkest places of my soul, that tomorrow wouldn't come. Those days had become more frequent as the truth of Brian's death became more difficult to ignore.

I had first arrived with my illusions fully intact, like an extra piece of luggage carried from the plane. When I had contacted the realtor that handled the renting of the cottage she had been very kind, the sound of her voice reaching soothingly through the distance. My parents had handled the cancellation of our plans to rent the house from May through October, and so she knew of Brian's death.

"Hi Jane, this is Sara Jensen. How are you?

"Why hello Sara, I'm just fine, you know me. It's so good to hear from you. I hope you got my letter. I was so sorry to hear about Brian. What a terrible tragedy. You two were such a special couple; we were so looking forward to having you up here. But I told your parents you didn't need to worry about a thing. I certainly hope you received your deposit. I sent it right after I spoke with them."

My voice caught in my throat. "Oh, yes, thank you, but, well I was calling because I wanted to know if the house had been rented or sold yet, or if it was still available?"

"Oh, well, yes it's available. As you're only too familiar with, the Carters aren't interested in having a lot of people moving in and out. And when they heard that you would not be able to…that, well about Brian, they were both quite saddened, and have so far refused any further discussion about it."

We had found Jane Kirby through a series of coincidences when we had begun asking around about the cottage. The day after our discovery we had mentioned it to our innkeepers and they had suggested we go to the real estate offices in town. But there weren't many, and the people in them knew nothing of the little house.

Finally, we had given up. Frustrated, chilled by a persistent drizzle and our waning mood, we had stopped at a coffeehouse for some hot tea, but ended up just staring into steaming mugs. Until, unable to help ourselves, we started talking about the house and the garden, and soon we were laughing at ourselves and the memory of our night there.

It was then that a woman had approached. She was tall and lanky with a thin face and gray eyes, and silver hair pulled into a bun that sat on top of her head, threatening with every move to topple over. I would have guessed, by her hair and fragile gait, that she was in her seventies, but there was something childishly vulnerable in her face and in the fullness of her lips, lips that promised to know more than they should tell.

"Excuse me, I couldn't help but overhear you talking about the old Carter place. At least I'm fairly certain that's what you're talking about. The little cottage out on Boon's Point?"

I looked from the woman to Brian, my eyes questioning his. He shrugged and turned to face her. "Well, we were talking about a cottage, but we're not sure exactly where it is, or what it's called. We're not from around here. It sits on a little hill overlooking the ocean, sort of pushed back into the trees, away from the rest of the houses on the street, and it has a beautiful garden in the back."

"Yep, that's it, the Carter place, no other place like it that I've seen." She smiled, showing all of her oversized, perfectly straight teeth.

"I can't believe it. We've been out all morning looking for someone who might know something about the place, but we've had no luck. And here we had just about given up and along you come." Brian was almost giddy. He stood up and pulled out a chair, gesturing for the woman to sit with us.

"Please, sit. Can I get you something, some tea or coffee?"

She sat but shook her head. "No thank you, I've just finished and was on my way out when I heard you talking about the garden. It certainly is wonderful. Mrs. Carter's pride and joy. I'm sorry; my name is Jane, Jane Kirby. I'm a realtor here and I manage the Carter property. I work independently though, so you wouldn't have found me in an office. And no, not too many people around these days who would know about the place, especially if you couldn't tell them Boon's Point."

Embarrassed that she might have heard our entire conversation, I flushed and quickly said, "We would love to hear anything you can tell us, Ms. Kirby. I'm Sara and this is my husband Brian. We're on vacation and just sort of fell across the cottage."

Brian smiled broadly and added, "It is so nice to meet you. And Sara's right, we'd love to know about the cottage. Is it vacant? Do the Carters still live there?"

"Oh no, they've been gone now several years. There was a time when they'd come back for vacations and summers, but as time passes it gets more difficult - they're a bit too old to be doing too much traveling, though you couldn't get them to admit it. But they keep the place up, have someone in there once a month or so to tidy up, and someone to care for the land, good thing, it's so beautiful." There was genuine affection in her voice.

"Why haven't they sold it, or rented it out at least? I'm sure they could get a nice return on it." That was Brian, always seeing "the return."

"They've been thinking about selling it, that's why they finally called me. I've known them for years, just a little girl when my family moved in a few doors down. I've been selling property here on the island forever, asked if they wanted me to put it on the market when they first moved to Boston to be near Katie, their daughter. They said they'd think about it, might just want to hold on to it for Katie. Ah, but she was never interested in the place, got away from here as fast as she could, went to college, been in the city ever since, always a bit too much energy for this place." She smiled inwardly at old memories of people and days gone by.

Brian and I sat captivated by this funny old woman who, within her bones, held the treasures and ghosts of a time long forgotten. I was struck by the math. How old must these people, the Carters, be, to have been living in the little house when this woman was just a child? I had not thought the house to be so old. So many stories, so much laughter and love. I heard the whisperings of generations echoing through me, urging me to add my own voice.

Picking up on my surprise, or reading my mind, Jane said, laughing, "Wondering how old they are, aren't ya? Closing in on a hundred I think, though it seems to me they've been alive forever, born before time, right inside that house. I really can't believe they ever left it, but I guess Katie insisted. Only thing they love more than that house and each other is that girl. She worried about them here, never trusted the sea...don't know how that happened. But I hear they went down there and moved right into a little house on the harbor. You can't take the sea out of people who are born of it, nope, it's impossible." She shook her head from side to side and I saw the twinkle of old wisdom lighting her eyes.

I could sense her nostalgia and how she loved to talk about the past, but there was also a vibrancy about her that spoke of a full and meaningful present. I liked Jane Kirby, quite a lot, and could imagine myself her friend, no matter her age.

"So the place has just sat empty for *years*?" Brian asked.

"Virtually, yes. As I said they came and stayed some the first couple, but that must be close to ten years now. Since then it's just sat up there on that hill, waiting for them to return."

"Ten years? They had to have figured out that their daughter didn't want it. Why'd they hold on so long?"

"Well, see now, that's quite a question. And you'd have to know the Carters to believe the answer." She sat back with her hands crossed over her chest, looking as though she was challenging us.

Brian raised one eyebrow and smiled at her. "Try us."

She stared intently, cocking her head from side to side as though measuring us up. We just sat and waited.

And then finally, after minutes had passed, she spoke. At first her voice was soft, almost a whisper, as if she was speaking to herself.

"Strange, but interesting." Then, her attention returned but the air of mystery remained.

"I'll do you one better. Yes, yes I will. The Carters are actually coming in tonight, first time in years. I'm not really sure why. Quite a coincidence wouldn't you say? They're planning to stay only a week. I'm having dinner with them tomorrow night. I think if you're available, you should join us. Ask them about the house yourself, and hear, from them, the answer."

Without hesitation Brian spoke for us both, "We would love to have dinner with you."

She clapped her hands together and let out a squeal, "Oh good, this should be fun. I can't wait for you to meet Beverly and Gil. And I certainly can't wait for them to meet you!" The youthful quality I had noticed upon meeting her took over her whole body. For that moment she seemed no older than I.

CHAPTER SIX

On the way to the bookstore it occurred to me how unsurprised Jane had seemed by my request. She had been more than happy to hand over the keys to the cottage for as long as I wanted, and assured me that the Carters, thrilled to just have me there, were in no hurry to discuss selling it.

Thinking of Jane, Bev and Gil brought a smile to my face, and lodged a lump in my throat. I had not seen any of them since taking up residence on the island. The Carters had not visited, as far as I knew. During the first few weeks Jane had called several times and left messages asking me to join her for lunch or dinner. Always I begged off, making up excuses I'm sure she didn't believe. She always understood though, and after a while stopped calling. But not before sending a note that read simply, "Call if you need anything, we will meet again when the time is right."

I drove on autopilot to The Next Chapter, the small, intimate bookstore that I had discovered on one of my few trips out on the island. It was in the beginning, when I still expected to find Brian here, believing that Maine would be the Heaven he would come to.

I had thought that he would be at the cottage, in the garden, on the beach. Racing from the airport in the SUV my brother had arranged for me to lease, I flew into the driveway, and barely turned off the ignition before running headlong into the house. Hurriedly I ran from room to room, calling for him.

"Brian, I'm here, I've come home."

From the family room and kitchen, to the master bedroom we had shared, I threw open every door expecting to see his face, feel his presence. I ran out the back door to the garden, where I finally slowed to breathe - arms stretched wide, eyes closed, face turned toward the afternoon sun, blood roaring in my ears. With every breath I said his name. "Brian."

But all I felt was my heart's own hollow beat.

I dropped my arms and opened my eyes. The squirrels and birds were there to greet me, but that was all. Brian wasn't there. I plodded down to the beach, still but barely holding on to hope. Reaching the shore, I walked along the water's edge, my mood growing darker with every step. Stopping, I stared out at the sea. It was deep blue and calm, the sky above cloudless.

I whispered into the air, "Where are you Brian? You must be here, somewhere."

Tears welled. I blinked hard and held my breath, determined to keep them at bay. I told myself he was there, that he was just being Brian and would never make it so easy – he would want me to look for him. Only slightly comforted, I headed back to the house.

Stepping in through the back door I moved without thought toward the fireplace, a knot forming in my stomach, my hands beginning to shake. Pushing the coffee table back, I sat in the spot where we had laid that first night. It was then that the creature first stirred.

The shaking gripped my entire body and in an insane instant some force took hold, ripping from my gut a primal beast. Burning heat pierced my stomach and chest, strangling my breath, and then a sound, deep and wild, came up from my abdomen and wrenched its way out from behind clenched teeth. With knees tucked under me, I lay my head on the floor until the sound faded, and left me gasping for air. I thought it was over, but then the tears came, sheets of rain, choking and sobbing.

When my strength was gone and the tears had dried up, I curled into a ball and lay staring into the empty fireplace.

And from that day on the creature had become part of my life, her hold increasingly more difficult to break, and her powerful message more difficult to ignore.

When I didn't find Brian in the cottage, I decided he must be somewhere on the Island. And so my search began.

I started in town, looking for him around every corner, retracing our footsteps, waiting for something to happen, something that would assure me that he was there, that I wasn't alone, that I never would be. There were stories of people having visions of a loved one they had lost, of souls hanging on after death to be near those they loved. That would be Brian, he would never let go - we would, one way or another be together forever. We had to be.

I had gone every day, but as each turned into the next I grew weary. Everywhere felt empty. Maine was still beautiful but now tarnished. I could not see or hear him, except in the dark of night, as I had at home. But not as I had expected to, not as I had literally bet my life on.

Not ready to give into the grief squeezing in around me, I continued to speak to my illusions, this time telling myself that I was looking too hard, that I had to be patient and he would find me. That was when I went to the cottage to wait.

It was on one of the last days of my search, a few weeks after my arrival, that I found the bookstore. I had decided to take to the trails, and to start with the last one we had done - the Acadia Mountain Trail, which looked out over Somes Sound.

The morning was cool and the fog lifting as I pulled the car into the designated parking area and made my way to the trailhead. But when I stood at the entrance I was faced with orange tape and a sawhorse that blocked the path. Nailed to it was a parched piece of driftwood with the words, "Trail Closed," written in large black letters.

For a moment I considered ignoring the sign, but then turned away and got back in my car. Where did I go now? There were other trails, but all I could hear was panic's voice calling me under.

I decided to just go home, but when I reached my turn on Route 3, I found myself continuing straight into Northeast Harbor, a small charming town held in a perpetual stretch, yawning and dropping its limbs tenderly around the water.

The road before me was imprinted on my mind like a map. Over the years Brian and I had explored every square inch of the Island, until we felt it running through our blood. I had always loved this area: the marina flocked with boats, the clank of masts answering to the wind, the shops and restaurants along the roadside, and the houses and inns snuggled into the landscape. Driving into town, I felt the arms of an old friend encircle me.

But then something inside lurched forward. A warning bell went off in my gut. Something had changed or was out of place. It must be Brian, he must be here, I had thought. Frantically I scanned the storefronts, but found nothing different or odd. After driving the short distance to the end of town I turned around and returned to the spot where the feeling had first struck. Pulling the car over, I got out and continued my search on foot.

Blindly noting the familiar landmarks, making a checklist in my head, I walked in circles, going nowhere, with the nagging sensation pricking like needles beneath my skin. I stopped abruptly on the sidewalk, overwhelmed by the desire to stomp my feet and throw myself down in a tantrum. The frustration of the day and the disappointment of the past few weeks heaved from the pit of my stomach, threatening to take control.

Just before breaking point, as I stood gripping the roots of my hair tightly in my hands, a woman passed in front of me and disappeared through a wall of green. Bewildered, but distracted from the madness that had nearly taken hold, I followed, timidly pushing aside the overgrowth of plants, surprised to find them concealing a narrow alleyway.

I kept on the woman's trail - a modern-day Nancy Drew on a new adventure. Just inside the entrance a small sign in the shape of an arrow pointed further down the alley, on it the words, "*It's time for The Next Chapter.*"

Noticing the return of the butterflies nesting in my belly, I continued down the walkway, until coming to an old brick building with an arched opening carved into the side, and a wrought iron gate pushed slightly ajar. Moss crept up the brick walls and the air held the musky scent of mothballs and spices.

After walking through the gate and under the archway, I was returned to the open air, delivered into a small brick courtyard shaded by a pergola adorned with lazily creeping vines. Planters sat all around, huge urns filled with flowers. The delicate sound of running water filled the space, mingling with soft music and chimes. A stone fountain stood in the far corner, and as I ran my hand over its porous surface the rhythmic pulse of water began to loosen the snake coiled tightly in my chest.

Startled by the tinkling of a bell, I turned to notice a door leading from the garden. The woman I had seen on the street had just come out, and a windchime danced above her head. She smiled and went on her way. When the door closed, I saw the sign: *The Next Chapter,* and beneath it, *More than a Bookstore.*

Like a gong on my nervous system, the words broke the spell I was under, and sent me scurrying back down the alley. I wasn't ready for "more" of anything.

CHAPTER SEVEN

The afternoon was proving to be a beautiful, if cold, one. The sun was out, the sky a flawless backdrop for Cadillac Mountain, which stood majestically overseeing the land below. With October beginning to fade, so were the leaves, the trees preparing for the winter ahead. I wasn't sure how prepared I was for my first northern winter.

The twisting road before me called forth fragments of all that had happened, winding them in and out and around the corners of my mind, until circling back to the present - to the bookstore. The tingling in my gut returned.

The street in front of the alley was unusually crowded with cars, a sign that made the tingling turn to a churning. "What the hell am I doing here?" resounded in my head. I was ready and more than willing to listen to the voice, to turn the car around and head for home, telling myself that it would be too difficult to park.

As I drove past the hidden walkway my eye caught sight of a sliver of purple beneath a dark cloud, floating along the sidewalk. Everything began to move in slow motion as I stared out the window, afraid of blinking and the image disappearing. Just before turning into the alley, the figure stopped and looked in my direction. Yes, it was the woman from the beach. Holding my eyes for only a moment, she smiled and vanished into the greenery.

A horn blared, and I looked forward just in time to slam on the brakes and avoid hitting the car in front of me. Every nerve stood on end and my heart pounded against the walls of my chest. Twice in one day I had seen this woman and both times she had managed to shake me from the inside out.

She was heading toward the bookstore, the same bookstore I was about to run from. What did I do now? I was crawling slowly down the street, surely annoying the person behind me, when the answer seemed to be given. A car parked just ahead pulled out.

I pulled in, to catch my breath if for nothing else. But instead I held my breath, while my hands, knuckles white, clenched the steering wheel. My brain froze. Every muscle went taut. Closing my eyes I finally breathed, releasing my grip enough to feel the ache in my fingers.

"Ma'am, are you alright?" My scream was faint but I jumped just enough to bang my head on the doorjamb. The man's voice came through the half-open window on the passenger's side.

"Oh…yes, I. I'm fine, thank you. I was, was just, well I was just resting for a moment." Unable to look at him, I fidgeted with the stitching on the wheel, trying to pretend my head didn't hurt.

"Okay, then, just checking. You have a nice day now." And he was gone.

Exasperated, I gathered together my purse and keys, pushed my sunglasses on top of my head and practically fell out of the car. "Idiot, you are such an idiot. 'Oh just resting sir.' What is wrong with me? She's just an ordinary woman, not a ghost or something. Oh good God Brian, you married a fool. And now I'm talking to myself. Maybe you should be put away Sara, there is definitely something wrong with you." Crossing the street, walking down the sidewalk toward the alley, I tried to compose myself. The man had sent Fear running, leaving only self-annoyance to fuel me forward.

Once inside the courtyard peace hit me like a brick. The odd spicy smell, incense I guessed, filled my head and clung to my clothes and hair. Gently falling water broke apart the tension that flowed through my body, and though my mind continued to race ahead, it simply bounced against the stillness and fell to the ground. The experience and the space were strange - frightening and comforting at the same time. I wanted to run as I had before, and I wanted to curl up and stay forever.

Instead I stood in the center of the courtyard and gathered whatever strength I could before venturing inside to become lost in the crowd. And before coming face to face with the woman in purple.

In some ways I was surprised when I first walked into the bookstore. I don't know what I expected, but it was something big, something that fed all the promises of anxiety that had been welling up inside. But instead it appeared to be a simple, charming place. The entranceway, thankfully empty, was narrow and lined to the left with an overstuffed bookshelf, on top of which plants lavishly grew and crept downward, their long vines reaching toward the floor. To my right was a counter with a cash register and a glass case displaying crystal pieces and jewelry made from various stones. Behind the counter was a line of casement windows, all opened to allow in the cool breeze.

Slowly the hum of voices infiltrated my awareness. I followed the walkway to the left, the bookshelf curving to guide the way. Streams of sunlight lit the path as I moved into the heart of the store.

When I rounded the corner and the bookshelf ended I found myself standing on the outside edge of a gathering of people. There must have been fifty men and women of various ages and races, talking, laughing and nibbling on tiny hors d'oeuvres. Comfortable chairs and couches, all inhabited, formed a large wide U in the center of the space. Bookshelves lined the periphery, except along one wall where a single window stood tall and long. The ceiling, low at the front of the store, rose upward several feet above the window and then curved, creating a great sweeping arch over the room.

I felt small, intimidated by the presence of so many who loomed so large. Their smiles seemed genuine, their eyes, joyful. There was nothing outwardly different or apparently extraordinary about them, but *something* definitely set them apart.

It was as though they shared a great secret, one that allowed them to smile and laugh, and mean it. I was sure the woman on the beach knew it and that's why she had come here. It was a secret that had somehow made its way to each of them, that whispered quietly beneath the chatter in the room and yet filled it with its hugeness. It stood in the midst of this place, floating amongst these people, laughing at me. Tears stung and threatened to give me away as the outsider I knew myself to be.

"Sara? Sara is that you? I don't believe it. Well, now yes, of course I do. I knew we would meet again. How wonderful it is to see you dear." Her gray eyes glistened, warm and loving, just as I remembered. We hugged and at once, to my surprise, I felt better, protected and safe in her long, bony arms. Why had I avoided her so long?

"Jane, oh it's so wonderful to see you too. I'm, I'm so sorry I haven't been in touch, things have just been, well..." I shrugged helplessly, fumbling for the right words, not knowing how to explain that I had not wanted to see anyone, including her.

"Don't you worry Sara," her voice grew quiet. "I understand. You've needed time to yourself; we all do at such times in our lives. But things will change, they must you see. Why, just stepping through that door," she pointed in the direction of the store's entrance, "you may just find that your life will never be the same again." She patted my face lightly and smiled.

Her words and demeanor threw me off balance. My hands shook as I smiled and nodded dumbly back at her. I had no idea what she meant, though I knew that this day had already been like no other.

Suddenly her manner changed. Her voice grew louder, her smile larger and her eyes less gray. "I'm so pleased that you found this place. It's quite special you know. It's your first time here." It was a statement not a question, but I found myself answering.

"No. Well, I discovered it a while back, but never came in, and then I got a flyer for today's event, so I thought I'd come. I guess you come here often?"

"Oh my yes. I'm a regular. Anna who owns the place is a gem. She's always doing things like this. Have you met Mark or Sheila? No of course you haven't, you've just arrived. Well you must. Come with me."

She made her way through the crowd with ease, dragging me behind her. She smiled at everyone we passed, patting the arms and shoulders of many, firmly imbued in her role as the presiding grandmother. Finally we reached the window, under which sat a wingback chair occupied by a remarkably beautiful woman busily signing her name to books that lay stacked at her feet. Her hair, red silk falling the length of her back, stood in sharp contrast against the black turtleneck she wore. Jade green eyes looked up when Jane approached.

"Jane," her voice was strong and feminine, "I was afraid you had left."

"No, no, just spotted a friend. Sheila Ryan, this is Sara Jensen. Sara, Sheila."

Sheila unfolded herself from the chair and stood with her hand extended. "So nice to meet you Sara."

"It's nice to meet you too." I wasn't sure what else to say, so I just smiled. Small talk had never been my forte.

Just then, Jane, who had snuck off, reappeared with someone new attached to her side. "Sara, this is Mark Wilde." When I turned around, stark blue eyes caught mine. Dark hair hung long over them, and curled just above the collar of his shirt. His face was tan and rugged, his jaw line square and strong. He looked like he had grown up outdoors - a child of wind and water, mountain and sky.

"Hi Sara, it's very nice to meet you. Jane has spoken of you often." His voice was deep, with just a hint of laughter. Immediately, I wondered what Jane had been saying about me. My mind started racing, imagining the worst, that everyone in the room knew that my husband was dead and that I was some crazy woman living alone, refusing to see anyone.

Horror must have registered on my face because Mark spoke again, throwing a life preserver into the murky waters where I tread. Placing his hand on my arm he laughed, small lines appearing around his eyes and mouth, and said, "Don't worry, she says only good things, how fond she is of you and that you're staying in Bev and Gil's old place. I love that cottage. I used to spend time there myself."

Jane piped in before anything more could be said. "Mark and Sheila are exquisite writers. They live here on the island and both have books published."

"Really? That's great. I...I love to read and I always liked to write, but I don't think I've ever met anyone who was published." To my own ears I sounded like a child and knew without a doubt that I did not belong here, and was quite sure that these beautiful, successful people knew it too.

But if either Sheila or Mark felt that way, they didn't let on. Mark just smiled, exposing a mouth full of straight, white teeth, and Sheila laughed, the freckles across her nose wrinkling together. "Well Jane is very kind, but it really is not as glamorous as it sounds. Bookstores like this one make the difference."

Her graciousness put me more at ease. The muscles in my neck and shoulders began to relax. Perhaps I would be able to string a few words together without embarrassing myself. But before I got the chance Mark excused himself, winked at Sheila and went to greet another man who had just walked in.

I watched him dumbly for a moment and then turned my attention to Sheila. "I'm afraid I'm not familiar with your work, what are the titles of your books?"

"Oh well here, let me get you one. I happen to be swimming in several of them at the moment." She leaned down and picked up one of the books she had just finished signing. Before handing it to me she opened the front cover, paused thoughtfully and then, with long lean strokes, added something to her signature.

"Thank you Sheila. But I'd be happy to buy it."

"No, please, my gift to you," and then conspiratorially, "just don't tell Anna I'm giving away books, she might not appreciate me undercutting her business." She giggled again and I knew she was teasing. "Actually it's amazing Anna can stay in business with all she gives away."

Just then a hush came over the room. The talking and laughter faded into silence and stillness resonated from the center. Sheila's eyes moved past me and her face smoothed into a softer, deeper smile.

I couldn't imagine what had so transformed the atmosphere. Hugging Sheila's book close I turned slowly around.

Never had I known a person to inhabit a space so completely, for a presence to live so loudly in silence.

She had entered through a hallway at the back of the store, on the other side of the large U. She wasn't very tall, but she held herself in a way that made her tower over the largest in the room. Her ballerina grace carried her to the center with delicate precision. Still untamed, her hair remained the only aspect of herself that seemed out of her control. She greeted each person she passed, touching them lightly on the arm.

It might have seemed like the entrance of royalty, as though this creature in purple was here to hold court, if it was not for the creature herself. Though she possessed an air, it was not one of superiority, but rather of openness. There was strength, but it was completely gentle in its power. "Total self-possession" is what occurred to me as I watched her, every move made without any assertion of will.

She came to stand in the center of the circle that had formed and carefully turned to look at each person. When her eyes fell upon me she paused ever so slightly, and I sensed the same energy from that morning rippling outward. Her eyes, clear blue pools, shot through me and paralyzed, I was unable to look away. Her beauty was awesome, more so because it was a beauty that radiated around her rather than one that lay upon the features of her face.

And then she surprised me.

With a bright smile and dramatic flair she threw her arms in an arc behind her back, bowing deeply. Everyone began to laugh as she threw her arms back over her head and laughed aloud, the sound, deep and full, rising above the rest. Then, like a young girl, she clapped her hands together and bounced lightly in place, giddy with delight.

"Speech, Speech." It came from someone in the crowd. I looked around frantically, wondering who would dare yell out at her. I was flustered and for some reason upset by the breaking of the silence and by her sudden change in posture. Everyone around me was whispering to one another, nodding genially and mindlessly clapping while waiting for the woman to speak.

I could not imagine a voice coming from her. She was such a mystery, a holographic image that came and went. I had followed her in here, hoping to discover who she was and why she kept appearing out of nowhere today. But as I stood holding my breath, waiting with the rest of the crowd to hear what she might say, it occurred to me that she was just a woman, real and obviously well known. Disappointment began to mount and at the same time, relief.

"Welcome friends. And thank you." Becoming still, hands held together in a posture of prayer, she bowed her head reverently. As she spoke, the room once again became quiet, the same arresting stillness taking over. Her voice, at once soft and strong, had the same effortless quality as her movement. My disappointment began to wane. So focused was I on the sound of her voice, I barely made out the words.

"It is wonderful to have each and every one of you here today. It warms my heart to see so many old friends and thrills me to see so many new ones. And for those of you whom I do not know, I bid you an extra-special welcome. May your journey carry you across our threshold time and time again.

"You have all come here today to help us honor our local writers. We have with us Sheila Ryan, Mark Wilde and Jeremy Rivers. Each has honored us by sharing their wisdom through the medium of writing. I am grateful for the opportunity to not only read their work, but to be blessed with their friendship. They offer us the chance to know ourselves more fully, to open our hearts and our minds to the beauty and splendor of our own truths. I thank them for being here and urge you all to continue to speak with them and with one another, for we each have something very special to share. At this time Sheila is going to share with us a passage from her latest work. Sheila, the floor is yours." Sheila moved forward and met the woman in purple where she stood. After embracing for an extended moment, the woman moved away and disappeared into the crowd.

Next to me I felt a presence. I was sure it was she, and when a hand touched my arm I jumped, as though lightning had struck.

Upon turning around I was again filled with disappointment and relief. Mark Wilde stood next to me. He didn't speak, but smiled gently, his touch returning me to the moment. I directed my attention toward Sheila, realizing I had missed both her introduction and the beginning of her reading.

"...our life. The landscape of our souls is much like a tapestry, interwoven threads that come together to make up the rich colors and textures of who we are. The patterns of the Self are complicated and intricate; often we see nothing but the big picture and tend to judge it as good or bad, instead of taking the time to come to appreciate the delicate beauty of each fiber, to wonder at the awesome hand that turned so many separate, distinctly different pieces into one magical whole.

"As you walk closer to a tapestry, or any piece of art, you discover that the whole disappears and what you see are the individual threads, or brush strokes, or words, each alive in its own right, but made only more magnificent when viewed in relation to the rest.

"This is what we must learn to do - to study yes - but also appreciate, hold gently in our hands and experience fully the different textures and threads of our selves. To wonder lovingly at each part, to not judge, but acknowledge, honor and be grateful for what they teach us, knowing that each has a purpose to serve. And in time, when we have heard what they tell us, when we have learned what they teach, then, as we do with our art, we may decide which pieces truly belong in the picture we wish to create. For unlike the woven tapestry, our landscape is not fixed, but ever changing, and we are both artist and masterpiece, creator and creation. Never alone, though, we are always guided by the One who designed the threads, mixed the colors and gave us the wisdom to weave."

Slowly, Sheila closed the book from which she read. For a moment there was not a single sound or movement. And then, like a crashing wave, applause. Sheila herself seemed frozen until the clapping began and people rushed toward her.

Throughout the reading I had listened intently, moved by the poetic fluidity of her words, yet had found it difficult to hold them in my mind long enough to capture the full meaning. I had been a little surprised, for some reason having simply assumed that Sheila wrote romances about beautiful heroines who fell in love with perfect men and lived happily ever after. I was not expecting to hear what sounded like something between psychology and theology. I didn't know what to think and was embarrassed that I had not been able to digest it completely. Obviously everyone else in the room had.

"Beautiful, wasn't it?"

It was Mark, still standing at my elbow. I had forgotten he was there.

I nodded, not knowing what else to say.

"She has a real gift with language. Look how embarrassed she is though by all the attention. She has trouble believing sometimes that she deserves it." He shook his head and smiled as he watched Sheila, obviously crazy about her. It suddenly occurred to me that they must be a couple.

I had not thought of Brian once since arriving. Guilt washed over me and was met with a tidal wave of pain. Seeing Mark's love for Sheila triggered the flood of a thousand memories, a thousand glances shared, looks filled with promises and passion. The ache was unbearable.

Unable to look at Mark again I turned to walk toward the sign on the back wall that read "Restroom," leaving him talking to the air. Blindly I moved, the sounds around me droning distantly in my ears. I watched the floor, not wanting anyone to see the tears welling up and falling down my cheeks. Jane called out, but I raced past the echo of her voice, intent on reaching my destination without having to speak to anyone.

The door to the bathroom slammed against the wall behind it, the noise breaking loose the pieces of my heart. All I could do was watch them slide down my body and fall to the floor. I didn't know how to pick them up, or what to do with them if I could. There was no glue to hold them together.

I sat on the toilet lid and sobbed. I couldn't stop it or quiet it. There was nothing I could do but let it out. Why had I come here? What had led me to believe that I was ready, that I would ever be ready, to meet new people, carry on normal conversations, or be anyone other than Brian's wife, Brian's widow?

Voices filtered through the crack under the door, the voices of strangers carrying on their lives as though all was right with the world. How dare they not notice that someone was missing, that the world was *not* okay, that everything was wrong? How could they laugh and chatter on without even *noticing*?

The door squeaked open, slowly and tentatively, as though someone wanted to warn me that they were entering. My sobbing caught in my throat. I sat perfectly still, hoping whomever it was would just use the stall next to me and quickly leave.

"Sara? Sara are you in here?"

It was Jane. She had obviously followed me and knew good and well I was in here. I ran my fingers through my hair and held my head in my hands. There was no escaping.

"Yes Jane, I'm here." My voice shook and cracked. I bit down hard on my lip to stop the choking sobs from returning.

She stood outside the stall. "May I open the door, dear?"

I nodded, and when she didn't respond, croaked out, "Yes."

The door swung out, revealing to Jane the carnage of my grief. My eyes, red and puffy, met hers. I didn't even bother to wipe my runny nose. There I was, sitting on a toilet, my pain naked and exposed for the first time to anyone since Brian's death. I was too exhausted to even be embarrassed.

"Well, let's see now. I think we should go and get some dinner. I'm starving and it's time to eat. I know a great place not far from here. It's usually pretty deserted until later, especially on a weeknight. The sun is about to set and if we hurry out of here, we might just make it."

As she talked she turned and locked the door leading back out to the crowd. Then, like a master puppeteer she stood me up and walked me to the sink where she proceeded to wash my face with paper towels and water. Like a mother to a small child she held a tissue up to my nose and I blew. Never did I resist her helping, nurturing hands. Neither did I say anything. I was just grateful that she had not acted surprised or appalled at my condition. If I was to fall apart in front of a virtual stranger, I was lucky it had been Jane.

The restaurant sat back from the road overlooking a fjord. Jane had been right, only two cars were parked in the lot when we pulled in. The dining room was floor to ceiling glass, and we were seated at a table in the corner with full views on both sides. I sat with my back to the door, facing only Jane and the windows, which invited me to gaze upon the sun as it headed for the horizon. A fireplace blazed not far from us and in time I felt myself free-falling into warmth.

Jane had whisked me out of the bathroom and the bookstore without a word to anyone. We had left my car there and she had folded me into hers. The ride to the restaurant had been silent, save for the sound of my nose-blowing and soft jazz coming from the radio.

Seated in the restaurant we didn't say anything for quite a while. I tried to concentrate on the sunset rather than the band of pain growing tighter across my forehead. Jane ordered our dinner and a glass of wine for each of us. I wasn't really a wine drinker but when it came I sipped slowly, allowing the alcohol to melt the tension that held my shoulders to my ears.

Finally I felt able to speak.

"Thank you Jane. For bringing me here, getting me out of there, and most of all for not saying anything about how pitiful I must have looked when you found me. I'm really sorry for taking you away from the party and for ruining your evening."

The candle on the table glowed softly over her face. "Oh my dear, you have not ruined my evening. I could not think of another place I would rather be. And as for how I found you, well, there is nothing that needs be said about that, unless you would like to say it. Well...maybe I'll just say this: we all experience rough waters, my dear, and we steer through them in our own way, using whatever means we have. There is no *wrong* way."

She laughed and waved her hand in front of her. "Oh my, see what living on the sea will do to you? You start talking in nautical metaphors. Forgive me please."

I laughed and it felt good. The wine, the fire, the sunset and the company of this funny old woman had been just what I needed. It helped that I knew that Brian had liked her so much. I imagined him sitting with us, arms crossed on top of the table, leaning forward to capture every word she said.

"Well, thank you Jane. I...I'm not sure that I know what to say about it. It's been such a long six months. I don't even know what I feel or think. It's like I've been in a daze since..." I lowered my eyes, "since the accident."

She reached over and patted my hand. "You two were so in love, that was easy to see. And my, he was handsome, and so sweet and interested in everything. So many questions. And I bet he was a mischievous one, something about him…" She laughed.

My eyes were wet with tears, but this time they were filled with the joy of memories, not the pain. "Yes, he was. He loved to laugh. I was the serious one. He lightened me up. And he made me feel safe. I've always been a big scaredy cat."

"Scared of what?"

"Life I guess, everything. But with Brian I didn't have to be. He made living look so easy." My gaze wandered to the sky, "It doesn't feel easy anymore."

Jane allowed me to stay with my thoughts until I was ready to return.

"You see, without him, I'm just a big chicken."

"I think you're very brave."

No one had ever accused me of being brave. "Well, you obviously don't know me very well, or you are just a lousy judge of people." I smiled to let her know I was teasing.

She acted offended. "I will tell you that I am a terrific judge of people, and if I say you are brave, then by God, you are." She smiled back at me and then continued.

"Really, Sara, how could you not see what a courageous thing you did, moving up here all by yourself?"

"Oh, but you don't understand. I, oh, this will certainly convince you that I'm crazy. I expected to find Brian here. I thought he would be waiting for me, that this is where he would be. Not that he was alive, really. I don't know how to explain it. I was at home, my parents' home, and I woke up one morning and was sure that I heard him telling me to come here. As far as I was concerned I had no choice." Jane nodded wordlessly, as though she truly understood, and waited while I went on.

"Anyway, I didn't know what else to do. I couldn't stand seeing my parents work so hard to convince me, and themselves, that I was going to be okay. I didn't know what to say to anyone, I was tired of feeling bad about it all. I've always liked to be alone. I'm pretty comfortable with it, there's no one to watch me say or do the wrong thing, no pressure I guess to get it right. Brian was the only person I felt I didn't have to work so hard around."

My own words caught me off guard. I had never voiced any of these things to another human being and yet they had just fallen out of my mouth. It felt good to say them out loud. But it also frightened me. I had held my feelings, my thoughts, and my life with Brian so close that they had become the very air I breathed. To give them away felt a little like a betrayal, and left me, quite literally, short of breath.

Embarrassed by my outpour, I said to Jane, "I'm sorry for rambling on. I...I don't usually do that. It must be the wine."

"Ah, we all need to ramble once in awhile. I do it all the time. Really, Sara, I feel quite honored that you would share that with me. Don't ever apologize for how you feel."

And with that, she changed the subject. I was tremendously relieved to move on to something else.

"What did you think of Sheila's reading tonight?"

"Oh, it was lovely. I can't wait to read the book." I had almost forgotten about the book and wondered if it had even made it out of the bathroom with me. I didn't want to delve too deeply into that topic, sure I would have little to offer in the way of interpretation or insight. So instead I asked her what I had been burning to know.

"Who was the woman that introduced Sheila, the one in purple, with the wild hair?" I tried to ask nonchalantly, while picking at my lobster stew.

Jane stopped mid-bite and looked at me across the table. "Why, that was Anna of course. Didn't you meet her? I'm sure I mentioned her to you. She owns *The Next Chapter*, or I guess she owns it. Anna and *The Next Chapter* are sort of one and the same, been around a long time. She doesn't seem to age though, all that healthy living I guess. Isn't she wonderful?"

Anna. Okay, I had a name and an occupation. Neither were too mysterious or exotic, or anything to be afraid of. So why had the butterflies returned?

I thought about Jane as I drove back to the cottage. She had insisted on paying for dinner. I felt badly because she had done so much as it was, literally saving me from myself. But she had no intention of taking no for an answer. We had driven back to my car and she had left me with a hug and an invitation to a dinner party at her home over the weekend. Assuring me that I needn't respond, she shoved the address and a map into my hand and told me to just come if I felt up to it.

The rest of dinner had gone smoothly, with no further talk of Brian, or Anna. I wasn't ready for more of either. We had fallen into easy conversation about the old days on the island. Jane talked openly about growing up, and her life with her beloved husband, whom she had lost many years before.

I was shocked when she said she had barely been beyond the borders of Maine, and rarely, if she could help it, left the island. When I asked her why, she said simply that she had everything that she could ever dream of happiness being. There was nothing to search for elsewhere. Her peacefulness moved me; one day I hoped I would be able to speak of Brian the way she spoke of her husband, without the hopelessness that seemed tethered to me now.

Before climbing into bed I slipped into one of the several shirts of Brian's that I had kept. They were hanging in the closet, waiting for him. Slowly I buttoned it and ran my hands along the soft cotton, remembering how it looked and felt on his lean body. Pulling the open collar to my nose I inhaled, hoping to catch a last lingering remnant of his smell. But it had faded long ago. Snuggled deep into our bed I wrapped my arms around myself and drifted to sleep.

CHAPTER EIGHT

I awoke in darkness. My eyes were open but I could see nothing. Blackness engulfed me. I was floating on a dark cloud - weightless and free from the bounds of gravity. I would have been scared but there was something soothing in the emptiness. Lying still, I listened, but could hear nothing - not the wind, nor the trees rustling against the sides of the house. Nothing but silence.

I realized I was holding my breath. I moved my arms and a cool wave rushed over me. My eyes began to focus. I looked up and a light shone in the far distance, its rays filtered through the murky haze. I reached for it, and air escaped from my nose, sending bubbles to rise in circles around my head.

My God, I was underwater, deep beneath the surface where it was dark and cold. All of a sudden I was terrified. Panic took over as the air pressed against the walls of my lungs, burning my chest. I could not hold my breath much longer. My entire body pulsed loudly, my head on the verge of exploding. What was I going to do?

And then it struck me. It was so simple. I was going to swim toward the light, or I was going to die.

Dying seemed like a viable choice. It would be so easy. I could just stop moving. There was nothing above the surface that I wanted anyway. Here, there was no more pain, just an endless, beautiful void.

I stopped fighting my need to breathe. Dropping my arms I looked down and slowly began to float toward the bottom of the ocean. The deeper I went, the more silent and still it became. Emptiness invaded every pore until even thought subsided. The last one I had, was the hope that Brian would come.

I was moving upward, quickly. Twisting and turning, I struggled to stop the motion, to free myself so that I could continue my descent. Reaching above my head I felt a hand. "No!" The word pounded in my skull as I traveled closer to the light.

But I was powerless – weaker than the force that held me. Obviously whoever it was wanted me to live more than I wanted to die.

Bursting from the water's surface felt like breaking through glass. Once there I gulped in air, my lungs starving for oxygen. I treaded water frantically, not sure I would have the strength to swim to shore. But then my feet hit bottom and I realized the water was only waist deep. How had I almost drowned, fallen so far, in such shallow water? I had no idea.

Remembering that someone had pulled me out I looked around, trying to find the person who had saved the life I had just tried to end. There was no one in the water.

Something caught my eye, a flash of color moving far ahead of me along the beach. As quickly as I could I waded in that direction. Raising my hand, I prepared to call out, when the figure stopped. Moving closer, breathless, I stumbled. Too weakened to move any further I collapsed in the muddy waters.

A hand reached out, grasped mine and pulled me to my feet.

I raised my head and looked into the stranger's eyes. Her crystal blue gaze met mine. Dark, curly hair, dry and wild, flew through the fingers of the wind, and her purple dress remained untouched by the waves.

She spoke but I couldn't hear what she said. I asked her to repeat it but she just smiled and began to walk away.

I tried to run after her but I kept stumbling...

With a violent shake I awoke, panting, heaving for air. A dream, it had been only a dream. But it had felt so real; I could almost taste the salt filling my lungs.

The clock read 2:11. The middle of the night. Desperately I wanted to go back to sleep, but was terrified of what might await me. Closing my eyes I became lost in remembering the cool, watery grave I had chosen for myself. I heard it calling. Peace washed against the shore of my soul and I was no longer afraid to return. Deeper and deeper, farther into the recesses I longed to go, the gentle emptiness lulling me back.

But then the drowning sensations returned and the need to breathe became stronger than the will to die.

My eyes flew open and I sat bolt upright in bed. The room, like the water, was dark and cold, but held no peace. Wind blew through the branches of the trees and they danced upon the roof. Every pop and groan of the house echoed loudly. The doors in the family room rattled, as though someone was demanding entrance. I watched my bedroom door, expecting Anna to appear. Thankfully, she remained adrift in the fog of my imagination.

I wasn't surprised that she had materialized in my dreams. It was her presence in my life that was disturbing.

Wide awake, I knew it would be impossible to go back to sleep, so I grabbed my blanket and book and headed for the couch, hoping a fire and a little reading would fend off the ghosts of night.

Fire blazing and hot chocolate in hand I settled into the couch, the blanket tucked snugly around me. I tried to read, but the novel couldn't hold my attention. So instead, I stared blankly out at the night.

Thoughts of the evening played upon the movie screen of my mind, the faces of Jane, Sheila, Mark, and of course, Anna, floating aimlessly about.

Brian would have liked these people. He would have been fascinated by Sheila's reading and full of questions. He would have known how to talk to her, to all of them. If he was here, we may have become friends with them.

I could see it – a group of us sitting around the coffee table talking, laughing, drinking beer and playing games. Maybe we would have gone hiking or out to dinner. That was the way it should have been. Not me left sitting alone in the dark, unsure if I'd ever see Sheila, Mark or even Jane again, and too painfully sure that I wouldn't see Brian.

"Enough of the pity-party Sara!" I said the words out loud – to stop the avalanche of woe-is-me thoughts I knew would follow.

Consciously I turned my attention to something Mark had said, about time he had spent in the cottage. I wondered briefly why and when that would have been. Often I had mused over the history of the house and the stories it could tell.

Bev and Gil had given away a few, but I had a feeling, not all. We had only met them once, at dinner with Jane. The memory brought back the odd flavor of the evening.

We arrived at the Jordan Pond house early and walked a little ways down the trail that rounded the pond, absorbing as much as we could before seven. Jane arrived first, explaining that the older couple had been delayed and would arrive as soon as they could. Happy to see Jane again, we sat at a table near the window and ordered drinks while we waited.

Conversation was easy. We chatted about the restaurant, the popovers for which it was famous, and the hike we had taken to Bubble Rock that afternoon. We tried to ask her more about the Carters but she said we'd just have to meet them ourselves, but she did ask that we not to bring up the cottage right away, due to the sensitivity of the subject.

Thirty minutes later a distraction stole our attention. A circle had gathered in the lobby and in the center an elderly gentleman was performing a soft shoe dance, and singing loudly enough for his clear baritone to echo through the dining room. It lasted only a moment leaving the crowd calling for more, but then the host broke through and began speaking quietly with the man. From where we sat I could barely see the pair, much less hear what they were saying. But the next thing I knew the host was slapping the old guy on the back and laughing. Together they walked to the podium and the host turned and pointed to our table. Jane, who had been smiling through the whole ordeal, was waving as the man approached.

So this was Gil Carter. He bounced, rather than walked, over to us, his gait lively and much younger than his years. A lean man with quick eyes that seemed to catch everything, and a shock of thick white hair that framed his face like a mane. Though he was of average height, his presence was immense.

Jane stood to greet him and they hugged warmly.

"Oh, Janey, how marvelous to see you, as beautiful as ever I must say. If you weren't such a youngster, Bev would have a run for her money." His eyes danced with joy, and laughter rose from deep inside and filled him up.

Jane seemed to actually blush at his flirtation, like a young girl swooning over the friend of an older brother, though to look at the two of them you couldn't tell who was older. It continued to astonish me that Jane had known these people when she was just a child. She had said they must be nearing the century mark, and yet Gil Carter was more vibrant than many young people I knew.

"My darling, what would Jane do with such an old, worn-out codger? I keep telling you that I am the only woman alive who could put up with you."

She had approached without producing the slightest sound, and stood at his elbow, the very picture of elegance and grace. He had to look up to gaze adoringly into her eyes.

Her hair, silvery-white, was swept up in a bun, leaving her long swan-like neck exposed. Only small lines around her eyes and mouth spoke of age. Her body was long and strong and she moved with the agility of the young. Unlike him, her nature was not playful and childlike, but rather quiet and still. Watching her was like watching a heron, fully self-composed and regal in stature. She was the kind of woman other women look to with awe and envy. The kind you were quite certain possessed the wisdom of the ages, and who, without arrogance, never doubted their own importance.

I was immediately drawn to him and intimidated by her, conjuring up all kinds of reasons not to like her.

"Hello Jane, we are so pleased you could come, and that you brought some friends." She squeezed Jane tightly and then turned her eyes upon us, "Please forgive us for being late. When you get to be our age everything takes a little longer." When she smiled her face softened.

Brian grinned widely, "No apologies necessary, we're just glad to have the opportunity to meet you and are grateful you allowed us to join you. I'm Brian Jenson and this is my wife Sara." He held out his hand to Bev.

Taking it lightly in her right hand and placing her left on top of it, she squeezed. "It's a pleasure to meet you both. I am Bev and this clown beside me is Gil." Her every word was enunciated and spoken carefully, even when she teased. She turned and took my hand and stared at me for a second before letting go.

Gil shook off the formalities and hugged each of us in turn. When he finished with me he took both my hands in his, stood back and whistled under his breath, "My my, Ms. Jensen, you are quite a lovely sight. I hope this fella knows how lucky he is."

"Okay, okay, enough of you mister. Let's all sit down." Jane beamed. It was easy to see that she dearly loved these people.

Dinner with the Carters was an experience like no other. He talked incessantly and laughed heartily, especially at his own jokes. His eyes were perfectly round and sparkling blue, and so wide they seemed never to blink. He was warm and witty and easy to be with, his love for life and the people around him illuminated his every gesture and word. She spoke rarely and when she did it was with precision and purpose. Each word carried depth and meaning and none were wasted. She was not cold or unfriendly, but where Gil lit up everything around him, Bev's fire burned in dark, private spaces, not easily seen, but nonetheless felt. It was as though she tended the flame and he carried it outward.

Both, I sensed, held secrets and stories rich with flavor, deep wells of wisdom to which access was guarded, but once granted, endless in its treasures.

We talked of everything and nothing, ranging from life in Boston, to Brian's job and island gossip, to the latest movies. They showed us pictures of Katie, a striking still-blond woman in her late sixties, and their grandchildren, all grown and leading lives of their own. However, the topic we had come to discuss didn't come up until after coffee, and a large dessert for Gil, had been served.

Early on we figured out that Jane had not even mentioned our interest in the cottage to the Carters. To them we were merely new friends whom they were more than pleased to spend time with. Both

Brian and I hesitated in broaching the subject, but finally, unable to wait any longer, Brian made the first move.

"Bev. Gil. Sara and I have a confession to make. We came tonight because we are very interested in learning about your home on Boon's Pointe. We came across it yesterday, and I'm embarrassed to say we did a little peeping in windows," he cleared his throat and I had to keep myself from laughing, "and we think it's a great place."

They both looked at Jane, and Gil shook his finger at her in mock anger. "Now I see your plan. You set us up. Inviting us to dinner under the pretense of missing us, just so you could try and persuade us to sell the place. C'mon, 'fess up."

"Now Gil, I just thought you might like to meet these people, they have mentioned nothing about wanting to buy the place, only that they stumbled upon it and wanted to know more about it." But with her arms crossed, sitting back in her chair, she looked like the winner in a chess match.

Gil began to speak, but Bev sat forward and the single movement quieted him. Placing her arms on the table and clasping her hands in front of her, she stared for a moment at Brian and then at me, before saying a word.

Then with her eyes resting fixedly on mine, she said, "You heard it didn't you?"

The steady calm of her gaze unnerved me. "Heard what?" My voice was a whisper.

"The house. You heard it." Her eyes drew mine like a magnet. I didn't know how and didn't dare move away from them. They reached in and pulled some part of me out that knew what she was talking about, even though it sounded crazy.

"Yes." The word escaped without my knowing it.

And with that she simply smiled and sat back, breaking the spell. But as she did I could have sworn I heard her say, "Finally."

Whatever happened in that brief, altered, moment changed everything.

Looking at Gil she nodded almost imperceptibly, as though to turn things over to him. He smiled at her and then at us, his big eyes beaming. Whatever tensions he had felt about Jane "setting them up" were gone. We had obviously gained entrance to their treasure chest. Taking the last bite of his dessert he settled into his chair and began.

"Let me tell you two a little story. I first came to this little piece of Heaven nearly seventy years ago. I was just a young man then, in my twenties, traveling for the summer with my parents. This was quite the resort area even then you know. Ah, yes, Acadia hadn't been a national park too long, and back then, well, it was something - the Rockefellers, Vanderbilts, so many names, who were then faces you could see around here." His eyes drifted inward, but with a slight touch from Bev he returned.

"Forgive me, I get lost in the memories. As I said, I was a young man then, not at all happy to spend a full summer with my parents. I would have much preferred staying in the city, trying to win the attentions of a certain young lady," he patted Bev on the hand, "whom I merely *thought* I was in love with, but my parents had insisted I join them.

"So here I was, stuck on this island. But soon after arriving I couldn't help but become enamored with it. I spent my days exploring the shores and mountainsides. I would walk for hours and sail endlessly, until I was arrogant with my knowledge of the place." As he spoke his hands danced wildly about, as though they alone could tell the story.

"One day I was walking a stretch of beach I had chosen as my favorite. It was always deserted and lingered forever in either direction. There were no homes built on it, or so I thought, and so I proclaimed it mine.

"Well, on this particular day I tired of walking and sitting and watching, and decided to go for a swim. So, looking around and seeing no one, I took off all my clothes and ran into the icy cold water. I swam out as far as I could and floated on my back. It's truly amazing how being held weightless in the water, staring up at God's great sky, can replenish the soul. Oh my, I had never felt so free, so much the master of my own world. It continues to stand out as one of the greatest moments in my life, and I have had many.

"But as inspiring as it was it lasted only a few minutes, because all of a sudden I heard splashing very nearby. In but a flash I was standing upright, searching for whatever it was that had startled me. And there to my left, I shall never forget the sight, was the most beautiful creature I had ever encountered. She was swimming right towards me with perfect, strong strokes. I didn't know what to do - my clothes were on the beach and I wasn't sure I was prepared to make a run for it."

Everyone at the table laughed. I could just imagine a young and handsome Gil, so full of himself, suddenly shrunk by the mere sight of the woman I knew to be Bev. Through the telling, Bev's eyes never left Gil's face. I was sure she too was lost in the memories of their meeting, and in the love that had so obviously come out of it.

"A few yards before running into me the creature dove beneath the water and disappeared. More than a little nervous I began to move slowly toward the shore, when all of a sudden she popped up less than a foot in front of me, smiling brightly. She was marvelous. There I was, embarrassed and self-conscious, (which I was in my youth), and there *she wa*s, grinning like a mischievous cat. And what does she say to me? As serious as can be, 'What, may I ask are you doing swimming in my ocean? And by the way, it seems you have lost your trunks.'

"Well, I couldn't help but laugh, her nerve catching me off guard. Plus the fact that I had already proclaimed this part of the ocean *mine*, so I said to her, '*Your* ocean? I'm sorry you must be mistaken, because this is *my* ocean. I have been here practically every day this summer and I have not seen *you* once.'

"To which she answered, 'But *I* have seen *you*, marching up and down the shore like a cat marking his territory. I have watched you think you own this beach, and it has been quite fun. Thank you.' My nakedness overwhelmed me. I felt completely exposed, imagining this girl watching me, unnoticed, invading upon my solitude. Then, I got angry. I couldn't believe her gall, no matter how beautiful she was, she had no right! So I told her so.

"And when I was done huffing and puffing, she just smiled and swam to shore. When she got to my clothes she picked them up, waved them at me and said, 'I suppose you would like these back? Well, I will give them to you if you will stop ranting at me; it is quite rude. Otherwise you will have to walk naked all the way to town, where they will probably arrest you and throw you in jail. And believe it or not, I would hate to see that happen. You may not know me, but I feel that I have come to know you, and I think that I might like you. That's why I decided to come down here and swim today. I had no idea that you would go skinny-dipping. That, I had never seen you do.'

"I was stunned into silence. I didn't know if I should be hopping-mad or wildly flattered. Here this gorgeous girl in a bathing suit was threatening to steal my clothes unless I behaved, and at the same time, telling me in her unusual way that she liked me. Well, in the end, let's just say I did what any good, red-blooded male would do - I gave in. I promised not to yell anymore and even apologized.

"Then she continued to stand there facing me, holding my clothes out, as though she was just going to stay right there and watch me! I decided to call her bluff and I kept walking. It was a game of chicken, one I had never had the thrill of playing. But just before I reached where the water, let's say dropped, *I* chickened out and asked her to please put my clothes down and turn around. She laughed but she did it."

Gil turned to look at Bev and put one of his wrinkled brown hands to her face. "She was, and still is, like no other woman I had ever met. She was gutsy and smart and way ahead of her time. From the beginning she seemed able to reach right in and pull the strings of my heart. After I put my clothes on she turned around and pulled off the swimming cap she was wearing. This long beautiful hair, the color of sunshine, fell to her waist. Without thought or control I grabbed her and kissed her, and haven't let go since."

Slowly and gently he leaned over and touched his lips to hers. She put her hand to his face and they sat that way, lost in the glow of the memory. It was a long moment before they remembered their audience and when they did, neither seemed the least bit embarrassed. They were perfectly comfortable being exactly who they were, two people in love. It was inspiring to see a couple that had been together so long and still had the look of new love in their eyes. I believed Brian and I would have that.

The moment was brought to an end by Brian softly asking, "And after the kiss?"

"Well young man, the rest is history. Bev and I spent what was left of my vacation together. We swam and sailed and walked 'our' beach, and when my parents packed up to head back to Boston I told them I was only going back long enough to get my stuff and then I was coming back, for good. They didn't like it one bit, but I was quite stubborn back then and determined to return. And return I did, but it took a little longer than I hoped.

"You see, before coming here that first summer I had been hired on as a teacher at a boy's school for the following fall, and I decided it would be best to work the year, save up some money and then return. I was lucky that Bev agreed to wait for me."

"Well, I had no choice, you begged so relentlessly." She smiled slyly.

He laughed heartily and nodded, "You bet I did. And the following summer I arrived on her doorstep, ring in hand, and asked her to marry me. She said yes, and from that day until this I have been the luckiest man in the world." Her look told him he was pouring it on a little thick, but he just continued to laugh and hugged her.

"And what about the house, where does it fit in?" Brian asked.

"Ah yes, the house, the whole purpose of the story, I almost forgot," but his wink told us he had not.

"As I told you, Bev had been spying on me that first summer," he looked sideways at her and she waved her hand, dismissing him. "What I came to learn was that she had been doing it from this wonderful little cottage hidden on the hill. It was *our* cottage of course, and just as I spent my days on the beach, she spent hers tucked away inside that house painting, that is when she wasn't taking pictures of me. Yes, yes, can you believe it? She's quite a talent, painter and photographer, and I had become her favorite subject. She would hide up on the hillside watching me, painting and taking pictures. These days she'd most certainly be arrested for such a thing. But back then, well, it was quite romantic and very flattering to my young ego."

Brian looked at Bev, "Did your family live in the house?"

"No, it had belonged to my grandmother, and when she died she left it to me. We were very close and I had always felt a special connection to the house; she knew I would take care of it. But my parents wouldn't allow me to live by myself - I was barely seventeen, so I used it as a studio. I spent every free moment there. And after we were married, we moved in."

"I taught at the local school and Bev began selling her paintings and photographs in a gallery, except the ones of me; I wouldn't let her. We had Katie and she grew up in the house then moved on. We lived there for more'n sixty years. And well, the rest, I say again, is history." Gil's eyes sparkled, but something within them belied the simplicity of the statement. It occurred to me that there was much more to be told.

Brian asked, "Wow, that's a beautiful story. Having seen the house I understand why you loved it so much, and I can only imagine how great it was to live there all those years, but why now, when you're no longer here to enjoy it, don't you allow someone else the chance?" He dug right in, challenging their sense of romance.

"Good question young man. Believe me, you're not the first to ask," he looked at Jane, "and we have pondered it ourselves. You see it's not that we don't want anyone else to live there, though I guess in a way we still expect to return. We have left it vacant, not out of sentimentality or greed, but because the time, the people, or perhaps the circumstances have not been... right, but it appears that all that has just changed."

By the time the check had been paid and we had all walked to our respective cars, the Carters had agreed to let us rent the house the following summer, and if we were interested, they would talk to us about purchasing it. We left the Carters and Jane with hugs and Brian and I drove off on a cloud. Heaven on earth, we believed, was to be ours.

By then I had forgotten all about Bev's talk of "hearing" the house.

Memories of the evening were bittersweet. The odd, old pair, so different than anyone I had ever met, had touched me deeply. It seemed incredible that it had been barely two years since I had first heard the story of the young lovers. It felt like a lifetime.

Sighing, I closed my eyes and snuggled deeper into the couch, imagining Bev in this very room, madly painting the portrait of an arrogant Gil she had yet to meet. I could see her watching him from the garden, careful not to be noticed, taking old black and white photos of the stranger on the beach.

I opened my eyes and they fell instantly upon a small painting that hung just to the right of the French doors. It was not the first time I had seen it, but it was the first time I had really noticed it since moving in. It captured the image of a young Gil walking proud and aimless across the sand, while in the background a surprisingly vulnerable Bev watched him longingly. It possessed a feeling of movement, like being washed over by the ocean, swirling blues and greens and a vibrant agelessness that could almost be touched.

Moving to stand in front of the painting, I felt the pull of the sea, the cold of the water and the warmth of the sand, as it must have felt that day. Tears blurred the colors. I wanted to dive into it, to feel the way Bev must have felt as she watched him from afar. I wanted to know the heat of that kind of love again, to stand in the garden, look down into the ocean and see Brian, swimming naked, alive and free.

The tears fell without resistance, and then they turned to sobs. I couldn't tear my eyes away from the painting, some part of me believing that if I stared at it long enough I could make it real. I wanted to possess it and all that it stood for, and I wanted to destroy it for all that it denied me. With an unfamiliar force I tore the picture off the wall. Turning the image away and holding it in both hands above my head, I stood ready to send it crashing to the floor, when I was stopped cold. Through my haze of grief and anger a light shone. Literally.

Hanging only inches from my face was something small and shiny, swaying back and forth like a hypnotist's pendulum. Confused, I looked up and discovered that the shiny article was a silver rope chain taped to the back of the painting, and from the bottom of the chain hung a locket.

The urge for destruction that only moments before had been overwhelming, drained away. Carefully I lowered the picture and removed the chain. Placing the painting on the dining table I carried the necklace and locket to the couch, handling it as carefully as the Hope Diamond.

It was shaped like a star and on each of the five points was a small amethyst. I turned it over in my hand, rubbing my thumb along the ridges of a circular carving that lay in the center of the star. Holding it in front of my nose I noticed an engraving inside the circle. I had to squint to make out the words: *A star to guide you home. Love, B & G.*

B and G. Bev and Gil. The locket must belong to their daughter Katie.

Inspecting further I discovered a tiny hinge on the top point and a delicate clasp where the two bottom points intersected. Ever so slowly I popped it open. Inside was an old black and white photo.

The picture was of a child, not more than five, with wet, dark hair that hung in ringlets. She wore a bathing suit and stood knee deep in the ocean, arms stretched wide and face tilted in laughter. She was a startling child, one whom even in a photo could take your breath away.

Remembering the pictures of Katie that Bev and Gil had showed us I somehow doubted that this was she. Katie was blond, but it was more than that. This child seemed to shine with wildness, a characteristic I had not sensed in Bev and Gil's city-dwelling daughter.

So, who was she? A grandchild perhaps? The photo seemed so old, and though the Carters did have grown grandchildren, I could not see them in the shadows of this face. The whole family was fair and golden, whereas this child was dark and earthy, more kissed by the moon than the sun.

Carefully I dislodged the picture and checked the back to see if anything was written there, but found nothing. I reinserted the picture, but continued to stare at it, until my eyelids grew heavy. After several suspended minutes I closed the locket, wrapped it inside my hand, curled up on the couch and fell asleep.

While I slept images of the child kept me company. I watched her play along the shore, splashing water and laughing. At first I was merely an observer, watching from the edge of the hill behind the house. In my hand I held a camera. Lifting it, I snapped a picture, just as the child stretched her arms wide and tilted her face to the sun.

All of a sudden Brian was there and the three of us played on the beach. We were a family. Perfect and happy. Then, without warning, the child grew serious and her eyes became hooded with wisdom and age. She pulled me to my knees so I could meet her face to face, and taking my hand, placed something in the palm and curled my fingers protectively around it. She said, "It's time for me to go. You take this; it belongs to you now. It will show you the way." And with that she turned and walked away, my gaze following her down the beach. Suddenly another figure appeared beside her. It was Brian. I called out to them, but they didn't even turn around.

I sat on the sand and stared sightlessly out at the water, unable to remember how to feel anything. And then a hand touched my shoulder. Anna was kneeling beside me. Gently she uncoiled my fingers to reveal the child's gift. Without a word she placed it around my neck, and sitting in front of me, placed her hands on my shoulders. "Wear it, and it will show you the way."

Around my neck hung the silver chain and from it dangled the star-shaped locket.

Dreams continued to haunt me past the hour of daybreak, though none so vivid as this. Mostly just faces, slivers of moments, postcard scenes. Flashes of Brian lying in front of the fire, Gil and Bev swimming in the ocean, the child laughing, Anna bowing under rainbows of light, Sheila reading from her book. The final image returned again to me, seated on the beach, Anna placing the locket around my neck, whispering into my ear the words, "It will show you the way." But when I turned around it was Mark Wilde who stood behind me, offering to help me up.

I awoke just as I reached to take his hand, shivering with guilt that it was Mark's image, and not Brian's, that clung on after sleep. Shaking off the memory I moved backwards to the dream about the child, Anna and the locket. Opening my hand, now crippled from my grip, I re-examined the delicate piece. The words rang in my head, "It will show you the way." "The way to where?" a small voice inside asked. But no answer came.

Wanting to shut the door on further questions, I began mechanically performing the regimen of the living dead that kept my head above water.

I started a fire and went to take a shower. Once bathed, I ate; once fed, I headed for the beach. I thought about taking out the kayak, but one step outside decided otherwise. The cold air, made colder by the gray sky, pierced maliciously through my sweatshirt.

Stepping onto the beach was like stepping into one of Bev's black and white photographs. Water reflected the gray of the sky and absently lapped over rocks, scrubbing them clean of color. Fog clung to trees, obscuring the view of the mountains.

I walked. I sat. I watched the tide come in and then go out. I breathed. One breath after another. I breathed.

With each intake of cold air I released the residue of the night. I wanted only to remember Brian, to see his face, feel his skin. I wanted to return to the embrace of my grief. I feared that if I allowed myself to drift too far there would be no return.

Hours passed. It grew colder and the fog thickened. I thought maybe it would snow. I imagined snow sitting on the water and wondered if I would be able to build snowmen on the ocean.

Brian and I had looked forward to our first winter in Maine, but now it was difficult to think much past this moment. Thinking about the future was about plan-making, and I didn't have any plans, nothing other than sitting on the beach and breathing.

The wind began to blow and the temperature continued to drop. Finally I got up and made my way back to the house, carrying the fog with me. Once inside I sat on the couch and just stared. Loneliness crept up and wrapped around me like a shawl. I pulled it close, comforted by its familiarity.

The day passed in a haze of gray. I read and napped, nibbled on the scant food in the refrigerator and did everything I could to avoid the locket.

I had put it in the dresser in my bedroom. I was hiding it from myself. It asked too many questions and demanded too many answers. It took me into a past that was not mine and threatened to carry me into a future that I was not prepared to enter. I thought perhaps I should contact Jane and find out how to return it to Gil and Bev, but even that felt dangerous. It asked too much of me.

While I busied my mind and body with the nothingness of the day I was able to ignore its plea to be noticed. On the beach I had barely heard it, but in the house its demand rang loudly in my ears: "Wear it and it will show you the way."

Its draw was like a magnet, pulling me deeper and deeper into its field. I knew that to give in to it would distract me, but I didn't want to be distracted and was relieved when darkness fell. In sleep I usually found the perfect hiding place.

I crawled under the heavy cool sheets, again wearing Brian's shirt, and stared at the shadows that stretched across the ceiling. Each time I closed my eyes images from the night before floated by, as if on parade. Fear showed up, fear that sleep would no longer be a peaceful escape, but would instead haunt me with the faces of strangers.

Eyes wide open I spoke into the darkness, "Please God, get them to leave me alone. Let me sleep alone tonight. The only one I want to dream of is Brian. Please God. Please."

CHAPTER NINE

My prayer was answered.

Morning knocked, easing its way into my awareness gracefully. First I heard its arrival, announced by the birds eating breakfast outside my window. Next I saw it, tumbling in on streams of sunlight.

The night had flown by, drenched in bliss. Brian had come. He had taken me flying over the mountains, then laid me gently back upon the bed where he held me until I fell asleep. Turning over I half expected to find him there. Sinking deeper into the bed, I allowed it to hold me in its large comfortable arms.

With a smile I realized I felt faintly peaceful. It was a very different sensation, difficult to define or explain, but for once I did not dread the day ahead.

Getting up I stood by the window. Birds crowded around the feeder. The trees dripped with dew, still moist from the fog and the showers that must have come in the night. Above them a blue backdrop stretched from one corner of forever to the next. Gone was the heavy grayness of the day before.

I opened the window and a breeze blew in, stinging my bare legs. It was cold but beautiful, a perfect day for a hike.

I had come to the edge of the world. Or at least it felt like it. Standing on a cliff overlooking the Atlantic I could imagine a no more perfect place on earth.

The trail was not a long or particularly difficult one, but it was my favorite, especially this midway spot. Being in the presence of both mountain and ocean reminded me that I was alive. It filled me up and echoed deeply in the caverns of my soul. Though I knew little of it, I imagined that this was where God lived.

I sat with my feet dangling over the side of the earth. Breathing deeply I thought of Bev and Gil claiming the ocean outside the cottage. In my heart I laid claim to this spot, forbidding anyone else to tread upon it, except of course Brian. Smiling, I imagined us planting a flag, declaring this our mountain. We would sit and watch the sun dip into the west. The night would wrap its arms around us and we would make love under the stars until everything around us disappeared.

I drew my knees to my chest and hugged them tight. The fantasies did not, for once, make me sad. Here in this place, I was happy inside them. Today they were not merely wishes, but living energies, and I allowed myself to let them be real if only for a little while.

With some regret I stretched one last time and picked myself up. Digging into my backpack I took out a bottle of Evian and took a long drink, then tied my hair back in a rubberband and set off on my trek to the top of the mountain.

It wasn't until I was nearly there that I realized I was talking out loud to Brian. Fortunately the trail was deserted, as most of the park was now that October was retreating. Laughing at myself I continued my conversation, talking as if he were beside me, commenting on the smell of the pines, how cold my hands and nose were, what I was hungry for, anything to keep the light from fading.

The view from the top of the mountain was breathtaking. The sun shone brightly overhead and glistened on the ocean below. I stood alone at the highest point I could find and turned in a circle with my arms opened wide. I came to a stop and reached my arms above my head, trying to touch the sky.

I felt freer than I had in months. Walking from the bottom of the mountain to the top had been like walking out of my own valley to a summit within that I had never known before.

"Thank you Brian, thank you for bringing me here. I had forgotten how beautiful it was."

The words bled from my heart and pulsed through my body, vibrating outward. The air became electrified. I closed my eyes.

Energy raced up from the ground and down from the sky, meeting in my center. My whole body shuddered.

And then the world stopped spinning. Nothing moved, inside or out.

When I opened my eyes I was almost surprised to find everything as it had been only moments before. Motion drew my eyes upward. Above me soared an eagle, wings outstretched and motionless. Suspended in air, effortless in flight.

I watched until the wind carried her toward a distant peak. When she was gone I slowly began my descent, touched by the way life had touched me.

Driving home I sang along to songs I didn't know.

I bounced into the house and immediately turned on the old radio that sat on the kitchen counter. I found the loudest, newest music I could and I danced. I danced around the family room, into the kitchen, through my bedroom and even out the back door. The beat of the music drummed in my blood and I moved until I could move no more.

Sweaty and exhausted I fell to the floor, chest heaving. Once I was able to catch my breath I reached for the dining room table to help myself up, and managed to dump a pile of stuff onto the ground.

A loud thump caught my attention. Kneeling to pick up the mess, my hand went directly to the book that Sheila had given me. I had forgotten all about it. On the cover was the silhouette of a woman sitting cross-legged, her hands resting on her knees. In the background was a surrealistic image of what I knew to be the mountains of Maine. The title, *Landscape of the Soul,* was printed boldly across the top. I opened to the title page and read Sheila's inscription, *Explore the landscape and enjoy the journey!* Intrigued, I shuffled randomly through the pages, settled on one and began to read:

> *When I went to the mountain I felt for the first time what it was to be alive. Life itself coursed though me. No longer was there mountain, sky, ocean, and bird, each separate from one another and from me. There was only one of us, each contained within the other and separate from none…*

My mouth went dry, my eyes moistened. I had not been able, had not even tried, to verbalize what I had felt standing on the mountain, but there it was, in a book given to me and written by a woman I had only just met. The coincidence was astounding.

I began to read further, but before I could a sheet of yellow paper fell from between the pages of the book and fluttered to the floor. Picking it up I immediately recognized Jane's handwriting and then remembered her shoving it into my hand as she said goodbye two nights before. On it was written her address and the date and time of her dinner party. Tonight. 7:00. I glanced at my watch. It was 5:45. Did I dare go? Suddenly hungry for company and struck by a bolt of courage I decided that yes, I would.

Jumping up, I ran into the bedroom, threw open the closet and fished around for something to wear. I had not worn anything nicer than a pair of jeans in three months. I pulled out a pair of black pants and a green sweater. It wasn't exactly glamorous but it would have to do.

I emerged from the shower with hair and body clean but with blood running down my legs from shaving too quickly. Make-up was easy - I hardly wore any and owned less. My hair hung long, straight and rather shapeless. Blow-drying livened it up a little, but anything more was useless. It had a mind of its own and not much to work with. Dressed and ready I studied myself in the full-length mirror on the back of the closet door. Not beauty queen material, but at least presentable. I decided jewelry might help.

Just as my hand opened the drawer I remembered. The locket. My eyes lingered on it for a moment but then I grabbed my pearls and slammed the drawer shut. Standing in front of the mirror again I held the pearls up to see how they would look. I reached back to clasp them behind my neck when the voice whispered in my ear, "Wear it and it will show you the way."

My hands shook. I looked around as though the voice had come from somewhere in the room. Slowly I walked to the dresser and opened the drawer. With a sense of resignation I put the pearls away, picked up the locket and placed it around my neck.

CHAPTER TEN

It was 7:15. I was late. I hated to be late.

My nerves bounced around the car. I was trying to concentrate on Jane's directions rather than obsess over what craziness had overcome me to be doing this at all. I had no idea who would be there, though it crossed my mind that Sheila and Mark probably would be, and maybe even Anna. I felt terrible just showing up, but Jane had insisted that I didn't need to respond.

The locket hung heavy around my neck but I had no room for it in my busy mind. My hike had left me with a sense of bravado; one I feared may prove false. I kept telling myself that I had a purpose in going - to ask Jane about the locket and find out how to return it to the Carters. It was a reason, if not an excuse, and it kept me from turning around.

By the time I found Jane's driveway it was 7:45. I prayed that dinner had not started and that I wouldn't make a scene by coming in late.

She lived north of downtown in a rambling old Victorian home that had once been a bed-and-breakfast. It sat low on the land, where a hill ran into the ocean. The driveway was long and wound its way through a thicket of trees. The dark made maneuvering curves a challenge but when I finally came out into the clearing of the lawn, the house was there to welcome me. It was not fussy or pretentious, but illuminated with history and promise, the perfect reflection of the woman in residence.

Candles shone in the windows and colorful spotlights set off many of the trees around the property. Cars lined the drive in front of the house, making it necessary to park a good distance away. I didn't mind. It allowed me time to psyche myself up and gain control of the tremor in my hands.

One slow step at a time I moved up the walkway to the front door. The blue clapboard structure eyed me slyly, giving away none of its secrets. Sidelights afforded me a peak inside before ringing the bell.

What struck me first was the brightness. There were lights on, but also a number of candles burned, providing an air of intimacy and warmth. The foyer, wide and long, flowed into a large open space in the back where most of the activity seemed to be centered. Off to each side were other gathering spaces but none appeared to be in use. Muffled laughter and music drifted under the door. My heart sank into my stomach. Mustering all the courage I could, I rang the doorbell.

I fidgeted with the clasp of my purse and forced myself not to watch through the glass, planting my body squarely in front of the door. When it opened I was surprised to see Mark on the other side. He paused only a second.

"Well hi, you came - that's great!" His smile was genuine, and though his voice was calm, I sensed that he was unsure of how to greet me, with a handshake or a hug. He chose quickly and stuck out his hand. As I reached to take it the image from my dream flashed before me - his eyes, his hand, his presence.

"Hi Mark, it's nice to see you again. I hope I'm not too late. Jane doesn't even know I'm coming, I uh, hope it's okay." Fumbling, stuttering.

"Of course it's okay, it's perfect in fact. She mentioned she had invited you and I know she was hoping you would come. And here you are. And here *I* am keeping you on the front stoop. Please come in." He stood to the side, sweeping his arm in a gallant gesture of invitation. Something nagged at the corner of my mind. He reminded me of someone.

"And don't worry, we haven't even sat down yet. You get a group like this together and it's hard to get them to do anything." I followed as he led the way to the back of the house. Along the way I glanced into the other rooms. There were deep rich tones and light airy spaces, all comfortable and inviting. The scent of vanilla mingled with the natural smells of age and wood. When we stepped into the main gathering area the aroma of baking bread and simmering sauces exploded, knocking everything else out of the way.

"Oh my." My breath caught in my throat.

"It is beautiful isn't it? Jane has quite a piece of paradise here. I keep threatening that I'm going to move in and she'll to have to adopt me." Light danced in his eyes and played around the corners of his mouth.

The room was exceptionally large and encompassed both kitchen and family room. A roaring fire took center stage in a large stone fireplace that covered one entire end of the room. Overstuffed couches, chairs and colorful floor pillows, all filled with guests, sat in front of it and around a square pine coffee table. Oriental rugs in hues of red and blue and brown enhanced the golden wood of the floor.

The kitchen was just as inspired. Cherry cabinets were built to resemble pieces of furniture and a large distressed armoire, painted in deep shades of green served as a pantry. Dark granite countertops and stainless appliances added a slight contemporary touch to otherwise classic styling.

It was all beautiful, but what immediately stole my attention were the French doors along the back wall that opened to a large brick terrace. There, several tables were set up with white tablecloths, silver candlesticks and bouquets of white roses. A pergola canopied the terrace and vines crept up the sides and across the top. They were barren now, but I was sure it was breathtaking in the spring. The backyard was well lit and the lawn rolled elegantly down to the sea. Trees lined the perimeter of the property, creating a natural privacy gate. Near the shoreline, off to the side, a large hedge partitioned off a piece of land. Into one side an arbor had been chiseled, providing access to what appeared to be some sort of secret garden. I made a mental note to make my way down there later.

Drifting through the center of the room I stopped before stepping out onto the terrace. I could feel Mark by my side. I turned to him and whispered, "It's extraordinary. It's so, I don't know, enchanting."

I barely noticed the guests that milled about. For just that moment it was as if Mark was the only other person in the room and for that same moment I was perfectly comfortable, and glad for his company.

Leaning in to meet my whisper he followed my gaze. "Yes it is, and you haven't seen the best part yet. That would be the garden. Maybe later, if you like, we could take a walk down there. I think you'll be impressed."

The moment was broken and reality returned. His closeness unnerved me. Then it confused and irritated me. Where was Sheila? I was sure she wouldn't appreciate him standing so close and asking me to take a walk with him. I didn't appreciate it. Didn't he see the sign on my forehead that read, "My husband is dead, please keep your distance?"

Looking around I saw Jane on the terrace. Without turning I said softly, "Excuse me," and walked away, my face burning. I was making a habit of leaving Mark talking to himself. This time I believed his behavior had warranted it. I was aware of his eyes on me. Stop it, I screamed at him silently. By the time I reached Jane he had wandered into the throng of people.

"Sara! Oh I'm so happy you're here. I was starting to think you weren't going to come." She drew me into her open arms. The people she had been talking to drifted away. "You look beautiful."

"Thank you Jane. I admit I almost didn't come, but I wanted to see you. Your home is absolutely beautiful. What a special place."

"Thank you, dear. I do love it. It's my sanctuary. I'll have to give you a full tour before the night is over. Have you seen anyone you know?"

"Yes, Mark answered the door. But I haven't seen Sheila; I assume she's here? That would probably be the extent of who I 'know.'"

"Oh, yes she's here somewhere. I'm glad you saw Mark. He's such a sweetheart, and so handsome. I have quite the crush on him."

Not wanting to continue a discussion about Mark, I said, "I thought you told me this was going to be an intimate dinner party. This looks more like a banquet. And look at these tables, they're gorgeous. How many are you feeding tonight?"

She laughed, her bun bouncing up and down on top of her head. "It's not that big really, about sixty. It's easy when someone else is doing all the cooking. And when you've lived here as long as I have, believe me, this is intimate."

Just then an older gentleman walked toward us, stealing Jane's attention. She transformed into a young schoolgirl, flushed with excitement. When he reached us she lifted her face and he pecked her on the cheek. I had no idea that Jane had a beau. She had talked about her late husband with such affection that I had assumed that she continued to carry his torch. I felt like I lost a little something.

"Hello Dan. Please meet my friend, Sara Jensen. Sara this is Dan Henries."

"Hi Dan, it's nice to meet you." He greeted me warmly, commented on what a nice evening it was, and then said, "If you'll please excuse us Sara I'm going to steal the hostess away for just a few minutes. I haven't seen her in much too long."

Jane smiled reassuringly and took my hands. "I'll be gone for only a moment, Sara. Make yourself at home, get a drink, and if you want, go tour the upstairs. There shouldn't be too many people up there. I'll be right back." She knew me well. I watched the two of them saunter off toward the garden.

Thinking I would be more comfortable with something in my hand, I went in search of the bar. It was on the far side of the terrace next to one of several outdoor fireplaces. A man in a white sweater and khakis served me a San Pellegrino with lime, which I drank in front of the fire. Looking around, I tried to appear at ease and felt completely obvious.

Absentmindedly, I reached up and grabbed the locket. I had nearly forgotten I was wearing it and it hadn't even occurred to me to ask Jane about it. Later. The cold smooth silver felt reassuring in my hand. To myself I whispered, "Okay show me the way, or at least give me the strength to get through this."

Glass in one hand, holding tightly to my purse strap with the other, I went into the house. I would have preferred going down to the water or to explore the garden, but I didn't want to disturb Jane and Dan's reunion. I could hold up the fireplace for only so long. It was less awkward to at least move and look like I had some place to go, or someone to find. The only person I could think to look for was Sheila, but I presumed she would be with Mark and I wasn't ready to see him again. I decided to make a beeline for the front of the house to find the stairway.

Crossing through the greatroom I noticed Mark out of the corner of my eye, walking in my direction. I sped up, keeping my eyes forward until I was in the front hall. I considered continuing straight through the front door, but thought of Jane, and the locket, and willed myself to stay.

The stairway was not in immediate sight so I ducked into the first room I found. It was to my right and it was empty. I guessed it must be the den. A small lamp, two candles, and a burning brick fireplace lit the room with an amber glow. There was a lovely wingback chair facing the fireplace on one side and a large overstuffed one, big enough for two, on the other. A built-in bookcase lined the back wall. The ceiling was wood, finished to match the floors, and the walls were painted a deep rose. It was a room to melt into, or hide in, which was my intention.

Perusing the bookshelf I was amazed by the collection of works. Classics intermingled with the latest bestsellers, a large assortment of poetry and essays, everything from philosophy to psychology to religion. Jane, I thought, may not be well traveled but she most certainly was well read.

I noticed Sheila's book, along with two others she had written. Next to them I was not surprised to see Mark's name. I tried to pass over it but found it impossible. I told myself it was simply curiosity, that all I wanted was to know what type of book he had written. Slipping it from its space on the shelf I went to the wingback chair, rested my glass and purse on the side table, and set the book on my lap.

The Mythology of Love. I was taken aback, unsure of what I expected, but sure it wasn't a book about love. Granted, I was probably making a sexist judgment - his exterior was so masculine and rugged. Obviously something else smoldered beneath the surface.

I remembered the affection in his eyes as he had looked at Sheila after her reading at the bookstore. Then thought again of how close he had stood to me, his intimate tone and invitation. Contradictions in character. Gentle in manner.

I stared blankly into the fire, lost in the ramblings of my mind. A chill passed over the room, and brought me back to the present. The heat of the flames licked the goosebumps rising on my arms.

I turned my head and my eyes came to rest upon her. She stood just inside the doorway. At first I thought she might be an apparition, conjured up in the midst of my daydream. Dressed in flowing layers of white, gold sandals on her feet, the embodiment of some mythic goddess.

The butterflies fluttered their wings and then enfolded them. There was nowhere to run or hide and for once I didn't want to. The anxiety created by anticipating this meeting had made me weary. I didn't speak or move. I don't think I was even breathing, half-expecting her to disappear in a puff of smoke, or turn and float away, half-hoping she would.

"Breathe Sara." She spoke the words softly, a reminder, not a command. And then she smiled and in her smile was the shadow of familiarity, but I could not place it. I heeded her advice, releasing the air I kept captive.

She moved forward and came to sit on the ottoman of the chair across from me. Even in sitting she held herself gracefully, poised but relaxed.

"My name is Anna, Sara. You probably know that by now. We have stumbled across one another several times in the past few days. Please don't be nervous, I'm quite harmless." Her voice was even, like the ocean in the early morning, before the wind has woken the waves.

She glanced at the book still sitting unopened in my lap. "He is a wonderful writer, don't you think?"

"I...I haven't read any of it. I just took it down and was about to..." I felt like a child incapable of forming the right words.

"I hope you do. His ideas are worth hearing." And then, "Is there anything you would like to ask me?" Her bluntness took me off guard.

A million questions banged around in my head but her open solicitation sent them scrambling for cover.

Desperately I searched for one to make itself available. "Well, okay. Who are you and what do you want?" It tumbled out, without censoring, and I was sure it sounded rude.

Rude or not, she was unfazed. "Good. I like that. It is best to move right into the center, not to dance around the edges. You seem aware that I am not simply a stranger that you keep accidentally running into. Or at least you think that there is more to it than that. Otherwise, why would you be so sure that there is something that I 'want'?"

Why *did* I assume that? What had she done to leave me believing that she demanded something of me? Had it simply been her presence, something about her that I assumed spoke specifically to me? Maybe I was wrong.

But no. If I was wrong, how did she know my name? And why had she come in here and asked the question?

"Please, I don't know what I know, but if you *do* want something from me, please just tell me what it is." I felt myself crumbling beneath the weight of her calm.

"Sara it is not my intention to upset or scare you. But I understand how you might react that way. You have chosen a path of solitude since losing your husband. You have been sad and alone and afraid. Yet in the past three days your world has been shaken. Actually it began long before, but you are only now awakening to it. You have begun to experience valleys of grief as well as peaks of exhilaration, each deeper and higher than you imagined possible. You have felt the draw of strangers, both wanting their company and resisting their call to change. And in me you have seen the reflection and shadow of yourself. In a short time life has brought you to the doorway of many mysteries. Now, I am inviting you to walk through."

"I don't understand. I'm sorry. Who are you? How do you know so much about me? Did Jane tell you about my husband? I'm sorry, I just don't understand any of this."

The anxiety returned. My body shook. The butterflies flapped wildly. The heat of the fire and the dark of the room became suffocating.

"There comes a time in each of our lives when we are ready to hear the truth. We may not know we are ready, we may not feel ready, but somewhere inside there is a deeper wisdom that sets the course and steers us forward. You are afraid. But you are ready. The time has come.

"You do not need to understand everything immediately. It is best if you allow the answers to unfold. I am here to help, to guide you through what may seem an extraordinary experience. It is the experience of discovering who you are. You have an important role to play and it's time you took the stage."

"Anna, I think you've made a mistake. I'm not anyone significant and I don't understand what you mean by 'ready,' ready for what? Time for what? I'm pretty clear on 'who I am' and it's not who you're looking for. I'm sorry to disappoint you, but you've got the wrong person." I was pleading with her, begging her to understand that I did not want to be this person. I did not want to be 'ready' for anything. I wanted only to run from the room, out the front door and as far away from here as possible, perhaps to the bottom of the ocean.

She reached out and touched my trembling hand. Her skin was cool, her touch kind. Beneath it my hand relaxed. I scanned the room, my eyes flitting nervously from thing to thing, landing anywhere but on her. She held her gaze evenly, patiently waiting.

When I had exhausted my search for escape, when no one had come to my rescue, I gave in to the pull of her stare. She didn't speak, just held my eyes in hers. It was as though she was pulling the restless, fearful energy out, leaving me exhausted, yet more relaxed.

"Listen to the voice rising from beneath the fear Sara. Breathe deeply and just listen. It will speak to you. It will tell you what you need to hear…"

Her voice receded into the distance. Lulled by its hypnotic flow, my breathing deepened and slowed. My arms grew heavy and then weightless. I sunk deeper into the chair and became lost in the empty spaces of time.

Much like sinking into the ocean, farther and farther I fell, but this time I was falling *toward* the light. As I grew closer my body expanded, stretching beyond the bounds of flesh, until all there was, was light.

White noise. Then mute space.

An astronaut possessed by the stillness of eternity. Held by nothing, to nothing. Free.

And then from a place in the center of no place a voice rose.

"You are more than you have known yourself to be. Your life is in the promise you made to remember this truth. Be not afraid, everything is happening just as it is meant to. All will be revealed in perfect time."

The words rang like a bell through my being, awakening not only my mind, but every cell in my body. Fire leapt through me, up the length of my spine, sending shock waves down my arms and legs and out through my fingers, toes and the top of my head.

Around and around, spinning, electrified.

And then with a thud I landed.

Disoriented, I held my eyes shut until wave after wave of nausea passed and I could once again feel the chair beneath me. I was unsure of how much time had elapsed or if Anna was still there, if she had been there at all. Maybe I had fallen asleep and the whole thing had been a dream.

I became self-conscious of my face, the way I held my mouth, the set of my chin. I looked down so that when I forced open my eyes they would focus first on my hands. Only when I saw her fingers did the feel of her touch register on the surface of my skin. They had not moved. She had not moved. Her blue-gray eyes rested easily on me and when I lifted my chin to meet them, she smiled.

"Welcome back. I hope you had a pleasant trip."

Sighing heavily I pulled my hands from hers and ran them through my hair. "That was the strangest experience I've ever had. What happened?" My voice surprised me. It only slightly quivered.

"You tell me."

"I remember you telling me to breathe deep and listen. Next thing I know I'm floating, and then I heard a voice. Actually it was my voice, but deeper, stronger, clearer."

"And what did it tell you?"

"It said I am more than I know and something about a promise I made to learn the truth." A light went on.

"No. It said, 'Your life is in the promise you made to remember this truth.' Whatever that means. But it reminds me of something." I shook my head, "No, that's too weird."

"Believe me Sara, someday you will believe that nothing is 'too weird.' Tell me."

"Well, the first time Brian, my husband, and I saw the house where I'm now living, I remember thinking that I heard the words, 'Life is a promise.' They sort of ran through my head, but at the time I could have sworn they were being whispered in my ear. It gives me chills just to think about it. And then when I met the woman who owns the house she asked me if I had heard it. Actually she seemed to know that I had. That's sort of spooky."

Anna laughed, the full-bodied laugh of one who knows more about a story than the storyteller. "Yes, I can see how that would seem 'spooky.' But really, it all makes perfect sense. You just can't see the bigger picture. Remember Sheila's reading at the bookstore?"

"Yes."

"She spoke about the parts that make up a whole, about how often we are not aware of all of the separate pieces, but only see what we believe to be the whole. She was speaking primarily about the different aspects of ourselves. But it is true for many things, on smaller and larger scales, and it is true of the opposite as well. Sometimes we see only small parts of a greater whole, a bit here, a bit there, but not until we are able to stand back and observe the entirety can we fully understand, or appreciate, the pieces. Yet, it is the pieces that lead us to the whole. It is a great cycle. You, Sara, have entered the cycle and have come face to face with a few of the fragments. Now begins your journey of putting them together. I promise, you will not be disappointed."

Dumfounded, I stared at her, then said, "I admit some pretty strange things have been happening lately. Things I don't understand and I'm not sure I really want to. Part of me just wants them to stop, to just go back to the way things were before. But I'm losing focus on what, or when, 'before,' was. The words I heard tonight take me back to the first time I saw my house, to possibly the happiest time of my life. Do I want to erase that? No. So what do I do? I have no idea. I'm tired Anna. Tell me, just tell me what to do."

"Do nothing but relax, Sara. Make yourself available to the process that is unfolding before you, within you. Try not to fight so hard. As I said, I am here to help you. You asked me earlier who I am. That is something you will come to know when the time is right. For now, I ask you only to listen to that voice within. Trust it, and if you can't trust it, then maybe try trusting me."

I couldn't help but laugh, the dam that held hostage the tension of the past few days breaking, sending it flowing like liquid energy through my veins. "Anna I'm not thinking very clearly right now. Trust is a big order. I have been terrified of you since the first time I saw you, and now I see why. I don't know what to feel about anything that you've said."

We stared at each other in silence for several moments and then I continued. "But I guess I am willing to listen – you've made it impossible not to. So, what now? You said to just make myself available. To what? Who? When? Where?"

Again, she laughed. "So many questions. What I said before 'make yourself available,' was 'relax.' Things happen much easier if they are not fettered by anxiety. But I know what you ask and I will give you an answer. Tomorrow. Meet me in Jane's garden at 5:30.

"Will Jane mind? Are we having dinner again?"

This time her laugh was not wise and knowing, but filled with delight. "Sara, I meant 5:30 *am*."

Without another word she rose and walked to the door. Before leaving she turned to me and smiled.

Although she had never seemed anything but calm, I saw in her at that moment a deeper, more profound calm - relief perhaps, as though whatever we were up to was as much about her as it was me.

CHAPTER ELEVEN

I was sure it was very late. It seemed that Anna and I had been in the den for hours. Life cannot completely turn on its axis in the matter of a few minutes.

After Anna left I huddled into the chair, pulling my knees up and wrapping my arms tightly around them, the way I always did when life became too large. I knew I should get up and go home, but was unable to move. Everything that existed beyond this room felt distant and unfamiliar. How did I walk out of here and step into there? It would be like crossing into another dimension. Or returning from one.

The fire continued to burn, a clue that not as much time had passed as I thought. Slowly the din of the party buzzed into my awareness. I couldn't believe it was still going on; there was no way I hadn't missed dinner. How would I explain to Jane why I had disappeared?

Uncurling myself, I returned Mark's book to the bookshelf and practically tiptoed into the hallway. Hugging the wall I made my way to the great room. Once there I melded into the corner and watched wide-eyed. It was as if no time at all had passed, or perhaps mere minutes. The tables were untouched, no one even seated. Guests were just as I had last seen them, mingling, chatting. Nowhere was there a gap, or the smallest sign that I had been missing.

"Stop trying to figure it out," I reminded myself. At least I wouldn't have to explain my whereabouts. I glanced around for Anna, but knew I would not find her.

Too overwhelmed to feel awkward any longer, I waded through the crowd, headed for the bar and ordered a beer. Drink in hand I wandered around the terrace admiring the tables. There were place cards designating where each guest should sit. I wondered if I would find my name scripted on one since I had shown up unannounced. But true to her style, Jane had seen that I was included. I was to sit between her and Shelia.

Unsure of when dinner would be called I decided to venture down to the garden, but just as I stepped away from the terrace a bell rang, beckoning the guests. Immediately people began to assemble around the tables, locating their names and taking their seats. With one last deep breath I joined them.

Several minutes passed before I saw Jane breaking through the crowd. Dan was no longer by her side. I watched with admiration as she hugged her guests, kissed them on the cheek and stopped to spend a moment with each. A first-class hostess.

I knew that she was a part of this, whatever it was, of which Anna had spoken. I wanted desperately to whisk her away and tell her what had happened, to ask her what she knew of it. But at the same time I knew that I wouldn't, not yet - it was mine for now.

She landed upon her chair, as lightly as a butterfly on a flower.

"You found your seat, good. I hope I wasn't gone too long. Dan travels so much, I hardly get to see him. He couldn't even stay for dinner, has a plane to catch tonight. London I think. He travels the globe and then brings it home to me."

"I didn't know you had a…a boyfriend, Jane." The word sounded odd when referring to a couple in their seventies.

She laughed, "Why yes. The human heart was made to love Sara. Ultimately it is all it knows how to do." Her eyes shone, almost convincing me that her words were true. Before I could respond, Sheila appeared and sat down beside me.

"Sara, hello. I didn't know you were here. Where have you been hiding?"

I tensed, not prepared to answer. But she kept going and didn't seem to notice.

"It's great to see you again." She placed her hand on my arm and turned away from me. With her other hand she pulled on the sleeve of a tall, square-shouldered blond man standing beside her chair, talking to someone else. Without turning he took her hand in his. While continuing his conversation he slipped into the seat next to her, the one I had assumed would be for Mark.

Sheila, still holding on to both of us, returned her attention to me. "I'm sorry Sara. I wanted to introduce you but he's caught up…"

"Yes dear?" The blond man interrupted. His features were sharp, chin square, lips full. Long bangs fell across his eyes as he swiveled his large frame in our direction. I was sure he played a lot of tennis, or maybe sailed in regattas.

"I wanted to introduce you to Sara. We met at *The Next Chapter* the other night." Sheila scooted her chair back so the man and I were face to face. "Sara, this is my husband Greg."

Stunned, my stomach fell to the floor, but I managed to recover enough to speak. "Greg. It's nice to meet you. Were you at the bookstore Thursday?"

"No, I couldn't make it. Unfortunately. I wanted to hear Sheila's reading, but Jane told me she did great. Did you enjoy it?"

"Yes, very much. Sheila was wonderful."

We continued with the usual Q & A of people meeting for the first time. He was talkative and funny, and obviously adored Sheila. I did my best to keep my attention on him, to meet his eyes and focus, but the entire time my mind was busy replaying my last encounter with Mark.

I felt terrible. My assumption that he and Sheila were a couple had led me to make all sorts of judgments about his behavior and character. His actions had been innocent. For all I knew he wasn't even aware that I was married. He may not have noticed my ring, or Jane might not have told him. Regardless, he had not said or done anything so offensive to deserve the way I had responded. I couldn't imagine what he must think of me. Neurotic came to mind.

And then, to make matters worse, as I turned to respond to Jane tapping on my arm I found myself face to face with Mark. He had slid into the seat across from me. Smiling hesitantly, his eyes held mine for an instant before looking away, first down at his plate and then, as if searching, at Jane and Sheila. He was doing what I was sure he thought I wanted him to, leaving me alone. And as far as I knew, he was right. That was exactly what I wanted. Still, I couldn't shake the guilt and embarrassment, or the sadness that crept in like weeds.

Not knowing what to do or say, I did nothing and turned my attention to Jane. By the time I found my voice she was staring intently at me, obviously having witnessed the awkward moment. Her eyes shone, a mixture of sadness and compassion, with just a dash of what might have been hope.

"I'm sorry Jane, did you ask me something?" I hoped my face wasn't too flushed or my voice too shaky.

"Oh, I just wondered what you found to do with yourself while I was with Dan. Did you tour the upstairs?"

"No. Actually I only got as far as the den. I just curled up with one of your books in front of the fire. It's a wonderful room." Though my eyes and words were aimed at Jane, my attention was directed toward Mark, his presence ringing loudly in my ears.

I was also careful not to mention Anna. I wasn't ready. The whole evening was becoming a feat to be taken one small step at a time.

"I'm so glad. It's one of my favorite spaces in the house. I've spent a lifetime collecting that library. Which book did you find to read?"

Dummy. My face grew hot. I could feel Mark's eyes boring through me like hot mercury. At least that's what I imagined.

"I...I'm not sure of the title. Actually, I didn't read much of it, I fell asleep." By the end of the sentence I was whispering, barely able to look at Jane. I was sure she could tell I was lying.

"Oh, well, that's easy to do in that room. I'm just glad you woke before dinner." She laughed and patted my hand lightly. And then she turned to Mark.

"Mark, you remember Sara don't you? I believe you met her the other night at the bookstore." Mischievousness laced her words.

"Yes, of course I do. We spoke earlier. Have you been having a nice time?" The last was directed at me.

"Um, yes. Thank you." I was at a loss. I owed him an apology but couldn't bring myself to speak the words in front of Jane and Sheila.

The rest of dinner passed in disguised awkwardness. Mark and I spoke little, but enough to be polite. Mostly he directed his attention toward Jane, Sheila, Greg, and the pretty young woman sitting next to him, who seemed a more than willing recipient. I didn't like my reaction and tried desperately to tell myself that none of it mattered, but found I was unable to concentrate on anything being said. Instead, my every sense was drawn across the table. Was he looking at me? What were he and the pretty young woman laughing at? Why did I care? All I wanted was to leave, to be through with this so that I could return to the cottage, curl up in front of my own fire and lose myself in imaginings of Brian. I was desperate for escape.

Course after delicious course it continued. Finally, somewhere between entrée and dessert I gave up the fight and withdrew from the table chatter to enter into the safety of my mind. My thoughts drifted to Anna and our meeting. The encounter with Mark and the whole dinner fiasco had served as a distraction, but as soon as I opened the door to internal darkness, there she stood, ready to remind me of the strange twist my life had taken in the past 72 hours.

I guess I closed my eyes, because when I felt them opening, Jane, Sheila, Greg, Mark and the pretty young woman were all staring at me expectantly. I looked to Jane for rescue.

Leaning in she said, "Lucy's right. That locket really is exquisite and so unique. And come now, you must tell us where you got it." I assumed Lucy was the woman flirting with Mark and for some reason she had brought the table's attention to my locket. Had I missed the entire conversation?

Feeling ridiculous, but grateful to Jane, I reached for the locket and glanced at Lucy. "Thank you. I, uh, actually found it in the house I'm renting. I felt a little bad about wearing it, but I figured it couldn't do any harm. This once."

Lucy smiled insincerely and nodded, her hand resting on her chin. After a moment she returned her attention to Mark, who seemed to bask in it.

I continued to grasp the locket protectively, not understanding the strange reaction from Lucy. Maybe I had misunderstood what had been asked or said. Helplessly I turned to Jane and whispered, "I'm sorry. I didn't hear what was said." My face was burning and all I could think was how foolish I must seem.

"Don't worry. Lucy just remarked on what an interesting piece it is." Then lowering her voice conspiratorially, "Never mind her reaction. She has had a mad crush on Mark for years and I think - well, it's rather obvious, that his attentions are elsewhere." Again the mischievous tone.

Flustered, I said ever so quietly so no one would hear, "Well that's ridiculous. He looks rather content to soak up her attention. Anyway, well, it doesn't matter anyway. I'm not interested. Ridiculous." The last word was more to myself than to Jane.

Before the conversation could go any further Sheila interrupted, "Sara, would you mind if I took a closer look at the locket?" Grateful for the change in topic I lifted it towards her.

"You said you found it in your house? How intriguing. Do you know who it belongs to?" Out of the corner of my eye I could see Mark begin to pay attention.

"No. Actually I had hoped that Jane could help me figure it out." Sheila released the locket and I turned to Jane who sat forward and took it in hand. Mark was now giving the locket his full attention and I couldn't help but think his interest was more than casual. Lucy barely hid her annoyance.

"It has a picture of a little girl on the inside," I said, opening it to show Jane. "There's an inscription on the back. See? 'A star to guide you home,' and it's signed, 'B and G.' I assume that's Bev and Gil."

Glancing over my shoulder at Sheila who was straining to see, I explained, "They're the couple that owns the house I'm renting, but I don't think the little girl is their daughter. At least she doesn't look like the pictures I've seen. What do you think, Jane? Does that look like Katie when she was little?"

Jane gestured silently for me to take off the locket. I did so and handed it to her. Her face was perfectly still, her movements slow and measured. The energy around us was pregnant with the unspoken. I could almost see her moving back through time, leaving this place, entering another, searching. When she spoke her voice was distant.

"No, this isn't Katie, no. Ohhh…well, my. Okay. Okay." She was speaking more to herself than to us.

It was as if collectively we were holding the breath of time, waiting for Jane. When she finally returned to the present I could almost hear the exhale, and the great clock began again.

"I'm sorry Sara, there is nothing I can tell you, but I will call Bev and Gil tomorrow."

Though I was sure Jane wasn't telling all she knew, I accepted her answer and said, "Thank you. I would love to be able to return the locket to them, or to whomever it belongs. Please let me know what you find out."

Sheila's voice drifted over my shoulder. "You'll have to let us all know Sara, when you find out. I would love to hear the story. I love mysteries." Greg nodded and voiced his agreement.

It felt good to be a part of something and to have a story to tell. For a moment I was taken out of myself and chatted comfortably with Sheila and Greg, telling them about the Carters and the first time I met them. In the midst of my storytelling I became aware of my own enthusiasm and animation. I felt alive. It had been a long time.

In my periphery I sensed Mark listening, watching. He said nothing but appeared to have fallen into a somber mood. When he got up from the table with a simple, "Excuse me," I stumbled over my words. His leaving weighed on my mood, which bothered me.

It was not long before the party began to break up. Looking around I was surprised to find that we were the last of the guests to get up from the table. Jane had snuck away right after her promise to call the Carters. For the hour after dinner she played out her role as hostess, inviting her guests to stay as long as they like and mingling amongst them. Some made themselves comfortable in front of the stone fireplace while others walked down toward the beach, but the majority said their goodbyes.

When Sheila, Greg and I made our way into the house we found Jane sitting on the couch, shoes off, feet up and wine in hand, talking to the small group that had congregated in the greatroom. Sheila and Greg immediately became involved in the conversation and sat down to join them. Jane motioned for me to sit next to her, but I had another plan.

"If it's okay with you I think I'd like to walk down and see your garden."

"Oh, you haven't been? Well you must. Let me get myself up from here and join you." Her words were sincere but I could tell she was tired.

"No, please, you stay where you are. I'm fine. I won't be long."

"If you're sure?"

"Absolutely sure. But I will say goodnight now, just in case it's too late when I'm done poking around."

I walked over to where she sat, leaned down and hugged her. As I pulled away, she whispered in my ear, "I won't forget about the locket. We'll talk tomorrow."

Taking her hands in mine, I squeezed and mouthed "Thank you." After saying goodnight to Sheila and Greg, with promises to get together, and nodding to everyone else, I walked out the terrace doors toward the garden.

The lawn sloped downward to the sea, an ocean of dulling green that dropped off to a rocky beach below. After walking a few steps on the grass I bent and slipped out of my shoes. I loved the way the ground, moist and cool, tickled my feet. The night was clear and the full moon kindly lit the darkness, allowing me to find my way. I walked slowly, grateful to once again be alone.

Before setting out I reached up, unclasped the locket and dropped it into my purse, releasing myself from its hold.

Embraced by the veil of night I felt freer, the weight of the evening lifting itself from my shoulders, like a heavy coat finally removed. With no noise to fill the spaces I could hear the clamoring of my mind, the voices of confusion and pain, excitement and renewal, fear, hope and promise, each tumbling over the next, vying for control. I stretched my neck from one side to the other while a maelstrom of thoughts and feeling spiraled through me... Mark, my guilt and embarrassment for the way I had treated him, and even more disturbing, the way I reacted whenever he was near; the locket and the anticipation of revealing its secrets; and of course Anna, the enigma

85

who had presented me with the challenge, the dare, to believe in my own salvation.

Shaking my head in an effort to clear it, I inhaled deeply, filling up on crisp, winter air. I was surprised that I wasn't cold, a Florida girl with water for blood, but the air felt pure and clean, and I imagined it washing away the soot left by so much thinking.

My thoughts turned then to Brian, who sat quietly on the edge of my awareness. I could see him, his kind eyes and smile, watching me, wanting to help. Drawing the image around me, I at once felt the familiar ache that defined my life. I missed him. Everything that had happened became instantly insignificant next to that one simple, consuming fact. It was easy to believe that all the fragmented pieces would make sense, would fit together, if only Brian were here.

Just as the thought took root a gentle breeze caught me in its grasp, kissing lightly the bare skin of my neck. I thought I would cry, would be attacked by the monster of grief living inside me, but instead, my heart lurched forward and was met with an astounding sense of peace.

"Brian is here," I thought. It was not the way I had envisioned in all of my searching - it was quieter, subtler, but at the moment, it was all I had ever wanted. With Brian close I could feel the world shift, the images of the evening recede, fear and uncertainty dissipate. I became more myself. The part of me that Brian had taken returned, if only briefly. I hugged myself, trying to latch on to the moment.

Continuing to walk I held on as long as I could, and when the breeze blew past it left me wistful, yet hopeful for its return. In its wake my step grew lighter and my breath came easier. Just as he had in life, Brian, from some distant realm, had managed to lift my spirits.

The garden was tucked gracefully into the land at the bottom of the hill. Square in shape, with an opening on one side, the corners had been carefully pruned into gentle curves. Before entering I strolled along the perimeter, amazed by the hedge that enclosed it, understanding how Alice must have felt when she fell into Wonderland. From the house it had been impossible to perceive the size and density of the living walls, but walking so close brought forth a profound sense of awe. They towered above like guards on watch, and I felt safe under their gaze.

I made my way slowly, dragging my hand along the close-cropped needles. When I came to the arbored entrance I stopped and looked upward. The archway peaked at least ten feet above my head, a good five feet above the tops of the hedges. I stepped back, completely enthralled. At that moment the night seemed to dim, to concentrate itself in this space, magnifying my sense of solitude. My pulse sped up, a trickle of fear making its way into my bloodstream.

Dropping my shoes to the ground I took a deep breath. Holding it, I stepped over the threshold, and that simple movement caused an almost instant transformation. No longer was I afraid. There was no room for fear inside the awe that overtook me. This was no ordinary garden. There were no rows of flowers or vegetables, or any such plantings. The path turned to dirt beneath my feet. Digging in my toes I stood perfectly still and listened as the sounds of the dark emerged. Birds and insects played their symphony, with the eerie bass of an owl providing backup.

Moonlight bounced about. The garden was like nothing I had ever seen before. The square border acted as a container for what I now realized was a circular design, about fifty feet in diameter. Walking straight ahead, hedges on either side of me, I could only go about ten feet before running into another. This one, like the ones to my left and right, was much smaller than those around the border, reaching only to my shoulder. The path then stretched and curved to the left until it disappeared around a corner. Before exploring any further I stood on my toes, curled my fingers over the top of the hedge in front of me, and peered over.

All I could see were more hedges, configured into a maze of some sort. At the center was an opening, but the green walls around it stood taller than the rest, not allowing me to discern what treasures lay there in wait. The other, quite astounding difference between the inner and the outer hedges were the flowering vines that climbed across the inner ones. Gazing over the tops of them was like standing on the edge of a rainbow. Flowers of every color swayed lightly in the breeze, their fragrance drifting almost visibly, dizzyingly about. I thought it quite extraordinary that anything, much less something so vibrant, colorful and abundant, would grow so well in the last days of October.

Entranced by rainbows and moonbeams I remained grasping to the edge, straining so as not to lose my view.

"Beautiful…night."

I lost my balance, nearly fell from my perch, and stumbled backwards. His arms reached out to steady me. I turned and we stood frozen in an awkward dance, until he let go and moved away, clearing his throat.

"I'm sorry. I didn't mean to startle you. If you'd like I can go. I know how nice it is to be here alone." He always seemed so silently strong and confident, but standing there, apologizing for his presence, he was sheepish and tentative. I couldn't blame him. Our previous meetings had both ended in my walking away.

Pulling myself together and remembering the power of speech I said, "No, Mark. Please. I…I was just admiring the flowers. And you're right, it is a beautiful night." I still couldn't bring myself to look him directly in the eye or say I was sorry for my behavior. I could swear my blood was shaking.

When he didn't say anything, but just continued to look at me as if awaiting something more, I rushed to fill the void, "I thought you left. You got up from the table so suddenly."

"I had a call to make, and I needed to take a walk. I went down to the beach, walked farther than I planned. I just made my way back up and thought I'd walk in here before leaving. I assumed everyone would be gone." He had regained his composure, remaining distant, the warm familiarity of earlier long evaporated.

"Oh. I hope everything is okay."

He smiled, small but grateful, "Yes, thank you." And then, "I guess I'll go. I've been here many times and I know it's your first, so I'll leave you to enjoy it. Goodnight." He turned to leave.

The word flew from my mouth, born of the knowing that I would regret letting him go without saying what was needed. How many times had I done that in my life? "Wait!" It came out too loud, too frantic.

He stopped and turned, looking both alarmed and relieved. He said nothing but waited.

Plunging in I said, "Please don't go. Not before I say something." My words got lost within the enormous walls of the garden.

"I'm sorry, Mark, …for earlier. I was pretty rude, just walking away from you in the middle of a conversation. And it's the second time I've done it. You must think I'm terrible or crazy. You've been nothing but nice to me, and I've been nothing but rude. And I'm sorry if I'm overreacting, you may have barely noticed, I just…" I stopped mid-sentence, aware that I was rambling. But I knew that if I kept talking he couldn't respond, and I was afraid of what he might say, and of feeling like an even bigger fool if he laughed.

Which he did, while shaking his head and running his fingers through his hair. I would have crumbled, embarrassed by my outburst, but in his laughter I heard kindness, an attempt to soften the moment and lay to rest the tension between us.

"Sara, I'm relieved, thank you. I thought maybe I'd offended you and that wasn't my intention. I would have said something but I got the distinct impression that you preferred for me to leave you alone. I just wanted to honor your wishes. Still, it would probably have been better for me to say something. I *am* sorry if I have done anything to make you uncomfortable." He drew his eyebrows together, sketching frown lines deeply between them, and shrugged, "Then again, maybe you just don't like me, and if that's it, well then, I am *very* sorry."

I was taken off-guard and began to laugh. He was making this easy and I was grateful, but even so, he was flirting - subtly maybe, but definitely flirting - which I wasn't sure what to do with. The moment between breaking the ice and moving forward was laced with silence as we each determined what came next.

And I knew it was up to me. "You haven't done anything. Believe me. I just, well it's a pretty long story, which I'm sure you'd rather not hear, so just take my word for it, the fault is all mine, and I am the one who should be, and is, very sorry." How did I even begin to explain the past few days, my behavior or my general state of mind? If I tried I was sure he would do the walking away this time, carrying with him a conviction that I was crazy. And I had been gripped with the sudden and palpable preference that he not walk away.

"And please, don't go on my account. This place is certainly big enough for us both. And really I wouldn't mind the company, unless of course you need to go?" I said it with an offhandedness that sounded as forced as it was.

Looking at his watch he smirked, "Hmmm...let's see, 11:00 on a Saturday night. *Where* am I supposed to be? No place I can think of, no place that I'd rather be. And just to remind you, I'm a writer. I happen to like stories."

Coming from most anybody else the words would have sounded contrived, merely an attempt to be charming, but somehow, coming from Mark, they sounded like simple truths. The lines around his eyes relaxed. For an instant I could see clearly how open and without pretense he was, had always been. Perhaps it was this purity that I found unnerving.

We decided to walk but didn't get far before realizing how dark it had become. A thicket of clouds had formed, obscuring the moon and denying us our only source of light within the garden walls. When we came to the first corner and stood in the blinding blackness, I became agitated. It was like being in a sensory deprivation chamber, the void too empty, too complete. I couldn't even see Mark, but I could hear the soft rhythm of his breathing, which did little to help.

When I suggested we walk down to the beach or back up to the house, I sensed only the slightest hesitation in Mark's agreement. The quiver in my voice must have given away my uneasiness, because he reached out and gently held my elbow, guiding me out of the garden.

"I'm sorry Mark. If you'd like to stay I can make my way back to the house."

"Certainly not. Forgive me if I seem a little disappointed. I was just looking forward to showing you the labyrinth. If you've never walked one, it's quite an experience. But we can do it another time. If you'd like, of course."

We had just stepped beyond the entrance when Mark's words caught up with me. I stopped and looked back at the structure, at once perplexed and intrigued.

"Labyrinth? Is that what it is? I've never even seen one, much less 'walked' one, and I don't know anything about them, except it's some sort of maze. I think I read about them in mythology, something about... the Minotaur was it? Oh I can't remember. It's been too long, high school English. How interesting that Jane would have one right here in her backyard. Why? Why would she have one?"

"Well I don't think it would be right to reveal all the secrets before you actually get to experience it, but once you do, you may understand how truly wonderful it is that she does. We are all very lucky to share it."

We stood together absorbing the mystery of the night, each lost in separate worlds, until Mark turned and walked toward the edge of the property, where a retention wall constructed of odd-shaped boulders provided a serpentine border between manicured lawn and nature's domain. I followed him and peered carefully over the side. Nothing but blackness stared back. I could hear waves tumbling over the rocks below. The tide was high. We walked a little ways in silence, enjoying the music of the ocean and the easiness that had settled around us. After only a few yards we came to a break in the wall where a stairwell, carved of rock and reinforced by wooden supports and railings, offered access to the beach. We took the first step down and looked at each other with the question on our faces. In unison we shook our heads, "Nah."

Instead we sat. The stone was cold and slightly damp from the sea mist. I barely noticed. Stretching my legs in front of me, I leaned back on my hands and looked up. Stars dotted the raven-black page of sky. Staring intently at one I imagined it a little hole torn in the fabric of night, from it escaping the light that lived beneath. What lay on the other side I wondered?

I could feel Mark's warmth next to me, and it, along with the stars, the soft glow of the moon, and the rhythmic melody of the waves, tucked into the spaces around me. I sighed heavily.

It was Mark who spoke first, softly, his voice careful not to disrupt the mood. He picked up in the middle of a conversation I had forgotten we were having. "You're right, about the mythology, by the way. It was Theseus who slew the Minotaur in the labyrinth. The story goes that Minos, the King of Crete asked Poseidon to send a white bull as a sign to prove to everyone that he was the true king. Minos told Poseidon that he would sacrifice the bull to him once it was sent. Well when the bull arrived Minos decided to keep it for himself, which made Poseidon very unhappy. Sooo, the king of the sea got back at him by causing Pasiphae, Minos' wife, to acquire a great, let's say, *fondness*, for the bull, so much so that she had Daedalus, an architect, construct a hollow wooden cow for her to hide in, to trick the bull into mating with her."

"Only in mythology and soap operas." I said, shaking my head. Mark arched his eyebrow, his expression playfully admonishing me for interrupting his story. I clamped my lips together.

"Well," he continued, "the bull fell for it, and, (this they wouldn't even do in soap operas) Pasiphae found herself with, well not exactly child, but pregnant nonetheless. And when the bundle of joy arrived it had the body of a man and the head of a bull."

"The Minotaur."

"Yep, the Minotaur. And when Minos found out he had Daedalus build a labyrinth in which he locked the Minotaur. And then he demanded Athens to send, every nine years, seven young men and women to be thrown in with it for food. This went on until our hero, Theseus, found out and volunteered to be one of the sacrificial lambs. When he got to Crete, Minos' daughter Ariadne fell madly in love with him and offered to ensure him a way out of the labyrinth if he agreed to marry her. He agreed, and Ariadne gave him a ball of thread to unwind as he went through the labyrinth, to help him find his way out. And it worked. Theseus went in, found and killed the Minotaur and led the whole group out."

"Did he ever marry Ariadne?"

Mark looked at me sideways, amazed and amused that after he had unfolded this whole story before me I had been most interested in a secondary point. "Yes, as a matter of fact he did. But then he abandoned her on an island."

"Ah, well, isn't that the way," I shrugged sadly and paused. And then, "You really know your mythology."

"Yeah, I enjoy it."

"So I gathered from the title of your book." The hidden confession surprised even me.

He looked at me openmouthed and then laughed. "So, it was *my* book you were snoozing over in Jane's library."

Embarrassed I grimaced and nodded. "Sorry, but I didn't really go to sleep, although I didn't get to read much. I just didn't want to…well it would have been a little awkward at the table. Anyway, I admit I was curious about what kind of book you had written. I was a little surprised."

"That it was about mythology?" He was baiting me.

"Well yes, I guess, but more so that it was about love." I was grateful for the dark; I could feel my face heating up and turning red.

"Hmmm. I'm not sure what to say to that."

Quickly I rattled, "I'm sorry, I didn't mean to offend you. I shouldn't have said anything, I just, well, I don't know what to say either…" Defeated by my own crudeness. I had said the wrong thing again.

"Oh, God, no. You haven't offended me. You'd have to, oh I don't know, walk away while I was talking to you or something, to offend me." He cut his eyes at me and grinned.

"I'll really try not to do that anymore."

"Good. But really, the reason I said I don't know what to say is that it's not an easy or small subject to launch into. It took me three years to write the book, and I'm still in the process of processing it. I guess I'm a bit surprised myself that I wrote a book on love. I'm no expert on it. And I'm not nearly the speaker that Sheila is, more of an introvert. I tend to live in my head. But as for mythology, the more I study it the more it intrigues me. It may sound like the ancients form of soap operas, and maybe in a way it is, but it has a lot to tell and to teach."

"Such as?" I was perfectly happy to leave behind the subject of love.

"Well for instance, all it took for Theseus to find his way out of a seemingly impossible situation was a piece of thread. Something so simple you would think it obvious. We're like that a lot, people I mean - we expect life, the answers to our questions and the way out of our 'predicaments,' or our agony, to be complicated, even impossible. Too often we give up before we've even begun, assuming we don't have within us what it takes to be the hero. And all the time, all it took was a piece of thread…the faith of a mustard seed…"

His words struck me like an arrow, puncturing a bubble of pain. I didn't like what he had said. Did he mean that pain, grief, sorrow should be easy to conquer? That all that I was going through could be fixed up with something simple, something right in front of me, something even inside me? Had I 'given up,' as he said? Maybe I had, but where was the string that would show me the way out of the nightmare? Where was the string that would lead me back to Brian?

"Did I say something to upset you?" He was watching me, worry hiding in the creases around and between his eyes.

"No. No, I'm sorry, I was just listening, thinking about the story. Listen, I better be going, it's late and I have to get up early. Thanks, for everything." I hurried to my feet, anxious to get away, and strode quickly up the hill.

"I know about your husband Sara." I stopped as if hit from behind, almost doubling over from the force. My breathing was hard and my pulse pounded in my ears. Slowly I turned around. He had stood up, but stayed where he was. The darkness framed him in a shadowy outline, the edges blurred.

I couldn't move, didn't know which way to go - to run away or return to where he stood. Or just crumble to the ground. Though my legs threatened to give out, I seemed unable to choose. I just stood, shivering, with tears rolling down my cheeks.

"Oh God," I murmured to myself, "not here, not now, not in front of this man."

Within moments his arms folded around me, slowly, gently. He didn't pull me to him or hug me tightly. He said nothing. Not, "It's okay," or "I know," or "Everything will be alright." He just held me in the circle of his arms, creating a cavern for my pain.

We stayed that way for a long time, or so it seemed, until the tears dried up and I could breathe once more. Even then I didn't move away immediately, but remained safely sequestered, listening, feeling the beat of his heart and the rising of his chest with each deep intake of breath. I fell into the rhythm of his breathing, and my own slowed. Closing my eyes I became lost in the gentle sound of his life pulse, selfishly drawing it in, wanting to steal from him his calm and his courage. I imagined that if I stayed long enough I would enter into his very blood and find the string to save me.

I knew that to move away was to break the spell of the moment, to reenter my life after having traveled into a place of solace. It was a feeling I had known once, in Brian's arms. The feeling of home. Here, under the moon, on this quietly beautiful night, held by a strong and gentle man, I could almost imagine him to be Brian, this to be us. To step away, to look into his eyes, was to remember.

Finally it was he who moved, slightly, almost imperceptibly, but making enough of a ripple to pull me back to the present. His hands came softly to my shoulders, holding us apart, and then with one finger he lifted my chin so that our eyes met. Blue-black hair fell across his face as he looked down at me. Mark. Not Brian, but Mark. The fact registered but didn't hurt as I imagined it would. His smile was searching, questioning, his eyes looking for answers behind my own. They wanted to know if I was okay, if I was ready to return, or if I needed more time.

We stood only inches apart, the space between us raw.

I began to speak, to apologize for once again making him the witness and victim of my grief. "I'm…"

His hand moved from my chin and his fingers came to rest lightly on my mouth.

"Please Sara. Don't say you're sorry. You don't need to apologize. At least not to me. I apologize to you though for blurting that out about your husband. It wasn't very kind, maybe a little desperate. I just, I didn't want you to go and I wanted you to know that you don't have to pretend or hide anything. You don't have to talk about it; I just want you to know that I know. You have nothing to fear from me. I'd simply like to be your friend, if you'll have me." He turned slowly and returned to where we had been sitting.

Baffled, I followed and sat down next to him. I couldn't help asking, "Why? I mean, I wouldn't blame you for politely excusing yourself and then running like hell." I made a meager attempt at laughter, but exhaustion was sneaking in and crying had made my body heavy and my mind foggy.

"Does there need to be a 'why'? Can you just accept that for some unfounded reason I would very much like to be your friend? The truth is I don't know. But ever since meeting you at *The Next Chapter* I've thought about it often, embarrassingly more than I'd like to admit. But I don't want that to scare you. I know you've been through a very painful time. I can only imagine what its been like for you. And you strike me as someone who has chosen to go it alone. I admire your courage, and I would never want to step upon your right to that, but I want you to know that if you ever get tired of carrying the load, I'm here, and I have a pretty strong back. I can also, believe it or not, be a lot of fun, so if you just want to get your mind off things..." He smiled, shrugged and stuffed his hands into his pockets, a teenage boy risking it all.

Shaking my head I ran trembling fingers through my hair. I fixed my gaze upon a distant spot, as though hoping to find there an explanation for the odd route my life was taking. The darkness grew the deeper I stared into it, until it enveloped me, and blocked out all but the void I longed to dive into. Blocking out even Mark, until his voice drifted through the haze.

"Sara, I will always try to tell you the truth. At least the truth as I know it. And what I believe is that in this life there are no accidents, that each person we meet, we do so with purpose. The purpose may be to learn or to teach something, usually both. And the relationships that we form with people give us the opportunity to see the best and the worst of ourselves, to experience the polarities of our own nature. We see, we learn and hopefully we grow. So all relationship is important, meaningful.

"But I also believe that there are those people who come into our lives to whom we are connected in some 'other,' deeper way. They are the ones who help us define the very stories of our lives. They are our greatest teachers. Sometimes these people are ones we think we'd rather not know. They challenge us, our thinking, our being. They force us to choose between their truth and ours. In the end, they are some of the most valuable relationships we ever have.

"But there are also those that feel more obviously like blessings. Those people that, when we meet them, we have the immediate sense that we are *meant* to know them. We may not know why, but we feel that it is important to be open to the natural unfolding of things, to be present to it. As though if we aren't, if we ignore it, we will be missing something. Although I'm not too sure that life would allow us to turn from it permanently. Does any of this make any sense? I guess the bottom line to all of this is that I feel that you are one of these people in my life, the last kind that is, someone I feel that I not only *want* to know, but am meant to, for some purpose that is yet to be revealed."

I listened, holding each word close. As I spoke I looked only briefly at him, then turned to the ebony sea. "Wow. I thought you said you weren't much of a speaker. I'd say you can hold your own. Actually you remind me of someone else I spoke with tonight. I'm by no means as articulate, or as obviously comfortable with this kind of thing as either of you, but…" I stopped, sighed heavily, rubbed my face with my hands, and continued.

"Mark, my life was perfect for a little while. It was exactly what I wanted it to be, what I had always dreamt of it being. And in one instant it all ended. I had no choice, no say in it. It just happened. I haven't figured out how to make sense of it. I came here, not because I am brave, as you and Jane seem to think, but because I was running. Away from something, to something, I don't know. Three days ago I think I could have explained it to you, and believed deeply in what I was saying. But now…well, in the past few days my life has taken too many turns for me to count. Things have happened that I have no idea how to explain or even begin to describe, though I'm getting the distinct impression that they wouldn't surprise you as much as they have me.

"The answer is yes Mark, to some degree I understand what you're saying, though I won't pretend to understand it all. But as for feeling, as you said, 'connected' to some people in a distinct way, yes I get that. I felt, still feel, a profound connection to my husband, and of course to my family and some of my friends. And when I first met Jane and the Carters I felt that I was meant to know them, although at the time I wouldn't have described it in those terms. And there is another person I met recently who may fit more into the 'challenging' category, but who I am becoming quite sure I am meant to know. At least she seems sure of it."

I wasn't looking at him, but I could feel him looking at me. I didn't know if I could bring myself to say what I knew he was waiting for. It was the truth, but it felt like stepping across a line from which there was no turning back. He had said it so easily, without fear for the consequences. But fear was the guiding force of my life.

The words were barely audible, "And I guess that it's how I felt when I met you." I continued to divert my face, but out of the corner of my eye I could see a smile play at the edges of his mouth.

His words were soft, "It's okay Sara. I admit I'm relieved that you share the feeling. But don't worry. It doesn't need to be scary. It's nice, to acknowledge a special connection to a person. Too often we choose not to, and I think that's sad. It holds only promise, the promise of whatever we choose. And choosing friendship is a pretty great thing."

It all seemed so natural to him, this forging of a relationship like none I had ever known. I found his openness, combined with his continual referral to friendship disarming, as if he knew that much of my discomfort stemmed from guilt for feeling *anything* for any man other than Brian.

The choosing to which he referred would be mine, that was clear. It would be up to me to set the boundaries. Without knowing why, I was certain that if I asked him to, he would walk away, no questions asked. And conversely, if I asked him to stay, to be my friend, he would. I dared not think to what extreme he was willing to be to me what I asked.

"Sara," Mark was leaning over his knees, stretching awkwardly to look me in the face. I had turned away from him, again becoming lost in my own thoughts. "It looks like you may be making this more confusing than I meant it to be. You're scrunching up your face as though I asked you to believe I was from another planet. Believe me, I'm not. Try, maybe, not to think quite so hard, it looks like it hurts."

The silly way he had contorted his body worked to lighten the moment. His handsome face, dark and close, exuded strength. The urge to reach out and touch it was almost overwhelming; my fingers twitched and began to flutter upward, then nervously drew back.

But I met his eyes. And the words came. "You're right, my head does hurt. This is all very weird to me, and quite honestly talking to you like this, just sitting here with you…it doesn't feel right, and yet it does. I love, not *loved*, but love my husband very much, Mark. So much that I ache with it, it is all that I am. Since he…died, I have felt as though I do not exist either, not in the way I did before. And now, since going to the bookstore the other night, everything's turned upside down. I do think maybe you're from another planet, but it feels like I'm the one that stepped off the Earth and landed in some very distant and strange land. Nothing is the way it's supposed to be or the way I thought it was. Jane, her garden, you and Sheila, Anna…" I hadn't meant to mention Sheila or Anna, but there it was.

"Anna? What do you mean Anna?" His demeanor changed, the shift filling the air around us with something bordering on panic.

"What's wrong?" My voice wavered, absorbing his energy.

The act of pulling himself together was almost visible. "I'm sorry, that was an overreaction at best. It's just that when you said Anna's name I was startled. I didn't know that you knew her well."

"I…I don't. I just met her. Actually she's the one I was referring to when I said your words reminded me of someone. Is something wrong?" The newly familiar tingle that had followed me the last several days, since first seeing Anna on the beach, was back.

"No, it's not that, not at all. It's, well…I'm sorry. I promised I would tell you the truth always, and here I am at a place where I'm not sure I can do that, not right now. I won't lie to you, my relationship with Anna is complicated, but it's not a negative one. It's just that, if you don't mind, I would like to *postpone* a discussion about her, just for a little while." Eyes filled with angst, the solid self-possession that had also reminded me of Anna faded.

With all that he had given me on this night, this I could give him, even though it meant hiding my own curiosity, and my slightly hurt feelings. I felt left out. And I was confused, where was the Mark of only moments before? The man so at ease with himself and discussions of feelings? Had I been wrong in believing I could trust him?

"Of course Mark. You don't have to tell me anything you don't want to. You've given me that freedom. I can certainly return the favor. Anyway, my own 'connection' to Anna is about more than I can handle." My intent was to soften the mood, to move away from the subject, but my last statement had the opposite impact. I watched as he viciously ran weathered hands through his hair and then covered his eyes with them.

Slowly he began to speak again, without looking at me, but leaning forward, forearms on knees, hands clasped together, staring sadly out at the night sky.

"What do you think your connection is to Anna, Sara?"

"Mark, I have to tell you, you're worrying me a little. Tell me Mark, is there something I need to know about Anna?"

"Oh Sara," he sighed, "all I can tell you is to hold on. Your life is probably about to change in ways you can't imagine." And with that I could tell the conversation was over. His gaze moved even farther away, beyond the sky to a place I could not follow.

Driving home Mark's words haunted me, as did the well of sadness they had come from.

He had returned from his inner journey after several minutes in which nothing seemed to move. He had smiled, but it was small and wistful, an attempt to erase, not his feelings, but the effect they had had on the space between us. He had stood and just as in my dream, reached out his hand to help me up. Together we had walked up the long lawn to the terrace.

I had sensed that there was something else he wanted to say or to ask. He had spoken no more of Anna, but she was present, as strongly as if she walked with us. When we had come to the terrace we stood awkwardly facing each other. After a couple of false starts he plunged forward.

"Sara, may I ask you a favor?" I nodded.

"May I please see the locket you were wearing earlier?"

Shocked, I stared motionless.

"I know, I know, it seems weird. But I would really like to see it if it's okay." His voice was smooth, his composure in the process of being regained. But somewhere behind the calm was the hint of loose threads.

Digging in my purse I said, "Well sure. Here." I held the little silver star out to him. At once he took it in his grip, respectful of its fragility, but also with an air of familiarity, like one finding a lost, beloved possession. Turning it over, he held it close to his face and read the inscription. Closely I watched his complete immersion. I doubted if I spoke that he would even hear me.

He opened the locket and as he took in the picture of the little girl I thought I could hear the pounding of his heart. His eyes moistened and he shook his head, as if receiving the answer to a question, and not sure he liked what he heard.

What, I wondered, was his connection to the locket? Did he know the little girl? Or was it Bev and Gil? Again I had been steeped in mystery. Would I ever get answers rather than more questions?

My head rang with such questions but I didn't know how to voice them. I hadn't been prepared for this, for any of it.

"Thank you," Mark whispered, and handed the necklace back to me, "it's a beautiful piece. An antique." The words were conversational, ordinary, but with each one I felt another thread coming undone. I wanted to help him, to understand what was going on, but something told me that this wasn't the time.

Before saying goodnight we looked back out at the garden. It all looked different now, like a place you know well, have traveled to and returned from somehow changed. It was forever engraved with this night's memory. No matter what happened when the sun rose, tonight would always be here. The thought floated through me and for the moment I was comforted.

CHAPTER TWELVE

It was after 1:00 am when I pulled into the driveway. The air was cold and I was shaking, though I wasn't sure one had anything to do with the other. My head was so full that no thought was able to form in completion before another began, the effect being a bottomless vat of no-thought.

Stumbling into the house, wired with exhaustion, it occurred to me that I probably shouldn't have come home at all. In four hours I would have to leave to go back to Jane's for my meeting with Anna. What was happening to me? Where was my simple life of only a few days ago? As I peeled off my clothes and crawled beneath the heavy coolness of sheets and blankets I longed to wake to the nothingness I had known.

In mere seconds I drifted away from the clamoring silence of my head and into the world of shapeless forms and formless images. Breathlessly I raced from place to no place, desperately searching for something, but what I didn't know. Everywhere I went a face appeared, none that I could name, but all that I knew, promising to give me what I sought, only to dissolve as soon as I put out my hand. Around and around I went, asking anyone, everyone, if they had what I was looking for. When they asked me what it was, I tried, but could not utter the answer. It was on the tip of my tongue, but would come no further. As soon as I thought on it, it vanished. Finally, I stopped. I just stopped. I was too tired and could go no further and after a long while I heard a voice in the distance, moving closer. It began as a whisper but the closer it came the louder it grew, until the words rang clearly inside my head. *"The answers are closer than you think. They are in the most obvious place of all."* And then even I vanished.

The alarm screamed, invading childishly upon the dark. Bolting upright I looked around anxiously, unsure of the surroundings, forgetting time, place, and even for a moment, name. Angrily I stared at the clock: 4:45am. Beyond the window the day had not yet woken, the eyes of the earth still shut tight.

Why in Heaven's name would the clock be set for such an hour? And then in a rush, like an avalanche gaining speed, memories of the night fell upon me. Backwards, like a silent movie in reverse, Mark looking at the locket, his arms comforting me, the garden, dinner, Anna...

Anna! 5:30. In the garden, or labyrinth as Mark had explained. In one swift swoop I was up and pulling on whatever clothes I could find scattered about, a "college clean" pair of jeans, turtleneck and sweater. A quick trip to the bathroom, brush through the hair and over the teeth. Socks, shoes, coat, purse, keys. Out the door in twelve minutes. Not an extra moment to think, to remember, to reconsider, to wonder what lay ahead, or to question the fact that I didn't recall setting the alarm clock.

But the drive to Jane's was another story. The roads were desolate, dark still lay heavy over the day and the air was thick with the smell of winter. The silence of morning was not, as usual, comforting, but threatening and lonely. It pressed against my skin, seeking a way to crawl beneath. It was *too* early. Like entering a room uninvited, and unwelcome. This was time meant not for humans, but for those mysteries unrevealed. I felt like a trespasser.

What was it about the isolation of early morning, about the dark, that triggered fear? Hands gripping the steering wheel, my mind gathered together all the remembered monsters of childhood and placed them along the roadside, beyond every bend and behind every tree. Even the music of the birds sounded forlorn, or berating, angry with me for intruding. I imagined my car as seen from above. A lumbering metal monster imposing itself, loudly and distastefully, upon that which sought a delicate equilibrium. Was it human nature to disrupt the balance? Was it our intent, design, or just a terrible misunderstanding?

I laughed nervously at my philosophical meanderings. They were better than the alternative, thinking of Anna and what awaited me in the labyrinth.

It was 5:20 when I pulled, or rather crept, into Jane's driveway. I could probably have pushed the car faster but I didn't want to disturb the house. Perhaps I should have told Jane about my meeting with Anna. After all, it was her garden. Maybe Anna had told her, or maybe this was a regular occurrence. I could just imagine Anna leading one innocent idiot after another into the maze. It wouldn't surprise me if what I found when I got inside was a Minotaur.

The thought blossomed into an entire fantastical imagining of me, as Theseus, raging against the man-bull, and against Anna as well, saving the lives of other hapless victims that had been lost in the garden's depths for eons. I would save the day, dismantle the mysteries and rid the world of this craziness that infested lives, leaving them disheveled and chaotic.

By the time I had parked and tiptoed around to the back of the house, I was knee-deep into my story, laughing out loud at my own brazenness in the face of whatever it was I was about to face. I guessed it was a little like picturing an audience in its underwear before a speech, the dislodging of reality helping to trick the mind into believing it was safe. Whatever it took to put one foot in front of the other.

"Good morning. And from the look of it you're having a very pleasant one already."

Startled I gasped, nearly fell backwards and came to a halt. Sitting comfortably in a chaise on the terrace, relaxed and fully alert, was Jane. Gone were the tables and bar from the night before and in their place was a full set of cedar furniture, table, chairs and chaise. Though it was still dark out an overhead light, dimmed softly, made it possible to see. She was bundled into a thick purple cashmere robe and on her feet were big wooly socks, the kind I used for hiking. Steam rose from a mug that she held in front of her with both hands.

"Oh my God, you scared me. I'm sorry. I didn't mean to startle you, if I did, you don't look startled. I know it's early, really early." I stopped and looked at her. Cocked my head and studied her. "You don't look startled at all. You're not surprised to see me are you? Are you always up this early?" The questions were disjointed, just like my thinking.

She laughed. "No and yes."

"So Anna told you I was going to meet her here? That's good, I mean I felt kind of bad just showing up and sneaking around." I walked to where she sat and squatted next to her, looking up into the kind, wise face.

"It's all so strange Jane. Everything, the past few days. I don't get any of it, especially Anna. Who is she Jane?"

A cool dry hand reached out and came to rest on my cheek. Like a child I wanted to crawl onto the chaise and curl up next to her, safe and protected under her steady, gentle watch.

"She is a woman, just like you Sara. She is also more than a woman, just like you. Don't be afraid child, there is nothing to fear, not really. It just seems that way. Everything is like that really, just seeming a way. Now go. I'll be here when you get back. Come and find me. We'll have a talk about that locket of yours." Her eyes widened, as if in anticipation of a great surprise. I wasn't sure how many more of those I could take.

With a final pat of my cheek she swung her legs to the opposite side of the chaise, stood and walked toward the door. My refuge gone, I also stood and moved to the edge of the terrace, where brick met grass.

"Oh and Sara,"

I turned. She was smiling at me.

"I haven't seen Anna. She never told me you were coming."

And with that she walked inside and shut the door behind her.

I was only slightly late, but wondered if Anna would be there and how long she would be willing to wait. I doubted long. Just a little more than five hours had passed since I had walked this lawn, and said goodbye to Mark. It felt more like a lifetime. It was different somehow too. Lonelier, emptier. Maybe it was just the morning stillness again. Whatever it was, it saturated my clothes and skin, and the closer I came to the garden, the denser it grew, until it showed itself to be that which it was, terror.

Fear was not new to me, but this was something more. It seized me in my center and moved upward, taking control of my breathing. Somehow, not of my own accord, I continued to walk, every step in direct opposition to the orders screaming in my head. Like a worm hole in space some greater force sucked me in, leaving me helpless to fight, helpless to do anything but wait to see where I landed.

The force I was sure was Anna. Or the promise she had made, the hope she had dared to give me. Her words came back... *"It is the experience of discovering who you are. You have an important role to play and it's time you took the stage,"* and the words that I had heard whispered in the void, *"You are more than you have known yourself to be. Your life is in the promise you made to remember this truth. Be not afraid..."*

How was I to not be afraid? The message itself terrified me, much less the idea that strangers seemed to have more of an understanding of my life than I did. A puppet at the mercy of their strings, unable to make or carry out decisions of my own volition. Should I run? Was this some dangerous masquerade being played out at my expense? But if so, by whom? And why? And if not, who was behind the curtain, pulling the strings?

Maybe if I clicked my heels together three times I would wake to find it had all been a dream, a sad, strange, terrible dream, and I would be back home, the home I had shared with Brian, and he would be sleeping soundly next to me. It was worth a try.

"In order for that to work you have to truly believe, and truly want what it is you are asking for, *know* what it is you are asking for. Do you?"

Why was it that people kept appearing out of nowhere?

Without realizing it I had reached the entrance to the garden. She stood directly beneath the arch, only a few feet away, barefoot and dressed in a long sheath of sky and cloud blue. Her hair was pulled back from her face with a headband and though it laid a little flatter than usual, wisps escaped and curled upward all around her head, as though rebelling against the attempt to be tamed. The sleeves of her dress were long but the fabric light. Was she never cold?

In the dim first rays of dawn her face was pale, luminescent as a china doll. Eyes made bluer in contrast to ivory skin. Sea, sky, clouds, sun and moon, all carried in the being of this one woman. Her shadow stretched for miles and I stood small and lost in the shade of it.

She was smiling, but I felt silly, having been caught in childish fantasy. Finding it hard to meet her eyes, I looked out over the ocean.

She had asked me a question. Was it rhetorical or did she expect an answer? My voice was soft, "No, I guess I don't know really what I want. And I'm not sure if there's anything I believe that much in anymore. Sorry I'm late."

"Are you late? I don't have a watch. It doesn't matter. You're here and that is what is important. You've been in the labyrinth?"

"Yes. Well, no. I mean, I came down here and started to go in, but then it was too dark, so I didn't get very far. I didn't even know it was a 'labyrinth' until…" I wasn't sure how much of last night I wanted to share with her, especially after Mark's reaction to the simple mention of her name.

"…until Mark told you?" I turned to face her. Bright steady eyes were fixed on me. Obviously she did not reciprocate the anxiety he had shown.

"Yes. How did you know?" I didn't really expect an answer.

"Let's save that for later. There is much to do. Are you ready?"

"I guess, but I still haven't figured out why I'm here. What I'm supposed to do? And what's the purpose?" It amazed me that she didn't seem to understand how odd this was, or how frightening she and her unnatural calm were.

Sighing, her smile holding an infinite amount of patience, the sort a mother exhibits with a small child. "Sara, the first challenge I offer you is this: allow this process, with all of its mystery and apparently hidden purpose to unravel naturally. You are welcome to ask questions, but you will learn only what you are ready to in each moment. We have not even begun and yet you wish to know the end, the outcome, all of the answers. When, ever, are answers to anything arrived at without undergoing the process of discovery? It is impossible to jump from the asking to the answering without a journey."

I sighed heavily in return, but mine filled more with frustration. Her wisdom always made sense but the kind that seemed impossible to follow. "Okay, I'll try to be patient. But, I don't even know what the questions are. It feels like I was yanked into this, whatever it is, without even knowing it. All of a sudden I'm just running into one weird experience after another."

"Let's sit a moment, okay?" She sat down on the damp ground, legs crossed in front of her, perfectly poised and relaxed.

I followed, not so poised or in the least bit relaxed.

A few minutes passed, both of us staring out at the shadows of the ocean. I sat with my arms wrapped around me, as a shield from the cold. I didn't know if she was waiting for me to speak, or if she was just comfortable with the silence. For me it grew deafening. I searched hard for something to say, something to do. Questions rose but I was too nervous to ask them. And then she spoke.

"Tell me about Brian. About your love for him."

The words made me dizzy. I sat speechless, shivering. Her tone was intimate, like that of an old friend, someone I could trust. But not even my oldest friends did I let into the wound that hearing Brian's name opened.

"I…we…he…I'm sorry Anna, that's not something I like to talk much about."

"I know. But try. Just relax, think about the love, and describe it to me."

Closing my eyes I pictured Brian. I had read in books that his image would begin to fade, that I wouldn't, in time, be able to see him clearly. But that had not happened. I could still call forth every inch of him - his eyes, mouth, hair. Strong arms and chest. His smell and the taste of his skin. It was these images that both haunted and gave me comfort in the night. But it was the way he had loved me that I wanted so desperately to pull from the memories, the love that continued to evade me.

"Brian was strong and courageous. He wasn't afraid of anything that I know of. But he was also good and kind and funny. He was always happy it seemed. I mean he could get mad or frustrated but he never let it stop him. And he loved me. It's so amazing, but he loved me. Just as I am. He understood. He kept me safe, protected me. I always felt safe with him." Opening my eyes I found Anna watching me, listening closely.

"Is that what it is to be loved? Safety?"

"In a lot of ways. To me at least. There's more to it than that of course, but yes, I guess I've always wanted to feel safe, and Brian did that for me."

"And what does it mean to be safe? Safe from what, or whom?"

"From the world and being alone in it. From pain and sadness, risk and failure. From my own weakness, my own inadequacy. Brian's love made everything all right. Somehow I never seemed to disappoint him. He shone bright enough for both of us. Being loved by him meant everything to me."

"And now?"

"What do you mean?"

"Do you feel loved now?"

"Well my family loves me and my friends, though I've managed to alienate a few of them. I'm loved, yes." I looked down at my hands in my lap as I spoke. For some reason I wanted to cry.

"Does their love make you feel safe? At night alone in your home, do you feel safe and loved?"

My bottom lip started to quiver. The tears were beginning to well. "No. No, I feel alone. That's what I feel. Alone, and empty," and then almost belligerently, "is that what you wanted to hear?"

"Sara, I'm not trying to hurt you. I'm just trying to understand the essence of your love with Brian, what it gave you and what losing him has taken from you."

"It's taken everything."

"You said that it was amazing that Brian loved you. Why Sara, why is that amazing? Are you so hard to love?"

Still I studied my hands. I needed a Kleenex. I wanted to stop crying. "It's just that he was so special and I, I'm, well, ordinary, I guess. There is nothing extraordinary about me Anna. I mean I have a pretty good mind, at least I was always told that I was smart, and I guess I'm okay looking. But nothing really that stands out, you know. Brian stood out. Everyone that knew him loved him and wanted to be around him. He had a way with people. Even so, with all of that, he chose me. With him, I was something. Brian made me special." A small smile tugged at the corners of my mouth.

"And without him, Sara. Who and what are you without him?"

The tears rolled steadily down my cheeks, comforting old friends. Slowly I lifted my face and for the first time met Anna's eyes. "I have no idea Anna. I have absolutely no idea."

CHAPTER THIRTEEN

"Do you know what a labyrinth is?" Anna asked me. We were standing back several yards from the entrance, trying to put the entire structure in our line of vision. In the dawn light it was even more astonishing than it had been under moonlight. Its mystery was still there, but different. The sky, in hushed tones of gray and gold, seemed higher and larger than usual, as formidable and immense as the labyrinth itself.

"Only that it's a maze. And Mark told me the story of Theseus and the Minotaur from mythology. That's about all I know."

"It really isn't necessary that you know all there is to know about them for you to experience what you need. But it's interesting, I think, to know a little. First of all, labyrinths are quite different from mazes. A maze is like a puzzle that has to be figured out. You have to make decisions and choices, and the wrong ones can get you lost or lead into blind alleys. A labyrinth on the other hand has only one way in, one way out. It can seem long and winding, it may even feel like you are getting lost, but really you aren't. You can't. With time and patience you reach the center and return back."

"Well that's good to know I guess, since I get the feeling we're going to be going in."

Anna continued on as if she hadn't heard me. "Labyrinths have been around for thousands of years. The origin is unknown, why they work as they do is a mystery. But they can be found throughout history, in a variety of cultures - different times, different places, the same basic design. The symbol of the circle can be traced to almost every religious and cultural tradition - from the Native American medicine wheel to Tibetan sand paintings, to the Kabbalistic Tree of

Life. The labyrinth has been found carved in rock, etched in sand, laid in stone on the floors of churches, and as this one, grown up out of the land. It is engraved on ancient coins and found inscribed on Grecian clay tablets that are thousands of years old."

"Why? Why are they so important? What is their purpose?" I was intrigued.

"They have been used in as many ways as there are cultures that use them. Always they seem to be sacred – a living template for a journey taken. An encapsulated pilgrimage." She turned her head to look out over the ocean. "In Scandinavia labyrinths were built close to the water, like this one. It is said that before they went out to sea, fisherman would walk the labyrinth to ensure prosperous and safe voyages."

"So it's superstition." My mother was very superstitious and had imbued in me a subtle underlying belief that my fate was shaped and guided by spilled salt, sidewalk cracks and my ability to decode, navigate and balance upon the tightrope of luck.

"No. Not superstition Sara. Superstition leads us to believe that there is a 'right' path and a 'wrong' path and that one little slip on our part will bring about calamity. In the labyrinth there is no 'wrong' path, no 'wrong' way. It is an ancient symbol imbedded into the very cells of man. Circles are the building blocks of life, from the smallest organism to the largest planet, they are the ordering component of the universe. We, as part of the great mystery, respond at a basic and primal level to this. It seems that we are always seeking the wholeness that the circle emblemizes."

"I've never thought of it that way." I didn't want to say too much, didn't want her to stop talking.

But she said only, "It's time now. The rest you discover on your own." And then without looking at me she walked back towards the mouth of the labyrinth. I didn't move, not yet ready to discover anything on my own.

I hesitated because I knew that everything else, all of the talking, had been merely a precursor to this moment.

Anna stood beneath the arch as if waiting for me to move forward. I was afraid, but I had made my decision and was determined to follow it through. Taking a deep breath I walked to where she stood, my steps faltering only slightly. When I reached her she held out a cool, comforting hand. Shakily I took it. Turning toward me she grasped my other hand and locked her eyes onto mine. Piercing blue pools that did not allow escape.

"It's time to walk the labyrinth. There is nothing to be afraid of. You will put one foot in front of the other and walk your way to the center and then you will return. Allow yourself to experience whatever it is you feel in each moment. Cry or laugh or do nothing at all but walk. Try to remember to breathe; it is the fuel of life.

"Walking the labyrinth is like walking the pathway of our own soul. It is a circuitous, sometimes confusing, journey. At times we believe it is leading us nowhere, except into the depths of darkness, where we are lost and alone. But if we just keep following the path we come to see that it has an exquisite order, a beautifully laid out route that leads to only one place, the center. Our center, our truth, our own splendid being lays waiting for us, waiting to be discovered. So take this journey in whatever way you need. Each of us travels it differently, our experience is unique unto our selves, created and breathed into existence through the moments of our lives, one at a time. Moment to moment, breath by breath. No matter how often we reach what seems like a dead end, or find ourselves turned around, no matter how easy or difficult the journey, we *will* reach the center. We all get there, it is impossible to lose our way permanently. One step at a time, you will find *your* way."

The soothing rhythm of her voice, like waves rolling onto shore, helped to calm my nerves. My hands tingled. Her touch, warm and electric, fed me energy. The air around us became charged, each inhalation a wave of electricity rising up through my spine and out the top of my head. It felt much like my experience on the mountain. My whole being alive, a swirling conduit of energy.

Slowly, as Anna stopped talking and released my hands, the feeling subsided, but I was able to remain relatively calm. Together we slowly walked the first ten feet, and then stopped. I looked down the corridor between the hedges that extended to the left. It stretched several feet before turning a corner. I could make it to the corner, but what lay beyond that?

Whispers of fear and doubt wiggled in around the edges of my awareness, tickling the walls of my belly and chest. But finally, with a long exhale I said, "Okay. Let's go," the words a sigh of resignation.

I began to walk, feeling every movement, concentrating all of my mental energy on the act of walking. Feet hitting the ground and rising, displacing patches of dirt with each step. Knees, hips, elbows, shoulders in synchronistic rhythm. Breathing in, breathing out. All the while watching the ground, like a child discovering the wonder of mobility.

I was halfway to the corner when I realized that I was walking alone. A flutter of movement drew my attention and I glanced up expecting to see Anna beside me. But she wasn't there. I turned around and found her still standing at the first turn.

The question was a tremor, a tiny earthquake of anxiety, "What's wrong? Why aren't you walking with me?"

Slowly she shook her head, a small smile lighting her eyes. "This is a journey you must take alone Sara. We each must. It is not a simple walk through the garden you are embarking on, it is a journey into your own soul. It is time you realized that you can walk the path alone, that you are strong enough. That you are enough."

She let the words hang in the air between us for what felt like a long, long time.

And then she continued. "But I will never be far Sara. And there is always support, always a force around us, within us, wanting and willing to hold us up, comfort us and guide us out of the dark. When you are in need, look for the light."

Tears stung the corners of my eyes, but I fought to keep them from falling. This was about courage. It was no time to cry. But I wanted to. Everything within me ached, reached out, desperate to be heard: "I don't *want* to be alone anymore."

But the words, screaming through my blood, came into the world as a silent prayer, heard by no one.

With Anna watching I continued my walk into the labyrinth. One step at a time. Each footfall sounding out the voices of my fear. My heart raced and I had no idea why. As I neared the corner my anxiety only grew.

Last night I had come this far with Mark, but the short distance from the entrance had not been so terrifying, marked only by the apprehension of his nearness. Today my skin was jumping, every inch, sense and cell alive.

Finally standing in the corner I remembered the anxiety that had been overwhelming the night before, the dark eerie stillness that had caused me to turn and leave. The morning though was bright and filled with life. In the soft waking sunlight, the colors - reds, yellows, blues and violets – burst from a deep green canvas. The song of birds announced the day while in the distance the ocean played its own baritone melody. Within the walls of the labyrinth it looked, sounded and even smelled like spring. Only the crisp cold air gave away winter's secret.

I stopped before following the path any farther. Hardly twenty feet and already I was exhausted. Everything - bone, blood, teeth and skin rattled. Looking back over my shoulder I was relieved to find Anna still there. I made a feeble attempt at a smile. In return, she said loud enough for me to hear, "Breathe Sara," and her own body visibly moved with deep inhalation.

It took several minutes of serious argument with myself before I decided to take another step. Desperately I tried to listen to the music of morning. It was so beautiful and yet none of it seemed able to touch the haunted dark within.

Staring down the long path I had just traveled I was alarmed by the strangeness of my response. It was a dirt path, nothing more. Granted I had never seen one quite like it, with skyscraper hedges marking its boundaries. But nonetheless it was benign, nothing to promote or justify my reaction.

And with that small thought, that seed of courage, I turned the corner.

But the seed wouldn't grow. The physical sensations of panic were stronger than my resolve, and were growing exponentially. Upon turning the corner I found myself staring down another long dirt corridor, more empty space and time, but now I was completely alone, Anna no longer in sight.

Briefly I tried to concentrate on the flowers and their dizzying colors, but even their beauty couldn't hold my focus. The thumping of my heart, like a native drum, called me within.

Little by little I became aware that only my body was awake, alone experiencing the panic. There was no thought, no emotion, no visions, ideas or memories, just physical sensations. The deeper into the labyrinth I traveled, the louder my body became. I could garner no control, the sensations flooding over and through me, brought alive by the rhythm of movement. Before I knew it I was rounding another corner, and immediately began to sweat. Cold air tickled my skin, but beneath it my blood ran hot. Walking, walking. Stomach clenched, chest heaving. And then tears, as though a faucet had been turned on. Falling unprovoked, unwarranted.

Walking, walking. Deeper, farther. Becoming body only. No mind, no thought, no feeling. Just physical being. Every move a complex system of responses. Every breath, step and heartbeat magnified. Racing heart, rapidly pumping blood, shallow breath, shoulders lifted to ears, jaws and hands clenched, a band tightening around my head, pain pulsing. A machine.

And then a subtle shift occurred, a slight change in the direction of the wind, and with sudden clarity I awoke to the voices of my body. For the first time I was completely aware of not just having, but being, my physical self. And with the simple shift of awareness I heard the strangled voice of my own breath. It was not the easy flow of wind, but rather the choked whistle of a clogged filter. The closer attention I paid the more clearly I heard the plea buried in the whimpering rasp: "Release me."

I came to a stop, the cries of my body reaching a debilitating crescendo. Muscles joined in, "Release me, release me," they demanded - an angry, wailing chorus pounding in my ears.

Another shift and I saw before me the living energy of my body, muscles, bones, organs, cells. Not like watching a movie where the images float distantly in front of you, but rather like standing inside of the movie, in the center of the action, and being the action at the same time. I was inside my body, inside every particle, looking out, and outside as well, looking in. And all around me was murky bog emanating from within, expanding outward, covering and infiltrating everything. Disease. The word rose out of the darkness. My own body betraying me, dying before my eyes.

"No!" The scream started low in my gut, the growl of a beast fighting for its life. When word met air the images crumbled, like glass shattering and falling to the floor. I began to run, back the way I had come, out of the labyrinth. Twice I tripped and fell to the ground, stumbling and clawing my way back up. The beast running from the hunt.

Anna was sitting just outside the entrance, facing the ocean, legs crossed, face tilted upward. So still and serene I almost ran over her.

"Sara. Slow down."

I ran past her with no intention of stopping until I reached my car. I wanted to get away, far away, from this place, these people and the foreboding images I imagined were chasing me out of the labyrinth.

By the time Anna's voice registered I was halfway to Jane's house, tears running, choking, blurring my vision. I didn't want to hear her. But like a magnet, her words pulled me back. At first I slowed imperceptibly, and then more, until I was walking. Finally, without turning around I stopped and slumped limply to the ground.

Anna's shadow stretched around me. I imagined her with the sun at her back, dark curls emblazoned with golden fire. The quintessence of strength. The truth of my own weakness cut like a sword. But it only galvanized the pain and I cried harder.

"Sara, it's okay to cry, to be afraid. You're out now and all is as you left it. If you can, try to slow your breathing, or at least start breathing." She was kneeling on the grass beside me, gently stroking my hair away from my face. "Relax. Breathe deep and slow. There, that's it, that's it. Keep breathing."

Like a child besieged by nightmares I fell under the spell of a soothing mother - allowing Anna to comfort me while I closed my eyes and drifted into the twilight world on the edge of sleep.

CHAPTER FOURTEEN

My eyes fluttered open. A leaf, brown and curled at the edges, sat only inches from my nose. It teetered in the breeze and rolled lazily down the hill. I, on the other hand, felt too heavy to move.

With gruesome detail I remembered what had brought me to this place where I now lay, curled like a fetus under a maple tree on Jane's lawn. It took great effort to pick up my head and look around, hoping against hope that I would see no one. Relieved when I didn't, I dropped my head back down and cradled it in my arms. Embarrassment and exhaustion covered me like a wet blanket. Though it had felt like only moments that my eyes had been closed I could tell that hours had passed. The sun was high in the sky, half-obscured by gray clouds that threatened to fill in the blue spaces.

A blanket had been carefully draped over me and my jacket had been tucked under my head. I cringed at the thought of Anna, and worse, Jane, standing over me, shaking their heads in pity. How nice it would be to just roll down the hill after the leaf, to be picked up by the wind and carried someplace far away.

For several more minutes I watched absently as one leaf after another followed the first. I wondered where they went, dead leaves missed by rakes. My mind ran the course of nonsense so often taken when it was too tired for any other thought. If I shut my eyes I knew I would fall back to sleep, and as tempting as it was I would only wake up later. What I really wanted was to disappear. To hide from what I knew was coming.

Just behind me I heard it, or rather her, stepping lightly over the grass. It would do no good to pretend I was asleep. She would only keep returning until I was ready to face her.

I spoke first. "How long have I been here?"

She sat with her back against the tree, an apple in her hand. She took a bite, chewed and swallowed before answering me.

"It's 11:15, about three hours. How do you feel?"

I remained in a fetal position, my back to her, "Stupid mostly. I can't believe I slept so long. Why didn't you wake me?" Feeling ridiculous I had decided to blame it on her.

"You woke when you were ready, that wasn't up to me. Do you want to talk about it?"

Feeling fragile and arthritic I uncurled myself slowly, my joints and muscles resisting every move. Bones cracked and popped loudly. As I went to sit up I felt woozy - head spinning, stomach bridling - a first-rate hangover.

"Did I drink heavily and forget?"

Anna laughed. "No. Not that I recall at least." She smiled down at me as I continued to struggle, and took another bite of her apple.

I settled miserably against the tree with legs sprawled in front of me and arms dropped limply at my sides like a worn out rag doll. It seemed my body was holding onto the memories of what had happened in the labyrinth. Like it didn't want me to forget.

"Anna, do you know what happened to me in there? What I saw and felt?"

"Obviously something that frightened you. I told you Sara, everyone's experience is different. Unique and perfect for them. You can tell me about it if you like." So casual and infuriating was her manner that for a flash I felt like knocking the apple out of her hand and shaking her.

Controlling myself I said, "It was horrible. If I had known what it was going to be like, I never would have agreed to go in. Why would anyone choose to do that?"

"How far did you go?"

"Far enough as far as I'm concerned," and then more meekly, "I don't know, I guess not very. But I couldn't stand any more. What if it had gotten worse?"

"What if it had gotten better?"

"How? How could it have gotten better? You don't know what I saw. I saw...I saw, it was me, my body..." I couldn't bring myself to say it.

"Dying?" She said it for me. She had finished her apple and was turned toward me.

"Well, yes, I guess. All inside me, around me, it was black - and painful. 'Disease' was all I could hear or feel. It was like I was inside my body, I mean really inside, looking at it, seeing this sick energy and I sensed that I was dying."

"We all want life to be easy and free from pain. We want to be happy. That's understandable, what greater purpose could there be than the creation of joy. But often the search is weighed down by worry, fear, expectation or need, and for many years we go about it blindly, unaware of our own motivations. So when we begin to pursue that greater thing, that purer truth of who we are, we must first travel through the residue left by all the other. We do die, in a sense, but only so we may be reborn to our larger selves. It is not easy and it can be painful. It takes courage and most of all, faith."

"Like in God you mean?"

"Well, yes, you can call it that, though there are many names. I am not talking about religion per se, but about calling forth faith in the larger order of things, in the knowing that there is an intelligence permeating every event and substance, and believing that you too are part of a greater purpose or plan.

"Do you still remember Sheila's reading from the other night?" I nodded half-heartedly. "She told us that we have the power to create our experience of who we are, to choose the palette in our life creation. But we cannot do that until we have seen the complete design, until we know what colors are offered. We have to take the time to witness ourselves in the light of truth, to love and honor the parts we like as well as those we don't. Those we don't teach us much of what we need to know. Within us there is both dark and light. Both are important, both necessary in creating a work of depth and contour, passion and brilliance.

"You saw in the labyrinth something of yourself you didn't like, or the beginning of something you assumed to be 'bad'."

"Well I'm sorry, but watching the darkness of death ooze out of me can't be good."

"The body, or our exterior life, is often the reflection of the soul, Sara. It manifests for us what we are unwilling to see otherwise. What you saw might not be literal, at least not yet, but it may very well be the image of things to come. Or at the least it may be showing you what your emotional life looks like, in physical terms, or perhaps what is required, before life can be regained. Regardless, it was telling you something.

"Do you understand what the darkness was about? Do you know why it was there? What it meant? Did you see it through to find out or did you assume the worst and react by running away?" Her tone was not reproachful but nonetheless I felt like my hand had just been slapped.

"You know what I did, I ran like hell. Maybe whatever it is I experienced is all in a day's work for you, but for me it was downright weird. Do you have any idea how strange all of this is? And how much at this moment I hate it?" The pain in my head and the nausea gripping my gut had made me ornery enough to say how I really felt.

She noticed the shift. "I'm glad to hear you say what you mean. And yes, I do realize that you are going through some pretty extraordinary experiences, though you are right that they are a little less 'weird' to me. But tell me this - do you want to walk away? Truly? Do you want to stop right here? Because if you do, if you, in the deepest shadows of your heart wish to, then it will end. That is, if you think you can. For sometimes it seems that once we begin to walk the road toward truth, that greater something, call it God if you like, draws us back again and again. We come to see that this 'force' directs our path and though we may steer the course in one direction or another we find that the current of the river is not in our control."

I was so tired. Tired of her voice, of the constant onslaught of lessons. But tired too, because I knew that what she said was right. Ever since I had first seen Anna I had known that somehow my world was about to be altered. Something inside of me had broken loose and released a flood of new thought and experience. Nothing in the past few days had been 'normal.' But it had, even with all of my fighting, been better than the alternative. It made me uncomfortable, moody, even angry, but at least I had felt more alive than I had in over six months, maybe ever.

I whined, like a child not wanting to admit they wanted to do something asked of them. "No. I guess there's no turning back. I've tried, believe me, and part of me wishes I could go back in time, stop myself from ever going to the beach that morning where I first saw you, go back and throw away that invitation from the bookstore before I ever decided to go. Because I think that's the only way I could truly get away from whatever it is…this is. Maybe it is God. To me God has always been, I don't know…distant I guess. Loving, but with some pretty high standards and just not all that interested in my little life. But when Brian was taken away…well that's when I gave up completely on God. I'll just never understand," and then more quietly, "or forgive…"

We sat silently while I turned it all over in my head, and then finally said, "Okay Anna, I'll keep going. I don't really know what else to do. I guess that means I have to go back in there. But I'm tired now. Do I have to solve the puzzle of my existence today?"

She laughed and moved gracefully to her feet. "No. I guess life's mysteries can wait another day."

CHAPTER FIFTEEN

Anna left me sitting alone beneath the maple tree, and it was another half hour before I had the energy or inclination to move. She had told me that the next step was up to me, that when I was ready to return to the labyrinth she would be there waiting. I, of course, asked how she would know, but she simply promised she would, and I let it go at that. Then she said she had some other 'personal' matters to take care of and disappeared.

It was hard to imagine Anna having a personal life. She owned the bookstore so I assumed she spent time there, but I had no idea where she lived or what she did when she wasn't turning my life upside down. I wasn't yet convinced she was altogether human, though I didn't have a grasp on what exactly that would make her. She just seemed outside the realm of real. But I did know that Mark played some sort of role in her life and I wondered if that was the 'personal' matter she had referred to.

When it became physically possible I slowly stood and stretched. I was used to creaky bones and sore muscles but nothing like this. Every part of me ached. My plan was to go straight home and crawl into bed and not wake until the pain was gone. When I reached Jane's house I tried to move quickly so as not to be seen, but my efforts were fruitless. Even if my body had cooperated I wouldn't have been able to avoid Jane, who was sitting in the same chaise as she had when I arrived, this time drinking something cold.

"No, I haven't been here all day if that's what you're wondering. See, I've changed clothes." Her hair was pulled back in its usual bun and she wore a bright yellow sweater and gray flannel pants. "Actually I was gone all morning and drove up just in time to say hello to Anna before she left. She told me you were still here. I hoped you'd have lunch with me, if you have no other plans?"

I couldn't bring myself to say no to Jane. So, accepting her invitation, I plopped down in one of the chairs.

Lunch was simple and delicious - tomato, mozzarella and pesto sandwiches accompanied by a huge bowl of fruit. We sat on the terrace and watched, as the day grew increasingly gray. Mostly I listened as Jane told me about how she and her husband, Peter, had come to buy the house and convert it from a bed and breakfast into their home, the reverse of what people usually do.

She had met her husband when he was on a trip to the area scouting out property to purchase for a summer retreat. He was single and successful - a newscaster from the west coast who had decided he needed a place to escape. Jane had just begun selling real estate and the handsome stranger was one of her first clients. She was immediately smitten and the feeling was obviously mutual. Their property search turned into a mere excuse to spend time together. They would drive for hours, with Jane playing tour guide, sharing with her rapt audience of one the history and culture of the island. It was on one such outing that they passed the hidden drive and Jane mentioned the bed and breakfast by the sea that had opened only the year before. It had been the summer home of one of the wealthy and infamous faces often seen on the island, but who had recently fallen upon bad times and had to sell the property. Peter asked to see it so they turned around and drove down the driveway.

They ended up spending the next three nights there, hiding away from the rest of the world. During the day they walked the beach, sat by the fireplace or out on the terrace, and evenings they spent curled up in the library. Every room became theirs as they explored and came to know each one. At night, tucked into the bridal suite on the second floor (they had told the owners they were newlyweds), they explored the terrain of each other's bodies and souls. When it came time for Peter to return to the west coast he simply didn't go. Instead he sent for his belongings, quit his job and bought the bed and breakfast. Neither he nor Jane desired to run it as an inn however, so they turned it into their own private oasis. They were married on the back lawn overlooking the ocean and together remained there until Peter's death. When he was gone Jane thought about selling but couldn't see herself anyplace else. For the past ten years she had lived alone, except for a live-in housekeeper, in the beautiful old home by the sea.

The story, much like Gil and Bev's, sounded too good to be true, like the fairy tale perfection of romance novels. The beauty of it touched me. Mine could have been one of these stories, but for the wicked turn of fate.

When we had both eaten the last of our sandwiches, we sat picking fruit from the bowl between us, and drinking herbal tea. The clouds continued to darken the sky but rain had not yet fallen, and over the ocean a small slat of sunlight glistened. I watched it, thinking how it was only a single ray of hope that I held on to in the midst of the storm. I hoped it was enough.

Lost in my thoughts I was somewhat startled by Jane's voice. "So, would you like to hear what Gil had to say when I spoke with him last night after the party?"

My scattered attention flew in from all directions to focus itself eagerly upon Jane. Leaning forward, elbows on table, eyes wide, I said, "Of course I do! I can't believe you went all the way through lunch without telling me."

"Well, when you get old, you love to tell your own stories to anyone who will listen. I figured I'd better tell mine first or you'd have no interest in it once I mentioned Gil." Her eyes were dancing.

"Oh please Jane, you're not old. You may have lived awhile, but old? No. And anyway I'll gladly listen to your stories anytime. Now, tell me what Gil said. Did he remember the locket? Who does it belong to? Does he want me to send it to him?"

"My, my, you're worse than a four year old with all of the questions. Let me just tell you what happened."

"Sorry."

"I called around 11:00 last night, after the last guest wandered out, knowing they would still be up. I raced through the chitchat - he's fine and I guess Bev's okay though he said she hadn't been feeling well, a bug of some kind, and was sleeping. And then I told him that I had seen you tonight and that you were wearing a wonderful locket that you had found in the house."

With her last sentence I laid my head on the table and folded my arms over it. "What's wrong?" Jane asked.

Murmuring into the table I said, "You told him I wore it. It wasn't mine to wear. I found it taped to the back of a painting, it's not like it was sitting on top of the dresser. I'm sure they wouldn't appreciate me snooping around. Especially Bev. And the thing is, I didn't just find it behind the picture, I actually had the gall to remove it and *wear* it for God's sake. Well, at least I didn't smash the painting to the ground, which is what I almost did. Don't ask."

"Pick your head up child, I can barely understand anything you're saying." And when I had, "Gil Carter could care less if you wore that locket. In fact, he feels that you were meant to. If nothing else Sara, you have to have figured out that there is no such thing as coincidence. Gil knows that. Whatever is happening, it's happening perfectly, things are always happening perfectly, even if it doesn't feel like it, even if we don't understand it. Can you see that?" Jane looked more intense than I had ever seen her, and yet she also grew more and more excited with every word, the sheer truth of what she said filling her up and bubbling over.

I couldn't help but catch some of her optimism as it spilled out and bathed me, like those stubborn rays of light over the water that reminded us that sunnier days would return.

"I hope you're right Jane, or my life is just plain strange. At least lately. I like the sound of those words - no such thing as coincidence. It helps to believe in the apparent chaos of life, that maybe it's not chaotic; it just looks that way from this perspective - that maybe, I guess hopefully, there is a bigger picture. I think that's part of what Anna is helping me to see. I just want to get to the place where I can see the bigger picture and have it all make sense."

"Enjoy the journey love, for when you reach the mountaintop you will find, undoubtedly, that there is yet another peak to conquer, a higher perspective still. It is the hike up that is important. I'm not sure we ever reach, on this plane at least, the place where we can solve the mystery completely. I have decided that the answer is in learning to appreciate the mystery, to accept that there is much we may never understand. Figuring it all out is a rigorous battle that I'm not sure can be won."

I nodded agreeably but all the while told myself that it was just Jane's age that made her choose acceptance over answers. I didn't really believe that I would ever be able to accept life without understanding it. That would mean accepting Brian's death without understanding it. If I was to come to believe that everything had purpose and meaning, including Brian's death, then I wanted to know what that purpose was, clearly and without question. As I sat there with Jane, mulling over the dismissal of coincidence and trying to formulate some kind of working hypothesis for my life, I came to one conclusion: I would use all they had to teach me to learn why Brian had died.

Keeping my newfound purpose to myself I returned to the question at hand, "So tell me exactly what Gil said."

"Oh yes, see, when you get old you're easily sidetracked. I blame everything now on getting old. It's quite a convenient excuse. Let's see, where was I? I told Gil you wore the locket and that you had found it in the house, and about the picture and the inscription with their initials. And I told him you were interested in knowing about the little girl."

"And?" She had stopped talking and sat staring at some internal chalkboard, her eyes darting across the notes written there.

"And nothing. He told me nothing, sort of pretended he didn't hear the question. He did mumble, as much to himself than to me, that it was right for you to have worn it, that it was very fitting. But then he just thanked me for telling him that you'd found it, that he would tell Bev and she'd be very relieved. He used that word, 'relieved.' Then he said to tell you hello, that he sends his love, and he hung up. Nothing more. But I know Gil and I have to assume that he has told me all he wants to and that I've done my part in giving him the information."

I stared at her in disbelief. "So that's it? That can't be it. What about the locket? What do I do with it? He didn't tell you who the little girl is? If you had pushed don't you think he would have? Maybe I should call him." I was astounded that she had just let it drop.

Jane watched as I deflated. She could hear the desperate plea in my voice that carried something far weightier than Gil's ambiguous answer.

I had given little thought to the locket in the past eighteen hours, it had been displaced by other, weirder phenomena, but now it was back in the foreground and nothing seemed more important. Mostly because it should have been an easy riddle. With a simple phone call Jane would find out from Gil and Bev who the locket belonged to and the story of the little girl. Just like that, mystery solved. One down, only a dozen or so more to go. Next to mythological labyrinths and curly-headed goddesses this was nothing, or should have been. With the piercing sharpness of a double-edged sword, I saw how nothing could be counted on to be simple, at least nothing that really mattered. Hope seeped from my pores. If I couldn't get the answers to this, how did I expect to figure out why my young and beautiful husband had been taken from me one sunny spring afternoon, at the very beginning of our story? I had hit a dead end.

Jane leaned toward me, mimicking my posture, and said softly, "No, I don't think you should call him, but that is up to you. I didn't push Gil because there was no reason to. He told me all he intended, I'm sure of that. Sometimes when we have followed a road as far as it will take us we have to trust that the next route will reveal itself at the appropriate time. Our job is to stay alert and be prepared for it when it happens. So my advice to you is, continue your work with Anna and whatever else you are doing, keep your eyes and ears open and follow your instincts. Instincts I said, not desperation. Instincts are quieter, clearer, and calmer, like mountain air. Desperation is more like city air. Also, be on the lookout for road signs showing you the right direction - they usually come in the form of people we meet, things we hear, or even just the clicking together of thoughts in our head, like finding the last piece to the border of a puzzle."

"You're in cahoots with Anna aren't you? Between her and you, I can't get a break." I smiled tiredly.

"Cahoots? Sure, why not. It's all a matter of tuning in. But if you're asking if we've conspired against you, then no, that we have not done. At least not yet."

In reply I grumbled, "Sure seems like it," and then to Jane, "Okay, I'll try to take your advice, though I can't promise anything. I'm going to go home now and get some sleep."

As I got up to go she said, "Up a little late last night? Funny, I thought you left early." Her grin told me she knew very well what time I left and whom I had been with.

"Don't start Jane."

"Okay, Okay, go home and get some rest. I'll see you tomorrow?"

I rolled my eyes and shrugged. "If I'm not abducted by aliens I guess, which at this point probably isn't out of the question. Anna said to come back when I was ready. That may not be tomorrow, or the next day, or the next - I don't know. I'll just have to go with my instincts." I winked at her and smiled. Then turned and left.

CHAPTER SIXTEEN

By the time I arrived home the sun was beginning its slow descent to the horizon. Barely able to keep my eyes open I slid out of the car and into the house. Never had a bed felt so good; within seconds I was asleep.

But my plan to remain unconscious was derailed by a persistent knocking on the front door. At first it was easy to ignore but after several minutes the hollow beat began to play on the inside of my skull, refusing to be dismissed. Lifting my head I peered through the window beside my bed. The silvery light of dusk barely bathed the sky. With great effort I pulled myself from under the mountain of covers and trudged, groggy and grumpy, through the house, and threw open the door in mid-knock.

He stood on my front stoop, his wide dimpled grin morphing into something between shock and amusement. Not until I saw his face did I become aware of how I must look - rumpled and swollen with a bad case of bed-head. Not to mention that all I wore was an oversized tee shirt with the word "Maine" written in big black letters, and bulky socks with holes in the toes.

"Oh, my God," was all I could say as I pulled down on the tee shirt self-consciously, though it already reached my knees.

But he didn't miss a beat. Quickly his smile returned, though his eyes crinkled a little too much with pleasure as he slipped passed me into the house. Maybe he thought I might close the door on him and run.

"You said, 'you and Sheila.' Not with pauses as though we were two separate people but all in one breath, like one thing," he said in greeting.

I had no idea what he was talking about, but my head was beginning to swim.

"Mark, what are you talking about? What did I say and when did I say it? You have to go slow here, I'm not following you or much of anything at the moment."

"Last night, you said that nothing was the way you thought, not Jane or Anna, and you said, or 'you and Sheila.' I got sidetracked by Anna, but when I thought back on the night, which has been difficult not to do by the way, I remembered that, and I told myself it was ridiculous to come over here to ask you why you said it that way, in one breath, but it kept circling around me, like a vulture, until I knew I had to ask you or drive myself crazy. So, why did you say that?" He was making me dizzy, talking too fast and pacing in circles. With his last words he came to a stop and crossed his arms over his chest. I vaguely remembered the words he referred to, but they seemed far away, belonging to some other lifetime. So much had happened since then. But standing there watching him, my body swaying, in threat of toppling over, I couldn't help but laugh. His ability to shake me up was at least consistent.

"God Mark, please. Can we at least sit, because if we don't I might fall over. Well wait, you go ahead, I'm going to put on some more clothes. Make yourself at home." I waved him over to the couch and stumbled to the bedroom.

I decided against even looking in the mirror, opting instead to splash cold water on my face and run achy fingers through flat lifeless hair. I couldn't believe he had shown up unannounced. Thinking back I realized I had not had one visitor since moving in, except my parents. No one had been invited and no one had dared to intrude, until now. And of all people, Mark.

After pulling on a sweatshirt, an old pair of Brian's sweatpants and other necessary garments for guests, I went to rejoin him in the family room. But he wasn't there.

"Mark?" Had I scared him away? I looked out the front window and saw that his black 4-Runner was still parked in the driveway.

The door leading to the back garden was ajar and beyond the panes of divided glass I could see him – his back to me, face lifted, looking upward into a tree. The room began to spin.

It wasn't that they looked anything alike, though both were handsome. Brian had been button-downs and loafers, where Mark was flannel shirts and hiking boots. And their personalities were a study in extremes. Brian had been an extrovert - witty and gregarious, someone with whom you always knew what you were getting, with no secrets lurking in hidden corners. Mark, on the other hand, was as confounding as the labyrinth. More quiet and intense, but in his own way, boyish and playful. He had all of these unrevealed rooms, some that he offered easy access to, while others he kept bolted shut. At one moment he was unfathomably honest and real, and in the next, distant and unreachable.

Standing at a safe distance, seeing Mark in my private garden, the differences between them vanished. It was their similarity that caught me off guard and buried itself beneath my skin - their maleness, strong and sure - reminding me of a presence I had once known. At that moment it was easy to forget all that had happened, to become lost in the meridians of time, to believe only what I wanted desperately to believe.

"Brian?" I said it softly, but filled with nervous anticipation. He couldn't have heard me, but still he turned, his eyes catching and holding mine. His smile grew slowly, tentatively, as though waiting for me to catch up, to see clearly.

When finally I did my face flushed. It took several breaths to harness the courage to move fully into the present and deal with this daunting, darkly handsome man in my back yard.

Mark tried to convince me to go out to dinner with him, but I refused on the grounds that I didn't have the energy to shower or change and I was not going out in public looking as I did. So instead he insisted on making dinner, and I watched with amusement as he hopelessly inspected cabinet after cabinet, searching for traces of something to fix.

"You do eat, right?"

"Of course. A lot, as a matter of fact. See, there's cereal and a little bit of lettuce and salad stuff. I just don't cook. I'm good at ordering out."

"Good God woman, you might not survive the winter. This is Maine remember? When the snow starts and the temperature drops to zero you won't want to run out to pick something up every night, and you'll wither away on lettuce. It's just a suggestion, but you might want to think about buying a few cans of something. That is if you have a can opener."

"Well of course I have one, I just don't know how to use it."

He stopped scavenging through the refrigerator, turned, picked up his keys from the bar and headed for the door.

"This is an emergency situation. I will be right back. Don't go anywhere, help is on its way."

"Yes sir." I said, saluting.

Just before closing the door he turned back and said, "Don't think I've forgotten the question I came here with."

He was gone for less than an hour and when he returned it was with an armful of bags from the corner market. I sat on the counter and watched as he unpacked the groceries. He opened and poured us each a beer and then began the ritual of preparing dinner. His moves were easy, completely unselfconscious, as though nothing more mattered than exactly what he was doing at that very moment. Cocking my head I studied him, really wanting to understand what it was that made people like him and Anna and Jane so comfortable with themselves. It was what I longed for most. I had seen it in Brian, had thought that through him I could acquire it, but it hadn't happened.

"Should I be flattered, or concerned that there's something large and green in my teeth?"

He didn't look at me or stop what he was doing, but obviously I was staring more intensely than I was aware.

Blushing I said, "Sorry. I was just wondering…never mind, it's silly."

"Maybe, but tell me anyway. Silly doesn't bother me."

"Well, I didn't really mean to be staring at you, I was more studying you,"

Interrupting he said, "Like a lab rat?"

"If you like that analogy. No, I'm just trying to figure out how some people, like you, can seem so comfortable with themselves, fit so well in their skin. It's a trait I admire."

For the first time he paused and looked at me quizzically, "You don't feel comfortable in your skin?"

"Not really. I never have. Not in the way it seems you, and others like Jane and Sheila and Anna do." I waited to see if he would react to Anna's name, and when he didn't I continued, "Or the way Brian did. I'm always, always self-conscious, at least around other people. I'm aware of my every word and action, worried that I'll say or do the wrong thing, because usually I have no idea what to say or do. So then I'm either over careful and become paralyzed, or I wind up saying or doing something that makes me feel and look foolish – or at least I assume it has. But none of you seem to have that problem. You're more natural. Does that make sense?"

"It makes sense, but Sara do you really believe that any of the people you mentioned, except maybe Anna, never doubt or question themselves in the same way?"

"I don't know, I'm just telling you how it looks."

"Well I can't speak for the rest of them, but I know I do. When I first got here tonight I told you that it was probably a ridiculous thing to do, just showing up on your doorstep, but I did it anyway. You have no idea how many times I went over it in my head - the different scenarios, what you might say, what I hoped you'd say and what I hoped you wouldn't. But in the end I followed my instinct. All I can really do is make decisions based on my soundest judgment, on what is most honest and authentic…and of course on what I feel capable of, which changes from circumstance to circumstance. It certainly doesn't mean I'm always 100 percent sure I'm doing the 'right' thing, but at some point I have to just trust – have faith you could say. Because if I spent *too* much time dwelling on it, and there was a time when I did, I'd never leave the house." He continued chopping mushrooms, onions, peppers and garlic, while waiting for a pot of water to boil.

"I've considered that tactic. But as you can see it leads to empty cupboards and eventual starvation. You're the second person today to talk to me about faith. Actually the third I think."

"Well they say when something is presented to you three times, you ought to listen." He smiled while he chopped and I couldn't help but linger on the square of his jaw, the slope of his nose. For some reason it wasn't as frightening to talk about these things with him, here in my own kitchen, as it was with Anna or Jane. The demanding tug of change didn't pull so drastically, or at least it felt a little less urgent.

"So you're saying all I need is a little faith, and then I'll feel more at ease in life?" It sounded a bit too simplistic, more like an overused cliché than a practical method for mastering my fears.

He stopped what he was doing and looked at me. "No. I didn't mean that. Faith isn't that simplistic. I'm not talking about a dogmatic kind – the belief in a man-in-the-sky faith. It's something deeper than that, a trust you come to by letting yourself experience what life offers, what arises in each moment and by responding to it with awareness. And well, by knowing there is something greater, some whole that you're a part of, some intelligent presence – God, if you like – that is always drawing you into wholeness."

Shaking his head, he smiled and went back to his work. Silence sat between us, some third entity waiting for our engagement. Finally, Mark began speaking again, puncturing the space as gently as possible. "It's funny, you know. I used to believe there was this big blackboard in the sky where God or whoever's in charge kept track of my 'right' and 'wrong,' my 'good' and 'bad.' That everything I said and did was of extreme importance to the running of the universe and that God – that man-in-the-sky kind of God - had something personally vested, and that whenever something 'bad' happened it was because I had racked up too many points in that column. I really don't know where I got that story, but it played in the background of my life for a long time." Looking up, he said, "But not anymore." Again, that smile.

"So what's your story now?"

Mark had sautéed the vegetables and garlic and was mixing them with a red sauce. Pasta boiled over onto the stove; he blew on it and it sank back into the pot.

"Now? Now, for me, it's foremost about awareness. About being awake to life around and within me, to my own behavior, motivations, choices and consciousness. I do like thinking of God in second-person, having a relationship with an Other that I imagine as a force of wisdom. It works for me. It's something I cultivate. But there are so many dimensions to the Divine worth exploring, both personal and transcendent. I'm not fooled into thinking that God is some man with a white beard who's monitoring my day-to-day activities and will reward or punish me based on them. No, what matters to me now is being awake – making choices in alignment with who I want to be and what I intend to create in my life. Life – God – responds accordingly."

"So you believe in a God, or a world, that doesn't really care? You think we're left to figure it and then Life 'responds accordingly'? Where does faith or trust fit into that?"

"Oh no, again, that's not what I meant. I define God as the very force of Life, the ground and source of it all – a force always moving in the direction of evolution, growth and wholeness. I just don't think He, She, It…is judging me at every corner. My choices are mine to make and their natural consequences are my guideposts, what direct me further down my path. Some will lead to aggravation, frustration, fear, anger and loneliness, while others to peace of mind, joy, love and happiness. All are opportunities for me to learn something and grow in some way, to evolve. And what I learn in one situation allows me to choose more positively, more productively and more graciously in the next. I've stopped thinking I have to get it all 'right' right away. It's all practice anyway. Not perfection. And God, I believe, is the force behind and inside it all."

"You make it sound easy."

"Oh, God, far from it," he looked at me and smiled. "I still get as worried and nervous and upset as the next person, but slowly I'm becoming better at recognizing my moods, the way I think and feel, and how it all works together. I've become a little better at letting go too, because in the end all you can do is act with consciousness, take responsibility and inhabit your life. Beyond that…there's only surrender. We can't control everything, or anyone. That's where faith comes in - in believing and knowing that no matter what, in the mind of God there is only Oneness, and we're part of the Beloved whole." He had dumped the cooked pasta into a colander and was shaking out the excess water. It amazed me that he was able to cook and articulate so clearly at the same time. Actually everything about him was becoming a wonder to me.

I didn't respond to his last statement. I didn't know how. I just sat and absorbed the wake of his words, the smells of dinner and the warmth of his company.

After a minute or so he looked up at me, pushed back the hair that hung long over his eyes, and said, "A little too heavy? Sorry. I tend to get carried away on the topic."

"No. It's okay. Just a lot of new information today. Guess I'm on overload." Getting up and going over to the refrigerator I asked, "Want another beer?"

"Sure. Ready for dinner?"

We sat on the floor leaning against the couch, plates and bottles of beer on the coffee table in front of us. I had started a fire and we sat quietly watching the flames leap and play, their shadows dancing across golden wood. The food was good, hot and heavy, and pulled from my bones memories of home.

Night snuck in through the windows, darkening the house, save for the fire. It brought with it a stronger silence, one that begged to be broken for fear of exposure. Obeying its command I got up and turned on the radio, the same one Brian had discovered on our first night in the house. Immediately the soft sound of jazz filled the air.

When I returned to my seat Mark turned to face me, placing one arm along the couch, his fingers only inches from my shoulder.

"Well, we've avoided it long enough. It's time you told me about the 'you and Sheila' comment. It seems kind of silly now, but I would like to know. Did you think Sheila and I were a couple?"

Grateful that I could hide in the low light of the room, I answered, "Yes."

"Why? What gave you that impression?"

Biting my lower lip I released my eyes from the hold his had on them. After a few moments I said, "A couple of things, but mostly the way you looked at her during her reading. It's a look I know – it was love. Of that I'm certain."

His head cocked to the side as it often did, and his eyes waited for mine to connect again, and then he responded, "You're right. It was – is – love. I love Sheila very much. I've known her most of my life, and yes, we dated once, long ago. But we always knew we were better friends than anything else. But even beyond that – I am in love with the spirit of the words she was reading. And that's probably the love you were seeing. Does that make any sense?"

I nodded, speechless, caught by a wave of guilt for how unfairly I had judged him. And by a wave of envy. How nice it must be to love something as simple as words.

"Sara," his soft voice lured me back, "did that have something to do with why you were so annoyed with me at Jane's?"

Sheepishly I nodded and said, "You were whispering to me about taking a walk in the garden and the whole time I assumed you were there with Sheila." I couldn't believe the words were coming from my mouth.

"Why didn't you say something?" His voice was soft, caressing in the near dark.

I shrugged, "I'm not good at that. Plus it threw me off guard," and then dropping to a whisper, "and it made me uncomfortable."

Turning away he didn't say anything for over a minute, and when he turned back his eyes were grave. "I can see why it would. I'm sorry. It was insensitive of me. I didn't mean to make you uncomfortable, but that's not the point. From the first time we met I hoped for the chance to know you better. I was responding from that place without giving thought to where you are right now. I told you last night that I would very much like to be your friend." With slow and gentle fingers he lifted my chin so our eyes met, "You're completely free here, you know. There are no expectations, no demands, no conditions. Do you understand?"

A tear fell unchecked and ran down my face, landing on his thumb. All I could do was choke out, "Thank you."

Smiling, sun worn lines burrowing deeper around his eyes and mouth, he wiped his thumb on his jeans and then used a napkin to wipe the tears from my face. When he finished I climbed onto the couch and nestled in deep.

We sat quietly for a while, until I looked down at him and asked, "Do you want to go for a walk?"

"I'd love to."

White light filtered through low-lying clouds, casting a gray hue over the beach. Round and plump, the moon drifted in and out of sight. I led Mark down the hill to the seashore where we walked along the water's edge listening to the call of night birds and the gentle lapping of water against rocks. A chilling breeze brushed against my face and cut through the heavy coat that was wrapped tightly around me.

"Maybe this wasn't such a good idea, it's freezing."

"Freezing? It's gorgeous out here. Look at the shades of deep blue and black on the water. I love nights like this, crisp, pure. It cleanses the soul, heals the body." With no coat, dressed in a flannel plaid shirt buttoned only to mid-chest and untucked from his jeans, he looked free, happier than usual, as though the moon pulled open every dark door inside of him and swept it clean. This land gave him life.

Laughing I said, "I'm from Florida remember, nights like this are rare and record-breaking."

"Oh, well I did forget. But come on, let go of the iron grip you have on that coat. Move around a little, let your blood flow. As tense as you are, all constricted and scrunched up like that, you're making it worse."

We had stopped walking. Mark was looking out at the water and I was huddled inside my coat, hugging it close, peering down at the rocks around my feet. Suddenly he was behind me, standing close but unmoving. I anticipated his touch. My heart raced from both panic and exhilaration. What would I do? I was afraid of the answer.

But the feel of his hands didn't come. He was breathing deeply, the sound of the air moving in and out of him close to my ear.

"It's a matter of attention," his voice was deep, yet hushed, a whisper of wind against my cheek, "don't close yourself to what's around you, open to it, allow your energy to meet it, not shrink from it." He reached around and with a feather light touch raised my chin so that I was looking out at the water and not at the ground.

"Breathe in the air that is right here. Not the air of your memories or your fear. Not the air of things to come, but the air of this moment. Let it sweep clean the things that weigh so heavily on your mind. Let it fill you up with its life-giving energy. Breathe in deeply - first to your abdomen, so that it pushes your belly out, then up into your rib cage, spreading it wide, and finally into your chest, expanding fully."

I followed the rhythm of his voice, of his breath, breathing deeply like I had never done before. Air flowed all the way to my toes, my body tingling with new life as oxygen spilled into my bloodstream, infusing organs and muscles. With each cycle, each inhalation and exhalation, another layer of tension was shed. Slowly my body relaxed.

Mark's voice drifted in through the sounds of sea and moving air. "May I touch your shoulders?"

Nodding was all I could do, afraid the reality of my own voice would pull me from this place. With strong yet gentle hands he squared my shoulders and pulled them lightly back. "Open your chest. Let your shoulders fall away from your ears and your ears move away from your shoulders. There. That lets more air in, gives us more room to move. Our bodies are starving for attention. They work hard to hold us to the earth. It's good to take time to appreciate them. They're remarkable works of art and can work miracles if kept vital. But they need oxygen to live. They need the breath to connect to the powers of healing and wisdom that reside within us."

His words entered me, as the air did, like water flowing lightly over pebbles along the shore. Penetrating through skin, bone, organ and muscle, washing away the scattered debris of my shipwrecked soul. Tears poured from my eyes, sprung from a well deeper than the wounds of grief, fear, death and birth. I was left both empty and full.

This was the release my body had cried for in the labyrinth.

The realization sent me spiraling back, dropping me hard onto the beach.

I wiped my eyes on the sleeve of my jacket and smiled. "That's it."

"What?" His volume matched mine, soft and whirring.

I turned to face him, backing up slightly to allow space for the air between us.

"I walked into the labyrinth at Jane's today, and it was horrible. My body ached - more than ached. All of a sudden I was so aware of how much pain it has been in. But it was worse than just tension. I could literally see how much damage was being done and I could hear it pleading with me for release. But I didn't know what it meant. I got scared and ran out, and I've felt like hell all day. But this, this is what it was asking for, what it needed to help let go of the fifty pound weight I carry around inside and cling to with all my might."

"Amazing isn't it, what a little breathing can do?"

"I always thought I knew what it was to breathe deeply, to relax, to let go, but I didn't. I had no idea. Thank you." My heart was bursting with gratitude. His gifts were subtle and unexpected, a gentle rain on a hot summer day.

"You're welcome."

"How did you know exactly what I needed? Did Anna tell you what happened?" I knew the chance I took, the possibility of dissolving the beauty of the moment.

"No, I haven't seen her lately." His gaze turned inward and I feared it wouldn't return.

"Well, it doesn't really matter how you knew, I'm just grateful you did. And you know what else?" I asked, wanting to lighten the mood.

"What?" He was smiling again.

"I'm actually warm, really warm," I said, shrugging out of my coat. Mark held out his hand as an offering to carry it.

"Thanks," I handed it to him, "My God you're right, it feels wonderful out here. Would you like to walk a little more?"

Before Mark left we stood at the open door of my home silently exchanging the energy of words we chose to leave unspoken. His fixed, direct gaze still unnerved me but little by little I found myself meeting it, absorbing its kindness and depth. Being left wanting to know what lay behind it.

As I settled into bed and stared up at the ceiling I was transported back to the beach, to the feeling of tension flowing like a wave out of my body, the sound of the wind and the sea and Mark's voice washing against me. Was it okay to feel so alive? The question went out into the dark, but it belonged to Brian.

CHAPTER SEVENTEEN

There would be a time, much later, when I would wonder if Brian did indeed answer my plea, but when the phone woke me the next morning my only thought was of how deeply and peacefully I had slept. The shrill intrusion of its ringing sent me tumbling from a place as dark and familiar as the womb. Blindly reaching for the receiver I slurred into it, "Hello?"

"Did I wake you?"

I was lying on my stomach talking into the pillow that half-covered my head. Upon hearing the voice on the other end of the line a ripple of pleasure swept across my nerve endings. I turned over and feigned wakefulness.

"No," I lied, and then, "well yes, but it's okay. You sound awfully cheery. I take it you're a morning person."

Laughter, followed by, "I am, yes, but it's hardly the wee hours. Do you have any idea what time it is?"

"Nooo…" With one eye open I stretched on my side to see the clock. "Oh my God, it's 11:30! How did I sleep so long? It's your fault for keeping me up so late." A nervous twitch in my stomach came close to shot-putting me out of bed, but I refused to go. Whatever it was I feared I should be doing would have to wait. All I wanted was to lie in the warmth of my bed and talk to Mark.

"I distinctly remember you making the call to keep walking, and it was only 12:30 when I left. Do you typically sleep 11 hours?" I could just see the crevices around his eyes widening as he smiled.

"No, but I had a very long, exhausting day yesterday. I would think a little compassion wouldn't be too much to ask. Or did you call with the express intention of being a smart-ass?" I yawned, stretched long and released, feeling better than I had in a long time.

"My, my, aren't we feisty this morning. That's good." His voice softened, "But no, I didn't call to give you a hard time. Actually I called to see how you are and to remind you to breathe, in case you forgot. But from the sounds of it you're doing pretty well. Got a good night's sleep at least."

"Mmmm... the best I can remember in months. Thanks to you. All that tension-releasing wiped me out I guess, let me sleep like a baby. I needed it. I am in your debt." Mark was, at the moment, the safest person I knew, and I was finding it easier to let my guard down with him.

"I appreciate the gratitude but I didn't do anything except remind you of something you already knew. But if you really want to repay me this imaginary debt, let me take you to lunch."

"No..."

"No? Okay. But if you change your mind the offer is good for...well, until I'm too old to feed or drive myself."

"I didn't finish. No, to you taking me out, but yes to going out. I take you though."

"Well that's even better. When should I expect you?"

"Expect me?"

"I might as well milk this for what it's worth. When will you be here to pick me up?"

"Oh you're something. But yes, I'll pick you up. You have to give me directions though. And I need about thirty minutes to get ready."

And so for this one day I allowed myself to forget Anna, the locket and the labyrinth, knowing they would soon knock again and demand my attention.

Mark lived in a small, cozy five-room house on a large plat of land that sat at the foot of a hill surrounded by woods, on the doorstep of a pristine lake. There were no visible neighbors, only wide, deep expanses of trees on either side. A thick line of pines along the front of the property hid the driveway, making an old tarnished mailbox with

'Wilde' printed in black letters the only clue that I was at the right place.

The house itself was a simple cape cod with a front porch and two dormer windows that were only for show, since there was no second story. The clapboard siding was painted cream with black shutters and white trim – the quintessential New England cottage. I loved it immediately. Once beyond the pines the yard was enormous, and obviously well maintained, even in the drying brown of early winter. I pulled to a stop at the farthest point of the drive, but instead of immediately getting out, I crossed my arms over the top of the steering wheel and stared through the windshield. From where I sat I had a full view of Mark's back yard.

The lake, long and curvaceous, stretched the length of the house and then ran from sight, teasing the eye with promises of places deep and wild. It reached up and held captive the sky, and anything else that danced in the eaves of the infinite. Just beyond, hills and mountains rose in varying degree, like the scales of a great sleeping dragon.

Mark, it appeared, had found his own piece of paradise. It occurred to me how homes truly were reflections of their inhabitants – Jane's stately, yet unassuming estate and Mark's simple, quiet dwelling, so obviously grounded in the earth. I wondered what my little house said about me.

As I reached for the door handle, movement on the banks of the lake caught my eye and I resumed my watchful pose as two figures came into focus. One man, one animal - Mark and a very large furry beast walked along the murky perimeter of the water. Not wanting to disturb the scene I remained in the car, enjoying the opportunity to watch the man unnoticed. He was dressed in his usual attire: hiking boots, jeans, and a black tee shirt, with a long-sleeved flannel shirt over it, unbuttoned and untucked. He was laughing as the dog ran in and out of the water, fetching and retrieving a stick that he threw. There was something primally beautiful about the carefree nature of them both. There was no loneliness here, not like in my home. It was just the two of them, but somehow it seemed enough, and at the same time, felt open to anyone who happened by.

I got out of the car and headed in their direction. Hearing my footsteps Mark looked over, stopped in his tracks and smiled. My heart fluttered at the genuine pleasure that crossed his face. He waved and threw the stick towards me.

The beast lunged forward. But just before plundering over me it made a sharp turn and snatched up the stick. I was standing perfectly still, braced for the tackle that didn't come.

"Hi!" He was only a few yards away and moving closer, his steps wide over the uneven terrain.

"Hi. Who's the beast?" I asked, pointing to the hairy monster now standing at Mark's side, panting and ready for more action.

"Beast?" He looked down at his companion, "Don't listen to her. She has no idea how gentle and demure you are."

"Demure? He almost pummeled me." We were like two kids flirting on the playground. Our faces would probably hurt later from smiles that were too wide and lasted too long.

Mark threw the stick, this time as far as he could in the opposite direction. The dog shuffled off after it.

"*She* wouldn't pummel you. I promise. I have her trained only to attack on my command, and so far I don't see that being necessary."

"Well, thanks." There was a moment of silence as we shifted gears.

"This place is beautiful. So peaceful." I turned my gaze to the distant mountains. His eyes followed.

"Thanks. I love it. My own private retreat. It's a great place to write."

"How long have you lived here?"

"Since my divorce."

He kept his eyes on that distant shore, but he could sense my shock. "You're surprised."

"I...I didn't know you'd been married. Well, as I told you, I thought you and Sheila might be, but other than that...Yes, I'm surprised. How long ago?"

"Oh, it's been ten years since the divorce. We were only married a little over a year. Too young, too different, too... unformed I think."

I looked at him quizzically then asked, "Does she live on Mt. Desert?"

"No, in New York. That was another problem. We got married right out of college, young and impulsive, but soon realized – well, she did anyway - how completely incompatible we were. She wanted to go to Manhattan and live; didn't want what she felt was a small life."

"And you wouldn't go." I couldn't imagine him in New York, or any big city. It would be like caging a wild animal.

"It wasn't that I wasn't willing to try. I could write anywhere. And I would have followed *her* anywhere at the time. But she didn't want me to try. She knew I wouldn't be happy, and she knew by then that she wouldn't be happy with me. So she left and I stayed. Me, my dog and my broken heart. Sounds like a bad country song, huh?"

"Do you ever regret it?"

"No, not anymore. I'm actually grateful for it, but it took a long time. I had a lot to learn – about myself and about love." He paused then continued, "Not that I think I've even scratched the surface. I just know I needed to get my heart broken. It was the only way I was going to stop long enough to pick up the pieces and examine them. Not a very easy or pretty thing to do."

After sighing deeply he said, "So, after she left I moved out here. It was a wreck and I bought it dirt cheap - spent the next few years fixing it up, working construction, reading, studying, writing, traveling - going on that infamous search for self."

"Is that what you wrote your book about? What you learned on your search?"

"Yeah. I started looking back and…" His eyes left the path of the past and rested again on me. "Hey, before I lay my life out on the table why don't I show you the house, if you're interested, and then we can get going."

"Oh, we're not going anywhere."

"We're not?"

"No, we're not. Hold on a sec. I'll be right back."

I walked over to the car, unlocked the trunk and pulled out a picnic basket.

"My plan was to take you to my favorite spot in the park, but now I see that you've provided us with the perfect location. I think we'll stay right here. If that's okay with you."

147

"Sounds great. I can't wait to see what you made." He grinned, mockingly.

"If you want to eat I suggest you don't tease."

Walking inside Mark's house was like curling up in an old down blanket. It was filled with the deep rich colors of the earth – brown, rust, dark blues and greens. Fading embers flickered in a brick fireplace while a stereo shuffled through modern CDs of old songs by Jackson Browne and Dan Fogelberg. Lighting was soft, provided mostly by diffused sunrays that fell through glass doors and windows onto dark oak floors. The lingering scent of incense and pine wafted easily about.

"My God Mark, it's…I don't know. I'm speechless."

"Well I'll admit I picked up some. I'm neat but not *this* neat." He was right, everything was clean and in its place.

"It looks great, but honestly I barely noticed. It's just so warm. It feels like a home. And it's not just the furniture or the colors; it's something more. I guess you might say it has great energy."

"Thanks. I think so. No matter what, I'm always happy to come home. There's not much to it – just this room and the kitchen, which you can see are connected." Gesturing to his left he said, "Down that hall is the bedroom and bathroom, and off from the bedroom is my office. And that's it. You're welcome to look around."

But I had already started wandering, touching, inhaling vibrations of things good and strong.

He asked, "Can I get you something to drink?"

I barely heard him. I had moved down the hall into his bedroom, which contained the same essence of masculinity and grace found in the family room. Something in me stirred and I pushed it away, unwilling to reveal it to my own eyes.

Everything in the bedroom and office was wood, earthy and real. His desk was more like a pine farm table, distressed with character. Papers and books piled high and a computer whirring in the center of the chaos.

"Like my filing system?" Mark leaned against the doorframe.

"Very nice. I'm sure there's order somewhere in the madness." My smile met his.

"I'm sure you're right, I just haven't discovered it. Would you like something to drink? Or did you want to grab a blanket and go outside with our picnic?"

"I've got everything we need, including a blanket."

"Then we're set. Whenever you're ready." His expression asked a question, wondered why I remained planted in his private domain.

The truth was that I was drawn to the place that contained the most of him, or maybe it was the need to be in the center of someone else, figuratively if not literally.

But how could I tell him that without it sounding like an invitation? Standing in his office, running my fingers over soft, pliant pine, and tracing the swirling patterns of grain, longings washed over me like crashing waves. The yearning to not only touch another, but to absorb their smell, taste, texture - to sink into their ocean and enfold myself in the blanket of their energy.

And not just the longing for *any* other, but for this man.

I couldn't look at him until the tides had passed, or at least receded, leaving in their wake the battle between past and present, heart and body. Brian's memory and his absence.

When finally the seas calmed I lifted my eyes to find Mark staring at me and I could sense his waters rushing forth to meet mine.

Drowning in a language once known but forgotten I could find no words safe enough to speak. But thankfully Mark was growing adept at handling my awkward moments. With his usual gentle manner he backed away from the connection. His smile softened and with a tilt of his chin he directed me through the door.

"Let's go see what's in that basket."

CHAPTER EIGHTEEN

"I think I would like to be a bird in my next life. I've always thought they must be the most blessed of creatures because they can travel closest to Heaven."

"Hmmm...could be true, who's to know. I'd like to think that maybe we can all travel to Heaven any time we like - that if we look close enough we'll be shown the way. And if not, maybe we'll find a way to grow wings and fly."

"Didn't we do that? I think it's called the airplane."

"Oh, yeah. But I'd rather find a way to power myself there."

We were lying on our backs staring up at the sky, which had been kind enough to stay blue. Warmth from the sun lightly caressed our faces, blending with the cold November breeze. I was splayed out on the blanket like a child about to form a snow angel. Looking up I imagined myself suspended far above the earth, carried by whatever invisible force had stitched the sky so seamlessly.

"Where do you think Heaven is?"

Mark was stretched out next to me, his hands tucked under his head. He considered my question before answering.

"Closer than we think."

I thought about making some clever remark. But I decided I liked his answer. It made things seem simple and hopeful. I thought of Brian. Closer than I think.

The lunch I had packed was gone, devoured with help from Mark's dog. Both of them seemed duly impressed by the spread - stuffed pitas, Greek salad, and a selection of cheese and crackers – until, of course, I confessed to buying it rather than making it. After eating we had moved with little effort into our supine positions.

Conversation came easy, as it had last night. Mark, like me, had little use for small talk, but he was good at finding something meaningful to say about almost anything – like the sky, or breathing, or Heaven. I liked listening to him talk, the way words sounded on his tongue, the way they reached across the air between us and landed on my skin. I liked who I was in his eyes - the stranger unraveling in my bones, who little by little was becoming more familiar to me than the face in the mirror. The lure of such pleasure and peace was magnetic - if only the incessant humming of guilt and fear that ran deep underground would cease.

"Sara? Are you asleep?"

Eyes closed I turned my head in the direction of his voice. "Mmm…hmmm," and then slowly smiling, opened my eyes. He was on his side, lifted onto one elbow, the heat of his body close enough to fall into.

"Do you want to go for a hike? There's a trail that starts at the base of the hill, not too long or tough, just nice for a view of the lake."

"Sure. If I can coax my body up off this blanket."

"We don't have to go. We can stay right here if you like. Believe me, I spend quite a bit of time just hanging out here. Sometimes I bring my laptop out and write. The quiet is powerful. Even more so when it's cold."

Stretching my arms above my head I said, "You're right. But I'd like to walk, see more of your world." Mark moved quickly to his feet while I struggled to sit. He stood over me and held out his hand, and as I went to take it I was once again reminded of the image from my dream.

The trail was well marked and cut through the center of the hill, winding its way gently to the top. Leaves, dead and brittle, crackled underfoot. It might have seemed depressing, with the landscape drained of color and the trees spindly in their winter wear, except for the continuous view of sky and water delivered by virtue of this very barrenness.

About an hour into the hike a side path veered toward the edge of the mountain and led to a precipice overlooking Mark's property. We laid out the blanket that had been stuffed into a backpack, opened a couple of bottled waters and sank down onto the earth. The lake and house were just below and from this vantage point it was apparent how truly private Mark's little sanctum was. Miles spread between the small dots that signified life.

"Do you ever get lonely here?" In the midst of so much space isolation was never far behind, at least for me.

"No, not too often. Not anymore. There was a time I thought I might die of loneliness, literally. But now I savor the aloneness. And the thing is, I don't feel like I'm ever really alone. Plus, I make a point to connect with other people. To get out and have friends over. And," he smiled, "if all else fails I have Lady to keep me company."

"How did you move from thinking you'd die, to not?"

"Oh, God, I tried a bunch of different things, from burying myself in work, to staying out all the time, to dating, and even drinking for awhile. I also traveled quite a bit. But none of it worked. Then I went the other direction and pulled in, never went anywhere, just decided to throw myself head first into solitude, see where it spit me out."

"And?"

"And at first I was miserable. I was mad at everything and everyone, mostly my ex-wife and myself. Then I got scared that I would never, could never, be happy. I cried a lot out of frustration and self-pity. Got 'writer's block,' or so I thought. Turns out I was just afraid of writing the truth, of seeing myself that clearly."

"How'd you get to the other side?" It sounded so familiar, all I wanted was to know how he had survived.

"Writing. I wrote myself to the other side. One morning I woke at 3 am, overcome with this desperate need to write, and when I sat down with pad and pen what came was page after page of pent up truth. Confusion, pain, self-loathing, anger and a whole lot of fear. I wrote for six hours nonstop. When I looked up the sun was up and I was halfway through my second notebook. But I wasn't done; I just kept going. And as the pen moved across the paper I moved deeper and deeper into my own soul. I was spiraling into a whirlpool of every memory, thought, feeling and sensation I'd ever had. I could see the images of my past, present and future in the air around me, circling my head, speaking to me across the currents of time. They were whispering the answers to my questions. Before long I realized that there was a force behind them, something guiding their words, guiding my words, placing them upon the page. I rushed on chasing it, not wanting it to slip away. I wrote and wrote, and then a word flew onto the page - 'Surrender,' and all at once I did, and instantly felt the most amazing peace I had ever known. My hand kept moving, but I had no control over it, or more accurately, I gave up trying to control it. Into the night I wrote and then finally around midnight the pen fell from my hand and I dropped onto my back, in the middle of the floor, exhausted and elated. I didn't move, but just lay there absorbing what had happened. My head was empty and so was my heart. For the first time in my life I felt free. It was that day I knew without a doubt that there is a God."

As he spoke he looked out across his land, his home. On his face was not the memory of a moment come and gone, but a peacefulness encoded into his knowing on that long ago day.

"So you had a vision? Some sort of divine intervention? What exactly did you find out?"

When he didn't answer, but remained absorbed in whatever inner tape was playing, I said, "I'm sorry, it's really none of my business."

Still he remained quiet. I rested my gaze upon his home below, imagining the magic that lived there. Moments turned into several minutes, and then Mark began speaking as if no time at all had passed.

"I wouldn't say I had a vision, or that anything 'extraordinary' happened to me. At least I don't think it would have looked like anything other than a psychotic break to anyone else. But whatever it was it was exactly what I needed. I've come to believe that we each have brushes with the Divine, and they're tailored perfectly for us. I met God on the page. We all encounter the dark, in one way or another, and often it is there that we meet the light."

"What do you mean, you 'met God on the page?'"

He looked at me and smiled. Something very old and beautiful fell in shadow over his strong features.

"Hmmm…good question. In that 24 hours I saw my life in total - every wound, every joy, and every prayer I had thought unanswered. I saw how all of it had worked in perfect accord to shape who I am, and how every circumstance, event and person in my life had been necessary in bringing me to that moment. And when I could see that, there was no longer the heavy weight of regret, or the hollow echo of guilt, or the fierce grip of self-pity and doubt. There was nothing except gratitude and peace and an understanding that something greater than myself had been at work, and that the picture was much larger than I could ever hope to see. At the very bottom of the well I came to discover that the most astounding truths were also the simplest. No longer was it a cliché, but a profound *knowing* inside of me that I am not now, nor have I ever been - nor will I ever be - alone. For so long I had sought that inner voice you hear about, and that night I heard it. It was the voice of God, and it carried the same tone and quality as my own. It ran like a stream that had been lost under the rubble of misconceptions and fear, but a stream that ran nonetheless. I just had to dig it out."

"And you were able to do it all in one night?" My battle was beginning to feel endless.

"Oh God no. Is that how it sounds? You have to understand that everything I had been doing for the *years* since Robin left, and even unknowingly for some time before, had been in preparation for this. Everything else I mentioned - the traveling, drinking, dating, the searching and crying - had been fodder for what was to come. I had been looking for God a long time. I'd been to India and Egypt, backpacked my way through a few countries and across several states, tried every church and temple around. Not to mention the mountain of books I'd read and the writing I'd done. For years my life had been dedicated to that search. So you see, it's not like I had this sudden epiphany and that was it. It was more like a big whack on the head finally waking me up."

"Waking you up to what?"

"To the understanding that what I'd been searching for had been with me all along, in fact it was me, or at least lived inside of me. I couldn't find God 'out there,' I had to find Him in here," he tapped his chest, "and She showed Herself through the act of writing."

"Maybe I should take up writing." I murmured.

"You could, but you might find that it's not the same for you. See, the point is that everyone's path is their own, you have to find the one that is designed perfectly for you. You just have to let go so you can find it, and then be willing to follow it. It's being shown to you every day, just look and listen carefully, you'll see it, feel it."

I didn't respond. He knew as well as I that I was in the midst of following, or more accurately fighting, a path that was giving more than subtle hints. Every day I was finding myself in conversations like this one, and though the source was different, the message was in many ways the same.

"The path for each of us is different, but in the end we all are brought to our knees. Some of us crash and burn and fall from the ashes, while others fall willingly, and there are those who are brought down more slowly, more gently - one knee at a time. It may take years, or even lifetimes, or merely a moment, but sooner or later each and every one of us will come to kneel before the altar of Love that gave us life and continues to feed us."

The tears began with this last statement. The image of the whole world on its knees in the name of Love broke the dam. As I wiped my eyes and nose on the sleeve of my coat I laughed and said, "Where in Heaven's name did you come from? I want to congratulate and thank whoever's responsible."

He surprised me with his answer and the sudden pained look he tried unsuccessfully to hide. "Now that is the million dollar question."

Stopping mid-wipe I looked at him, studying his expression for signs of philosophical flippancy, but there were none. He was serious. Puzzled I said, "I don't understand."

With large weathered hands he rubbed his face. "Oh, I'm sorry Sara. You know it seems like all we do is talk about me, or listen to my soap-box speeches. I think it's time we talked about you." Weariness nestled into the lines around his eyes.

"Oh no you don't Mark Wilde. Not this time." I shook my finger at him, then pulled my knees in and hugged them. Continuing, I said, "You say we talk about you, but you know good and well that everything we talk about is actually *for* me. You have been kinder to me than I deserve and better for me than you could possibly know.

You and Jane and Anna have come into my life to help me…heal, I guess. You have given me so much in such a short while and, as difficult as it is at times, I am beginning to let myself open up to your friendship. And now, like the other night at Jane's, something comes up that obviously bothers you and you won't let me be there for you. That's not fair Mark."

For the first time I reached over and touched him, placed my hand flat against his unshaven cheek. His skin was warm and rough, the feel of his flesh activating every sense, grounding what had, until then, been an attraction of energies.

"Mark, do you not feel you can trust me?"

The frown deepened between his brows. "No, it's not that, it's just…" He put his hand against mine and held it to his face, closing his eyes. And then he let go. My hand moved along the side of his face and over his hair. Electricity flowed up and down my body, concentrating itself in the center of longing. Then not knowing what more to say or do, I sat quietly and hugged my knees again. I stared out over the cliff and watched as afternoon gave way to evening, the veil of night close on the heels of the sinking sun.

Suddenly, as if having debated the issue and made a decision, Mark turned his entire body to face me.

"Sara, I've told you quite a bit about myself and maybe it has sounded like once I had this great experience everything fell into place. But that's not true. For a long time afterwards I tried to recreate the experience, but I couldn't, not exactly. I got frustrated and had to slow down, remember what I had learned, have faith that it was real and move forward – return to a daily practice, one in which steady cultivation is key. What I also didn't tell you was what came before all of it, exactly what your question referred to – where I come from. The truth is, I don't know, not everything anyway. And the hole created by not knowing is what I, for so long, was trying to fill, and sometimes that hole still haunts me."

"What do you mean when you say you don't know where you come from?" I turned to face him, but kept my distance, giving him space to connect his thoughts and words.

He sighed deeply. "Okay, when I was twelve years old I found this picture. It was old and faded, in black and white. It was of a young girl, no more than fourteen. She was beautiful, haunting. Something about her reached out to me. Yes, I was twelve and going through puberty, but it wasn't hormonal. It was something more delicate, more familiar. Anyway my mom found the picture in my room one day and asked me where I got it. She was nervous. Not mad, but very upset, though she tried to hide it. I told her I'd found it in a box in the basement, which was true. I asked her who it was and she stumbled over her answer, telling me it was an old picture of her cousin. I accepted what she told me, but never really believed her. I knew there was something more. She took the picture away from me." His face twisted in painful memory and I could see the little boy's confusion etched there.

I listened intently, using my eyes to urge him to keep going.

"A year later my parents sat me down and told me I wasn't theirs by birth. I was shocked and angry. Adolescents are pissed off by nature and this just validated mine. But in time I allowed them to tell me the story. I wasn't adopted exactly, more like 'relinquished' into their care. They didn't know who my father was, and knew next to nothing about my mother, only that she was the woman in the photograph I had found." I could feel in the air between us the red-hot scar of his wounding.

After several long deep breaths he continued. "They told me that they were in the process of applying for adoption when they met this woman. They shared with her their desire to have a child and the struggle they were encountering inside the system. A few days later they ran into her again and she said she might be able to help them. Three months later they had a bouncing baby boy." He half-smiled and shook his head, answering to my confused expression. "I know, I know, it's crazy. Or so it sure sounded to me at thirteen. I asked them all the things you're wondering. Who was the woman? Where did she get me? Was it legal? Well, I never got an answer to the last one, but I'm pretty sure I know what it is, and I'm still looking for a more complete answer to the second. But they did tell me who the woman was."

He wanted me to ask. "And?"

"Bev Carter."

"Bev Carter? My God, you're kidding. Did you know Bev at the time?"

"No. I had heard her name from my parents, and around town. The Carters were pretty well known, well respected and a little feared I think."

"Feared? Why?"

"They'd been around forever, and always been way ahead of their time. Well you know them, there's just something about them that keeps people guessing. And people are afraid of what they don't 'get.'"

"I can attest to that. I'm terrified of a lot of things, especially lately. And I don't 'get' any of them. So what did you do once you found out about Bev?"

"I didn't do anything but mope around and stew in my confusion and anger, I was thirteen remember. But it didn't last long. Two weeks later I get this note in the mail. It was written in very formal script and signed, 'Your Friend, Beverly Carter.' In it she invites me to her house for tea on the following Saturday, to get 'better acquainted.' She invited my mom and dad as well, but I told them I wanted to go alone. They were so heartbroken by the whole thing they would have agreed to anything I asked."

"You were pretty brave for thirteen."

"Not brave. Just young. I stubbornly, dramatically decided I was an orphan and would have to make it on my own. My parents are wonderful people and I love them dearly, and no matter how close we are now, I know I hurt them back then. But I was so hurt and angry and confused – stuck on the idea that I had been given away by one mother and lied to by another. My thirteen year old heart was shattered."

Tears welled in his eyes as he recalled the child that still lived in his bones. I reached out and touched his hand. He wrapped his fingers around mine and held on.

"Thanks." He looked at me and smiled, a quiet, wistful smile made sadder by the deepening shadows of night. But instead of revealing any more about Bev or his visit with her he said, "Are you hungry? Because I am, or will be soon. Would you mind if we head back to the house? I'd love for you to stay awhile. We could light a fire, have some dinner? That is if you don't mind eating two meals in one day with me."

Something soft and fragile blanketed my heart. "That sounds great. But you're in charge of dinner, you ate everything I brought."

Neither of us moved. Our fingers were still intertwined and our eyes locked. Then finally, he squeezed my hand and pulled us both up.

By the time we got back to the house the last remnants of day had dropped under the horizon and night had come, cold and clear. Stars had helped guide us down the trail. We had walked close, telling each other it was safer that way in the dark, but knowing it had more to do with the energy flowing and swelling between us. As we hiked Mark taught me about the birds, whose lonely calls we intercepted, and the trees, who danced naked in the moonlight. He knew every species and spoke with a knowledge born from the wisdom of the earth, not merely recited in the pages of texts.

The warmth of the house melted the chill I hadn't been able to breathe away. Even Mark was thankful to get inside. He immediately set about starting a fire while I fumbled around the kitchen scouting out the wares for making tea.

While waiting for water to boil I watched him, his back to me as he knelt before the fireplace. Layer after layer he opened his soul for me to see. And my own soul seemed to respond. How could that be? How could I give in to the draw of this man whom I barely knew? Guilt and shame hovered near, whispering accusations in my ear. Brian's wounded voice was the loudest, demanding to know how I could so easily forget and betray him? Only a week ago I had dreamt of death's sweet embrace. And now I stood in another man's kitchen, feeling myself reaching out from the fertile soil of inner landscapes I was only coming to know. It took all I had to fight the sweeping tides of desire that threatened to swallow me whole.

The urge to bolt out of the door rushed over me, and I almost followed. But then Mark turned, and I knew I would be going nowhere, not yet at least. I didn't want to. I needed this, the company of another, of a man. I needed his strength, his courage. I wanted to know his story, to tell him mine.

"Are you okay?" He was walking towards me, concern contorting his features.

"I…I'm fine, just tired I guess."

"Now who's avoiding?"

I closed my eyes to block out the intense blue of his, but it only tuned in the smell of wind and wood he wore, and Jackson Browne's luring voice urging me to "…abandon your sad history and meet me in the fire…" I was dizzy. There was a harsh ringing somewhere in the distance. Mark's hands gripped my arms. "Sara, what is it?" He turned off the teakettle and the ringing stopped.

The universe returned to center. Embarrassed, I opened my eyes and smiled sheepishly. "I'm sorry Mark. It's just that this, all of this, is a little overwhelming. Can we sit?"

"Of course." Quickly he poured our tea and led me to the couch that sat facing the fire. It was deep and soft and safe and I sunk into it willingly. Mark sat in the opposite corner and waited patiently.

I couldn't look at him. Instead I stared into the fire, entering the blue center of the flame. The soft rhythm of Mark's breathing fell in line with mine and for a while we just sat together.

I had to begin somewhere. "Brian died the day we were supposed to leave to move up here. We had rented the Carter's house for a few months, hoping we could buy it. Three months after he died I decided to come without him. Well, that's not true - I came thinking he'd be here. I came to find him. I actually thought I heard him tell me to come." I turned wide, pleading eyes to Mark and begged, "Does that sound crazy?"

"No, Sara. It sounds like you knew what you needed, or some part of you did. It might have been funneled through actions and voices that felt desperate and true at first and strange and crazy later, but ultimately the deeper wisdom was there, guiding you. Didn't you say you've come to believe you came here for a reason – to heal?"

"Yes."

"Well then, maybe it *was* Brian telling you to come. Just not to literally find *him*, but to find what you needed to heal. And maybe, in time, to find some other knowing of him."

I tried his words on like a new outfit, seeing how they felt and if they fit. It was comforting to think that it *had* been Brian, that he had reached across Heaven and spoken into my heart. But large dense pieces of rock remained, on which were chiseled the contract I had made with grief. They would not budge, and I found comfort in them as well.

"Sara? Can I ask you a question?"

Tentatively I replied, "Yes."

"You said this is 'all a little overwhelming.' When you say *this*..." he placed his hand on his chest, "do you by any chance mean me? Am I coming on too strong? Hanging around too much? Making things harder for you?"

It seemed I never ran out of tears. Tears of grief and pain, tears of sorrow and longing, tears wrung from the sweet touch of hope and kindness.

"I wish I could say yes Mark, I really do." A golden light danced around the room and landed peacefully on the shadows of his face. My words came easier when I watched my hands, the fire, the floor, anything but his handsome face. "But it wouldn't be fair. Or true. In the kitchen just now I was watching you light the fire, thinking how nice it is here, how good today felt, how much I like being with you, near you. All of a sudden I realized I was happy." The tears started to fall and once again I turned pleading eyes to him. "Mark, I can't be happy. Not yet. Maybe not ever. It hurts too much. And it's not right."

I don't know if it was the force of my plea or the force of his compassion, or perhaps simply the force of that which is inevitable, but before the next breath could be taken I was wrapped tightly in his arms. We had come to our knees on the floor, our bodies pressed together, the fire leaping and spitting around us. He did not move to kiss me or to do anything other than hold me, but I could feel his pounding heart beneath the soft flannel of his shirt. Or maybe it was my own. Closing my eyes I inhaled deeply. He smelled of the outdoors and stale cologne and firewood - things real and warm and good. I held on, afraid if I loosened my grip, he'd let go.

When space sought to separate us we drew our arms tighter, in silent promise to hold one another up. I tried not to make a sound or move in any way that might indicate I was ready to release our embrace

But just as the tide flows, so must it ebb. Our drawing apart happened just this naturally. Mark moved his hand to my neck, and then to my face, pulling back far enough to look at me. His eyes, wet with his own tears met mine for only a moment and then moved on to study every freckle, line and feature of my face. Fingers followed eyes, lightly touching, seeking, finding. He traced the invisible path of tears until he came to stop at my lips. Softly, slowly, he outlined their curve. They trembled under his touch.

"You are so beautiful."

I reached up and held his fingers to my lips. Kissing them I tasted the salt of our tears. Our hands folded together, and then, like images in a mirror, met palm to palm. We watched them in the firelight – so different, one large and leathery, the other thin and pale – forming between them a single prayer.

Ever so slowly we laced our fingers together. And then even more slowly slid from our knees to sit on the floor, side by side, holding hands.

In silence we watched the fire burn. There was nothing awkward about the silence, nothing empty in it. Words were not necessary or even adequate; they would have been too small and only fallen short of truth. Like trying to fold the sky into a box, or get to Heaven in an airplane.

CHAPTER NINETEEN

"Tell me about your book." I was the first to send sound into the silence. I did so quietly, so as not to disrupt the delicate balance of the night.

We were still in front of the fire, our fingers still intertwined. The orange flame was the only light in the room. Mark had risen once, and returned with sandwiches and fresh hot tea.

"What would you like to know?" He picked up my hand and placed it on his denim-clad thigh.

"Whatever you're moved to tell me." Yawning, my head rested comfortably against the back of the couch. I rolled it lazily to the side to look at him.

"Hmmm…well…it's about love. And mythology, in a sense. My take on the topics at least."

"Oh, well okay, that clears it up." I wrestled my hand free and playfully slapped his leg. "I got that from the title."

"Oh, I'm sorry, you wanted the long version." I was getting very used to the curve of his smile.

"Yes please."

Running his free hand through his hair he looked up at the ceiling, searching for some invisible cue card and once done, turned back to me.

"Okay. Here goes. Not verbatim mind you, just the general ideas and how they were formed." He sighed, the air releasing from his lungs slowly. Propping his elbow up on the cushion behind him he cupped his chin in his hand, his face so close to mine I could feel the space left by the air he inspired.

"When Robin left I fell apart. I looked around and couldn't find any fragment of myself in my life. Everything I was and did and wanted was tied up in her. I had long before decided that to love someone was to give yourself over to them, and in turn they would fill you up with their love. It was the idea – the popular myth - of being made whole through someone else, and the belief that love was something to be found – sought for, discovered and received, in precious and limited quantity. And without it, without that other, you are left broken and incomplete, and void of love."

With each word he dropped into the air he wrote the next chapter in my book of lessons. I could hear the echo of my own story, and I didn't like the direction it was heading.

Wanting to defend what I thought to be the honor of love, I looked up at Mark and said, "The truest, most beautiful thing I have had in my entire life is the fact that Brian loved me. And I always liked the idea of being completed through his love. I thought it was what perfect, true love was about – finding your 'other half'- literally." Even as I spoke, the other truth registered somewhere in the center of my heart. Since Brian's death I *had* felt broken, lost, and yes, void of love. But wasn't that the price you paid for the blessing of having been loved?

I wasn't sure if what I had said would hurt Mark, if he would pull away or loosen his grip on my hand. But he didn't. He seemed to accept whatever I had to give. "Sara, please know that it is, in no way, my intention to question your love for Brian. The book was based on my own experience. These are my beliefs, they don't have to be yours, or anyone's." He shrugged, smiled and cocked his head to one side. The right side. He always tilted his head to the right.

"If you'd rather, we don't have to talk about this anymore."

"No. I want to. And I want you to be honest. It just hits close to home and I'm finding that happening a lot lately. But I can't run from every little thing I don't like, though that's easier to say than do. I've been running from things all week, as you know only too well. But I can make the decision not to run from this. Please, go on. I want to hear." My thumb stroked his, liking the feel of his skin.

"Okay, but if you want to shut me up at any time, just say so. My feelings won't be hurt." He squeezed my hand tightly for a moment.

"So…when Robin left, I was left searching for something else to fill me up. That's when I went and tried all those things I told you. I'd go out, meet a woman, bring her home or ask her out. It didn't matter, the outcome was the same. I'd do my best to ingest as much of someone else as possible, each time falling a little bit in love, or so I thought, and thinking if they'd only love me back I'd be okay again."

"I assume it didn't work."

"No. Not at all. Afterwards I was invariably left emptier than I'd been before. So on top of that I took to drinking – a lot. I had always been a social drinker, but that was before I'd forgotten how to laugh or have fun. This wasn't about fun. Every night I'd go out with a bunch of guys, or a woman, and drink until I could hardly stand. For a while I went the whole macho route, looking, not for love now, just sex."

"It's hard for me to imagine you like that." The image was a little disturbing because it reminded me of so many of the men I had dated before Brian. I wondered how many of them had been as confused and hurt as Mark.

"Yeah, well, it wasn't a pretty picture, but as I said before, I see now how it was necessary, just another step in my journey. I saw what I was capable of, how desperate and lost I was and how scared."

"Scared of what?"

"Of looking inside and finding nothing. Of discovering that without Robin there was nothing real, worthwhile, or true about me. And yes, I've come to see the connection to finding out about my mother, to the search for a woman's love. Regardless of all the archetypal complexes, the bottom line is that I was convinced some critical piece of myself was missing and that only a woman could fix it, and if love wasn't to be found, then whatever else was available would have to do."

"Is love such a terrible thing to want?" I sure hoped not. It's how I had spent the greater part of my own life.

"No," the slightly roughened edge his voice had taken on, softened, "not at all. But it can be a dangerous thing to need. At least as desperately as I did. That kind of love has nothing to do with what you can give but everything to do with what you can get."

The words clanged against my own history. "So, what changed?"

"Well, nothing immediately, but after years of that kind of fruitless, self-destructive searching I decided that maybe what I needed was to look for answers in something more spiritual. My own background was sparse where religion was concerned. My family had gone to church but I had never felt completely comfortable. I tended to ask too many questions and not be satisfied with the answers. For a long time I had turned my back on the whole thing, but when my world fell apart I found myself on my knees, calling out for help, pleading with some invisible force to heal what I couldn't.

"That's when I took off for India, Egypt and a score of other places, with nothing more than a backpack stuffed mostly with books on spirituality, religion and philosophy. I saw myself as a modern disciple, willing to bow before any altar, or any *one* who would tell me who to be, how to live, and more importantly - how and where to find love. My motivation, regardless of what I told myself, was to find that magic something that would fill me up inside, answer all my questions and lead me to someone who would love me. Or, if not that, then lift me out of the darkness of desire. And yet, after months of traveling, studying, and following every path that I could find - ancient and modern – I still felt empty. I mean, I learned a great deal, had some peak experiences and met some incredible people who seemed to possess what I sought. But for me, there was something, some understanding that was still missing."

"So after all that, you didn't find what you were looking for?"

"Yes and no. As I said, it was an invaluable learning experience. First of all, it was my introduction to being alone with myself, if only physically. But it was more than that. I was changed forever by the richness of the cultures and spiritual traditions I encountered. I learned to appreciate their differences and their similarities, and began to see the beauty of the grand design at work. No matter where I was or who I prayed with, or to, I could see in the eyes and feel in the hearts of every person a similar quest. I came to believe that we are all seeking, in one form or another, the same thing – union, or maybe it's re-union. I don't know." He sat quietly reminiscing and I watched in wonder, feeling how small my life had been next to his.

"It's amazing how much you have done and seen, in a relatively short time. I would never have the courage to go out on my own like that. Shoot, I have trouble leaving the house these days." He turned to me and smiled, deep and kind. Without speaking or releasing my hand he pushed himself from the ground and pulled us both onto the couch, where we settled into the thick soft cushions.

While stretching limbs that had been folded up for too long he continued to look at me, brows furrowed and mouth pinched into a curious smile, preparing for what else he had to say.

"When I told you about my 24 hour writing frenzy, you joked that maybe you should take up writing and I said that it might not work for you because everyone's path is different. It's the same thing here. Just because I've been to a lot of places doesn't mean I received something that everyone else doesn't, in some other way. At the time I thought it would mean just that. I thought somewhere out there I'd find the one *right* way - *the* path to complete and utter bliss and that I'd just follow it and there I'd be. And once there I would never be confused or hurt or angry or lonely again. Just imagine what it would be like to have gone almost literally to the ends of the earth to escape suffering, and not be able to do it."

"Well, if you put it that way…I only went a few thousand miles." I grinned proudly. "How did you finally decide to give up and come home?"

Smirking, he answered, "I was in Scotland, nearly broke and barely able to stand myself another day. I'd spent the night on a bench and woke to the stench of stale booze and vomit. And then there was this voice, rough and gravelly, and this hand pawing at my shoulder. At first I shoved it away, without even opening my eyes. But it was insistent. The voice kept saying, 'Get outta here, this is my place. You gotta find your own. Everybody has their own and you can't just go around takin' somebody else's.' Over and over, the same thing. And then, like the striking of a gong, the words registered, and my eyes flew open.

There, hovering above me was this man, dirty and half-drunk – just my kind of guardian angel. I sat up and asked him to repeat what he had said. He spoke in a slurred accent and looked at me like I was a lunatic. But actually I was saner than I had been in months, years, maybe ever. As he said it again, word for word: '*...this is my place. You gotta find your own. Everybody has their own and you can't just go around takin' somebody else's,*' an understanding began to take root in my mind. When he finished I laughed, kissed him on the cheek, thanked him for teaching me the one thing I had been unable to learn in all the churches, temples or ashrams I'd been in and asked him what I could do for him."

"And what did he say?" The smile that radiated across the years was contagious.

"Well after almost slugging me, he sort of puffed up a little, looked in my eyes and told me that I could quit stealing benches and go and find my own." Mark's eyes were wide, like a child looking into the world for the first time.

"You're kidding?" It took all my willpower not to laugh.

"I swear. Then he asked if he could have my coat."

"And?" I asked.

"I gave it to him of course. Small price to pay for an epiphany."

"Okay, let me get this straight. What you're telling me is that you traveled halfway around the world, for how long? Months? A year? Only to be told by an inebriated homeless gentleman to get off his bench. And that, you believe, is the gem you had been searching for?"

"Makes perfect sense don't you think? I know, it sounds ridiculous, or at least like I was grasping at straws, but I'm telling you – something about that moment resounded somewhere deep inside of me. I heard not simply his admonition for stealing his bench, but a deeper meaning behind the words. Maybe he was just an innocent messenger, or maybe he wasn't, I don't know. Looking back I realize that I had been given the same message a million times, in who knows how many languages, but not until it came from that man was I able to hear it. Don't you see? It was necessary for me to experience all that I did, to take every step I had in order to find myself on that bench at that moment, to be spoken to by that man. I find it absolutely, wonderfully, blessedly brilliant - and painfully, agonizingly infuriating - the way the universe works. I just love it, when I'm not hating it of course." I had never seen Mark so animated.

"So you believe that the universe, or God, or some greater force led you all over the planet to find that bench?"

"Yeah, I do." And he seemed okay with that.

"Do you think that's the way it always is? Do we have to jump through hoops in order to know some peace in our lives, in order to just be happy? Why would God do that to us?" I really wanted to know, needed to know.

"I don't think God does do it. I think it is part of our soul's journey of growth. For all I know we choose what struggles we'll encounter before we're ever born, or they're the product of our free will. But one thing I truly believe is that God, the Universe, Life, whatever you want to call it is constantly giving us signs and guiding us toward the becoming of our greatest Self. And even though our souls may see and understand the signs, our smaller selves have a harder time accepting them. We've been programmed to more readily accept fear and judgment, and to mistrust our intuition, which is one of God's greatest mechanisms for communicating with us. But we doubt it more often than not. So consequently we are given our messages over and over, in different ways and forms, until we are ready to hear. And I'm not sure what makes us more ready in one moment than another, but as the saying goes, 'When the student is ready the teacher appears.' If I had caught on earlier in the game I may not have had to venture so far, but then I wouldn't have learned all that I did or met all the people I did. So in the end, nothing is lost. I've got to accept that there will be things I will never understand, about the way it all works or the timing of perfection. I'm just glad God seems to be infinitely patient and persistent."

I let his final words fade into the firelight. I wanted simply to sit with all he had shared, to let it settle into the air around me, so that I might breathe it in and make it a part of me.

But even as I allowed myself to be carried on the tide of Mark's conviction, some part of me remained doubtful. As hopeful and positive as his outlook was, it offered me no understanding of Brian's death, and like Jane, professed that some things would never be fully understood. It was a reality that still felt too large, too dark, and it just seemed wrong such pain and loss should be accepted as a steppingstone in anyone's evolution.

He read my expression. "You're not convinced?"

"I'm trying."

Gently he responded, "Don't. There's no need to push yourself to believe anything that doesn't feel right to you. Take it from me, anything we push too hard to possess has a way of staying forever out of reach. It's when we just slow down and stay open that God has a chance to catch up to us. Like my bench story. It wasn't until I was at rest that I heard what God had been saying all along."

"So tell me, what exactly is it that you heard?"

"Simply that I had to find my own path to God and ultimately to love, the way that was real and right for me, and that I couldn't just hang on someone else's coattails and get what I sought. I first had to sink in, face myself and the demons within, and engage with God in the silence and emptiness of my own being. Then, I had to figure out how to go out there and live more consciously. Daily, in my relationships, in my work, in the world, the best I could. That's what I work on now. It's really nothing different than what I said about the writing and the traveling.

"There is much to be learned from every religion and spiritual path out there, and I had immersed myself in quite a few of them, which prepared me to immerse myself in the living of my own life and the forming of a relationship with God that was more personal and intimate. I had no idea what it would look like or how I would do it, but I sensed that if I just showed up, God would meet me on the road and show me the way. And I figured I had little to lose since I'd tried about everything else. It was time to get to know myself as well as I knew what others had taught me."

"Didn't you say that after all your searching you came home and isolated yourself? Was that what you felt you had to do?"

"Well...as you've probably gathered, I did little in moderation. I'd swung the pendulum so far in one direction it naturally swung as far as it could in the other. So, yes, I came home, got back to work on the house, stopped dating and drinking – altogether for a while - and just threw myself into being alone. And as I said before it was a miserable experience at first. I wasn't used to being that kind of alone, even traveling had been different – louder, more distracting. Here, with only myself and Lady to talk to, I could barely stand it after the first week. But I had a sense that it was exactly what I needed, to get used to my own nature, the rhythms of my moods, discover what it felt like to be me apart from anyone else. And then I had the experience with the writing." He was beginning to look a little tired, but at the same time at peace in the company of all he had done and learned.

"And you got to the point where you were no longer lonely? No longer needed the company of another or to be filled up and made whole by someone else? Is that what it taught you about love, that it isn't necessary?" I had a hard time buying such a possibility, but if he was able to give me a way to forget wanting Brian's love, forget needing it to make living bearable, then I was willing to listen.

A look of total surprise wound its way across the landscape of his face. And then, with the back of his index finger he stroked my cheek, from temple to chin, slowly, softly, as if trying to answer my question with the pureness of the act.

With a voice that matched his touch he said, "In no way did I mean to imply that love is not necessary or that it is not the most beautiful, most absolutely perfect blessing of life. My entire voyage through foreign lands, both external and internal, was about discovering just how awesome Love is.

"You see Sara, what I came to understand is that Love is not something to be acquired. Love is free. It's abundant, and in no short supply. Love is not something I had to be given, because it is something that I *am*. It is *all* that I am, all that each of us is. It is impossible to be without, and therefore it is unnecessary to go out and seek or steal it. It is the very stuff of which life is made. I believe that Love is the energy that makes up our cells, that holds our physical bodies together and is, through and through, the flesh and blood of our ethereal bodies. It's as though God took into hand the energy of Love and fashioned from it the entire universe, every organism, leaf and pebble, man and woman. And then She breathed Love's power into His creation, and Life was born. Father God the builder, and Mother God the midwife."

Breathless I whispered, "That's beautiful Mark," and then, "but hard to believe. I mean look around, look at your own story. If what you say is true, then why *do* we go out in search of it, why do we all feel so alienated from it?"

"The sun is so bright, so full of light that we cannot look directly at it. We close our eyes. I think it's the same with Love, at least partially. It is around us and in us in such massive quantities it's blinding. So much so that we cannot see it, or if we do, we look away.

"Also, there is nothing beyond or outside the realm of God. What we think of as the dark is no less part of the whole. Without the dark we wouldn't know light, without fear, love. God makes no distinctions. Only we do. Still, somehow, somewhere along the way, we became almost blind to the light and to love, became more comfortable in the dark, wrapped in fear and its illusions, almost content to passively accept its drug of pain, thinking there is no other choice."

"But I don't think most people *want* to be unhappy. They – we - just don't know how to stop the hurting." Tell me Mark. Tell me the secret.

"Of course we all want to be happy. Somewhere inside of us there's the truer part that knows that we are Love and that we have, and are, all that we need to live joyfully. But because we have gone to sleep, allowed the noise to distract us, we are able to hear and see only a fragment of the truth and we miss the bigger picture. We think in order to ease our suffering we must find someone else, some other wounded soul, who will both need us and fulfill us. We take our broken, disempowered selves into the world, in search of love, in search of our 'other half,' hoping that maybe then we'll feel whole, because two halves make a whole, right?"

"I get the feeling the answer is 'no,' but I don't know Mark. I always thought that was the case. Brian was everything that I wasn't and it felt like together we were complete." I was inside his words, devouring them. At any other time I might have ached with sadness, feeling like Mark was tearing apart the only piece of grace I had known. But instead a duct had opened, letting in, one drop at a time, the fresh, life-enriching waters.

"Again Sara, I don't mean to question or take anything away from what you shared with Brian. I'm just sharing my thoughts with you."

"I know you are and I'm not upset, really. I'm just trying to understand. Please, keep going."

"Well, I think the image of two halves coming together, fitting perfectly into one whole is what feeds our popular idea of love, and quite honestly it is a beautiful image. It's how I felt and what I imagined for Robin and myself. But it didn't work. Because ultimately, we aren't merely someone else's half – we're whole, and of course a part of a greater, even more complex whole. The entire Universe is filled with all the energies of existence and we belong to that great web. But we tend to see ourselves as static, containing only what we have somehow come to believe we are, thinking that our stories are written and that's it. We don't understand that our potential is much greater than we can imagine and that there are stories yet to be written in which we have a hand in scripting.

"We tend to think that some of us are strong and others weak, some practical and others creative, some reasonable, and others passionate. But we each carry the coding for all of these things, in varying degrees. We are dichotomous creatures, thriving vats of opposing energies, masterfully blended into unique personalities. We are light and dark, masculine and feminine, capable of anger and forgiveness, love and hate, sorrow and joy. Some qualities outweigh others naturally within us, but others we have just chosen or been told we are supposed to be, or not be. So in the process we often end up disowning those other things we've decided we aren't, or been told we shouldn't be, and then end up seeking them out in another."

"Can you give me an example?"

"Okay, I've always been pretty emotional, sensitive, whatever you want to call it. I used to be an extreme of those things, easily getting my feelings hurt, working hard to be liked and appreciated. I manifested and dealt with it the way little boys are taught to, by sucking it up and pulling within. Regardless, it's what I was, and so, when I went on my hunt for completion I chose, completely unconsciously, a woman who 'complemented' me by providing the traits I felt I lacked. She was strong and assertive, and didn't question

173

everything the way I did or seem to feel things as intensely. She didn't think everything to death and wasn't as plagued by life's larger questions. Everything was a challenge to her, and she loved it. I was a writer who loved the ocean, the sky, and things simple and quiet and she was an executive-to-be, who preferred skyscrapers, city streets and all the latest and best that life had to offer. Neither is right or wrong, but I see how I used her to be for me what I wasn't able to claim inside myself."

I saw too, how I had relied on Brian to be what I couldn't. Or had felt too afraid to be. But I knew that our love had not been just about possessing unrecognized traits. We had connected in too many ways.

"You don't think you and Robin had anything that was real?"

"I know that we did, we had much that was wonderful. We made each other laugh, we were both passionate people, both liked movies and books and hiking. We also challenged each other to learn and experience new things and think in new ways. I'm not saying that the people we gravitate to in our lives don't share common ground with us, and that we can't truly and deeply love them, or that we aren't meant to learn from them. It's all about our motivations, what we're trying to 'get' from the relationship. If we're hiding from our own power or beauty or gentleness, if we've attached ourselves to another in order to take from them what we need to feel better, then we deny ourselves the fullness of our own nature, and eventually, when our plan doesn't work, we are left, once again, feeling discontent and unfulfilled. And the cycle begins all over - or worse, it doesn't and we just give up and wither away."

"So what do we do?"

"I can't say what's right for everyone. But the best thing I ever did for myself was simply begin to listen to, notice, question and acknowledge my own thoughts, feelings, actions and especially my motivations. I stopped siphoning out those things I didn't want to face or hear or see. I got honest, with myself and with God. It was painful. I had to look at all the ways I manipulated and how needy and fearful I was. I saw it all – the good, the bad and the ugly. The bad and ugly were easy to drown in and for a while I did. And then I got angry and even threw some things around. Bottom line was that there were things I needed to change, to do differently…ways I needed to grow.

"Little by little I also began to see inside myself the seeds of those things good and valuable, and the seeds of those qualities I thought I could only get from Robin. I could be strong. I could be assertive when I needed to be and I could be practical and decisive, and still embrace my own creative, sensitive, loving nature. Seeing this helped me to accept myself more fully - my strengths as well as those traits I had judged as weaknesses, and it allowed me to appreciate Robin for who she was without it meaning anything about me. I could also let her go and know that I would survive. More than that, I would thrive, and at the same time come to appreciate her for being one of the greatest teachers I have ever had. It hasn't been easy and I continue the process each and every day of my life, but now, more often than not, I love the journey."

"And love?"

"The greatest thing of all is the way it has expanded in my life. There are more days, more moments, when I feel connected to the energy of Love that is within me, and connected to the energy of Love inside of everyone and everything around me. I finally see that Love is ever-present. I'm the one who was missing for so long." He was beaming, in a quiet, settled kind of way.

And then he laughed, "It's sort of like when you can't find your sunglasses. You search all over the house, in your car, everywhere you can think to look, only to discover they've been on top of your head the whole time. I went from one extreme to the other, looked under every rock, in every star, and not to mention in quite a few eyes, for the experience and knowing of Love, only to find it in the one place I never imagined it to be – living inside my own skin."

I had to admit that he had struck me, from our first meeting, as a completely self-possessed, self-assured person. He also seemed happy, and content. But still…

"It still sounds lonely to me Mark. It sounds like you've decided there's no need for an intimate relationship in your life. That you are everything you need and there's no room for someone else."

"Oh, but you're so wrong. I want very much to share my life with someone. But the key for me is to go to someone, not with misdirected needs, but openly, freely, honestly, and already filled with love – love that I can give, without fear, without the ulterior motive of proving myself worthy or even without the expectation of being loved back. Without expectations or demands, especially for that person to be anything but who and what they are. I hope at least to love more unconditionally, more honestly, and be able to show and share my whole self, flaws, vulnerabilities and all. I'm human and I know it's a tall order, to love in such a way. I fully expect to have to work at it, until I don't have to anymore. But that might take another lifetime or two." He laughed at himself – a man who accepted the ebb and flow of his own tides.

"And I realize my vision of love sounds somewhat unromantic, because it doesn't fit with our pop culture's unyielding definition of love as 'painful longing.' Listen to the radio and all you'll hear are songs dedicated to a love that is causing more tears than laughter. But I think my vision has the capability to be *more* romantic. I know at least that I feel more passionate, more alive and more able to connect with someone emotionally, mentally, spiritually and physically than I have in my entire life. To me the idea of meeting another, as two wholes rather than two halves, holds the potential for a pretty incredible union. It won't be easy, probably filled with new and different challenges, but hopefully I'm more prepared to meet them. And, quite honestly, I now have enough inner strength to know that if a relationship doesn't work, I'll be okay. No matter how much it might hurt, I will go on and still have the capability to know and feel love. And that means as much to me as anything."

When I didn't say anything, but sat silently studying the vein lines on his hand, he squeezed gently until I looked up at him. "Are you okay?"

"Yeah, I just…I don't know. You seem to have it all figured out. I've spent my whole life believing I didn't really exist except through the eyes of someone else." Tears had formed but didn't fall. I had returned my gaze to his hand, the first hand to hold mine since Brian's.

I uncurled our fingers and held them flat against one another. For some reason I was drawn to the line created by our touching flesh.

He remained quiet, knowing I wasn't finished. When I spoke again I raised my head and stared over his shoulder. "Since moving up here I've lived alone, but all I've done is search for Brian and wander aimlessly from one day to the next, at first working hard not to feel or think too much, embracing a numb void of sorts, and then standing by as grief threatened to devour me. The idea of being truly happy, of laughing and crying and living a life separate from Brian, or beyond his death, feels implausible."

Pausing, I sighed deeply, and continued. "But then, this past week…I don't know. All of these things have happened, things that have pulled me away from the fortress I had so carefully designed and constructed, and introduced me to you and others. And every one of you seems destined to teach me something new, about myself, Love, God, living – no matter how much I resist. And a lot of what's happened has been…weird, almost magical, or surreal, and yet, in some ways it's felt more real than the rest of my life. I don't know. It's hard to explain. It terrifies me, and at the same time I can't help but be drawn in. I keep running away, and somehow end up right back in it. It's like it won't let go of me, or maybe I'm the one holding on."

Exhaustion swept over me. I laid my head against the back of the couch and closed my eyes. Once surrounded by the dark, the tears escaped and fell soothingly down my cheeks. They were tears of grief, and tears of bitter truths recognized. Mark had seen into my heart - my need and my longing - and he had exposed them to my blinded eyes. Foremost was my intense dependence on Brian – the way I had literally fed my starving soul with his energy. And with honesty unfamiliar to me I saw how I had already begun to do the same with Mark, craving his masculine power and spiritual strength.

And as if hearing and answering the call of my soul, Mark's hand moved to my forehead and rested there, cool and comforting, before gently running down the length of my hair.

And that's the way we remained for a long, long time.

I left Mark's house reluctantly just after one in the morning. We said goodbye at my car door with Lady looking on. We dared not hug but fed our final desire to touch by running fingers along patches of exposed skin – faces, wrists, hands, necks.

Driving the road home, I replayed the day. Every word, every touch. The longing, the pleasure, the guilt and the pain. Our conversation on Love clung like mist to my skin. I could feel it more than hear it. It laid like a shadow over my past, while spreading a thin film of promise over the breaking of a new day.

It seemed that every shade of light was edged with dark, and on the corners of the dark were the glimmers of light. I wondered if this was the way it was supposed to be, if it wasn't at least better than drowning in the dark.

CHAPTER TWENTY

Morning came softly, sneaking in on lighter shades of gray. It was the sounds that first crossed the threshold of my awareness, each one tuning in like a different instrument in an orchestra. The flutter of wings, the whir of the paddle fan, the low whistle of wind cutting through trees, and behind it all a constant hum with no known origin, the white noise of life.

Keeping my eyes closed, I listened. The sounds of motion, of the world going about its business. Awaking to a new day was like buying a ticket to the show, to add the tune of my own instrument to the symphony. I knew mine was badly off-key, but at least I felt willing to try.

Just as I moved to stretch and join the music, a note - closer, more human than the rest - sent a needle across the record, and my eyes flew open. Replaying the noise in my head I tried to place it. It took a moment but I got it - the shuffle of feet through fallen leaves, the occasional snapping of a twig. Red numbers glowed from the clock on the nightstand. 6:30. Too early for anyone to be walking around behind my house. Fear swelled like a balloon.

"Okay, calm down, breathe like Mark showed you. Maybe it's just him, maybe he came over but didn't want to wake you up. No, it's too early; he wouldn't do that. But who else could it be?" My mind babbled through every possibility, benign and threatening.

Heart pounding I crept from my bed, threw on last night's outfit, thick with the scent of Mark's cologne, and tip-toed into the family room, staying close to walls, feeling like I should have something menacing in my hands. When I got to the kitchen I stood behind the bar and peered across the great room, through the French doors.

A sliver of cream caught my eye. And then the ivory arm that stretched outward from it. Someone was sitting in one of the wrought iron chairs grounded into the corner of the garden, just to the right of the doors. There were two of them positioned on either side of a flat-topped rock sculpture that acted as a table. Matching breaths and steps I moved across the room and slowly opened the door.

The sight of the long slender figure perched lightly on the chair took me completely off-guard. A new day, another surprise.

"Bev?" She was the last person I would have expected to find on my back doorstep. But there she was, impeccably dressed in winter white, hair pinned on top of her head, swan neck tilted slightly to the left. Wide alert eyes focused on me. She was as regal as I remembered, calm and poised, her demeanor casual, as though it was as natural as the sun rising for her to be sitting behind the house at 6:30 in the morning. It did look natural, even to me, and I had to remind myself that it was I who now lived here.

Dumfounded, I plopped down in the other chair. My thoughts went immediately to Mark's story about his mysterious parentage, about the role Bev had played in giving him to the Wildes, and to the story's still unrevealed end. Could I ask her myself? I would have loved to give the truth to Mark. But I knew it was not my place, even in the light of the intimacy we had shared only hours before.

My attention returned to the woman sitting across from me - this woman, who held in her possession the answers to secrets recently lain at my feet, whose home I now lived in. I wondered how many more ways our paths could intersect.

"Bev, I don't know what to say - Good Morning? Would you like some coffee, or tea? Do you want to come inside?" Not knowing what else to do, I turned to my mother's instructions on being a good hostess.

"Why thank you, it's kind of you to offer, but no. I'd just like to sit here for a bit." She made no reference to why she was here or to the hour, or to the fact that she had nearly sent me into a panic attack, and she seemed not the least bit aware that there was anything highly unusual about her 'visit.' I started to say something, to convey my confusion, but no words would form.

Bev sat, ageless hands folded in her lap, surveying the land she owned and loved. I felt like an intruder and wondered if I should leave. It was her property, but then again, she and Gil had rented it to me and that had to afford me some rights, like the right to know why she was here, and which mystery had drawn her to my doorstep. I struggled with what to do and finally decided I would go inside and make some tea. I was quite sure Bev was not someone who would feel the need to explain herself, unless she chose to, and then it would be in her own time. In that way she reminded me of Anna.

But just as I rose to leave she held out her hand and turned to look at me. A hint of sadness lit the edges of her eyes. "Please, don't go. I'm here to see you. But I love this spot and wanted to absorb it for a moment. If you don't mind, stay and listen to it with me."

"Of course, whatever you like." An ache reached out from low in my chest and a shudder passed through me.

We sat for nearly an hour, and I did my best to 'listen' to what she so obviously heard in the language of the wind. But I heard nothing, save for my own racing thoughts. I tried to breathe and though it helped to slow me down a bit I was unable to fend off the tide of anticipation that kept rising. There was no way she could know about my conversation with Mark, though I was sure she knew about Jane's phone call concerning the locket. That had to be why she'd come. But why would she travel so far instead of call, or, if she wanted it returned, have me send it to her? Especially considering Gil had told Jane that she wasn't well. She looked well, though there was something almost haunting in her stature and her stillness.

When gray began to reluctantly give way to subtle hues of blue, Bev returned from her voyage within. Turning once again to me she said, "Thank you for letting me just sit here. It is what I have needed. How are you?"

I wanted to laugh. "I really have no idea, to be honest with you, Bev. You would think that's a simple question. At this moment, however, I admit that I am confused and curious. I mean this is the first time I have come out to find you sitting on the back porch at the crack of dawn, or anytime for that matter."

To my surprise she laughed. Out loud and heartily. I wouldn't have believed she did anything loudly, ever. "It is a bit odd, isn't it?" Followed by, "You look shocked. You thought only Gil laughed so, didn't you? You forget I am the same woman who spied on him from this very house and held his bathing trunks hostage. It is I who *taught* him spunk."

Even as her posture softened she retained an essence of elegance. But I was warming to the spark she had released.

"I never told you how much I loved that story. It's the kind that fairy tales are made of."

"Dear, love is as real as we let it be. It is we who have sadly relegated it to the pages of myth and lore. But it is never without mess and a share of darkness, even for Gil and me. We have had our troubles, our knock-down-drag-outs, and our moments of forgetting. Still, the truth is, Love is available in every breath we take."

"So I've been told."

I had missed Bev's kindness when we first met. I had been too intimidated by her strength, believing they could not live side by side in such degree. Now I was glad she was here, for whatever reason.

"May I please make you some tea or offer you something to eat? My kitchen has been recently restocked."

"Tea would be lovely, but only if we can drink it out here." As I opened the door leading into the house she casually added, "And when you come back out would you please bring the locket with you?"

I returned as quickly as I could, balancing mugs of steaming green tea and holding the silver chain tightly in my grasp. Carefully I set a cup in front of Bev and placed the locket in the center of the table. Curled up in my seat across from her, legs tucked under me, I waited for her to speak.

"Exquisite, isn't it?"

"Yes. It's so...delicate...but not fragile." Much like you Bev, I thought.

"Yes, you're right, that's the perfect way to put it." Neither of us touched the locket. Instead we watched it shimmer in the morning light.

"I'm sorry about removing it from the picture and about wearing it. I had no right to."

"Of course you did Sara. The locket is yours now, you were meant to have it."

Before I could protest she raised her eyes to me and said, "Do you remember at dinner that evening my asking if you had 'heard' the house?"

"Yes."

"What did you hear?"

I studied her a moment then said, "Well, I thought I heard the words, *'Life is a promise.'* At the time I assumed it was my imagination. But after the week I've had, I'm not so sure."

She nodded, got up from her seat and walked a few steps down the stone path until her back was to me. I thought she might continue all the way to the beach, but she came to rest in the center of the garden. I imagined her inbreath, filled with the pleasure of returning to this place, the home she had shared with her beloved for over seventy years. So often I believed I could feel the living energy of their memories, hear the laughter and the lovemaking, the echoes of dreams made and lived long ago. Having her here was like bringing the past forward, giving birth to the spirits of yesterday. She stood, flesh and bone before me, but appeared as a mirage, fluid and unfixed - the symbol of, in the language of Kahlil Gibran, "Life's longing for itself."

She remained with her back to me. "It was almost fifty years ago that I first heard the whisper of this house. I was standing right here in this very spot. I had woken early and had come to sit, to listen to the wind and the ocean. The smell of the sea always seemed strongest in the morning. I could never get enough of it. I would sit and breathe it in and let it wash through me like a wave. On this particular morning I had wakened with a start, to the sound of someone calling me. But when I opened my eyes I decided I must have been dreaming and tried to go back to sleep, but something - some nameless, faceless something - kept nagging at me, demanding that I get up. At the time I wasn't a big believer in such things, but this need in me to rise left no room for skepticism. So, finally I did and without even thinking I came out here, in nightgown and robe.

"I remember that light was just beginning to break. It was this time of year, cold and damp, but I hardly noticed. I did, however, notice everything around me, acutely - every sight, sound and smell, as though it was being chiseled into my memory. I can see and feel it now as clearly as I did then, as though not a day has passed. The outline of the trees like pencil sketches on the sky, the last of the leaves clinging to bare branches. I recall thinking to myself how I hated when everything turned brown and died.

"I was drawn, like a disciple to the light, to this spot. I stood and waited, for what I had no idea. But I knew, as strongly as I had known anything in my entire life that I was supposed to be here. Then, the pulling on my insides calmed and peace filled me. The wind fell away, the earth became silent. For a brief moment I truly believe that life, all of life, stood still. And when the moment passed a breeze brushed up against me and spoke in my ear. It was the clearest, truest voice I had ever heard."

I was holding my breath, waiting for her to speak the words. I dared not move, not ask.

"*'In the midst of death new life is born. No end, no beginning. Life is a promise held in your heart eternally, home is the Love that made this promise. From Love you came, to Love you will return, and in Love you will live forever. Fear not the dark but bless it, and love it in equal measure with all things, for it is the shadow of the light. And know that there is nothing you need that you do not have and nothing you have that is not blessed.'*"

Absolute quiet trailed in the wake of her voice. Her words came to rest upon me, as Mark's had, seeping into my skin, searching for space to plant themselves, for openings in my heart where they may burrow and wait to blossom.

She still had not turned around but I knew that her eyes were closed, focusing on another day so many years ago.

"I was brought to my knees by the beauty of what I had heard. Tears ran down my face and fell into the earth. I looked down and watched as they soaked into the moist soil, rainwater of the human heart feeding the bulbs of spring. Never would I look at the coming of winter the same way. From that moment on I saw it as the most beautiful time of year - when that which is old gives way to what is waiting to be born.

"When I looked up my eyes fell upon the pathway before me and again I was urged to move. There was more to what I was to discover on that day. When I woke that morning I had no idea that my life map was about to be altered. Until then my purpose for living had been to love Gil and Kathy, to paint and take pictures of the life around me. It had been enough, more than enough, and all that I wanted. And I still believe that those things are the simplest, purest treasures to be found. If I had continued to live as I had, I would have died knowing the meaning of grace. You see, I had known more than my share of light and even though the voice had moved me beyond measure I had not understood the reference to the dark. But what I didn't know was that I was being given words to guide me through what was to come, not to explain what had been.

"What I discovered on that day changed my life drastically, giving to it a dimension I had never imagined. It was on that day that I found the reason I came to this earth."

Bev turned then and smiled gently at me. Tear streaks stained her cheeks.

"Come. Leave the locket." She held out her hand and waited as I moved obediently toward her. When I stood just behind her she grabbed my hand and held it firmly.

She continued to speak as she led me nimbly down the path, ducking under low-hanging branches, stepping sure-footedly around rocks and fallen twigs.

"The instinct to move pushed me forward along this path. I had walked it a thousands times before. And really that day was no different. I followed the steps I had taken every day of my life, until I came to stand here." We stood on the edge of the hill, the thicket of trees at our back, the beach below us, the ocean - deep green, touched lightly by a halo of morning gold - stretched before us. The same waters that had licked the shore fifty years ago. A chill swept over me, the bands of time colliding, rolling one over the other.

"I watched the water for several minutes, overcome with memories of all the days and nights Gil and I had spent in our private paradise.

My heart ached with love and gratitude. I had been given so much and never before had I taken the time to embrace it fully, or to give thanks to the land, the sky, the sea, and whatever force it was that had so blessed me. With the power of a rip current I was taken down again and again into the depths of love, to the yearning for connection to everything around me, everything my eyes, my thoughts could touch. And deep inside the joy was a pinlight of despair - for not seeing sooner, for having missed something without even knowing it, for all that lay beyond what I could envision and imagine, for that which I *could not* touch. For the first time I was aware of the enormity of life, the magnitude of Love, and I longed to devour it in its entirety, to hold onto it forever. And yet somewhere in my very human body I knew there would always be more, forever something that lay beyond my grasp. I would never understand or experience it all."

She had grown taller, wider, fuller. And holding her hand I too could feel the expansion. Rooted to the earth I grew upward toward the sky, filling in all the spaces in-between. For a flickering moment it occurred to me that maybe I *could* experience love the way she and Mark spoke of it. I thought of the mountain and knew that perhaps I already had.

Eager for more I remained riveted to the story Bev was unfolding.

"I am ninety-two years old and I have lived a remarkable life. And from that day to this I have come to understand a few things more clearly, and between each sunrise and set I learn more. But even now I am aware that there is ever more that I do not know, do not understand. I no longer seek to shape and mold sense from what is. Today I feel no despair, for one of the things I *have* learned is that the most ecstatic and awesome truths are touched on the edge of mystery."

After a prolonged silence she continued, "I absorbed both the joy and the sadness, believing I had landed on the recognition I was meant to have. But then, once again, I was prompted to continue. It was an overwhelming desire to walk along the beach, to be as close to the floor of the earth as possible." We climbed down the hill onto the rocky shore, as she had done that day.

"Something kept me from walking along the waterline. Instead I stayed nearer to the face of the hill." She moved as a woman in a trance, egged on by the inner echo of a voice she heard calling from the past. In silence we walked, retracing footprints only she could see. A half an hour passed and I wondered if she was heading for any particular destination. I tried to concentrate on my own movement and breath, consciously willing myself to relax. Just as I entered my own trance, hypnotized by the purr of the water lolling against the shore, Bev's gait slowed and she touched the air around my arm.

The terrain had changed slightly, the gentle sloping hill turning into a sharper wall of rock, rising steeply above us. Ahead I could see where a piece of the wall jutted out several feet onto the beach. Its center was hollow and the opening at either end was just wide enough to walk through, but it bowed widely in the middle, creating a deep cave-like space.

Bev continued, "How many times had I walked past here? I couldn't count. But that day, even before I could see it clearly, I knew it was where I was going. The colors of the rock, the striations, were richer, more pronounced, every groove and marking alive. I know now that it wasn't any more spectacular, but rather it was my seeing that was different, my attention and perspective. *I* was more alive and therefore able to see the life bursting from everything else. But I didn't realize that then; I truly thought that there was something different about the world."

She paused briefly, refocusing, and then continued. "I approached slowly and when I reached this point," we were about fifteen feet from the entrance, "I stopped. Movement in the mouth of the cavern startled me. I remained very still, holding my breath, waiting. And then…" She put her hand to her chest, every emotion, every moment playing on her face. I too watched the darkened hole, fully expecting something to happen.

"…a figure, small and dirty, appeared. It was a child, no more than four. She was extraordinary, absolutely extraordinary." Her voice had become a whisper. "When I first saw her I was speechless, breathless, unable to move. She was so young, but there was wisdom in her wide-eyes that left *me* feeling like the child. She was standing perfectly straight, like a little soldier, completely composed and unafraid." Shaking her head in a gesture of remembered awe, Bev began to take slow careful steps forward.

"When reality finally registered I ran and kneeled before her. I wanted to ask who she was, where had she come from, why was she here, but these were not the questions of priority. Instead I asked her where her mother was, her father? I feared she wouldn't understand me or be able to answer. Before she had the chance, a sound, low and guttural, came from inside the hole. My first thought was animal, my instinct to protect myself and the child, but then it came again and I realized it was the deep, primal moan of human pain. The child looked back and then again at me, pointed and said, 'My Mommy is sick.' I remember putting my hands on either side of her face, wanting to comfort her, but she did not seem to need comfort. Her words had been meant to answer my question, not as a child's frightened plea for help.

"I took her small hand in mine and went inside," we copied her moves, as if rehearsing for a play. "There, lying in a shallow, rounded-out hole was a woman. She was dressed in light cotton, wrapped in a threadbare blanket. Next to her was a small ration of nuts and blueberries, and an empty, dented thermos that had been knocked on its side. Her hair was damp and stringy and clung to her face. She was skinny, her eyes closed, moaning with each exhalation. I sat beside her and touched her forehead. It was burning. She smelled of all things dark and human - sweat and waste and the salt of tears. My own tears formed and fell.

"When I smoothed back her hair, she opened her eyes, tiny slits of white and blue. They were more alert than I expected. I asked her if she thought she could stand, walk? If she could not I would have to leave her and go for help, get my husband to come and carry her back to the house where I had a warm bed, food and a phone to call a doctor. I told her I would take care of her, that she would be fine. I was terrified. But I also understood that I had been led here to help them, to save this woman from the shadow of death that hovered." She looked at me then, returning to the present, "I had forgotten what the voice had said: '*In the midst of death…Fear not the dark…*' I assumed instead that I was to be the light in this darkness, keeping it at bay."

I was sitting in the spot that would have been just above the crown of the dying woman's head. With eyes closed I thought I could feel her shivering body, smell the ugliness of decay. How I wanted her to live.

"Over and over I reassured her, telling her help was here. And just when I moved to rise, having decided she was in too much pain to answer and that I best go and get Gil, she spoke, her voice a hoarse whisper. She said, 'No, I prefer to rest here, by the ocean. I am not going anywhere.' The force of her words, the finality of the last five, told me that she knew she was going to die, and that she wanted to do it next to the sea."

For the first time since Bev had begun telling her story I spoke, not able to bear to believe that she would allow the woman to die.

"What did you do?" Almost accusingly.

"I scooted around behind her, tucked my bare, half-frozen feet up under me and held her head in my lap. I stayed here, right here with her, all through the day, as the sun traveled overhead on its journey to the other side of the world. She slept mostly. And as the day grew old her animal moan began to change, to transform from the haunting cries of anguish into an ancient chant of life. It caused my heart to ache it was so beautiful. I knew she was sliding away from this realm and entering into another. Part of me envied her. I wasn't sure why, but I think it was because it was that same part of me that knew where she was going."

I was crying. "And the child?"

"She sat near her mother the entire time, rubbing her feet, her arms, her head. Her touch was compassionate and loving, well beyond her years. She would talk to her, in the simple vernacular of a child, soothing, tender, often playful. Whole conversations that I couldn't understand, as though they were forever in the middle of a private talk. Never did she cry or whine. She simply took care of the woman, as she obviously had been doing since before I arrived. It broke and touched my heart in places I had never known." Bev sat quietly, remembering.

When she spoke again her voice was filled with fifty years of living, sprouted from the seed of one day. "As light began to fade I thought of Gil, knowing he would have spent the entire day worrying, but also trusting that he knew me. There had been more than once that

I had taken off before he woke, camera and sketchpad in hand, and not returned until dinner. Perhaps I should have gone back to tell him, to get him so he could be there with me. But I never did, never even really considered it. I was completely consumed by the woman and her daughter.

"The lower the light became the softer her chant. At some point the child had fallen into tune with her, their voices echoing softly in the dark cavern. I watched and listened to them, and to the silence behind their song. I did what I could to keep her comfortable. I expected that at some point she would simply quit breathing, but there came a moment, a blip of time when something altered. All of a sudden the child rose and walked outside, down to the water. I thought I should go after her, make sure she was safe, but before I could the woman's eyes opened. She was trying to speak. Stunned I leaned over, my ear close to her mouth. 'Take care of the child. I have done my part. I have brought her here. Now you must do yours. Raise her, teach her, and when the time comes, let her go. First into the world and then again, to return home. You will both know when those times have come, but you must listen, and help her to not forget how to hear.'

"And then she closed her eyes. Of course I wanted to know more, but how could I fill her last moments with questions? Also, I was a bit unsettled. Throughout the day it had waded across the waters of my mind - what would happen to the child when her mother died? I could see what I had truly been called to do - find safety and shelter for this motherless girl. And though I had played with the idea of taking her in I had given no grounding anchor to the thought. Now I had been directed, clearly, definitively. Did I have a choice? I thought not. Here, that night, the sounds of death and life so near, there was no room for practicality, for doubt, and certainly not refusal."

"I told her I would do as she asked. Then the child returned and reclaimed her place as caretaker. They resumed their chant. It wrapped around me as I stared blankly into the void. I don't know how long it was before I awakened to a single voice, going out into the night, the lone song of an orphaned child."

CHAPTER TWENTY-ONE

We made our way back along the beach, moving farther and farther from the past. It followed us though, with its gross sadness. Bev had said no more, though I knew there was more to be told. She seemed less weighed down than I, for she knew the rest, understood the significance, whereas I remained lost in the suffocating coil of death.

"It's all so unfair." I couldn't help breaking the silence. The story of the woman had slingshot me back down the road of my own despair.

"It seems so, yes. From our limited perspective. There's so much we don't see and so we're afraid. I think it's the sheer size of truth that scares us into smallness. After that woman died, when the moment had passed, I forgot that there had been beauty in it. I forgot the peace that had spread over her face when life no longer dwelt there. I forgot the sound of the chant, both haunting and sublime, voices raised in the ennobling act of release. Most of all I forgot the words: 'In the midst of death new life is born…'

"Instead I was scared and angry. Angry at, as you said, the unfairness. Angry, too that I had been 'chosen' to not only witness it, but to be handed the enormous task of raising another child. I was forty-two. I had no plans for more children. All at once I found myself standing over a dead woman and her toddler. It was like waking up from a dream, but there was no forgetting this one. I can still feel the anxiety, the urge to run and leave them there, to return to my home, my bed, and wait to wake to a new day, pretending that none of it had ever happened."

Her words struck home. "I know what you mean. I have felt like that almost every day for the past six months, just wanting to pretend that the day Brian died and every one since didn't happen. And in a way I know I have done what you wanted to - I ran and hid. The past several days have been the same, and different. They've scared me, shaken me up, sent me running, and made me see how much I have come to rely on my sadness, how comfortable I am with it. For so long I thought that all I wanted was to keep the grief at arm's length, ignore the fact that it was stalking me and ignore the truth that Brian was dead. But at the same time all I want to do is stay inside of it and keep alive the…" I struggled for the word, "the *experience*…of his death." The tears came freely, "It's all I have left of him, the only way I know to be near him."

I sighed heavily and wiped my eyes. "These past few days I've been yanked and pulled, kicking and screaming, from the comfort of hard won isolation, and into a world I don't recognize. I see how I'm always running from whatever it is that's in front of me, inside of me. It's exhausting."

"Sometimes our pain, our wounding, becomes our closest friend, the one thing that never deserts us. We cling with all our might to whatever it is we believe connects us to this world, even if it is the same things we say make us unhappy. Fear is our greatest inhibitor and our greatest motivator. We resist the calls life gives us for fear of losing ourselves and because they don't come in the forms we would like. But, the truth is that in answering the calls we often find ourselves. I learned, Sara, that in order to get over the fear, I had to go through it. There was no alternate route, no trick door to take me under or around it. Not even wings to fly above it."

It was true. As much as I hated it I knew what she said was true. "So you took her home? And you and Gil raised her? I assume it's her picture that's in the locket."

Bev nodded and walked in silence for a bit before saying, "She was a remarkable little girl and grew into an extraordinary woman. She taught us as much, more I think, than we taught her. We didn't raise her as much as give her the space in which to blossom, to mature into whom she already was. Not that it was always easy. She challenged us every step of the way."

"How?"

"By not allowing us to squeeze her into our preconceived notions about growing up, children, life, ourselves. She was given into our keeping, not into our possession. We were asked to teach her, not mold her, and we did our best. I grew in ways I had never imagined possible. I stretched the limits of my own boundaries, my own understanding of…well, everything. I was forced to empty myself of every firmly held judgment and obstinate opinion I had ever had, to awaken to a new way of seeing each day. Life ultimately became more beautiful, more confounding, more miraculous and more inspiring. And, in no small measure, more frustrating and difficult." The smile on her face told me that what she had gained had made it all worthwhile. The light had truly carried her through the dark.

Envy flooded my veins. Followed by shame and then a tiny particle of joy. It nudged softly, trying to awaken me to the bold light of truth that shone all around, just waiting for me to come and stand within it.

Curious for more I asked, "What was she like?"

"All things really. Serious and funny, strong and vulnerable, stubborn and pliant. Mostly she was free. There was a wildness about her, a fierce independence from the start. She was unlike any child, girl, woman or human being I have ever known. Still is."

"What happened to her? Her mother said you would have to let her go twice. Did you figure out what that meant?"

Again she nodded, slowed to a stop, bent over and rummaged through the rocks near her feet. When she stood she held a piece of smooth blue glass, the most difficult color to find. Holding it in her open palm so that the sun would catch it she said, "She was, is, one of those rare souls who are born to this earth without forgetting the truth of who they are, who is here to remind others of their own grace and the truth spoken to me at the house: '*From Love you came, to Love you will return, and in Love you will live forever.*' And the truth spoken to you as well."

"Me?"

"Yes. You. You asked me if I had had to let her go. Of course I did. All parents do. But with her it was different. It wasn't when she went off to college or to get a job, or to get married. It just happened one day. We woke to find her gone."

"That's it, she just left? Did you see her again? Did she leave a note? And what about the locket?"

She smiled, closed her fist around the glass and resumed walking. It took me a few seconds to fall in line beside her.

"Yes. I saw her. I still do occasionally. Letting go didn't mean forgetting, it just meant that we had to know when our job was done, when to allow her to move into her own work, claim her own wings and fly. And no, she left no note. We had talked often of the day she would go. On her seventeenth birthday, five months before she left, Gil and I gave her the locket. I think we all knew it was coming. We were very close and as odd as it may seem, goodbyes were not necessary."

We walked on. Morning was giving way to the noon hour, the sun settling into its highest place in the sky. It was clear and cold.

"Letting go the first time was difficult but at the same time exhilarating. We had done what we had been asked to, and had been given so much in return. But opening our eyes was only a small part of what she was meant to do. I was thrilled to have her move on and continue to bring light to others. All things move in cycles, letting go is part of the cycle."

She quit talking but I had the feeling she wasn't done, so I waited.

"But, still, the second letting go is more painful. I know it doesn't need to be, that there is nothing ultimately sad about it, but I am human. I have been holding my breath for so many years, waiting. And now that the time is coming I am relieved, and at the same time, grief-stricken." She stopped again and turned to look at me. Her eyes were pools of deep water and in them I could see the history of all things gentle and hard.

"It's why I am here Sara. To tell you this story and to say goodbye. Because now it is necessary."

I was shaking, not from the cold, but from somewhere deep inside.

"Why?" I asked, unsure if I really wanted to know.

She breathed deeply, bringing in the air she had been unable to for all those years. "One night, about a year after she left I came out to the beach and found her standing on the shore. I had not seen her in several months and though the sight of her filled me with joy I knew something was wrong. Never before had she possessed such an aura of sadness, as though a weight rested on her heart. I didn't speak, knowing enough by then to wait until she was ready. When she was, we sat together on the rocks, holding hands as mothers and daughters do." She dropped slowly to the ground and gestured for me to join her. When we were seated Bev took my hand in hers and stared out across the ocean.

"She then laid before me the heaviness she bore. 'Bev,' she said, 'you have always known that I came here to fulfill a purpose, and I have walked my path joyfully, always believing that I would be prepared for where it led. And I have been, for the most part, but now something unexpected, even to me has happened, and something else has come forward, not unexpected, but unnerving nonetheless.' Then she laughed and said, 'For the first time I feel overcome by my humanness.'

"I didn't offer any motherly cooing, that had never been our way. But still, my heart was breaking. She was not a child of my womb, but she was a child of my heart and soul, no different than Katie. I ached to sweep away her angst. But I resigned myself to wait, to hold her hand and listen. And in her time she revealed the rest.

"First, she was pregnant. I was shocked. Not upset, the way the mother of an unwed eighteen year old would be, for she was no typical eighteen year old. Rather, I was astounded that she had attached herself enough to someone to become pregnant. It was not a turn I would have ever, in a million years, imagined for her. But when I told her that I understood how such an unexpected twist had caught her unawares, she looked at me, smiled and said, 'You don't understand. What is unexpected is my resistance to do what must be done.'"

A lightning bolt struck the center of my chest. Shaking I asked, "And what was that?"

"She didn't tell me, not then. She never came to me seeking answers, only to be heard by human ears. I often thought how difficult it must be to align such an open spirit with the tide of emotions such as fear, doubt and attachment. To walk the earth, bound by flesh but able to see the illusion, and yet still get caught in the net. I am not sure whether it is harder to see truth or be blind to it. Still, I would choose seeing any day."

"So, she did tell you at some point, right? What was it? What did she have to do?" Oh God, it had to be. I held my breath.

"Ah, patience. All things in their order. Perhaps we will return to that, but now I want to share with you her other piece of information."

Feebly I answered, "Alright." I was resistant to let go of the first, but knew I had no choice. Before speaking Bev searched my eyes, for what I didn't know, but the intensity made me squirm and glance away.

"Oh my Sara, it is with great faith that I leap forward, trusting you are ready to hear what I must say."

The drumbeat of my heart played upon every cell. Breathless, robbed of speech, I forced myself to look at her. A well of compassion and love met my gaze.

"You don't have to say anything. Just listen. That night, I sat here as I do now with you, and listened to another young woman claim the inheritance of her soul - without regret, but with newly experienced fear. Years before her mother had told me that I would have to let her go, not once, but twice. I had allowed myself the privilege of forgetting, but on that night, fourteen years later, this extraordinary woman-child, reminded me.

"She told me that she had been awakened by a dream, a dream in which she witnessed herself handing the locket we had given her to another woman. She said to me, 'I pressed the locket into the woman's hand, telling her that the time had come for me to return home, and that now she must begin the work she was born to do. She was scared. She refused to take the locket at first, but then a light shone between us and in it she was transformed. She reached out, took the locket and put it on. She smiled, and in her eyes I could see clearly the turn of things to come, and my own, much older reflection. I felt a great wave of peace and I knew it was as it is meant to be. When I awoke I understood what my final act in living would be - to find, teach and prepare this woman for her calling. And that my own calling home would be foretold in the meeting of this other, the one chosen to continue my work.'"

The shivering had grown worse. My hands would not be stilled. I knew at the deepest levels of my being what Bev was saying to me. I knew and did not want to know. It was too incredible, too orchestrated, too coincidental, or it was none of these. And that scared me most of all.

"You said she was afraid." I wasn't sure if I was asking a question or just trying to keep her talking.

"Yes. One, she was experiencing doubt over some aspect of the pregnancy and two, she was afraid of facing the knowledge of her own death. She didn't know how long she had or exactly when it would happen, but she knew it would. And that filled her for the first time with an awareness of her own humanity, her mortality and the feelings that go along with it. Most of us spend our whole lives avoiding or denying our feelings, especially the darker ones. Some of us learn to face them, fewer to embrace them, and even fewer attempt to complete the cycle by learning to detach from the tumult of them. Here she was, born with full understanding and yet still, in the midst of deeply human experiences, felt the sting of emotion."

"What did she do?"

"She had to, like the rest of us, start at the beginning instead of at the end, to learn to see the beauty buried inside of pain, to recognize it as opportunity. To know choice, and then choose according to the greatest good, while loving her humanity at the same time. Not an easy thing to do."

I looked out at the sea, longing for escape. Unwinding my fingers from Bev's, I ran them through windblown hair then pulled my knees to my chest and hugged them close. There was nowhere to hide.

"Bev, you told me earlier that the locket was mine now, that I am meant to have it. Gil said something of the same to Jane. I have dreamt of a woman putting it around my neck." My words unfolded slowly, their significance growing as the picture of the puzzle came into focus. "Bev, what was the child's name?"

My eyes remained on the waters in front of me, as did hers.

"We called her Anna."

PART TWO: AWAKENING

CHAPTER TWENTY-TWO

A great chasm split open, an earthquake force that began as a shudder and spread violently outward. Entire walls crumbled while massive chunks of rock dislodged and fell noiselessly into an abyss. Small clefts grew into gaping holes of darkness, from which demons and ghosts flew in ecstatic release. And upon the ocean surface floated the debris.

Images of my life with Brian - our wedding, our lovemaking, his laughter and protection – floated by in a mist of foam, much like the images in a dream. I reached out, desperately grabbing for them, believing that they would save me, somehow sure that if I held on tightly enough I wouldn't have to follow the rocks into the abyss, that the creatures of darkness would not descend.

But the moment my fingers took hold of the images they vanished, melting into the sea, leaving behind the pungent scent and taste of blood. Repulsed, I pulled back my hands. Blood flowed from the center of each palm. I watched, terrified, horrified and fascinated as it formed red rivulets along my forearms, dripped from my elbows, and pooled at my feet.

I stared into the wound of my left palm. Black universes swam in a circle of ripped flesh. A tiny speck spiraled forward from the depths and stood suspended just inside the darkened hole. It was a seed, small and perfectly round, with a smooth, unflawed shell.

Suddenly, the shell cracked open and fell away, exposing a tiny fetus floating in the vast pool of space. It lay curled on its side, expanding and contracting with every beat of its heart. My tears watered the small life.

The interior caverns of my being continued to shatter, the blood continued to run, and I continued to cry. Tears fell into the blood and were washed away. And the seed of new life continued to grow.

Then a light filled the universe within my wound and cradled the fetus.

From inside the light came a voice: "In the midst of death, new life is born."

And in the flash of an eternity it was over.

CHAPTER TWENTY-THREE

The glare of a fading sun pressed sharply against my eyelids. With a start my body flew forward. I had been laying against the rocky shore, floating in an empty, silent sea, when suddenly the world tapped on my shoulder and shuttled me back to the third dimension. Words and images flooded in and my eyes opened, as the memory of flesh, wounded and woven in red, dripped into consciousness. Frantically I searched my palms, and then the horizon.

I thought I might throw up. My stomach was heaving, waves of nausea rolling over organs, muscles and bones, brought up from the pit of my soul. I bent my knees and held my head between them, the roots of my hair gripped in trembling hands. I was shivering, inside and out.

Bev was gone, or at least nowhere in sight. A heavy woolen blanket had been placed over me but I had thrown it off. I was angry that she had left me passed out on the beach after razing the last of my life's fragile foundation, and I was surprised that all around me weren't strewn the bits and pieces of my shattered identity. But most of all I was shaken by the desire for the earthquake to return, to finish the job it had started by blowing apart the final filament of awareness and deliver me into oblivion.

I waited, not knowing what else to do and feeling incapable of speech or movement. The piercing echo of a trapped scream rang in my ears, but remained, choked and strangled, in the cavern of my heart. Tears didn't even come to comfort me, only the cutting wind that accompanies the dying of day. I had no idea how long I had been out, but judging by the sun an hour or two.

A sound to my left, distant and faint, caught my attention. Turning my head so as to rest my cheek on my knees, I squinted in its direction. Someone was walking along the shore, moving purposefully closer. I was still shaking and racked with nausea, and my heart began to pound, but I hadn't the energy or the strength of spirit to move. I was paralyzed by the fear that it was Anna.

But it was Bev. When her shadow fell across me she knelt and stroked my hair.

"Get up Sara."

I shook my head violently.

"Come, I'll help you stand. I must go now and I'd like you to walk with me inside." It was not a command, but at the same time left no room for defiance.

She held out her hand and I took it, but my legs buckled under the weight. I tried again and this time was able to hold myself semi-erect and walk stiffly up the hill, down the path and into the house.

I knew I had questions, more to ask, to say, to protest. But I could hold no firm grasp on any one thought, could not bring to light the images, the story or its implications. Gone were the small specks of hope that had been with me over the past couple days, gone was my willingness to at least consider that the sun might rise on my life again. With one story everything changed. Now I could see only the shadow of things to come, the weight that had been placed, like a yoke, around my neck.

"*… the one chosen to continue my work.*"

I realized I wanted Bev gone and I wanted to be away from the house, from Maine, from anything that reminded me of the past week. Adrenalin pumped through my veins as a plan to run formed. As soon as Bev left I would grab only what was necessary, get in the car and drive. If I couldn't get a flight to Florida I would drive there, but no matter what, I was leaving.

We stood in the middle of the family room. I still had not spoken, my restlessness growing in the shade of her placidity. With arms crossed over my chest I avoided her searching eyes.

"I told you that I came here to tell you the story of the locket and to say goodbye to Anna. The first I have now done and must go to do the other. Do not think that I don't realize the magnitude of what I have shared with you. I do." She reached out and found my hand. Holding it between hers she added, "Just as I wished I could sweep away Anna's confusion and fear some thirty years ago, it is my wish that I could make this easier for you, perhaps even make it disappear. But I cannot. The greater course and purpose of our lives has long been written."

I said nothing. But I raised my eyes to hers and in them I know she saw the deep and brutal combat going on within.

Together we walked to the door, where she turned before leaving and once again reached for my hand. Into it she pressed the locket, and an envelope.

She walked down the sidewalk toward her car, but halfway there she stopped, and returned to where I stood. For the first time, age held her in its fist.

"Sara, I do believe that our greater stories are held in the heart of God, but know too that we have been given the power to choose. You stand now at the point where the circle both begins and ends. You must decide which way you will walk – into the dark or into the light. The trick is in realizing that each contains seeds of the other. So be careful in your choosing and do so not under the dominion of fear."

Her smile was warm but worried. She knew that some choose to turn from faith in the unfolding of life's promise, embracing instead the deceptive lure of calmer seas, those that hide in their waters the monsters of illusion.

"You may not be able to make it disappear, but I sure can." I spoke to Bev's retreating car. Once I was sure she was gone I ran inside and closed the door, the simple act carrying with it the resolution to lock out her words, as well as anything to do with Anna, the labyrinth, Jane, the locket or whatever force was trying to impose its will on me.

"It's crazy, they're crazy. And I don't want to be crazy. I just want to go home. Mom was right. It's better not to spend too much time alone. Crazy things start to happen. Like you let people fool you into believing in purpose and destiny and a God who cares. You do that and sooner or later the demands are made, the conditions set." I was walking around the bedroom, throwing clothes into a suitcase. I didn't expect to take everything, only enough to get away. The rest could be sent later, or maybe I would just donate it all and be done with it.

I moved without thinking, without alighting my mind on any face or feeling, until finally, with suitcase, purse, and keys in hand I stood at the front door, ready to go, and not looking back. I didn't want to remember, to stay too long or say goodbye. I had come to expect the unexpected. It was best not to give it time to occur.

As I turned the knob a photograph I had taken of Brian flashed before my eyes. It was my favorite, taken on our first trip to Maine. We were on Gorham Trail and he was sitting on a large rock facing the ocean. The picture captured his profile in perfect silhouette against a sky awash in the rosy light of dusk. Never had he looked so peaceful. I had left the picture on the bedside table, abandoned in my hurry to escape.

Without a second thought I dropped my bag and ran into the bedroom. Grabbing the picture I held it to my chest.

"I'm sorry Brian. You're the only thing I want to take with me from this place."

I tucked the photo under my arm and was scuttling through the door when my eyes darted toward the dresser. I kept moving forward, but something had registered and like a magnet drew me backward, returning me to the bedroom.

The room was growing dark, dressed in the pale colors of twilight. Colors that only served to illuminate the white and silver objects that demanded my attention. The locket and envelope Bev had pressed into my hand - discarded immediately, thrown off as if they were poisonous. Unfortunately I had gotten them only as far as the dresser.

"Damn. Damn you. Damn. Damn. Damn," I cursed the objects and all that they represented. And then with a sigh scooped them up, shoved them into my purse and headed toward the front door. But once again my attention was deterred. This time by the blinking red light on the answering machine.

With a grunt I slumped over to it, frustrated and irritated at being held back.

Into the air I said, "Okay, whoever's at the controls, stop it. I'm leaving and that's it. I'm checking out. I'll check this message, but nothing more."

I pushed the button, praying to whatever power might be on my side, that the message would be innocuous, like a solicitor or the IRS. My mother's voice was both a comfort and a relief. Never had I been so happy to feel guilty.

"Sara? Are you there? It's mom. Well, please call me. I don't know where you've been. We haven't heard from you in nearly a week. You haven't returned our calls, or your brother's. Please call and let us know that you're okay. Well, we love you. Bye." I hadn't been ignoring their messages, only too consumed to return them. And I didn't want to take the time to call now, to have to explain where I had been and why I was coming home so abruptly. I knew that if I just showed up and said I was home to stay, they would be thrilled, and wouldn't want to ask too many questions. If I couldn't get a flight I would call from the road, at a time when they'd most likely be out, so I could just leave a message. Ah, avoidance – my old friend.

After my mother's message ended I reached to turn off the machine, but before I could it beeped again and another voice filled the room. It floated about like remembered cologne from a time long past, one that awakens forgotten dreams, hopes and desires.

"Hi Sara, it's Mark. Just calling to say hi and, I admit, to hear your voice, even if it's just on the recorder. I also want to thank you for sharing yesterday with me. It was…great, though that's a pretty inadequate word. You'd think as a writer I could come up with something better. But I can't seem to. I'll work on it. Give me a call when you get a chance. Take care and I'll talk to you later."

"Oh God." I could feel it rising in my chest, pounding on the walls, demanding control. The creature. I couldn't let her free or she would hold me captive. My bottom lip began to tremble, hands to shake and eyes to burn. I stood in the center of my seaside home and fought the urge to scream, to fall to the ground, pound my fists and rage at the Heavens.

Like a hallway of doors shutting, one after the other, I tuned out the sound of Mark's voice, the feel of his heart pounding next to mine, the comfort of his arms and the fire in his eyes. In making the decision to leave it had been mandatory to fend off thoughts of him. They complicated both my reasons for going, and any I had for staying.

Somewhere in the murky bog of my mind was a truth I refused to shed light on, but it told me that my going was as much for Mark's sake as my own.

The sobs broke loose when I spoke, looking at the answering machine as if he could hear me. "I'm so sorry Mark. But I have to go. I can't say goodbye, because I might not be able to. I just have to go. I'll call you when I can bear to. I promise." My fingers were on my lips, trying to contain the surge of pain that was rising. I breathed deeply, kissed my fingers softly and lay them on the answering machine. With eyes closed I took one more breath, turned, picked up my suitcase and ran out the door.

CHAPTER TWENTY-FOUR

I got almost as far as the strip of Route 3 that connects Mount Desert Island to the mainland. All I had to do was follow the road to Ellsworth, then take Route 1 into Bangor. It was hardly more than an hour trip. I'd done it a dozen times before.

The radio blared and through quivering lips I sang to the music. Anything to drown out the voices in my head. Traffic was light. There weren't too many people left on Mt. Desert. It was cold and sunny. An all around beautiful day. One of the worst I could remember.

But it had all the makings of an easy trip. I was sure getting a flight to Boston would be a breeze, and from there it was little more than a two-hour flight home. But as is often the case, flights of fear are met with obstacles. Mine never even got off the ground.

The stop sign came from nowhere, a pebble in the shoe of my focused distraction. I plowed on the brakes, sending everything in the seat next to me hurling to the floor – jacket and books and all the contents of my purse. There was no one coming in either direction, so the stop was basically a moot point, but it succeeded in shredding my already frayed nerves. With shaking hands I pushed loose strands of hair behind my ears and wiped my tear-lined face. It was hot to the touch. Instead of pushing onward I put the car in Park and laid my forehead on the steering wheel and tried to breathe.

"Oh God, help me please. I have no idea what I'm doing."

I stayed glued to the steering wheel for several minutes, forgetting I was parked at a stop sign. When I raised my head I didn't change gears, but just sat numbly staring at the mess on the floor. After unhooking my seat belt I bent down and began to pick up the insignificant pieces of my life that had spilled from my purse: hair brush, broken sunglasses and crushed lip stick tubes, loose change, scraps of paper with numbers I no longer recognized and meaningless scribbled notes to myself on the back of old receipts. Amongst the clutter were hidden a few significant items – a picture of Brian, the key to our home in Florida, and a silly toy ring he had once given me. I took a moment to hold each item, hoping their solidity would remind me of what was real, but there were only textures and shapes, no stirrings, no connection – nothing.

Before shoving it all back into my purse I leaned down one final time and swept my hand beneath the seat. It knocked against something. I grabbed on and pulled. The locket.

I clenched it in my fist, wanting to squeeze tightly enough to break the delicate silver star, to crush its history and abolish its future.

With all the energy, anger and resentment I could muster I threw it back to the floor. It didn't break or disintegrate as I wanted, but it did pop open, exposing the picture of a young and already wise Anna. Immediately I bent, picked it up and cradled it in my hand.

The creature began to stir.

I moved to sit upright, and as I did, noticed the corner of the envelope peeking out from beneath the passenger seat. I bent again, retrieved it and placed it with the open locket on the seat next to me. I sat up again, put the car in Drive, turned right and quickly found a place to pull off.

It was inevitable. I was beginning to accept that at the very least I was going to have to read what Bev had written. But I could do it in my own way. So, I held it for a long time, and debated with myself about opening it or simply throwing it out the window. I even held it out the open window for a minute. The debate was inane, done only for my own satisfaction.

Finally, slowly, I slid my fingernail under the flap, reached in, unfolded the lightly scented, lavender paper, and began to read:

Dear Sara,
I write this as you journey inward to places I cannot follow,
along the pathway of your soul's search for answers. I wish

that I could tell you, and have you believe, that it knows where it is going.

Yes, Sara, what is happening is beyond the scope of usual understanding. Beyond the range of everyday comprehension. I am sure that your life, until recently, followed a certain pattern and that you trusted it to look a certain way. And now the landscape has drastically changed.

As we grow up we are given guidelines, or rules, by which we are to live. Early on they are set doggedly in place, steering us, helping us to navigate, keeping us on 'track,' and planting us firmly into the soil of our existence. They are given to us by our parents, reinforced by our society, religion and peers. They attempt to tell us who we are and who we should become. And some of these boundaries serve us well, at least in childhood.

But many of them only keep us from discovering the fullness of ourselves. They demand from us conformity - the unquestionable allegiance to what has been collectively deemed acceptable, 'normal,' and safe. They advocate ideas such as 'you must see it to believe it,' 'don't ask too many questions,' or 'don't doubt what you are told,' and judgments such as, 'women are weak and men are strong,' 'love is conditional,' 'there is not enough money, love or joy to go around,' and any others that cause us to believe we are small – less than we think, not more. Any that cause us to believe we are separate from one another and from God.

In order to uphold such doctrines man has developed rules and laws governing behavior, beliefs and most astoundingly – love, and these laws he calls truths. And the strangest thing of all is that he assumes his laws are identical to God's laws, which I believe, are more in line with the laws of nature, than those created by man.

So, all in one breath we are told that we are powerless before God, and yet that we must accept and believe, without question, that what has been written down by mortal men, in the name of fear, is God's truth.

Is it any wonder that when we experience something that we have no previously created context for, that is in direct opposition to what others have taught us and say is so, that is beyond explanation and scientific hypothesis, and which causes us to experience ourselves as powerful, purposeful and, brilliant, that we resist, shrink back and deny its validity? Denying our validity in the process?

I read through my tears, the pages shaking with the tremor of my hand. I could feel again the chasm within that had split. Nothing stood firm anymore. I resisted and applauded, turned away and ran toward.

But blessedly there comes a time for each of us when the mysteries call us forward, when a door opens and everything we have ever believed is called into question, from the ground beneath our feet, to the sky above.

And yes, my child, it means the tearing away of our entire foundation, which is probably what you have felt happening. And when this occurs we are left staring into the black hole of our lives asking, "Who am I?" and "What is left?" And it feels that there may be nothing more than a mass of unformed life and bits and pieces of rubble.

But, I give you this seedling of hope Sara – when you peel back the folds of illusion, you will find your truth.

"Yes, Bev, yes," I whispered to the flawless script, "all that is left is the rubble." Sighing I added, "But I don't understand. What is my 'truth' and how am I supposed to know the difference if illusion has always looked like truth?" Desperately I sensed there was nothing familiar to cling to.

And then, as if in direct answer…

I am aware that the concept of truth may seem vague, because it is not a fixed and tangible element. And though I wish I could, Sara, I cannot tell you what your truth is, except that it lives in your heart and you will know it when you hear or see it.

But I will tell you what it is not: it is not blind belief in what everyone else tells you or adherence to their expectations and roles set for you. And I can tell you what I believe about it – it lives in the fulfillment of your highest purpose. No one else can know or dictate what that is for you, just as you cannot know or dictate it for another.

Each person's truth is their own, it is the whispering of God within, the contract made between each of us and the creating force of the universe, which is forever guiding us toward the knowing and being of Love. So when you are trying to find Truth steeped in a world of illusion, listen and pick out the voice among the many that remains when the rest have run in fear, for that is the voice of Love, the one that comes from God.

And when I speak of love I speak of Love that is unconditional, that does not seek reward, or anything else, but only gives of itself freely and without restriction, expectation, limitation or fear. It is Truth and Love that open the doors to our destiny, it is that which guided you to Anna, to the locket, to this house, this town, your marriage – every step that has led you here, and will lead you forward.

If you listen you will hear, if you watch closely you will see the next step set before you. It's already there, you need only step out in faith and it will rise to meet you. But you must take the step, Sara. It is only by becoming involved in the process that you will ever experience the current of truth in your life, the current that promises the greatest knowing of joy available.

Ultimately, the choice is yours.

It is time for me to go. Now, from this page, and this home on the sea that I have loved. And soon, I know, from this life. My body is old, in human terms, dear Sara, and it is beginning to grow weak. But the timeline of the body means nothing. The truth is that I have done my work here. I have been given a blessed many years and God has been generous in Her gifts. It is, as this season taught me long ago, time for that which has come before to make room for that which is coming into being.

And though there is much that I will miss, I will go to what awaits with a full and open heart, and with open arms greet the next adventure. I do not know if I will be there to meet Anna, or she me, but there is a profound joy in knowing we will be together.

And in knowing that only Love is real.

> *With Love and the Blessings of Light,*
> *Bev*

The words dissolved in puddles of blue. Though I couldn't see them, they rang in my ears. My heart, my head, my very core, ached with sadness and longing – the longing to move forward, to go backwards, to forget and to remember. These women – Bev, Anna, and Jane – accepted life and all its light and darkness openly and without fear. They were happy, like I had never been. They were brave and strong and filled with the energy of the earth and the Heavens. They believed in an essential goodness and grace, a divine and noble force that would forever lead them to Love.

And two of them would soon be gone.

How could I accept what they were trying to teach? How could I ignore the burning acid in my stomach that demanded to know why everything beautiful in life died? Why the good perished and every lesson had to hurt so much.

And why was it that life suddenly asked so much of *me*?

An entire history and so many lives siphoning into mine, placing their future upon my shoulders. I wasn't strong enough to hold the weight.

My insides were itching. I had to move. I threw open the door and jumped out, wanting to run, to feel my blood pumping and muscles working. But I couldn't disrobe my self-consciousness. The creature continued to writhe, to seek escape. I had to do something. Looking around and seeing no one I slipped into the car, closed the door, gripped the steering wheel, and screamed, long and loud.

It was a wail that reached out across the fibers of time and space, and was echoed back by the voices of all whom had ever heard Life calling, and knew not how to find, or rather feared, the answer.

The creature grew silent, but did not sleep. Throwing the car into Drive I swung around and headed, not towards Bangor and the airport, but in the opposite direction. I drove, letting my hands guide the wheel. Blurs of browns and greens flew by me, sleeping trees, and homes with smoke curling from chimneys – pieces of life that had no room for me.

All I could see were shards of images coming at me like daggers. Slivers of conversations, fragments of stories told, fitting together in a tale as unbelievable as any Greek myth or Grimm fairy tale. What I realized as each particle slipped into place was that it would never go away. A painting was being emblazoned on the canvas of my life and I in no way felt like the artist. Someone had made a huge mistake in choosing this path for me, but I seemed unable to get anyone to listen. I was terrified. I had no idea how to accept what was unfolding, and had no idea what to do with it. What I needed was someone to tell me, to hold me up and play Geppetto to my Pinocchio. But who? Everyone I knew here was somehow touched by this mystery.

...one chosen to continue my work.

...one chosen...

...one chosen...

The words drummed a foreboding beat on my cells. Everything within and without vibrated with a terrifying energy.

As I drove, clouds gathered above, dark pools that made the black of night more ominous. I drove without seeing, without willful direction. But led, nonetheless, in purposeful direction, inspired by unseen forces that had picked up the strings and were now mastering this puppet show.

The car sped across asphalt, shadows whizzing by, and just as it spun into the drive the skies opened up. Rain pummeled the windshield. But it only added power to the energy that pulled me forward. Squealing to a stop I shoved the car into Park and flew out into the rain, oblivious to the stinging cold nettles striking my skin.

I ran, full throttle across the lawn, down the hill, until I stood drenched and breathless before the labyrinth.

Tilting my face upward, I welcomed the icy bullets of rain. My chest heaved and with each breath the walls of the prison crumbled, until the sobs came. I fell to the ground and clawed my fingers into the mud in front of me.

Anger, like a match ignited, flared upward, and lifted me tall onto my knees, fists raised in challenge to the forces of nature. With rainwater and tears flowing over my face and neck I screamed into the sky, "Why are you doing this? What do you want from me? How dare you 'choose' me for anything! Who am I that you would do this?"

I expected, truly expected, something, some voice or thundering answer. But there was nothing. Only the sound of wind and rain. And my breath and heartbeat.

But I refused to go unheard. If there was a God, He or She was going to listen.

"Come on coward. Whoever you are. You've played with my life long enough. Tell me, damn you, what do you want from me?" My hands moved to my face, smearing it with gritty mud, and ran through my long wet hair. The creature invoked.

Bringing dirt-streaked arms out in front of me with wrists up, as if in offering, I demanded, "My blood? Is that what you want? My flesh and bones?

"Or is it my soul? Is that it? My soul?" Choking sobs racked my body until my arms fell limp by my sides and finally I melted to the earth, chest lowered to knees, my face in my hands – bowed, spent and broken, at the altar of my demons.

I stayed curled in that position for several minutes, waiting for the hand of fate to be dealt. The rain continued to fall and somewhere in the distance thunder grumbled. The Heavens roaring at my blasphemy.

A chill passed through me and slowly I raised my head. As I did a short spasm of blue light filled the sky, illuminating the path stretched before me.

"Fine. Whatever it is you want, take it." And with a resolution empowered by sheer desperation I moved onto my hands and knees and crawled the few steps to the entrance of the labyrinth.

CHAPTER TWENTY-FIVE

My feet retraced the steps taken only two days before. Hollow darkness saturated my skin with as much brutality as the rain. Cold seeped malignantly through my clothes and into every pore, washing away all that was within, until I was turned inside out and emptied. Until all that was left for me to do was blindly follow the trail wherever it would lead.

Sparks of lightning were my beacons. As I rounded the first corner the sensations of body that had possessed me on the first journey began to take over. A vibrational shiver started low and moved upward and outward until I was shaking uncontrollably. The air was frigid but I had become numb to it, blind to all but the experience of walking. The shaking magnified to the point that I feared that my heart, and all other organs, might explode. It was as if something inside refused to stay restrained and still any longer, something nonphysical that required greater space than flesh would allow.

The sensations – palpating heart, sweating, trembling hands, strangled breathing – were intensified by the storm and night. With each step I returned to the depths of my physical being. Just as before I spiraled through layers of skin, muscle, bone and organ, into a black hole of space in the center of the self. Into the void the voices whispered and then wailed, "Release me, release me, release me." And with the plea came the images, the visions of my pained and imprisoned body.

It took every scrap of will I had not to run at the first sight of the dark murkiness named Disease. But instead I moved deeper, swallowed by the nothingness. Pain ripped through me, and I was brought to my knees. Gasping for air I clawed at the walls of my tender, aching, inner cavern. And just when I thought I could take no more another voice broke through my body's haunting cries. It was Mark's voice, carried in on a wave of new memory.

"*...don't close yourself to what is around you. Open to it, allow your energy to meet it, not shrink from it...*"

Breathe. He had told me to breathe.

"*Our bodies are starving for attention...they need the breath to connect to the powers of healing and wisdom that reside within.*"

Ever so slowly I brought my attention to the moment. I moved to my feet and planted them firmly. With courage I did not actually feel I raised my head, pushed back my shoulders, and inhaled deeply. The stench of neglect brought tears to my eyes, but I didn't waver. Again I pulled the air around me deep into my lungs, filling them from the bottom to the top, and exhaling fully. Over and over I repeated the cycle.

At first each outbreath caused my body to convulse. But little by little it subsided. Until all there was, was the quiet swoosh of air coming in and going out. Everything else faded benignly into the background. The shift was subtle, happening the way daylight turns to dusk.

Breath by breath I watched as my body responded. First the pungent smell became diffused, weakening, if not disappearing. Then the voices, once so frightening, began to alter, taking on a tone of impassioned liberation. Like a chorus lifting its song to Heaven and feeling the breath of the Divine upon its face.

Looking around I saw the walls of my organs and bones, my entire inner structure moving in rhythm to my breath. I could feel how starved it was, but the longer and deeper I breathed the more relaxed the beat became. Tears ran down my face.

When the symphony moved into a new and developing harmony, I began to breathe more naturally, more deeply and slowly. There remained a degree of pain and darkness, but by standing in the is-ness of what was, and not running from it, I had perhaps taken the first step toward healing my outer self.

Could the scars of the spirit also be so healed?

The thought echoed around me. As I tried to hold it in my mind I blinked, and when my eyes opened I found myself returned to the labyrinth.

Disoriented and bewildered, the raindrops, plopping into puddles at my feet, served to pull me back. I was shaken, afraid that either madness was taking hold, or that it wasn't. And I wasn't sure which was worse. But either way, I couldn't go back, of that I was finally sure. There was no other choice but to continue deeper into the labyrinth.

So, with a fleeting hope that the worst was behind me, I looked down the path and prepared to put one foot in front of the other.

It seemed to happen in exact concert with my foot hitting the ground on my first step. The hostile missiles of unyielding rain slackened. Not enough to escape their aim, but enough to feel a difference. I took it as a hopeful sign, that perhaps the center was closer than I thought.

But before my third step was taken the next blow was thrown, this one striking like an uppercut to the gut. I doubled over, struggling for breath. When finally I could stand upright again I squinted into the menacing darkness in search of my attacker. Shadows danced about mockingly, punching and jabbing – sleek, agile enemies of the night. Blindly I walked with my arms out in front, fending off invisible monsters, not knowing where or when the next would strike. Images of the Minotaur ran through my mind.

With each footfall the night grew darker, colder and a sharpened sense of fear escalated. It wrestled itself around my throat, cutting off the scream that rose from the gutters of my inner well. Like a shroud, terror came and lay upon me, its heaviness suffocating.

I had bumped into Fear and fallen headlong into his open arms, which seemed to be awaiting my surrender. At first I struggled to free myself from their powerful embrace, but they fit like a straight jacket, pinning me against the wall of my inner fortress.

My arms and legs were rendered immobile, useless without the ability to flee. I closed my eyes, my ears, whatever I could to keep from facing Fear. Every time I turned my face from his he would run long, cold, bony fingers down my cheek, digging sharp blackened nails into my neck. If I tried to scream he held his hand over my mouth, forcing me to swallow the bile of terror I wanted to spit out. From side to side I whipped my head, refusing to give in, to do what he wanted and let him inside of me.

For my entire life I had felt his presence, forever walking beside me, behind me, dancing around me. He taunted, threatening every moment of joy with his power to destroy. Fear was the great blackmailer who dared me to trust too much in goodness and love, in faith and God, and most especially in my own power and worth, for if I did he would descend and whisper in my ear the hymn of the undeserving, the sermon of the selfish, and with a gleeful laugh demand homage to his altar. For if I did not remember him in all things, he would see to it that everything I wished for and loved would be destroyed. And I would be left alone. Sacrificed for my irreverence.

And so I had always, even in the midst of being happy, remembered to be a little afraid, like I walked perilously on a tightrope between grace and annihilation. And it was my adherence to the Laws of Fear that kept me from being pushed over the edge. He had been the deity I had chosen, but I had kept him at arm's length - agreeing to supplicate my will to his, but refusing to look him in the eye, to see his face in full form and know from what depth he had been born.

I hated him. Not because of the demands he made upon me, but because he had not kept his end of the bargain. I had been his blind and unwavering servant. And still Brian had been taken and my life destroyed. Where was the justice? I had been good and compliant. Never asked too many questions, or demanded too much from anyone. I had worked hard to keep conflict at bay, to please the gods of fortune and peacekeeping, to be seen and not heard. I had done all that Fear wanted me to, and he had betrayed me.

Anger rose. Dark and primeval. From the lowest places in my being it began to squirm and vibrate into life. With every hot and foul breath that Fear shot into my face, Anger grew. Until I no longer felt the shape of my own mind, but was given over completely to the creature that had for so long stirred within. I had never known it by name, never allowed myself to get close enough, even in those moments when it reared its head. But now it had taken over, and there was no way to dismiss or deny it, or to turn away. Its name was Anger and it held me in its jaws.

It surged upward from the bowels of Hell, and with the force of an inner tidal wave plunged through my blood, stretching into my limbs, wearing my skin as a wolf does fur. A sound, not scream nor sob, but wild and animalistic – a howl as base and primal as man's origins – rose from murky, bottomless depths and pushed out, as though birthed from the womb of creation.

I did not simply feel anger - I was Anger. With his voice and power coursing through me I drew myself up and turned toward Fear with the fierceness of a wild animal held captive. It came in gut-wrenching sound, in clenched fists swinging and legs kicking; it came from the center of my physical self, and the center of my soul, in wave upon wave of venomous, repressed rage.

Before my eyes flashed the fuel of my fire – images of death: mangled cars, ripped and bloody clothes, and Brian, lying too still on a cold metal table. Images of nights spent alone with no one to hear the scream reverberating in the hollows of my chest. Images of my parents, my family and friends, tiptoeing around me, their scared, worried faces, protecting their own discomfort more than mine. Images of laughter never to be heard, tears never to be shed, children never to be born, and love never to be made.

I swung with a force I'd never known I had, the force of fury that had lived inside my cells, trapped and hidden from the light of day. Fury that had been pounding against the walls of my flesh, demanding release. It had been Anger, at least partially, that had been ravaging my body. Anger that my breath had given life to.

I punched and howled. The images continued, each slashing deeper and deeper, past the surface of my psyche and into the black hole of my soul. If I had been able, I would have been horrified, would have asked myself what right I had to feel such things, especially towards those who loved me. But Anger saw to it that there was room for none of this, for nothing but his pure, unadulterated release. And the images only became more horrifying.

There was Brian. Not his death, but him. And the image of his beautiful face made me mad. Viciously mad. The beastly noises turned for the first time, to words.

"Damn you. How dare you die on me! How dare you leave me here alone! You know that I need you, that I don't know how to do this without you! Damn you. I hate you for leaving. Do you hear me – I hate you!"

Before the last word was spit out, the image changed. It was of me, lying on the dirt floor of the labyrinth, quivering with fear, tears streaming down my face. Again the viper hissed.

"And you, you I hate even more. What the fuck is wrong with you? You are so weak, such a child. Get up, damn you, you coward, get up and fight! Don't just lie there drowning in your own tears. Can't you do anything for yourself? Are you that weak and worthless? You are, aren't you? No wonder your life is falling apart. No wonder Brian left you."

And then, for the final time, the scene shifted.

I was in a church, kneeling at the altar. It was a church I had never seen before, a moment in time that had never occurred, but the words I heard myself mumbling were words I knew well. It was less a prayer than a plea, sent out to God, begging to know why Brian had been taken, why I had been left.

As I focused on the cross that hung above the altar Anger surged upward once again - stronger, deeper, as though the bottom of the well had been reached. All at once I felt it swell, mount and rush forward, through my abdomen and into my heart, where, with a white-hot force, it exploded. I lurched forward, as if hit by lightning, and fell hard to the ground. Anger, its head tilted to the sky roared, with a volume and intensity that shattered the fragile veil between realities.

When the sound waves had skirted past perception I opened my eyes, and found myself actually kneeling before the altar. Above me hung the cross, suspended from the ceiling, glinting in the refracted rainbows of stained glass windows. There was silence, the silence of the absolute and infinite, found only in the void of space and time, its pureness painful to the ears.

I was shocked by where Anger had taken me. He was still present, fuming beneath the surface, but I had been given into the keeping of something even more powerful. I looked up at the cross and began to cry.

The tears were as silent as the space around me. With each one that fell I could hear Anger's now desperate whisper.

"You were supposed to take care of me. You were supposed to protect me, and Brian, but you didn't. You took him from me. Why? Why did you do that?"

My chin fell to my chest. My fists clenched, but when I spoke, the words were barely audible. "I am so angry at you. So angry I don't want to believe you even exist. Because if you do - if you do, then you must have taken him purposefully, knowingly. And you must have created me to be weak and fearful. You must have given me all of this hateful fear and guilt. You must have abandoned me. And why would you do that? Are you that vengeful, that cruel, that uncaring? Or is it me? Is it what I deserve? Did I not do everything I was supposed to? Have I not been, am I not now, good enough?"

And then beyond even that, beneath the anger of Brian's death and life's injustices, lay the seed, wrapped in sheaths of anger to hide the bottomless well of sorrow. It came, bringing with it rivers of sadness, pain, confusion, and fear. It came as a memory of home, the home before the womb. It came, in the end, as longing, and as love.

"Oh, my God, my dear God. Why did I have to leave your side? Why did You send me away? I love you so much, and I long to return to your arms. I want to come Home. It is too hard here. Too empty, lonely, disconnected. Nobody remembers. Even I've forgotten."

And then, with one final burst of fury I lifted my chin, fixed my eyes on the cross, and screamed.

I screamed until I was empty and spent, until there was no line between sound and matter. I raised my voice and sent it into the silence, where it was picked up and carried into the web of the collective, to become part of the symphony of anguish and alienation that had been recorded over the course of all history, and still traveled through the ethers.

When the last note had left my throat I crumbled to the floor, and came to rest on marble steps that led to the altar. My forehead lie against the cool stone now soaked with tears. The scream's echo reverberated through my mind, and when it finally faded, the sound of the silence was startling.

What could be left in such emptiness? I had gone past exhaustion, past the flesh and blood and bone of Anger. I had descended so deep into my own waters that I had reached the place, I thought, where nothing could live, where only the dark survived.

But there was something there, something small that lay shivering upon the sandy floor. It was helpless, rolled into a ball, and more frightening to me than the cold hands of Fear or the fiery breath of Anger.

And yet, when it slid silently inside of me it felt almost comforting. It brought with it images of Brian and all that I had ever loved and believed was lost.

It wrapped itself around my heart, squeezing until it was absorbed, until my heart began to bleed, the blood released in the shape of tears.

I cried and I sobbed. The pureness of Grief, of Sadness and Sorrow - for what had been and was no longer, for what would never be, and for all I still longed for and knew not how to find – rolled through me like the crashing waves of the sea. I gave unto the emptiness all that was left of who I had believed myself to be. And when no more would come I entered willingly into the void, opening my arms, my legs, my body and being to welcome the vacant hollow of sweet nothingness.

I sensed the presence as much as felt its touch. Somehow I knew who it was, knew that I could never have run fast or far enough, or hid well enough to escape his clutches, not even in the void. Even when I thought there was nothing left, it was still there.

Slowly I turned to look at the hand that had settled on my shoulder. I expected it to be gnarled and ugly, to clench my flesh tightly in its cold, unfeeling grip. I expected to be whipped up and thrown back to the ground, to be trampled and pummeled, and left to die. But I was mistaken. I had always been mistaken.

The hand that rested on my shoulder, the hand of Fear, was small and fragile. It was the hand of a child. Shocked I moved to touch it, to feel if it was real. The pale, delicate flesh was warm beneath my hand. I raised my eyes and turned.

She wore a robe of black, the hood pulled low to hide her features. Several times I reached out to push back the hood, but each time stopped short. It was she who finally, with timorous hands, removed the cloak.

When I came to look upon the face of Fear, an avalanche of understanding fell upon me. It was the face of a child. And she was me.

"I have spent many years trying to catch up to you. To get you to hear me, to look at me. But you would never slow down, you would always run away."

My voice was a shudder. "But who…what…my God, you look exactly like me as a child. You…you even sound as I did."

With sad, ageless eyes she studied me, and then answered. "Don't you see? I am you. I am the you that holds the fear, that was inseminated with it and gives birth to it each and every day."

She may have looked like a child, but her essence was both tired and wise.

"I…I don't know what you mean."

"Yes, you do. You just choose not to. You have chosen to see fear as a horrible monster over which you have no control - no relationship or responsibility to. But the exact opposite is true. Only you have the power to release me. You see, I was born centuries ago, the same time that Love was given to earth in human form, but I remain a child because to grow up spiritually – to live one's own truth - is to transform fear into Love. I am the wounded child that lives inside each human being. And inside all of human consciousness. I do not mean you harm, though that is what you believe. In truth it is through man's continued misunderstanding and forgetting of Love, through the harm you do to one another and to yourselves, both consciously and unconsciously, that I was consummated and am fed.

225

"Every time, when you were young, beginning before you can even remember, that you were denied love, I was nourished. Every word, look and deed that said to you that love has to be earned, that it is only given under specific conditions, that whatever another did or felt is your responsibility, sent energy to me. Every feeling you had that was labeled unacceptable, every intuitive response belittled, every honest moment denied, became my playground. Until there came a time when I was given the reigns and asked to rule the kingdom. When this was done, you moved into my world."

My heart lodged in my throat, my words small and burst forth on a wave of pain, "Your world?"

"Yes. In my world the walls are thick, the sky low, the rules rigid. In my world, you are safe, but you are not free. As long as you live under my dominion, you will be as close to death as you are to life."

"But then how...how do I break free? How do I let go of you?" And then, helplessly looking around at the elaborate setting, "I mean, my God, I don't even understand how any of this is happening. I have no idea what is going on or how to begin to..." The words were breathless, desperate and as I spoke I realized that my hands clung to the black wool of her robe.

She knelt before me on the floor and took my hands in hers.

"We - you and by reflection I - have always sought to understand, and yet feared the understanding. For to understand this," she swept her arms wide, "is to believe in a world far larger, far deeper than ever imagined. It also asks more from you – expects you to live a larger, deeper, truer life, and that is only done by stepping out of my world and risking it all - your heart, your relationships, your very life. It means walking to the edge and raising your voice to the wind and trusting that it will be heard, and knowing that though you might stumble, you will ultimately experience a life free from the chains and shackles of fear. But it also takes understanding that fear is a gift, given to show you what you yearn for most, for encased in our fear, is our greatest longing. And ultimately it is about believing that you deserve what it is you long for."

Before I could respond she withdrew one tiny hand and placed it on the top of my head. Immediately a jolt of energy pierced through me.

"You ask how to let go, how to free yourself from me. You are asking the wrong question. I have followed you, haunted you for so long, not because you have failed to get rid of me, but because you have refused to see me clearly. Understand, you *cannot* get rid of me. That is not the answer."

Her open palm remained on my head, the energy sweeping across my inner terrain. As she began to speak again, in hushed whispers, she moved her hand so that it rested over my heart.

"Open your heart, and with it look into the heart of the child you were."

Memories of days past uprooted from my cells and drifted across the mind's movie screen. Still moments of the child I had forgotten, of the girl and young woman I had left behind. Some so small they barely registered as a ripple in the ocean, but whose accumulation over the years had altered the natural direction of the water's flow. Scenarios of rejection, words of judgment, looks of disdain, expectations unmet, disappointments felt, dreams abandoned and a lifetime of unexpressed truth. I watched as a persona was created at the expense of authenticity, for the sake of a peaceable kingdom. It was, in a sense, the creation of Camelot. Brick by brick the walls went up – safeguards against a world where a sensitive soul could easily perish, where wanting too much or diving too deep meant drowning under the weight of illusions carefully erected by Fear's henchman.

Resentment flared. Voices of blame rang out, seeking to destroy all who had participated, all who had helped to lay the brick. It seeped out of dark dusty corners and raced into my bloodstream. The release was exquisite. Resentment, like Anger, was something I had never dared feel.

But the surge of emotion crested and rolled away, as another layer was peeled back and I was allowed to see behind the facades of those at whom I had pointed fingers. Behind their proclamations of contentment, behind broad smiles and reproaches for tears, behind their demand that I keep beat with Convention's Army, was the small timid face of Fear. The fear of breaking cadence and walking a path alone, unprotected and unaccepted by the masses, the fear of speaking, acting and living truthfully, of embracing Love as readily as they had

Fear. Looking closely I could see her in the shadow of all the faces of those who marched blindly in step, following a well-worn path and further marking it for generations to come.

And even deeper, alive and cradled protectively in the arms of Grace, I could see their longing, pulsating to their inner beat. It was the longing to do just what they feared – to step away from the pack, to bid farewell to those things that drew lines in the sand, and walk into the stream of unlimited potential and possibilities, to live an untethered life that followed the passions, the rhythms, the ecstatic dance of the Spirit. And manifested it - lovingly, wildly, compassionately - through flesh.

A life that honored the truth. A life that answered the call. And in doing so remembered that Love was all there had ever really been.

Like a flower blossoming in the spring, my heart opened. So clearly I saw the pain and the fear that ran underground, a current flowing beneath humanity's history and its present, threatening its future. I saw how it held my loved one's in its grip. How I too had been held and had chosen to follow, to deny and eventually become deaf to my own inner murmurings, and ultimately refusing to take courageous responsibility for this life that had been given to me.

Compassion came in on the wings of understanding. The chains that had bound my heart snapped and a great rush of Love spilled forth. I began to sob, not the sobbing of personal pain but sobbing for the universal whole that vibrated with a single yearning, but so wrongly felt itself to be alone and without choice.

And then, looking again into the marching crowd, I saw my own small, fragile frame – the image of the child I had been before Fear had completely taken control. She followed, her steps out of line, trying desperately to get it right. Watching her, my heart ached. How hard she worked to stay in step, to fit in, to keep from getting run over. Several times she tripped, stumbled, and started the count again, glancing about embarrassingly, hoping no one saw how lost and lonely she was. I wanted to run to her, hold her in my arms and gently guide her away from the group. I wanted to tell her that it was okay to walk at her own pace, in her own rhythm. I wanted to tell her I loved her and I was sorry.

Could I? Could I return to this child and fill the gaps left by so much time? Was I strong enough, good enough to love and support her, to tell her what she needed to hear and make her the promise she deserved? I didn't know, but if I was ever to try, the time was now.

Tentatively I moved toward my younger self, the image becoming real as I neared. Amazed, I stood on the periphery of the marching masses, and found sickening the sound of their heels clicking in unison against the pavement. At first I couldn't find her in the crowd, but with gathering strength I persisted. Suddenly she was right in front of me, as though she had been looking for me all along.

I grabbed her the way you would snatch someone from a burning building, concerned only about saving the life they had yet to live. I kneeled before her, held her delicate shoulders and looked into eyes filled with terror. And relief. Somewhere inside she understood what I had done and she was grateful. In wonder and amazement I studied her. Could I have ever been so young, so innocent, so real? Had there really ever been a time when my own rhythm was more natural than the one prescribed by others?

Yes! With a sudden burst of joy I knew there had been. Leaning down I hugged her tightly, love and compassion overflowing, moving from my heart into hers. Beneath my embrace she first resisted, went rigid and then slowly melted and wrapped her skinny arms tightly around me. Small warm tears drifted down my neck. My own fell over her hair. Lovingly I stroked them away.

Into her ear I whispered, "I am sorry for your confusion and your pain. For your loneliness and your fear. You are not alone. I promise you. Just look inside your heart – there is a strong and loving force within you that will carry you forward, that will give you what you need to face whatever you must. And when you get down the path a way, I will meet you, and when I do, I make you this promise: I will honor and love you; I will remember that force and use it to continue the journey. I will not return to the march but will grow, will move ever more into the natural rhythm of our own step. I will walk in quest for what is true, and I will do my best to courageously claim our place in this world – according, not to convention, but to the compass inside of us that is guided by God. I have ignored it, but I know, I know it has not stopped working." Hugging her closer, crying tears of loss and purification, I felt us begin to merge.

In that instant I was filled with the wisdom of all I had ever known, and saw how much I had misunderstood, misinterpreted, and forgotten. But instead of being possessed by Anger, Resentment or Fear, I felt only the beautiful truth of Love, the healing force of Compassion.

When she looked up at me and smiled I could see in her eyes a knowing, a re-membering with Love.

Together we looked back at the parade of soldiers. My eyes fell upon a face that was not directed straight ahead, but rather peered over the shoulders of the others to see what lay beyond. He noticed us, his expression holding the longing openly, but he didn't move. As we scanned the crowd I started to notice other eyes meeting mine, some cautiously, but others firmly, holding the gaze, silently passing to me the message that there were those carrying the flame and passing it on. The longer I watched the more I became aware of this faction of revolutionaries. They walked on the edge of the crowd, disengaged but still part of the whole. Some of the faces began to look familiar – teachers, friends, acquaintances whose paths had crossed mine. And there they were: Sheila, Greg, Jane, Bev, Gil, and Mark. I laughed – the truest, deepest laugh I had ever known. I wanted to jump up and down, wave and tell them that I understood.

But before I was able, another face caught my attention. It seemed to glow, illuminated by a golden light that reached out to touch me. As he passed, his eyes connected with mine, and he winked. Love and longing swept over me. I reached out to meet the light, but he just smiled and continued his stride. Brian. My beautiful Brian.

My heart swelled and threatened to burst, touched by the exquisite grace of what I was witnessing, the hope embedded in what had appeared as tragedy. I saw how there were and always had been keepers of the flame. The brave and devoted, those who were willing to fight the good fight, using love, forgiveness, compassion and truth as their only weapons. Brian was one, even now. And the numbers were growing. Someday they would outnumber the harvesters of Fear, and when that happened the shell would crack, the march would stop and…the possibilities sent shivers up and down my spine.

Next to me my child-self fluttered. To my astonishment, without even a glance in my direction, she walked back into the mainstream.

"No!" I screamed and grabbed for her, but the image had become only that, no longer tangible. All I could do was watch helplessly as she returned to her faltering step. But then I saw that there was something, some small shift in her gait, in her carriage.

She had taken her place. As much as I hated it I knew that it was what was necessary, what was right. My eyes kept pace with her for several steps until she moved passed me and all I could see was the back of her head. Just before she moved out of sight I noticed next to her a violet ripple. Focusing, I smiled. Above the purple haze was a tangle of black hair. The last I saw of them was a strong, slender hand reaching out to take a small, timid one.

And the last thing I heard before darkness descended, like the curtain at the end of a show, was the voice of Fear.

"And now the challenge becomes for you to choose – will you take *your* place? Will you keep your promise? Will you remember, or once again forget that there *is* a choice? Whatever happens, I give you this: I, Fear, am not your enemy, any more than Anger or Sorrow, or Grief is. There is no choice you can make that will ensure you freedom from us, for we are, at least for now, a part of the human experience. You may either give us control through your very resistance, and thereby remain on life's sidelines, never knowing the real prize. Or you may embrace Compassion, for yourself and others in the face of suffering, while accepting and learning from us what we can teach, and discovering within yourself the spark of Divinity that will ensure your survival, and much, much more. But you must choose. Each and every day, you must choose…"

CHAPTER TWENTY-SIX

There is always the memory of waking.

First was the feel of the earth, made soft and supple from the rain that was now all but gone. Like an old favorite glove it held me in its palm. Next was the infusion of the dark into every sense. When my eyes opened it was as if they remained closed. And only then came the realization that I wasn't scared. I was, in fact, visited by the finest shroud of peace I had ever known. It rested upon my bones, its filaments reaching in subtly and binding to my blood. There resided in my heart a seed that began to sprout and grow. It was the long lost, long awaited return of Calm. Not passivity or paralysis, but a calm imbued with delight.

I lay on the ground, covered in the mud of the labyrinth floor, drenched and alone in the middle of a winter's night. And never had I been as content. There was, to be sure, the inclination to run out and find whomever I could, to tell them what had occurred, what I had seen and heard. Like Scrooge on Christmas morning I had awoken with new understanding and was eager to share the news. But more than anything I wanted simply to absorb the gift I had been given. There were still many questions, things I did not understand, but for the moment none of that mattered. All that mattered was the extraordinary peace and hope that I felt.

So, for an indistinguishable amount of time I allowed myself to just be. To lie inside the rapture, letting the almost erotic fingers of joy caress my body and soul. Every breath was like a drink from life's cup of grace. Greedily I gulped. With each sip another part of me awoke until my senses were on fire, resurrected from their deathly slumber. I inhaled deeply the sweet, languid scent that drifted in from the sea to be expired by the dew. I became aware of the way the air, carrying with it all of it's memories, smells, tastes and sounds, settled upon my skin, brushing the fine hairs, rolling over my nose, eyelashes and ears.

Drawing fingertips together I was entranced by the heat flowing between them. The energy of life. It was everywhere, all around me. Examining closer I thought I could actually see the threads of the web – an intricate interweaving of energy, alive between my hands. There, in that small, encapsulated space was the stuff of all life, pulsing with heat and humming with song. I wondered at, with a child's delight, and at the same time knew, with a new wisdom, the source of the music. And in that knowing, for the first time in perhaps my entire life, I felt both truly safe and completely free.

At some point the hand of either time or awareness or another force unseen, was placed upon my shoulder, reminding me that I had farther to go. Part of me eagerly anticipated what was yet to come, while another, slightly larger part, resisted. I didn't want to lose this moment, this feeling. What if it didn't come again?

Without even realizing it I began to walk, all the while caught up in the questions, the doubts, the worries. How did I go out into the world without forgetting and keep the feeling of freedom and faith alive? How could I be sure I could keep my promise, that I would have the strength each day to choose courage, compassion, truth and love? Especially in the presence of those and those things that countered everything I had seen and learned.

When finally, startled by the loud cry of a bird, I looked up, and out from the churning wheels of my mind, I was shocked to find that light had begun to yawn. I could see what was before and around me, and how far I had come.

Wide-eyed I stared. All of the trappings of fear, a habit hard lost, melted like wax from the heat of a candle flame. I had been given my answer. A cross, like the one I had seen earlier, stood in the labyrinth's center. Entering the space was a sacred experience in itself. It had been carved into the shape of a six-petal flower, and in it there was nothing but the cross - even the flowers that grew along the labyrinth walls ceased blooming. The eyes I had begun the journey with would have been disappointed, seeing only barrenness and loneliness, but the eyes with which I beheld it saw exquisite beauty in the simplicity.

Above, the clouds had parted, creating a hole in the silvery sky from which shafts of white light flowed. The rays, like beacons in the dawn mist, reached out and landed upon and around the cross. I moved toward it, each step stripping away the remaining debris, leaving me naked and unafraid. When I stood under the shadow of the cross I cupped my hands and dipped them into the light. Bringing them to my lips, I imagined I could drink in its source. Humbly I stood, bathed in the purest, most beautiful presence I had ever felt, or imagined to exist.

Speechless, breathless, I fell to my knees and cried. I thought of Brian. Of how beautiful it all was. How I wished him there. And I cried.

And into my mind the words sounded. *"In the center, beneath the all and the nothing, there is the still, simple truth: all is Divine, nothing is lost, and Love is the source. God is above you and around you, but most of all, God is within you. You are, and have always been, the creation and the creator...the monster of your own nightmares, and the savior of your dreams. In the end, as in the beginning you are held in the hand of Love. Forever and ever, Amen."*

Kneeling, my hands held in prayer, I felt the warmth of the light pouring into the top of my head, like water from a pitcher, feeding every cell. And when I believed I must be full and no more grace was possible I sensed a shift. No longer did it feel like the light was being given to me, but rather that it was being pulled up from within. The sleeping snake at the base of my spine wriggled into life and slowly ascended, until it met with the point of light at the crown of my head. Everything within drew up and opened.

It was then that I turned, knowing that someone was there.

"Hi Sara."

Before that moment, I am quite sure I would have fallen to pieces at the sound of my name. I would have cracked open and split in two, unable to cope with the gentleness of the eyes that looked so lovingly into mine.

Instead, my heart opened wider and every ounce of love and gratitude I believed possible welled up and overflowed. Tears sprang to my eyes and my hand flew to my mouth.

"Oh my God. Oh my God." Reaching out, my trembling fingers stopped just before touching him.

"It is you isn't it? You are really, truly here? It's isn't just my imagination?"

"Yes, I'm really, truly here. You called for me, and I came, as I always have." I knew as he said it that it was true.

He looked as he had in life, but not quite - there was something more, the essence of wholeness that is sacrificed for skin. It was as if all the pieces lost in the process of living had been restored, and now Brian dwelt in the center of the light.

"Can…can I touch you?" My voice quivered, thick with love and the yearning to hold him close. All of it - the months of aching for him, of denying his death, and of simply missing his nearness - came back and flooded my senses. I felt it in every acre of my soul and upon every inch of my skin.

His smile deepened as he moved toward me. No amount of trying could make breath come. When his hand touched my arm I was certain my heart, for at least that moment, stopped beating.

"Oh my God." It was a whisper and all I could say, the words coming through tears, through shaking voice and trembling limbs, and carrying with them the force of every wish I'd ever made in Brian's name.

But then the trueness of what was happening came through. I felt once more, the ground beneath my feet, the beating of my heart, the chill upon my face and the softness and familiarity of his touch. And I felt too the distances we had both traveled since last meeting, and the lands that lay between the few short feet we stood apart. He was still my dear and beloved Brian, but he was now a son of the light, and I was still a daughter of the earth. This, no held-fast illusion or wishful thinking could change.

With tears running down my cheeks I looked down at his hand. Tentatively I placed mine over it and its warmth startled me. When I looked back into his eyes, it was with a deep sadness and a resolute knowing.

"You know that I thought you would be here when I came – to Maine, I mean. I thought you'd be waiting for me, and that it was all a big and terrible mistake."

"I know. But it was good that you came. There was so much waiting for you here. You see that now don't you?"

"But...but all I ever wanted was to be with you."

"And I with you, Sara. But not everything ends with the dying of the flesh. I have come every time you have thought of me, missed me or asked me to. It's just that this is the first time you have been open to seeing the truth. To seeing me. I love you Sara. I always will. Sometimes Love calls for us to stay, and sometimes...for us to go. Everything that has happened has happened perfectly, for both of us. It is taking us exactly where we are meant to go."

"So...so you died so that I would learn all that I have? To force me to open my eyes? But that's not what I wanted, that's not fair. I'm so sorry, so sorry for being so weak." A terrible ache settled into the center of my chest. I thought I had excavated all the pain possible, but I was learning that the human well of emotion is a bottomless one.

When Brian moved his hand to wipe away my tears, a faint and translucent light followed in its wake. "Oh Sara, I am sure you have figured out that nothing is quite that simple. But no matter all the reasons for my death, what matters for you is what you are able to take from it. If through grieving for me you are learning of your own magnificence, then you have discovered in it the purpose for you. There is no fault, no blame, only blessing."

I could not speak. I bowed my head and placed my hand over his, holding it against my cheek. For so long I had awaited his arrival, never really believing he would come. But on this day I had walked through my own fires, stripped away all I knew of myself and believed to be true of life, and come naked into the center. And there I had found him, where he had always been. Where I knew he would always be.

Now, I had to choose. Just as Fear had said. I had to choose between living and dying. Between embracing one or the other. Could it be that we all made the same choice each morning that we awoke? How many dawns had come and gone without my noticing, without my passionate participation? Was not noticing, not loving the very act of breathing, the same as choosing death?

I spoke to the ground. "I have not wanted to live without you. I have not felt brave enough to face the world alone. I see now that I am not alone, but I have a feeling it will still feel that way sometimes and I am still afraid – of failing, of not being accepted, of not doing the right thing, or not knowing what to do. I have never stepped out there before, without you, my parents, or someone, to hold me up."

"But now you see that there is always something holding you up. You never needed me Sara, you just thought you did. And truthfully, I liked it that way. But now, now I'm here, and always will be, cheering you on, wanting you to rush wildly into life, to live it beyond the edges of joy. And to love in every way your heart is called to."

With his last words I lifted my head, knowing my expression asked the question.

"Yes Sara, I want you to love, to fall in love if it is what happens. If you deny yourself the experience of Love's full and unconditional expression, you will not be truly living."

And then holding gently the sides of my face and smiling, he said, "He is a good man Sara."

Without thought or hesitation I fell into the space inside his arms that I had always called home.

Into his ear I whispered, "Are you happy? Tell me please, that wherever you are, that you are happy. Then maybe I can begin to live."

He did not answer, in the language of words at least. But as we stood, heart to heart, the answer came.

And no more was said. He pulled gently away, folded my hands together and held them over his heart, while smiling the smile, that cockeyed grin I loved so. And then he winked at me, and disappeared.

CHAPTER TWENTY-SEVEN

When Brian died we had a funeral – a memorial service they called it. Everyone said it was an opportunity to say goodbye. When it was over we had a party. They said that was an opportunity for everyone who loved him to get together and share memories. Then they all went home, and said it was time to get on with life.

I hadn't bought any of it. Goodbye was not an option for me. I didn't need a party or other people to help me remember him and as far as I was concerned, without Brian, there would be no life to get on with.

Never had I imagined what changes the course of time would bring.

I was standing, I could feel it, at the very point where the circle of my life ended. Which was, as well, the very point where it began. Like winter's shedding I was peeling away the layers of the past, making room for the blossoms of spring.

Goodbye was still not an option. But I saw now that it also wasn't necessary. It was true that I would not be able to share my life with Brian, but it didn't mean I had to stop loving him, or that I was supposed to forget him - "get over him." It would not be the same, it would not be what I had wanted or planned, but Brian would forever remain a part of my life. He had never left, not really. Not *actually*. They had always liked to say, "He's still with you." I had nodded. They had nodded. None of us sure if what they said was so.

But it was, in ways we had dared not imagine. Brian was here. Not just in my heart or my memory, but in the very air that I breathed – in the wind that caressed my face, in the morning light that settled over the day, and in the dark of night that would enfold me in its arms.

When his image no longer stood before me I felt a piece of my heart take wing and fly. I bid it farewell, knowing that it went to dance in places I was not yet meant to go. Knowing too, that it, and he, would be waiting when I was.

I sat beneath the cross for a long time, humbled by its purity, its presence and the unconditional force of Love that had offered its protection to me. I spoke to it, to the God of my new understanding, and to Brian. I told them of my experiences, of what confused and still frightened me, of the ache and the joy that filled my heart, and I talked to them of the choices I knew I had to make. In that space, that small circle of grace, I took the first steps toward reshaping my relationship with Brian, with God and with myself.

The choices were easier then they first seemed. I proclaimed them out loud: "I choose to live. I will follow this path you have set me on, wherever it leads. I will do my best each day to choose Love, to choose Truth, to choose Faith. I will do my best. And that is the only promise I know for sure that I can keep."

With the saying of the words, doorways, dusty from neglect, swung open inside my heart. Laughter gurgled up from depths unknown. I leapt to my feet, threw off my soggy clothes and danced. I danced and danced, all around the center, moving freely, gracefully, sensually, attuned to a new rhythm. Like a gift, I understood for the first time what it was to be completely, wildly, freely, one hundred percent - me.

I knew the time would come when I would walk the path again, this time traveling outward – out of the labyrinth, out from my own core and out into the world. It was one thing to make the choice, another to live it. And it was in the living that true freedom would be found.

When the time came I went willingly. But before doing so I stood once more before the cross. Cold air swirled around my naked body and the growing morning light shone upon me as I focused all of my attention on the sacred symbol. Breathing deeply I exhaled my gratitude. With the next inhalation, I was given a deep and kinetic understanding.

Crucifixion and Resurrection. In every moment we die and are reborn. In a lifetime we experience the cycle over and over again, in small ways and large. And if we are to ever truly live we must first hang on the cross. Only through the death of those things that bind us to Fear are we born into a larger life. Only through surrender are we made free.

I saw too the way the cross, by its very form, merged the Earth and the Heavens, the Human and Divine. Through life we are given the blessed duty of being that which joins each with the other.

A surge of emotion overwhelmed me. Stretching my arms wide I lifted my face to the rising sun and shouted, "I Love You!"

The echo reverberated around me, as though Life had not only heard my declaration, but returned it tenfold.

CHAPTER TWENTY-EIGHT

Walking the path out of the labyrinth was, in its own way, as powerful as walking into it had been. But rather than being carried out of my senses, to foreign lands within, my senses were heightened. Spiraling inward I had experienced the sensations of body, heart, mind and spirit separately, layer after layer peeled back until I reached the center. With each step outward I felt the merging of the separate parts, each being returned like pieces of clothing of the self, integrating into the whole. All working, walking, moving and breathing in unison. The ground more solid, more real. My skin finally fitting. My heart's beat stronger. Inside the labyrinth everything was more alive. Flowers, birds, sky, colors of all things, all smells and sounds - magnified, more vibrant, more of themselves. Just as I was. It was like seeing, hearing and smelling for the first time. Step after step, piece after piece clicking into place.

Behind it all I sensed that awesome creating force, the sound waves of God that I could not translate, but could nonetheless feel as they entered my bones.

Then I came to stand at the spot where it had begun. Again the circle had come back to the point of both origin and ending. And beginning once more.

It was a new day. The rain was gone and had taken the clouds with it. Above me the sky was a sparkling blue. The sun hovered behind the mountains to the west. It was early, and upon the ground rest droplets of leftover rain and dew.

Beyond the walls of the labyrinth nothing bloomed, but rather stretched and curled dreamily to sleep. Never had anything appeared so beautiful as the world withdrawing into winter - recuperating, rejuvenating, and preparing for new life.

She stood facing the ocean, leaning her lithe body against the wall of stone at the property's edge. Her hair flew wildly about and in her posture was a profound serenity, and a deep pleasure.

I walked over and stood next to her. Together we silently soaked in the ocean's wisdom, until there came a time that I could see us from a distance, until there was no distinguishing between she and me.

But I was not Anna, and I knew this. I was not the child that had been born with and had never lost the knowledge of her divinity. But standing next to her I could sense that we were profoundly linked, bonded together by a strange and unfolding history, and by that which had shown and offered itself inside the labyrinth. I was also reminded of the story that had brought me here, and of the unknown future it held out to me.

Continuing to look toward the horizon I whispered, "You were right. The farther I went, the more I understood, and the less afraid I became. I don't even know what to say Anna, it was…it was…" I fell quiet, unable and not wanting to bring words to the experience.

She nodded, understanding. We allowed the silence to settle once again.

After a time I breathed deeply, invoking the energies of the cross, gathering courage, and said, "So much has happened since I last saw you. It feels like years have passed, lifetimes even. And I know that with all that has happened, it has merely brought me to the doorstep, to a beginning. But Anna, I still have no idea where I'm to go from here. What it all *means* about my future. What I am to do or what role it is I am meant to play."

I let the words drift between us, knowing she would answer when she was ready. Before she did she sighed heavily and smiled, still not looking in my direction. "You still, and may always seek to understand more than you are meant to, to unmask the mystery. But that's okay, it keeps you open to those answers that *are* waiting and willing to be revealed. But as for what happens next – simply keep your eyes and heart open, notice what is happening around you and listen to the voice within. You know now that you will be guided, you must just trust enough to follow."

I weighed her words silently for a moment and then said, "I guess you know that I saw Bev, that she told me…about you, and your mother, about finding and raising you, and about the locket, the dream – and your pregnancy." I let the words hang between us.

She turned toward me and I met her gaze more steadily and evenly than I had ever been able. "Yes, I know. It is what she was meant to do, share the story with you."

"To be honest with you Anna, as grateful as I am for what I just went through in the labyrinth, I'm still concerned and frightened about what she told me." I felt strength in telling the truth.

"What about it, exactly, are you afraid of?"

With a sigh I plunged forward. "Well for one, the words '*the one chosen to continue my work.*' I'm that *one* - the woman from your dream - aren't I? The one you said those words about?"

"Yes," was all she said.

I shivered. "You have to know how cryptic that is. It carries some kind of duty and responsibility, but I have no idea *what* kind. What it means I am supposed to do. If I'm even capable of doing it. And why, in Heaven's name, *I* have been '*chosen.*'" I stopped speaking, expecting her to say something, to give me the answers, or at least offer some wise teaching, but she didn't. She just continued to watch me, the teacher waiting for the pupil to see the light.

I tried to focus inwardly, but the effort just brought further questions. Beginning to become exasperated I concentrated instead on my other concern. "Anna, Bev also told me what your finding…me… would mean for you. I sat in the center of that labyrinth," I said gesturing to the august structure behind me, "and felt the exquisite truth about death. And yet I cannot bring myself to readily accept playing such a role in yours."

Into her face came the most radiant compassion. "No matter our understanding of death and its divine nature, as humans we hold on, even in the smallest degree, to a fear of our mortality. It is our love of individuation. We work our whole life to find out 'who we are' and then in death we are returned to the cosmic kettle, united with the All

There Is, the One. When we get there we find that it is the most glorious freedom we have ever known, but in flesh we have forgotten this and from this perspective we imagine it as a loss of the self. Or worse, an end to all being.

"As for your role in my earthly departure. Dear Sara, we – you – are powerful beyond measure, and at the same time, perfectly, wonderfully, powerless. You can turn from here, try and run as you did last night, but most likely you will find yourself unable to, once again. And even if you do, I suspect you would merely travel far and wide only to find yourself returning to this place, or one much like it. For once we have glimpsed the Mystery, felt the call of larger living, it is virtually impossible to turn back for long. Our soul remembers, and with each taste of Truth it is strengthened. I know you feel a large responsibility has been placed upon you and that you are not yet sure what it is you are supposed to do. But know, I would have it no other way. You are following the path of Higher Will, and you are doing so courageously and with a heart filled with Love. You have been called, as have I. Never would I expect or ask you to dismiss or ignore that which you are called to do. There is no life better lived than one that follows the call of the soul. It is not always the easiest path, but it is the one of greatest integrity, and ultimately, deepest joy."

She studied me, dismantling heart, mind and body, until I imagined she reached the place where thought originates and could read mine before even I knew what they were.

"Ask me the other question. That story I will tell you."

CHAPTER TWENTY-NINE

The 4-runner sat tucked beneath the baring branches of a maple tree. He was home. My heart beat faster as I pulled slowly to a stop in front of the house.

It was my first challenge, my first opportunity to keep my promise, to tell the truth and face the consequences. To be brave. The universe didn't mess around.

A full day had passed since I had left Anna at the labyrinth. I had gone home and slept, not waking until the sun had risen on another day. I had slept soundly, dreamless – my mind, body and soul exhausted. At dawn I had risen, gone down to the beach and cried, in gratitude and in awe. I had been afraid that I would find the world less wondrous than I had left it the day before, but I had not.

For an hour I walked and sat and prayed and listened in return. And then, after eating everything I could find in my kitchen, I had simply showered, dressed and gotten in the car, knowing what came next. I was still scared. The only difference was that now I made the choice to risk truth rather than hide behind illusion.

Before getting out of the car I breathed deeply, said a silent prayer for strength, one for a little luck, and then without allowing another thought walked to the door and knocked.

There was no answer, so I tried again, but still no answer. Tempted to use it as a sign to leave, I almost headed back to my car. But I didn't get far. I knew he was there. I could feel him.

I followed my pounding heart around to the side of the house, and shielding my eyes from the sun, scouted the land around the lake and even squinted up into the mountain, thinking I might actually see him sitting on the ledge looking down at me.

Something large and solid knocked against my leg. I didn't need to look to know that it was Lady. "Hey girl, where's your dad?" I bent down and asked as I stroked back her ears.

She turned around and walked toward the back of the house. I followed, and found him sitting at a small round iron table set in the middle of what, in spring, was probably a colorful garden, but was now a rectangular patch of dirt dissected by brick pathways and bordered by faithful evergreens and naked aspen. On the table was a laptop computer surrounded by several books and pages of scribbled notes. Classical music floated about, coming, I guessed, from speakers either disguised as rocks or hidden somewhere under the shallow overhang extending from the roofline.

He was typing, lost in the rhythm of his thoughts. So focused was his attention that he didn't even notice me standing at the edge of the garden, or Lady, for that matter, who rambled over and wrapped her burly body around his feet.

For a long moment I just watched him – the way he played the keyboard like a piano, or a lover, and the way his jaw tightened at the smallest hesitation in his fingers. His hair, as usual, hung low, shadowing his face, and between his eyes were the deep grooves of concentrated thought. I could have sat down and watched him for hours and become as engrossed as he. There was something so beautiful about his intensity and the meditative quality with which he worked, as though he wasn't really there, but rather lost in the space between words. Taking dictation perhaps from the voices inside the silence.

I hated to disturb him so I turned around to tip-toe quietly away, telling myself I wasn't running but simply waiting for a better time. But with my first retreating step, Lady barked, loud and with purpose.

"Sara?" I turned to find Mark rising from his chair, looking dazed.

"Hi." I waved.

"How long have you been here? Why didn't you say something? Were you leaving?" He seemed out of it, having been pulled abruptly away from distant lands, awakened mid-dream.

"You're busy, I don't want to interrupt. It looked like you were pretty deeply involved."

Laughing, his smile bringing to life his handsome face, he said, "Well, you're right. When I'm working and it's going well, I tend to fade away. But please, don't leave. I mean, seeing you is certainly a distraction, but a welcome one."

"Thanks." I give you the right to retract that later.

"Would you like to sit down? Or go inside? I know it's pretty chilly out here, but I love to work when it's like this."

I moved past him into the little garden and over to the table. "This is really lovely Mark. How come I didn't see this the other day?"

He shrugged then grinned. "I don't know. It's prettier in spring and I guess I was keeping it in my back pocket, just in case I needed some lame reason to see you again."

Shaking my head I laughed. "You're too much." Not knowing quite what to say or where to begin, I walked aimlessly around the garden, lightly touching the needles and bark of the trees. I felt different and so did everything else. It was scary. I wasn't sure how or where I would fit into the world now or exactly how to live day-by-day in the light of what I had experienced. Somewhere inside I still longed for the safety of another's arms.

"Something's happened. Something's different." His voice was gentle and smooth. I turned and met his gaze.

"Yes." I nodded.

Without a word he held out his hand, and I took it. We walked through the back door into the house.

He started a fire. I made tea. We came to sit side by side on the couch.

I had come to tell him a story, the truth as I knew it. I had to tell it all, but I wanted first to unfold for him my journey through the labyrinth.

So I did, one amazing petal at a time. I told him of the darkness, the rain, the way I had called desperately out to the unknown. I told him how his lessons in breathing had helped me release the external layer, allowing me to move beneath the surface. I shared with him the faces of Fear, Anger, and Grief – and all that they, especially Fear, had taught me. I told him about the altar and the cross and the sorrow I had laid there. I described for him the parade of the masses, and the hope I had been given. I told him I had seen him there, and I told him I had seen Brian too. I even told him that Brian had come to me, and how beautiful it had been. I told him I had met God out walking.

Tears ran down my cheeks as I relived the journey to my center and laid it out for this man to see. Through it all his eyes never left mine. He listened, not only with his ears, but also with his heart. Never had I felt so open in the presence of another human being. When I finished we sat silently, fully alive inside the energy of Love that flowed between us and held us in its hand.

Just as I wished that he would, he reached out and held his hand against my cheek. I closed my eyes and drifted inside of his touch. Reopening them I met his gaze and in his eyes saw all the roads of the past converging into this moment. Weightless, thoughtless, emptied of past or future, I leaned forward to meet him. Our lips found each other and we opened ourselves in that first kiss to the passion forged in the meeting of body and soul.

It would have been so easy to follow the longing, to hold on and not let go. It would have been so easy to forget that there was more to say. So easy, because I knew that what was left would change everything. Might even change the way he felt about me. But I knew that I could not forget and that Love called for me to tell it all, and let him choose.

Tears stung my eyes, a wave of regret washing over me as I brought our kiss to an end and pulled slowly back from his embrace. I smiled and touched his face, memorizing every detail as though I might never see it again.

"Are you okay?" His voice was thick.

"Yes," I said stroking his face and hair, and then bringing my hand to rest on my leg, "and no. There is more Mark that I have to tell you. I would like to say that the story began and ended with what I've already said. It would make everything a little easier, but it didn't. And I want to, have to, be honest with you. Completely. There is more to tell, and if affects you as much as me."

Softly, and without pulling away, he said simply, "I'm listening."

And so with one deep breath I began.

PART THREE: ILLUMINATION

CHAPTER THIRTY

It was the story of a woman, one like no other. She was beautiful and smart, compassionate and strong. Both Warrior and Goddess. She had come to this earth one final time, and though she would not stay long she would do much, for she had come with a purpose. And though she came into the world as all children do, conceived by man and woman, she did not, as most do, forget, in the transference of spirit to matter, why she had come.

As a child knowledge came easily to her, pouring out from her deeper well of Wisdom. She heard the voice of all things as she walked through the world, the voice of the wind and the water, the trees and the sky, the voice of God speaking clearly to and through her. She was unafraid and never doubted that her every step was led by a loving force and that all that happened was perfect and meant to aid in the fulfillment of her purpose. Even in the face of what others would call suffering, she lifted tears of gratitude to Heaven.

As she grew, her footsteps followed the course of God's wishes. Each one she accepted with an open and joyous heart. She embraced and released loved ones, knowing they were never truly parted and she considered all whom she met loved ones. She danced through life in the arms of the Beloved, leading and following as necessary. She enjoyed the body and gave thanks for the experience of living it allowed her. She thought woman the most glorious of creatures, and gratefully, openly, passionately knew love in all its forms - sensual, physical and spiritual. She was saddened by the ways in which It was misunderstood, belittled and judged.

But she knew the winds were changing, that someday all would step from behind their skin and into the light of ecstatic truth. She was

251

here to help it happen, just as those sent before her, and those yet to come. And the countless that awoke each morning to hear the call.

She walked through life barefoot and free, sharing with every soul she met the grace and beauty of Love, Beauty and Truth. Her work was done breath by breath, in small, magnificent gestures that echoed far and wide. She transformed everything and everyone she touched, leaving in her wake a trail of light, of hope and a band of spiritual pioneers.

From a very early age she had known that she would not live long, and that hers would be a solitary road traveled with specific intent. She had returned to the land of flesh by her own choosing. Her soul was very old and was meant to soon remerge with the All. But there were things left to do, things to be taught and shared. It was an exciting time on the earth plane, one of healing and spiritual unfolding, and she had wanted to be a part of it, if just once more.

Her final journey would last only little more than fifty human years. But in order to ensure that Balance and Order were maintained, a pact had been made. A pact with another soul who would hold the seeds of Remembrance and pass them on, to be planted again.

So it was in all times, souls in collusion...one sent to awaken another who would awaken another who would awaken yet another...

When she heard the words, one early morning as she knelt on the ocean's shore, she had not been surprised:

"The time has come for the next chapter to begin. Walk slowly, watch carefully, and you will find what you seek." It was time to go home.

She had walked miles, patient and alert, before she had seen her, the woman from the dream sitting upon the shore. She knew her, had known her for lifetimes, and in-between lifetimes. She knew too that the woman would not recognize her, would have forgotten the pact they had made. But only the human part had truly forgotten, not the soul. It was the soul that had led the woman to the beach that morning and the soul that would unravel the veil of illusion, one thread at a time, ensuring that the pact was kept and that the will of the Greater Plan was followed.

And so had begun the end. She was prepared for what she must do and joyfully anticipated her departure. Perhaps things were not as far along as she would have liked, but they were continuing to evolve. She had done her part, had served as intended, and that was all that mattered.

Her time had been short but substantial. Looking back there had been few quivering moments of uncertainty, tempting lures of earthly illusion. But in the end there had been only one true regret.

It reminded her daily that even she could not escape the Mystery.

She had loved him. That was certain. She had recognized him, his soul as familiar to her as the wind's whisperings. There was no mistake in their meeting, in its form or its brevity. They shared only one night, and in the course of those twelve hours they merged skin-to-skin, heart-to-heart and soul-to-soul. When morning came they parted, the seed of their union planted in her womb.

As the child grew inside her, she grew – her heart and spirit expanding to heights and depths even *her* awareness had not fathomed. She loved the child she carried, the boy and the man he would become. Before he was born she gave him a name, simple and strong. Mark. He would be a seer of truth, a lover of all things and peoples, a teacher and a strong and steady light through the darkness.

The night she dreamt of the woman she also dreamt of her child. The Heavens parted and he was born, through her but not to her. In her dream she was shown what she must do.

Upon waking she had cried, in grief and in seething despair. She had cried until her tears formed a river in which her child would be forever cradled. And when there were no more tears to be shed and she was empty, the light of Grace refilled her.

She did as she was meant to…she gave her child into the keeping of another.

She was, however, given the gift of watching him grow from a distance, and watch him she did. With every day her love for him deepened. She watched him stumble and fall, and rise to try again; she watched his heartbreak and his battle to heal, and she could see the determination of his soul to prevail.

When he was a young man she was even allowed to touch upon the corners of his life, to know him as mentor and friend, to influence the course of his learning, to plant seeds that would later blossom and grow.

But she could not, as a mother, reach out and brush away his tears or hold him in his grief. She could not call him son.

She knew when he discovered the truth of his adoption and the anger he felt. She knew the hole it left in his heart and all that he did to try and fill it. His agony made her own heart ache. And in the ways that she could, she reached out to him – through the powers of energy, of love and compassion.

In all ways human she regretted this part of her path. She did not like the pain and the suffering it caused this blessed child of her womb.

But in all ways Divine she understood that he himself had chosen this course - that each soul follows its own journey to awakening, and that facing such challenges, such forms of suffering, is still the route humans take to remembering the seat they hold next to God.

She wondered often if she would, before dying, be led to offer him the truth of his parentage.

Her answer came on the same day she was called Home.

She had invited him to the bookstore – the other earth child she had bore – for a signing. She knew the woman would be there as well. What she had not been prepared for was the vision.

They came regularly to guide her in her work and assist her upon her path. This one though was about him, his work and his connection to the woman, and the course of things to come. The work they were meant to do.

During Sheila's reading she had stood in a corner, hidden from view. Her eyes had wandered to the woman, who looked afraid and confused, her soul trying desperately to be heard, though there was so much working to extinguish the light. And then he had walked over and placed his hand on her arm. It was in that instant that she saw it, all of it – in that instant that she knew and understood. And her heart danced with joy, and quivered, ever so slightly, with sorrow.

CHAPTER THIRTY-ONE

Even as I told Mark the story, as much of it as I knew, I marveled at it. With all that I had experienced in the labyrinth I still had trouble grasping the fantastic truth about reality. Planted on the earth I had learned that magic was an illusion and that rationality, real – not the other way around. And yet I believed, with all my heart, with every cell and to the depths of my soul that the story I told was true.

I knew too, that there was much that Anna had not told me. I knew not her purpose for coming to this earth or who the man, Mark's father, was, or what the vision had been, or the information it had given her. She had not expounded upon the other lives we had known together or the pact we had made. She did not reveal to me my part in the plan or the plan's intention for me.

And she had not shared with me the sadness the final knowing brought her. That I had seen in the shadows of her face.

There were no words when I finished my telling.

Only a boy's pain cracked open and a man's struggle to survive the truth. His tears came easily, openly and courageously. I held him in my arms as he cried, pouring out the grief and anger of lost years, and all that lived in the dark, empty places inside. My own heart responded, and I too cried, for him, Anna, and for myself.

Evening came early, announcing itself only through the light that faded softly away. When our eyes had dried we lay wrapped in each other's arms and fell asleep.

I awoke in darkness, enfolded in Mark's warm embrace. My face rested against his chest and for a while I just followed the rhythm of his heartbeat and his breath, not wanting to disturb the gentle life force I felt there.

As if sensing my waking he stirred, moving his hand to the back of my head and combing my tangled hair with his fingers.

"Hi," he whispered.

"Hi," I responded, shifting my position so I could see his face. I didn't know what to say - there was no precedent for what we were facing. I just reached up and kissed him softly on the temple then held my hand to his cheek.

He smiled, tired and wistful. I wondered if he had slept at all.

"Long day, huh?" He tried to sound light, but fell short.

"Yeah, what time is it?"

Craning to see the hands of a clock on the bookshelf behind him, he said, "Looks like just after midnight. Would you like to go in and sleep on the bed? I can stay here."

"No. I kind of like this if it's okay with you. Unless of course you're uncomfortable." I wanted to stay close, to hear his heartbeat through the night.

"No, I like this better too." And then we were quiet again, neither sure how to bridge the chasm between what had been and what was now emerging. I felt though that I owed it to him to be the strong one this time, to at least make the effort.

Propping myself up on one elbow I looked at his unshaven face and bloodshot eyes and said softly, "Mark, I dropped a lot on you today. I'm…well, I just want you to know that if you want to talk about it, any of it, I'm here, and I'd like to listen."

He said nothing but smiled wearily again and lifted his hand to my face, tracing my cheek.

Tears welled and I smiled back, and with quivering voice, added, "And I understand if you would rather not talk to me about it or about anything. I'd understand if you'd rather not see me after this."

He brought his finger to my lips, closed his eyes and whispered, "Shhhhhh."

And then pulling me to him and squeezing tightly, he said, "Not now, not tonight. Tonight let's just stay like this, holding the moment. Tomorrow will come soon enough."

And so it did. And when awareness swept in I found myself alone on Mark's couch. The clock read 5:30 and darkness still permeated the room and my head, which was thick and foggy. It felt as though I had been sleeping at the bottom of a well - someplace deep and dark, warm and quiet - and hadn't been ready to be pulled out.

But something had tickled the edges of consciousness. I was sure it was Mark moving, leaving a space large and empty beside me.

Struggling to focus, I sat up. While waiting for my eyes to adjust I listened carefully, straining for an audible hint as to where he might be. Only the dust particles of silence answered back. When I could, I got shakily to my feet and began searching the house, assuming, sadly, that he would be in his bed. But it was empty, just like the kitchen, his office, the bathroom, and the garden.

Deciding he obviously didn't want to be found, I returned to the couch and lay down. But I couldn't sleep. All I could do was stare blindly into the space in front of me. My stomach turned over nervously.

It was starting, I could feel it – and almost hear it – the clicking of the final pieces into place.

"Get up, get up now." The voice was firm, but calm and kind. I didn't know how long I had been lying there, but light, faint and gray, was creeping in under the door and through whatever crevices it could find. I didn't think I had fallen asleep, but felt like I was being woken up. The words slipped by, slivers of sound.

"Get up, get up now." They were repeated, more firmly. This time they were clear, and I sat up and glanced around sharply, thinking someone - a woman, for the voice was feminine – must have come into the house. Slowly I realized that the voice was coming from inside my head. I had heard it before, but never so loud and resolute.

I did as it said.

"Go now, it's time." And in that instant, with shockwaves of dread, I knew where to find him. And I knew that he wouldn't be alone.

CHAPTER THIRTY-TWO

It was winter in Maine and everything was under risk of exposure. Left to die away or to be transformed.

The thought chilled me, more so than the biting wind, as I made my way along the shoreline. Above, the sky was painted in tones of shimmering silver and gray, tinged haphazardly with bold strokes of deep rose and burnt orange. It was a long walk in the cold. I felt like an actor coming to the stage, to play out the final scene of her life's most important role.

Just when it seemed I had gone much too far I found that I had arrived. Looming before me was the rock cave, the place where Anna's story had begun. What had come before the day Bev had found her tending to her mother's frail and withering body was to remain, I imagined, a mystery. But what was to happen here on this day, I feared, was another such ending and beginning.

The closer I came, the slower I walked. The sun was rising, greeting the dawn with subtle beauty. There was no fog or mist and yet I could not, for some reason, see the space around or in front of the cave clearly. It was brighter than the rest of the beach and like a mirage, ebbed and flowed obscurely. I squinted my eyes, trying to focus. There was something on the shore, something white dancing in the wind.

Just as I became aware of it, just at the moment it caught my attention, the energy reached out and touched me, and I became a part of the distortion, held inside the higher vibration. And disappeared.

For one fragile instant of eternity I became the We, the All, and the One. No body, no single mind, no thought. Only Being. Pure, Joy-filled, Creative, and Loving.

And when it was over and the fingers of energy had retreated, I stood once again on the periphery - feeling slightly, almost imperceptibly fractured, and at the same time, restored.

Again, the scene before me was unfocused.

"Come closer," a voice inside the anomaly said.

I walked forward, both afraid and wanting for it to embrace me once more. But with my every step toward it the vibration visibly slowed, and the space, wave by wave, became clear.

Rocks had been displaced and pushed back to form a circle, several feet in diameter. In the center a fire blazed, its blue-hot flames extending upward, engulfing all that it could of the brilliant energy that was still present, if not so readily seen.

And standing just in front of the fire, facing the ocean, was Anna - bare feet spread apart and arms in movement – stretched outward and coming together, to rest, palms touching, in front of her chest. She wore a sheath of white. Crossing her forehead was a sequined band of silver and another rested at her hairline and flowed into a long veil of white silk. I stood breathless watching her, this living Goddess, in ceremony of prayer. It was the most beautiful thing I had ever seen.

She did not turn, did not look at me or move her lips to speak but still I heard her, clearly in my mind.

"Join me, Sara."

Without word I walked trembling into the center of the circle and stood beside her. I wondered what it was I was supposed to do.

As if in answer I once again heard Anna's voice, floating like a breeze through my mind. "Relax Sara. Allow yourself to simply be. Let go of seeking what is to be done. There will be time for 'doing' later. Now, now is time to fully enter into and witness this moment as it arises and falls away, to breathe into the spaces between the lines of thought. Only by doing so will you discover your greater story, the inner poetry written by God upon your soul in the moment of your birth. Within these verses lives every answer to every question you have *ever* asked about yourself…your gifts, your purpose, the ways in which you are meant to move and be and give voice to your being. The embodied life is a journey of learning to read that poetry, and one of sharing it with the world. But only in the resting place of the soul can you begin to find your way there. And when you arrive you will discover that you are, and have always been, the pure poetry of God, present always in the company of Love."

In my core I felt an opening, a response to her words. My inner poetry, pulsing to life. How I wanted to read those words, to know now what they said, where they led. I tried to let the impatience flutter and fall. Breathing. Breathing.

Yet…

Not knowing if it would work, I thought out my questions, hoping she would hear.

"But Anna, you said I was 'chosen.' Chosen for what exactly? If I don't figure it out, I am in danger of not honoring my part of our pact. Is that possible – that I can fail something so important?"

No answer came, only the sounds of the sea and the wind. I sensed she had heard, and her answer was silence. I waited, but nothing came. I grew uncomfortable. The clarity I had experienced briefly, the release, evaporated. My mind began to spin. I wondered where Mark was, and considered stepping out of the circle and looking for him. I thought of my family, realizing I hadn't called home. The fire grew hot on my legs, the air cold on my face, and my shoulders ached. Then, admonitions crept in. I should be breathing, praying, being, anything other than complaining. All ran through my head, each thought rolling into the next, my mind unable to quit, my body unable to move.

Time passed slowly, moments like hours but probably mere minutes. My eyes closed, time passed, thoughts turned into memories, then wishes, hopes and desires.

I felt the fire not only on my legs, but also on my back, my neck, the crown of my head. Rising above me, it moved over and around until I was engulfed in a circle of flames. From some distant perspective I could see the energy of my thoughts, feelings and actions, sense their power rising out of my body, up through the top of my head, and into the web of energy that connects everything together. Almost instantaneously they returned in the form of my experience and added to the cumulative experience of the collective. I understood, too, in that moment, the complexity of life. My inner life, the outer world, those around me...everything from the genes in my body, to my history and the history of the world, to my own perceptions and those of all who touched my life, and even of those who came before and shaped the context of all I knew...all played a part in who I was, who I thought myself to be. But beneath it, within it and beyond it all...was the body of God. There, all melted into One. Yet, from the One came the Many – the singular, unique expressions of humanity and all existence.

A great wave flooded through me, carrying me from the individual identity I knew as Sara to the transcendent realm of the Absolute, to the ground of all being. And in the center where the two met, I felt the labor pains of new life.

Traveling through inner dimensions, I knew myself the vessel through which energy poured and originated. On the edge of my awareness, shapes began to appear, at first vague outlines, gradually vibrating into physical form. Looking up and out I was astonished as faces came into focus: Jane, Sheila, Greg, Gil and Bev. Out beyond them more appeared to my even greater surprise...my own mother and father, my brother, other friends and family members...a sea of familiar faces. And even farther still stretched an ocean of unfamiliar ones...hundreds, thousands of strangers of every race, age and culture. But they didn't feel like strangers. Though I did not recognize the faces, the eyes reflected ties deep and long.

No one spoke aloud but in my mind I could hear their voices rising in harmony, all in eternal prayer.

Before I could move or speak or dare to do anything at all I felt Mark's presence. When I turned, he held out his hand. We walked into the center of the crowd, rooting ourselves in the web of connecting energy and adding our own. I wanted to reach out, to speak to my family and all whom I knew and loved, but no sooner did I introduce the thought did a shift occur. The chorus of voices grew, the beauty of their rhythm and words filling my head. And then the ceremony began.

Attention was focused on the beach, on the circle in which Anna stood. She began to move, to dance. It was the dance of a goddess – graceful and poetic. Her voice rose above the rest, not a song but simply sound, set free from the soul to fly upon the wind. The voice of a woman in Love.

Mesmerized, as I always was by her, by the way she embodied both what is feminine and what is powerful, and all that is wise, I watched. Her entire body took part in the dance - feet, legs, hips, shoulders, arms, head and hands. As she moved and sang, enfolded in the song of souls, another beat began to play. This one much lower, much deeper, more primal and instinctual. It was the beat of the earth – the music of creation that forever plays.

I felt my own body respond. At the deepest level I could feel it, could hear the resounding, healing rhythm. And I began to move. The entire body of creation, within and around me, began to dance.

The light surrounding us grew brighter as sound gave way to silence. I looked toward Anna. She ceased moving and stood once again in posture of prayer, the fire behind her growing. Brighter and brighter the light became, pulsating between and around every piece of matter. Each began to vibrate, faster and faster, until flesh disappeared and all that was left was light. Millions of points of light, first separate, then merging into One.

In the spark of that instant, I would swear to the end of my days I saw the gates of Heaven open, and at them stand Brian, and through them walk Anna.

And in the next instant all was consumed by the fire.

CHAPTER THIRTY-THREE

From the ashes rose stillness. Not the Absolute of earlier, but the peaceful emptiness of a clear night sky or the ocean at dawn. Beneath me was the earth, above me the Heavens, and in-between, like the space between breaths, I stood - child of both, conduit for each to the other.

And through the conduit came the chorus of voices. Countless spoke, but I could hear clearly those of Anna and Brian:

"Yes, Sara, you have been chosen. Chosen to carry forth truth -the truth as it has been revealed to you, the truth as you have felt and known it in these past days and nights. You ask, 'But what exactly am I to do?' And the sons and daughters of the Heavens and the Earth say to you this: Do nothing, Do what you will, Be who you are, or even who you are not. It matters not. For no matter what you do, don't do, no matter what you choose, or whom you become, you are, and forever will be, the poetry of God. What you know of Life in the confines of individual identity is but a wink in the eye of Divinity. The truth, the glorious truth of Life is that there is no death, and furthermore, there are no conditions or expectations to be met - for when flesh becomes ash, your spirit will return to the One – sourced and forever dwelling in Love.

"But Sara, to live joyfully, *to live in* Truth, *is not found in* doing *anything, but in waking up. In cultivating awareness of the totality of that which you are, both human and Divine...and coming into communion with the energy of Love. Waking up, dear Sara, to the is-ness of each moment, and living from the center, from the place between form and infinity.*

Through awareness then flows right doingness. The inspiration of your calling, the guidance you will need, will come from the signature of God written upon your soul. You will know it when you meet it. You will live it because nothing else will do. It is that simple, and that complicated.

"And yet your human self still begs to understand why you have been 'chosen,' just as many, including you until now, have begged to understand why they have not.

But listen closely dear Sara to the whisperings of the angels, their voices found in the stirrings of the wind... for they whisper into the ears of all creatures, all beings of Love, all children of God, saying to each and forgetting none, though most do not hear... 'You are chosen, You are chosen.'

And that is the promise of God."

PART FOUR: FULL CIRCLE

CHAPTER THIRTY-FOUR

I awoke slowly, coming into awareness one second at time. Warmth registered first and then the softness beneath me. Sounds filtered in and then light. Visions swept across my closed eyelids, words rang in my ears. My eyes jolted open.

I was in my bed, tucked deeply beneath sheet, quilts and comforter.

A dream, had it all been an exquisite beautiful dream? Tears welled at the thought. But if it had, where had the dream begun, for I did not remember last crawling into bed. Moving as little as possible I looked suspiciously around the room.

Bare branches from the tree outside the window played a shadow game on the wall, while beyond its spindly arms was drawn the clear blue of sky. It was day. That was the only thing I seemed to know.

My mind raced, trying to latch on to some lost piece of the puzzle, anything that would prove it hadn't all been a dream. Snuggling deeper into the bed I closed my eyes and sought comfort in the wanderings of my mind as it settled on what I remembered, or imagined I remembered, about the experience on the beach. It was like trying to recapture the fragments of a dream you don't want to forget.

I could see it all so clearly and it felt real.

"Keep the promise, keep the promise." I said the words to myself, referring to the promise I had made in the labyrinth, or thought I had made. They were to be the mantra I used to find my way to courage. But had that been merely a dream as well?

Lost in the lines between realities, I was unsure where to find the fulcrum to keep me afloat. *The breath.* All I could think to do was return to the breath. Focusing on the soft whir of each inspiration and the release of every exhalation, my body began to loosen. My mind continued to seek cover from the confusion, but everything lessened in degree.

Finally, a fragile whisper asked, "If you were to choose faith over fear, what would you do?"

Smiling, I nodded and threw back the covers.

It was a calm, clear day. Still. Unusually, especially still. Almost as if the earth had taken a breath, inhaling the movement of life, and had not yet released it.

The moment I saw him in the distance, a lone figure perched upon the shore, I knew, indeed, that it had all happened just as I remembered. I approached slowly, quietly, not wanting to disturb his solitude, and not having any idea what to say.

As I drew near, Mark turned to look at me. He was smiling softly, his eyes glistening with tears already spent. I said nothing, but sat so close to him our shoulders and legs touched, and I was relieved when he didn't move away.

After a few moments in silence I asked, "Are you okay?" It was a silly, clichéd question, but it was a starting point.

"Yeah, I guess." But his voice said differently.

A knot formed in my heart and moved into my throat when I tried to speak. Afraid of falling apart I looked away and closed my eyes.

His hand, surprisingly warm, covered mine. "It's okay Sara. Look at me, please. Really, it's okay."

Tears blurred my vision as I turned to meet his words. With a smile he wiped them away.

"It really happened didn't it? Right here, this morning?" And then, my voice barely audible, "Anna's gone, isn't she?"

Fresh tears filled his eyes, "Yeah, she's gone. And yes, it really happened. It was...amazing, wasn't it?"

"My God, Mark, I've never...I mean...my God, it was so...beautiful, so incredibly beautiful. Do you think it's like that for all of us?"

Suddenly he laughed, a delicate peace settling over his face, "I don't know, Sara, I have no idea. I guess we can only hope."

He grew more serious, shook his head and looked out over the water. "I thought I knew so much, thought I'd actually figured some of it out. And then this morning… It seems like the onion just keeps getting larger the more layers I peel back. The biggest question of my life was answered, and yet, I don't know…I feel like I know less than ever." Turning back to me he asked, "Does that make any sense?"

I couldn't help but laugh. "Yes it makes sense, the only thing is – I don't know that I've ever known, or thought I knew, anything. From the minute I stepped off the planet, I've been freefalling. But I have this strange sense that this morning I landed."

We stayed on the shore a long time, neither of us willing or wanting to rush whatever was to come next. I sat alone on the rocks, letting the cold clarity of the day penetrate my mind and heart. Mark had gotten up and walked back into the cave and then farther along the beach in the opposite direction. I sensed he needed more time alone before heading back to the house. When he returned I raised my eyes to his and smiled.

Then he held out his hand, as he had so many times before. But as never before, the touch of his flesh sparked a crack in the edges of time and space. It was not simply déjà vu. Not just the memory of my dream. For in that brief moment everything changed - the landscape behind him, the rocks beneath me, the clothes he wore. Framing him was the dry, rocky terrain of an ancient desert, the hand he held out dark like the Mediterranean night, his shirt ragged and torn. The eyes holding mine were a deep mocha, but in them I could see the imprint of the man I knew. Everything lived in the space between seconds, moving in slow motion. I looked down at my own clothes and skin and was unsurprised to see them changed as well. In some strange way it all made sense. I understood that a million different scenes could play out before me – times, places, names and faces. Every moment a memory circling back to its own completion. I wondered, as time shifted again and blurred into focus, back to the beach: how many times had he been there to help me to my feet? In how many lands had we played out this very act? How many lifetimes had there been? How many more would there be? I smiled, calmed by the knowledge of his eternal presence, and that change was as much an illusion as everything else.

As we walked the shoreline in silence I became aware of the current of my thoughts. I had been taught so much, but I knew, as Mark had said, that there was only ever more to learn. Only weeks ago I had vowed to unlock the mysteries. Now the idea almost made me laugh. The only thing that seemed clear was that the more I opened my mind, eyes and heart to the secrets of the Universe and the more that was revealed to me, the larger and greater the Mystery became. As though each doorway into the soul led deeper and deeper into the mind of God. And to that there was no end.

By the time we reached the house I was grateful for its protective arms. It was growing colder. Dark came early in November and would arrive shortly. As soon as we stepped through the back door I busied myself with making a fire.

I was a little afraid that Mark would leave immediately. Not a word had been spoken during the walk back. He had seemed preoccupied, lost in his thoughts, as I had been in mine. I wanted to reach out and bridge the gap between us, but knew I had to let him, when he was ready.

He wandered the house, and I felt his unease, though I didn't know its source. He didn't move to leave but he didn't settle in either. When the fire caught I warmed myself for a moment and then turned to tea-making – my two rituals of northern living. It wasn't until I handed him a mug that he broke the silence.

"Thank you." He held my eyes in his – strong and steady - and said, "Do you have any idea how much I care about you?" There were tears close to the surface.

My hand began to shake, the tea threatening to spill over. His words and the heat of his closeness reached for me. It was several seconds before I could speak.

"I…no, yes…I guess the only thing I *know* is that we are strangely, strongly, connected." More quietly I added, "And that I care very much about you."

It was a moment of exposure, the exposure of truth and Self. It was all that was needed to open the next doorway of understanding.

With a mixture of relief, and what could only be called angst, he closed his eyes and sighed, and when he opened them again I saw in the shattered fragments what he did not say. He began to speak, to say the words, but I shook my head and placed a finger to his mouth, "Shhh." I knew what was to come, or could at least feel the essence of it, and my heart wept.

But it wouldn't be tonight. That, my only solace, was all that mattered.

I reached out and took the mug from his hand, and put it with mine on the dining room table. After exhaling the last of any doubt I curled my hands around his neck, stretched upward, and with the taste of tears on my lips, kissed him.

He met me openly, with a gentle, trembling wonder and an almost painful appreciation. Drawing back I took his hand and moved toward the bedroom. He resisted and when I turned, his face beautifully vulnerable, asked the question. *Are you sure?*

"Yes," I whispered.

The body knows the nature of longing, but not alone does it possess the power of it. Or the means with which to touch its center.

It is in the melding of Spirit, Heart, Mind and Matter that ecstasy is truly tasted.

Every moment passed as an eternity, every spark of time alive, forever frozen in the blink of perfection.

We knelt upon the bed, only our breath between us. It had grown dark and I had lit a single candle. The room filled with the shadows of the flame, dancing over our bodies and around those things that live in the corners of the night.

We touched softly, tentatively at first, as though afraid of shattering the truth of the experience. Like travelers in a holy land we explored one another's bodies, awed by the beauty found in what is real, and humbled by the magnificence of that which is offered most freely.

The more familiar we became, the hungrier we grew. Moving with tenderness and strength, Mark came to hover above me, his face cast in shadows. In his eyes I saw the light of his soul and knew mine was rising to meet it.

He entered, not only my body but the deeper caverns of my knowing – places warm and wild, where Goddesses run with the wind in their faces, and their feet bare upon the ground, places reached only outside the limits of space and time, and found only in the shimmering rhythm of Oneness.

The fire, which at first raged hot and low, swept upward, encompassing and igniting each center of life – from the base of the spine to the crown of the head, from the primitive to the Divine. Until there was no longer he and me, until all that was left was all that there had ever been – one, single light.

And it was only after we came crashing upon the shore of the present that I felt the tears that had never stopped flowing.

Afterwards we lay clutched together, neither able to speak, both caught in the final flows of passion. In time the waves of intensity calmed, settling into a place more intimate, far beneath the roots of hunger.

I will never forget that night, its purity, and the way that Love came to settle upon us, like a blanket to keep us from the cold. It nestled into the small spaces, more a remembrance than a discovery. It needed no words, and asked for nothing but the joy of giving itself. And when I became aware of its presence, my heart leapt, aching both with waves of gratitude and with the pain of growing beyond what it has known.

I thought of Brian and felt pangs of regret, not for loving Mark, but for the ways I had not known to love him. Though I had loved Brian completely, I had needed him even more, to save me from Fear, to protect me from life, and to fill in the spaces of my own fractured Self. I had expected so much and given so little, and none of it without cost. Some part of me realized that it had all happened as it had with purpose, but I knew too that I would forever carry a sliver of that regret, and a sadness for the stakes lost at the hands of ignorance.

But for now, in the deepening of night I allowed the regret to flow gently away, bidding it farewell with the promise to return occasionally to its shores – in those times when I needed to remember the greater wisdom of Love.

I had taken Mark to my bed, had taken him inside of me, knowing that it may be the first and last time. I wasn't sure how I knew, or from where the strength came to give myself over to loving him fully and freely, with no thoughts of tomorrow. But somehow it didn't matter what the sun would bring, only that Truth and Love be lived in the moment of their emergence. If every decision was a choice between Love and Fear I wanted to believe I would begin to choose Love more often.

So it was that I turned on my side, nestled back against him and drifted into the twilight of sleep, with no declarations, no promises, no coaxing of assurances.

And just before the void came for me, a whisper of breath crossed my ear, carrying with it the words, "I love you."

CHAPTER THRITY-FIVE

It was still dark when my eyes opened. Looking out the window, to the stars beyond, I thanked God and Anna and Brian for taking such good care of me. Mark's body, strong and solid, was warm against mine, his even breath comforting on my shoulder. He held me close, his arm curled around my waist. The night was quiet and I was grateful to have woken into it, to catch a glimpse of life off-guard.

But I only thought that I witnessed it alone.

"I think it is in those moments when we get closest to the perfection and we actually see into God, that our human hearts feel the deepest ache." My skin tingled as his breath brushed the fine hairs on the back of my neck.

In answer I snuggled closer, wrapped my feet around his legs and whispered, "Thank you." Nothing more would pass the lump in my throat.

His laugh was deep and low as he turned me towards him and kissed the hollow space behind my ear. He moved to my chin, my lips, my cheek and brow. "Mmmmm. No, Sara, thank you." Then he just pulled me close and held me against him.

After a few minutes I shifted my position so I could once again see out the window. Neither of us spoke for a long while.

And then, "Sara."

I knew by the tone what he was going to say, and I wasn't ready. Not yet. Just a little more time.

Interrupting, I said, "Tell me what happened when you went to see Bev when you were thirteen, tell me about Anna, and about what happened last night. Tell me the rest of the story."

When he didn't answer I turned to meet his eyes. "Please, Mark. Will you just tell me the story now? There's time for the rest. I just want to hear your voice, to hear you and feel you and know all there is to know, before…" My voice cracked at the last and I turned away, burrowing farther into the cavity created by his body.

Moving as close as flesh would allow, he said softly into my ear, "Okay beautiful Sara, I will tell you the story, the parts of it that you didn't tell me."

I went to Bev's as she had requested, which was, as you know, right here in this house. We sat on the back porch. It was summer and I remember it being warmer than usual. But it didn't matter, we still drank tea. I guess it's just what you do.

I was so nervous, but refused to show it. All puffed-up, determined to be the one in control. You can tell I didn't know who I was dealing with. Bev Carter is not, nor was she ever, one to be controlled. It didn't take long to figure it out.

She didn't tell me who my mother was, only that she had been young and beautiful, and though she loved me she had other work that she was meant to do. That isn't exactly what you want to hear about your mother, that something else had been more important than you, so when Bev said it, it only further validated my anger. I became sullen and pouty. And then she said something to me that I will never forget.

She leaned forward, her face so close I could feel her breath. I tried to back away, but she would have none of it. She put her hands on my shoulders, looked directly into my eyes, and said, very softly yet with great intent, "Listen to me Mark Wilde, and listen carefully, for I will tell you this only once. Once in your entire life, and so you do not want, in your anger and immaturity, to miss it: You are the child of a Goddess, here to do the work of Truth, and as such you too are called to great things. There is not time, nor place, for self-pity or anger. There is too much to be done. You will go from here and be grateful to the Wildes for offering you protection and love and all that is necessary to grow. You will be grateful for this life and for the very act of living. And most of all, for Love. And though it may be many years before you understand what I am telling you, you will feel these words every day, deep down in your heart and one day, when you are ready, you will understand and you will step forth and claim your heritage. And on that day, I promise you, she will be there."

If you know Bev you know that when she has said what she has to say, she is done with it. Never again, in all the years I have known her, has another word been spoken between us about my mother. And when she finished, she simply sat back, smiled and asked if I'd like some more tea.

I was completely shaken. I was only thirteen and nowhere near ready to hear what she had said. But some part of me had heard, some part I was, until then, unfamiliar with. At the time it felt like I'd been taken over by the 'body-snatchers.' My head was fuzzy and I was more than a little spooked. But at the same time my bubble of hate had been popped, replaced by this wave of deep and heavy sadness. I started to cry. I was so embarrassed and tried to get up but Bev just waved me down, handed me a Kleenex and said, "It's okay to cry Mark. Don't ever be afraid to cry." It seemed strange coming from this perfectly poised woman, but nonetheless, it touched me, and never again was I afraid to cry.

She allowed me a few minutes to recuperate then simply went on to other things. She didn't ask me about school, or my friends, or other typical thirteen-year-old stuff. Instead she talked about art, history, and philosophy. She told me about the house and photography. She told me about love, and how she and Gil met. It was amazing when I look back on it. She treated me like an adult. Spoke to me about things she thought were important for a person to know, and not condescendingly, but as a teacher who has great faith in the student.

"Did you see her again after that? I remember you saying the night I met you that you had spent time here. I wondered why or when, but, well, never asked." We lay spooned together, deep beneath the blankets, watching the night, and his story, unfold.

I think now that it was Bev's intention, above all else that day, to become my friend, teacher, or perhaps surrogate grandmother because she did in fact become all of those things. After our visit I met Gil, and well, Gil is Gil, and he won me over immediately. I went home kinder than I had arrived and it is undeniable that I was changed, be it by Bev's words, or by whatever mysterious energy the two of them possess. It is easy to see that though I didn't know it, the seeds of my spiritual journey were sown on that day.

Still, I was an adolescent, and though I was kinder to my parents and not so openly hostile in general, I was, in a way, more agitated. I remember lying in bed reciting Bev's words to myself and thinking, 'The child of a Goddess – what the hell does that mean?' I figured she just meant my mother had been a good person. Which was nice to know, but didn't explain why I had been so dispensable. Bev was right - it would be many years, until this very day in fact, before I would even begin to understand. She was also right that Anna would be there when I did.

But I'll get to that in a minute. You asked about my relationship with Bev. It did continue. With Gil as well. I became a regular fixture at this house. I would actually come and stay for weeks at a time during the summer. Bev taught me to take pictures and tried to teach me to paint. Gil taught me about trees and birds and the history of the Island. Together they taught me about integrity and kindness. I have to say I wish I had learned what they had to teach about love, but I guess some things are only learned through experience.

The three of us would take walks on the beach and they would talk about whatever came to them and I would just listen, absorbing all that I could. It was Bev who urged me first to write. She would give me book after book to read and then challenge me to think beyond the author's text. When I left for college they threw me a party and gave me the possession I value most.

Mark paused and breathed deeply, his chest rising and falling against my back. When he didn't continue I squeezed his hand and looked over my shoulder at him. His mouth was curled into a half-smile.

"Well, what was it? Tell me."

To my dismay he got out of bed, his body replaced by a funnel of cold air.

"Hey! Where are you going?"

Before he could answer he was slipping back into the space beside me, his hand curled around a small object.

"Just to get something out of my backpack."

This is where things begin to connect. After everyone left the party the three of us sat in the family room drinking a final glass of wine, reminiscing and laughing at Gil, who tells stories better than anyone. It got late and I knew I needed to go but hated to leave. I was going to miss them and I somehow sensed that things were never going to be the same. There had been talk of them moving to Boston. They said they weren't going anywhere, but I had a feeling that Katie would win in the end.

I was sitting there blindly watching Gil tell his story and tears just started running down my cheeks. He stopped talking, looked at me with this incredible depth of kindness and said, "You know that we love you, don't you Mark? You need not ever feel that you are alone."

Then Bev, who had slipped from the room, came back in and knelt on the floor in front of me. She didn't say anything, just took my hand and put this in it.

He reached over and placed the little object on the bed in front of me.

It was a very old, silver compass, shaped much the way a pocket watch would be – small but thick, and circular.

"Turn it over."

I did as he said. On the back of the compass was the etching of a star and in its center the words, "A star to guide you home."

Of course at the time I didn't know anything about Anna or the locket. I was just touched by the gesture and by their love. I keep it with me always.

It was after Robin left that I first saw the locket and first met Anna. That is something else I will never forget.

Bev and Gil had already moved - it didn't take Katie as long as everyone thought it would - and by that time they were rarely visiting anymore. I was in the vacuous place between being tired of my binging phase and not too sure what came next. Without Bev and Gil there to set me straight I felt lonelier and more lost than I had in my entire life.

One day after breaking down and calling Robin, promising whatever I could to get her back and having her tell me, in not so pleasant terms, to stop calling, I huffed out of the house, got in my car and just started driving. I ended up on the other side of the Island. I did a hike to blow off some steam and was heading back through Northeast Harbor when I stopped to pick up something to drink. That was when I saw a sign for The Next Chapter and decided to wander back.

I went in and there was not another soul in sight. I wandered around awhile, then sank into one of the chairs and just sat there, feeling horribly sorry for myself. I guess I went into a sort of trance because the next thing I know there's a book being tossed in my lap and this voice saying, "It's time for this."

Stunned, I looked up and there she was. Anna. I swear my heart stopped beating and I couldn't breathe. She was incredible. Beautiful yes, but more than that there was this energy about her... and something else. In that first moment I knew...I knew it was her, the woman from the picture. She was at least twenty-five years older, but I had no doubt.

Until of course the next second. Then, I wasn't sure of anything, including my own name. But she of course wasn't fazed, or didn't seem to be. She just casually glanced at me and said, "You read that and then come back and we'll talk." And then she walked away. I tried to find her before I left, to pay for the book, but she was gone. Well, you know Anna.

"Yeah I do. So what happened? I assume you read the book, and went back."

You'd think. And I did. But it took me a good two months before I even opened it. I put it on my dresser and every day would look at it but that was as far as I'd get. It wasn't so much the book I was afraid of but what I sensed it was going to do to my life – the path that it, and she, were going to lead me on. It wasn't going to offer me a quick fix. I had a feeling something was going to be asked and expected of me – change, for one thing, and I wasn't ready, or willing.

"Been there." I laughed and leaned back to kiss him.

Well believe me, you're not the first or only one to resist change. Especially the kind from the inside. But when I finally started reading the book I couldn't put it down. It spoke to the kind of man I wanted, but was afraid to be. It took me less than two days to finish it, but another two weeks to go back to the bookstore. Reading a book was benign next to facing this woman who I was so oddly drawn to and somehow afraid of. I still had the picture I had found when I was twelve and I spent a lot of time just staring at it, trying to convince myself in one minute that it couldn't be her, and in the next, that it had to be. In the end I decided that it was wishful thinking and I needed to get over it.

So, I went back to The Next Chapter with the intention of simply thanking her for the book and insisting to pay for it.

"Silly you."

To say the least. When I got there she was, of course, nowhere to be found. So I looked around, sat in the chair again for a minute and then got annoyed and decided to leave. Just as I got up and headed out I hear, "Not very patient are you? Good for some things, not for others. Come back and sit down."

I did as I was told, as you always do with Anna. It was when she sat down across from me that I first noticed the locket. It hung around her neck and I glanced at it for the briefest moment, just long enough to file away the detail.

We talked about the book and I asked her if she had another to suggest. I remember she stared at me for a long time and then asked, "Why? What is it you're looking for?" Her eyes were so intense…

"You have the same eyes."

Oh. Really? Well hers made me very uncomfortable that day. I sort of mumbled some ridiculous, completely dishonest, answer, like, "personal growth" or something. Whatever it was she laughed at me. I was so humiliated. But her laugh wasn't really unkind, it just exposed how far removed I was from the truth. I really had no idea what I was looking for. All I knew was that something in the book had reached me, and I wanted more of it. Anna knew that and when she stopped laughing she started walking around the store pulling books from the shelves. When she finished she piled them into my arms and said, "Go. Find out what you really want, and then come back."

I went home, began reading and before I knew it was stuffing the books into a backpack and taking off for spiritual lands far and wide. You know the rest of that story.

When I got back, nearly a year later, I went straight to the bookstore. It was then that Anna and I began our real friendship. I told you that when I came home I isolated myself. That was true, with the exception of Saturdays that I would spend at the bookstore. Every week I'd go and we'd talk and read and argue well past closing.

I could hear the tears in his voice, the choked sound of a heart in pain, as he recalled times now past.

She became my mentor, my own personal sage. She called me on my shit and challenged me to be better than I thought I was. She also encouraged my writing. I'd read my stuff to her and she would tell me what she liked and what she didn't. It was the most honest relationship I had ever had. So many times I wished it were she in the picture. I would look at it, squint my eyes, and try to convince myself that it might be. I think I wanted to believe that I could come from such a person.

"So what happened?"

"What do you mean?"

"That night at Jane's when I mentioned Anna you got very uptight. It seemed like you were upset about something, at her even."

All of this, my weekly visits to the store, started years ago. They stopped shortly before my book was published. The day I went to tell her that it was going to be published, she said, "Of course it is." And then I went to sit in our usual place and she said, "No, no more. It's time for you to move on now."

I was devastated, but like Bev, when Anna said something, that was it. So I left. But I was angry and hurt. Much like I had been at thirteen when I found out my mother had given me away. I felt abandoned again. That was nearly two years ago.

I see now that she was giving me what I needed – it was time to grow up, to move out from under the wing of those like she and Bev and fly on my own. At the time though, I was just hurt.

But then everything changed the night of the signing, the night I met you.

Goosebumps covered my arms. I remembered how strangely Anna had talked about that night. "What do you mean?"

First of all I was surprised by the invitation. It came in the mail, hand-written by Anna. Actually it was more a command than an invitation. I barely saw her the whole night, until the end. It was after you left. Anna came up to me and said that she would be stopping by my house the next day and that it was very important that I be there. There was a look in her eyes that I had never seen before. I don't know how to describe it, it was somewhere between excitement and dread. I didn't sleep at all that night trying to imagine what was so important that she was coming to my home.

She arrived at eight o'clock in the morning. In her hands was a box. She came in and as always was her style with me, got right to the point. She handed me the box and said, "In this box are threads of a story, a true story that must be discovered and shared. It is a story that will change the lives of many...perhaps all. It is a story for you. You will find it and you will share it."

I turned to look at him, "My God Mark, what is it?"

When he continued his voice grew very quiet, as though it tiptoed upon the night.

I don't know. Not yet. See Sara that's what I need to tell you. What you know and don't want to hear. But let me explain the rest first.

I tried to get Anna to tell me more. I asked her to explain what the story was, how I was supposed to find it, what it all meant. She told me only to read the papers and then she left. I sat down immediately and devoured them. It was like an archeological dig. They were mostly letters, written in a language I don't understand. I have no idea how old they are, I'm afraid to guess. There are fragments of symbols in them, maybe religious in nature. I don't know Sara. All I know is that it is important and it's been dropped in my lap.

The night I saw you at Jane's I saw Anna as well. Probably right before or after you did. She told me what I had somehow known, that I was going to have to follow the story where it led, and that it would take me far from here and that it would change my entire life.

Then, when we were at dinner I noticed the locket around your neck, even before Lucy did. When you explained how you had found it and recited the inscription, I almost fell off my chair. Too many 'coincidences.' A locket from Bev - the woman who had given me to the Wildes - with the same inscription as my compass – a locket that looked exactly like the one I had seen on Anna years before. Too many connections. Then when you showed it to me and I saw the picture of the little girl... I knew it was her. It was like a tidal wave came up from inside and swallowed me whole.

But at the same time there was you. And you were undeniable.

He pulled me even closer and we lay in silence for several minutes, watching the darkness pass over us and feeling what was real – our bodies and our breath.

Every moment I haven't spent with you, I have spent with the papers and the picture. And then you came and told me the truth. You will never know how grateful I am for that and for you.

And then last night I was awakened by a vision of Anna. She was standing in my house telling me to come to the beach, to let you sleep and to come. So I did. When I got there she was in the cave. We sat together and she told me that she loved me, that she had always loved me. And then she told me that it was time for her to go but before she did she wanted to spend time alone with her son. We talked a little, laughed, cried, but mostly we just sat, sharing space. She told me about the ceremony. And she told me about you.

She said she knew that I loved you and I would know what was right when the time came. And...here I am. I don't know what is 'right,' only what I have to do.

...You do know that I love you don't you?

Tears had filled my eyes. "Yes. I know." I turned over so that our faces were only inches apart and looked him in the eyes, "And I love you too. But you have to go. Whatever this work is that she asked you to do, you need to do it. I won't tell you that it's easy for me to let you go, but I have to, I know that. You helped teach me that. The best way I can love you right now is to let you go." By the time I finished I was choking on my tears.

His tears flowed too as he stroked my face tenderly. "I would ask you to come with me, but there is more here than just the work. My heart is broken right now. I'm not afraid to share that with you but I feel in myself the old ability to cling so tightly that I would strangle you, and eventually our love. I don't want to do that, not with this. If I go and do this work, I will also be going to remember myself, to find the pieces of myself that Anna held. And when I come back..."

I put my fingers over his mouth. "No. No 'when.' Just 'I love you.' That's today, that's now, and that's all that matters. The rest we'll leave for its own time."

The love we made was as honest as the sorrow that filled our hearts. With the passion of a lifetime that may never be, we opened ourselves and gladly swam in the warm oceans of the only promise we could make.

We held each other that night, until the dawn came and reminded us of what we had, for a little while, allowed ourselves to forget. And when it did, Mark went home, to begin preparing for the trip that would take him away. After he left I lay in bed and cried. I cried until my body ached. I cried until the pain devoured itself and left me empty.

It was when I reached the emptiness that I was able to Remember. I remembered the faces of Fear and Grief; I remembered their words and knew that only in accepting them honestly and embracing them fully, would I ever be lifted into the arms of Joy and Love.

CHAPTER THIRTY-SIX

I didn't go home for Thanksgiving, or for Christmas. When I called my parents it was difficult not to tell them all that had happened, difficult not to see them as they had been on the beach, their voices raised in prayer and celebration. Maybe one day I would be able to share what I had found on the other side of the veil. One day when I was strong enough.

They were disappointed with the news that I was going to stay in Maine for the holidays. My mother was nervous about my being alone, but surprisingly, she didn't argue with me. I think perhaps that she could hear in my voice the echo of the new construction going on inside. She was a good and loving woman, and beneath the fear she only wanted me to be happy.

It wasn't that I didn't want to be with my family or that I didn't miss them terribly. I just knew that I wasn't ready. As long as I was with those who had traveled this journey with me I felt supported and comfortable in my raw and developing identity, but in order to step back into a world that knew only what had come before, time was needed – time to not simply *know* myself, but time to *become*.

Mark and I spent every available moment together. As November passed into December the days grew shorter and colder, but we took from them all that we could, and savored the gifts to be found in long stretches of darkness. When the year's first snow came in the second week of December I watched in awe as white draped itself around the land I loved, holding it close.

I came in those days and nights to know Mark in ways I had never known another human being, even Brian. While Winter watched from the window, we would talk for hours, about the most essential things we knew or about nothing at all. It found us most days nestled into opposite corners of my couch or his, our feet keeping contact as we read, stopping often to share those things that made us laugh, cry, or otherwise touched us.

It was common, too, for It to catch us simply listening to the silence, seeking out God's breath between our own. And when with tired eyes the day would fold into night, we would follow, chasing every moment and holding it close.

Mark left before Christmas. We had hoped to spend it together, but in the end it was a matter of flight schedules, reservations and other absurd practicalities. As well as the ironic timing of the Universe.

He left on December 21st - the Winter Solstice - the longest night of the year. The day the earth bathes itself in darkness, preparing for its slow return to the light - the moment of final death, on the other side of which life awaits.

I took him to the airport, Lady and I that is. She was mine now. He had turned over the keys to his house to Jane who would rent it out until given further instruction. We exchanged gifts the night before, neither surprised by the other's. He gave me his compass and I gave him Anna's locket. And then we lay together, waiting for the morning to come, no words between us, only the silent flow of tears.

The plane would take him first to Boston, to Bev and Gil's. Bev was doing well but we both knew how fragile time was. He would stay with them for a few weeks or however long he felt necessary to reconnect and learn what they had to share about Anna. From there he would visit his parents who now lived in Virginia. There were things, he said, that needed saying. Things as simple as 'Thank you,' and 'I love you.'

Then he would move on to the mountains of North Carolina where he had rented a cabin where he would begin to reassemble the pieces of his soul, remembering what he knew of himself and what he knew of God. And when he was ready he would turn to the legacy that Anna had left him. He was prepared to devote whatever time necessary to unravel the threads of the story she had given into his keeping and go wherever necessary to search out the missing pieces of the puzzle. When the research was complete the larger work of sharing what he learned would begin. It was a blind mission and he had no idea where he would be led or who he would be when he reached the other side.

We both knew that our roads were leading us in different directions. And so as we said goodbye under the glaring lights in the airport terminal, we did our best to release expectations, let go of promises, and in the corners of our all-too-human hearts, hold on to hope.

CHAPTER THIRTY-SEVEN

In the end, as in the beginning, there is the memory of waking.

It came flowing in on a tide of dreams. Corridors of the labyrinth disconnected and strewn about, moving into place, finding center. Images of those I had known and loved, those now gone. And the image of another, one who lurked in the shadows at the edge of light, waiting to be revealed, to be fully embodied. I tried to move toward her, tried coaxing her out, but she remained cast in silhouette. Slowly though the shadow began to fade, or perhaps the light began to grow. Yet, just at the moment of recognition, I awoke.

The first thing I became aware of was the empty space next to me, the absence of Mark's warm and welcoming body. I ached deep inside.

Lady rose from her spot under the window and came to rest her large furry head on the bed next to me. She understood.

It was cold. Bone cold, I thought, as I made my way down to the beach with Lady. We walked slowly, every footfall landing on another memory, calling back another voice, another day, another promise.

I decided that I loved winter in Maine. It was raw, naked, exposed – stripped of the final remnants of what had been. Winter, the great purifier. I knew the need for purification.

Looking out over the ocean it occurred to me that I had come full circle. I stood now at the exact spot where I had sat that morning when I first saw Anna. They were all gone now - Mark, Anna and Brian – but I was still here. So much had happened, and it all came back to this spot. How different it looked.

Yes, everything had fallen away. But I wasn't alone, and that was the difference.

Warmth settled over me or came up from inside. I'm not sure which. Watching the water I was comforted by the familiar fingers of foam rolling onto shore. The heat around me grew more intense and stretched out toward the water, coming to pool in a single spot a few yards out. It was as though the space opened up and beckoned me.

Without thought I shrugged off my coat, threw off my sweater and shirt, stripped away everything I wore until I stood naked on the beach. Then I walked into the water and lowered myself beneath the surface. I let myself fall toward the light, and in its center saw the face of the woman in the shadows become illuminated. I reached out my hand and her fingers touched mine.

As I broke the surface of the water and took what felt like the first breath of life, I knew I had come home.

www.ingramcontent.com/pod-product-compliance
Lightning Source LLC
Chambersburg PA
CBHW070308260626
47160CB00003B/763